Broken

J.E. Irvin

Broken

J.E. Irvin

**The New
Atlantian Library**

ABSOLUTELY AMAZING eBOOKS

Manhanset House
Dering Harbor, New York 11965

bricktower@aol.com ■ tech@absolutelyamazingebooks.com
■ absolutelyamazingebooks.com

Library of Congress Cataloging-in-Publication Data

Irvin, J.E.   1. FICTION / Mystery & Detective / Hard-Boiled
Broken   2. FICTION / Thrillers / Crime
p. cm.   3. FICTION / Romantic/Suspense

ISBN: 978-1-955036-27-3, Trade Paper
Copyright © 2021, J.E. Irvin
Electronic compilation/ paperback edition
copyright © 2021 By Absolutely Amazing eBooks
September 2021

For every heart that has broken,
For every heart that is lost...

~~~~~

...“what’s past is prologue” ...
William Shakespeare, *The Tempest*

I should have done the research, but if I had, I might not have made the journey. Then every broken part of me would have remained broken and the tempest of my life uncalmed. Bloody Will...always ahead of the game. Unlike me, Riley Finn, who only read the article a year later, after the killer struck again.

WANAKENA GAZETTE...June 5, 2017
Murder In Our Midst
by
Mariah Kimby

Tragedy visited our quiet hamlet last night when Ranger Josh Waylon, completing his daily trail patrol, discovered the body of his ex-wife, Amanda, along the path leading up Cat Mountain. The State Patrol at Gouverneur responded to a 911 call relayed from Ranger Waylon through the SAT line at Janack’s Landing. Investigators arrived on the scene shortly before midnight, but they did not bring the body down until early this morning. Interviewed by this reporter in Wanakena, Officer Sandra Kellerman refused to release any details, citing “the ongoing investigation and the need to preserve evidence.” Josh Waylon also declined to speak for the record. Rumor has it that the ex-Mrs. Waylon died by strangulation, possibly at the hands of someone who knew her. Here in the Adirondacks, under our very noses, a murderer lurks. Be careful out there, Folks! Everyone’s anxious and asking one question. Will the Wilderness Strangler strike again?

Chapter 1

... when the universe speaks...

On the last day of May in the year of our Lord 2018, I agreed to meet Warren Carstairs at Heidi's Café, the expectation of a double chocolate latte and a proposal pinging in my head. I know what you're thinking. But I was so sure it was my time. I don't gamble, never play the lottery, but I decided to place a bet on the ace of hearts that day.

I had just pulled on running shoes when my cell phone pinged. Warren's text made my heart stutter. *Can you meet me at H's? Important.* Who could blame me for thinking the moment had arrived? We'd dated for three years, shared Thanksgiving dinners with our respective families, and vacationed together. Yes, we had sex, but not very good sex, and not often. I thought it would get better once we were married. Once or twice, he asked me what I thought about friends who planned destination weddings instead of saving money and celebrating at home. Earlier that month, I found a brochure from Michaelson's Jewelers among the magazines on the bathroom reading shelf. A formal commitment seemed the inevitable next step.

Peeling off my exercise gear, I stepped into the shower, then grabbed the only clean outfit in the closet. On the way to the café, I ordered myself to stop grinning and obey the speed limit. My mouth and my foot refused to listen.

The late spring sun teased the east with streamers of scarlet and purple so bright my eyes teared up. I squinted my way through the intersection of Market and Main, ignoring the goosebumps crawling up my spine. My father's favorite saying sprang to mind: Red sky in the morning, sailor's warning. I shrugged off the thought and parked my Civic next to a handicapped spot. Then I gathered my excitement and my purse and crossed the street. I took two slow, deep breaths, practiced my best *Yes* under my breath, and turned the handle of the heavy wooden door that graced the entry into the old Victorian house Heidi Pomeroy had turned into Hopewell, Ohio's gathering place. The early morning professionals hadn't yet arrived. Several high school instructors whom I recognized only by face were lined up in front of the counter. Just one waved. Third-grade teachers like me didn't show up on their radar.

"Morning, Riley." Heidi stuck a pencil in her curly brown hair and turned to fill another order. I clamped down a pang of jealousy. When we'd played doubles together in high school, Heidi had trouble remembering where she'd left her racquet. Now a successful entrepreneur unfazed by an extra thirty pounds of baby weight, she worked six days a week at her restaurant/catering business, boarded racehorses on her farm property, and was raising three kids under the age of six. Yet, she didn't have a wrinkle on her face or a smudge on her white chef coat. I smoothed down my un-ironed blouse and the panic that surfaced like a wave inside. My life resembled dirty laundry, all crumpled and waiting to be sorted.

"Morning," I called back.

"You run today?" She set a tray of raspberry scones in the display case.

"No." I blushed, my excitement overriding caution. "Something came up."

Heidi looked like she wanted to say more, but a buzzer went off in the kitchen. She waved as she hurried away. Someone in line shoved me hard in the back. I tripped forward and caught my elbow on a basket of straws, which sprayed out like champagne. The woman who pushed me rolled her eyes and smirked. I glanced around again, but I didn't see Warren. I stared at the chalkboard announcing the day's specials, wondering whether to indulge in a *pain au chocolate*. I had almost reached the Order sign when he called my name.

"Riley! Over here, Ri. Let's go up."

I backtracked to the bottom of the stairs leading to the second floor. Warren, his crisp white shirt, sedate yellow tie, and creased dockers mocking my casual style, held two cups above his head as he climbed. I'd never seen him in jeans, not even on vacation. I wondered what he'd look like with mud between his toes. When I stood on tiptoe to kiss him, he turned away.

"I can't be late today, Riley. Got a bus fight to mediate." As the assistant principal, Warren Carstairs handled discipline at Hopewell High. No one wanted to be on the receiving end of his displeasure, including me. I followed him along the narrow hall to the empty second-floor meeting room. We threaded our way through the crammed-in tables and chairs. Lyrics from an Enya CD drifted through the air. I settled into a seat by the back window.

"I got you a chai," Warren said, setting the to-go cup in front of me. "Only a grande. Hope that's all right."

I wrestled off the lid and took a sip to hide my disappointment. Chai? When had he ever known me to order tea in the morning?

"What's new with your parents?" He blew on his coffee, then took a big gulp and smacked his lips. Not his usual elegant move. I wondered if he was nervous, too.

"Same old, same old." I traced the angle of his head, the way his short, muscled body stretched against the high-backed wooden chair, one of a set Heidi had rescued from an antique dealer in Lebanon. A nerdy piece of info, right? But I wanted to remember every detail about this day. "I'm going to see them tomorrow. Want me to tell them anything?"

"Riley." Warren set down his coffee. As he rested one hand over mine, his warm brown eyes teared up a little. My heart did another quick flip, the second one this morning. I put a hand on my chest. No, I ordered, no jumping out of rhythm, not now. I took three quick breaths, and the fluttering stopped. Warren didn't notice.

"I know we've been dating for a while now." His fingers stroked mine.

"Thirty-six months, two weeks, and five days." I giggled as I said it. Giggled. What a dope. "But who's counting?"

"I didn't realize you kept such close track."

"You know I'm a math junky." I blew on my tea and took another sip.

Warren sighed. He took his hand away and straightened his tie. "The thing is, Riley, I've come to realize how much you mean to me. How much I want to protect you. And I can't do that if we go on dating."

My purse slipped off my lap and dropped to the floor. The lip gloss and Chapstick rolled out. Ignoring the urge to pick up my stuff, I waited for Warren to go on.

"This is so hard." He stood up to pace, but the cramped floor plan only allowed him to move from one chair to another. "You know, I think you're terrific, Riley."

And then I got it. He wasn't proposing. This was a brushoff. A break-up. A thanks-but-no-thanks speech. I stood up, too, bumping my hip on the table. My chai sloshed over, staining the tabletop with a wet brown smear.

"Just say it." I bent over to retrieve the fallen items so he couldn't see my face.

"I like you, Riley, a lot." He reached out to grab my arm. Stunned, I didn't even pull away. He lowered his voice to a whisper. "It's just that, after one failed marriage, I'm not ready to risk another. I don't want to go through that again."

"Warren." I choked on my saliva. I tried calming myself with a sip of tea, but that just made it worse. When I finally stopped coughing, my eyes were watering, and my nose dripped. I fumbled for a tissue, playing for time. I wanted to say that we would be different, that I could make him happy, that I, Riley Marie Finn, didn't have a thing in common with his first wife, the bitchy Yolanda Markey. But the words stuck in my throat. He mumbled something about being sorry. I shook off his apology and rushed down the steps, clutching my chai tea (grande) and the realization that Warren Carstairs didn't want to marry me after all.

My father's old saying returned as I unlocked the car and scrambled in. I should have paid more attention to what the sky was trying to tell me. Rolling down the window, I tossed my cup on the sidewalk. Now I wasn't only a jilted lover. I was a litterer. Slaloming around the construction barrels lining Main Street, I drove up the hill toward Hopewell Elementary. Drove like a bat out of hell, shaking with anger and shame. Loose coins jangled in the cup holder while I processed this change in my relationship status. Emma. I needed to talk to Emma right now. But my best friend and co-teacher, Emma Pearson, who used to spend the half-hour before classes sharing gossip and advice with me, had turned up pregnant a month ago. Now, while I covered our bus duty, Emma spent the time before class throwing up in the bathroom. Maybe I could throw up with her. My life had suddenly acquired a decidedly nauseating aroma.

*

Afternoon recess arrived with a bang. I stood on the curb, one foot scuffing at the asphalt parking lot, as I considered effective ways to torture a forty-year-old, once-divorced, twice-shy ex-Marine who suddenly decided to remain unattached. The ball, when it hit me, knocked me to my knees.

Thirty yards away, Jaden Scott, scourge of the playground, stood with his hands over his mouth while the soccer ball he'd kicked directly into my right temple bounced toward the storm drain. Temporarily blinded, I glimpsed the bleakness of the next year of my life in the black floaters dancing behind my closed eyelids. No Warren. No ring. No happily ever after. When my vision returned, I collared Jaden and marched him to the secretary to await further punishment. Then I staggered to the nurse's office and filled out an accident incident report. On my way back to my classroom, I experienced yet another inner shift. Some might call it a revelation, although it felt more like resignation. Hopewell was no longer a good fit for me. My heart fluttered. I leaned against the wall, hoping the irregular beat would reverse itself quickly, then hoping it wouldn't. If I ended up in the hospital... No, damn it, pity love wasn't what I wanted. I didn't want a heart condition either, but the universe doesn't care what we want. It just follows its own plan.

Inside the classroom, I booted up my aging computer and drafted a request for a sabbatical. I could go back to school, work on a Master's degree, a doctorate. My heart stuttered again. I took three deep breaths and kept typing. *Don't think, Riley*, I muttered to myself. *Just do.* I slipped the letter into an envelope and headed for the principal's office just as Emma, her short red bob bunched up around her ears, staggered out of the bathroom.

"What the hell?" Emma covered her mouth as she burped. "You look shell-shocked."

"You know that guy I used to date?" I balled my hands into fists, crumpling the envelope. A blush of shame and embarrassment crept over my neck and cheeks. Tears threatened. I squeezed until my nails bit into my palms. "Well, not anymore."

"Warren? He broke up with you? That rat bastard." Emma put her hands on her hips. "Tell me exactly what he said."

"He likes me. He wants us to be friends. He doesn't want to get married again. Yadda, yadda, yadda." I swiped at my eyes with the backs of my hands.

"Oh, no." Emma stepped forward and hugged me. She smelled strongly of throw-up. "Do you want me to kill him for you? Because Gary knows a number of hitmen. His work in undercover narcotics left him with some very dubious connections."

"It's all right, Em." I didn't want to smile, but my mouth betrayed me. Emma always knew the right thing to say. We stood there, hugging and laughing like two crazy women. When the fit passed, I waved the envelope in the air. "No, don't kill him...yet. I'm asking for a sabbatical. I think I'll go back to school."

Grabbing my shoulders, Emma marched me into her reading resource room. "Just because one stupid man decides he's not right for you doesn't mean you should quit teaching, not even for a year. Besides, didn't you read the email?"

I grabbed a tissue and blew my nose so hard it honked. "What email?"

"You sound like a goose." Emma patted my shoulder. "The one about the meeting after school today. Something's coming down from the school board. With the last levy failure and our contract negotiations, it doesn't look good."

"What's that got to do with you and me, Em? I mean, we've been here for," I paused to do the math, "seven years, not counting this one. They won't fire us."

"No, but they can RIF us. You know, Reduction in Force, take those lowest on the seniority list. Release us, then call us back if the issue passes in August."

That got my attention. Emma and I, along with Shelley Wollenhaupt, who taught first grade, were the most recent hires. We'd be the first ones to go.

"Well, Hopewell's a nice place, Emma, to settle down and raise a family and walk your dog and be happy, but none of those things are happening for me. Maybe it's time to go." I didn't know if I meant it. I'd already lost Warren. I couldn't lose my job, too.

"You just haven't met the right person, Riley. He's out there. I know it."

"Sometimes," I shook loose from Emma's grasp, "the universe punches you a ticket, and you have to get on board."

Emma shut the door and leaned on the desk. "But what will you do? With all this belt-tightening, teaching jobs are hard to find. Where will you go? More to the point, what am I going to do without you? We're a team."

I heard the plea in her voice. She was counting on me to be her labor coach and part-time nanny since her husband was gone so much. Feeling guilty, I fell back on cliché. "I'm taking a leap of faith here, my friend," I said. "Time to be wild and crazy. I'm sick of tame and predictable."

Emma sniffed her blouse, trying to judge whether any bits of vomit had escaped her attention. Then she distracted me with a quick hug and snatched the envelope out of my hand. "Your brain's just a bit scrambled right now. And this thing with Warren," Emma paused. "Does anyone else know?"

I shrugged. "I don't know, but they will. There were plenty of teachers in Heidi's this morning. Someone's bound to mention what they saw, and I'll look like the world's biggest idiot."

Emma tap-tapped her nails on the desk. "It's a lot to process right now. But you have a life here. Your parents. Me. Just think about it."

I grabbed Emma's hand to stop her drumming. Her argument joined forces with the fear of change pushing its way through my resolve. I worried my lip and reached for the envelope. "No, Em. I don't have a life here. It's time I looked elsewhere."

Behind me, the kids in the special education reading group pushed into the room. Emma shoved my request letter into the top drawer of her desk and slammed it shut. Then she shooed me out.

"We'll talk later," she whispered. "Don't do anything without discussing it with me first."

In the hall, I tightened the scrunchie on my ponytail and headed back to my class, a deep bell of sorrow clanging in my ear. *For better or worse.* I had intended to speak those words with Warren. Now they pointed out the direction my life was headed. Right into that sailor's warning.

Chapter 2

...when the fog clears...

Smokey lifted his head as I entered the apartment, disinclined to change his position atop the window ledge. I scooped him up, cradling his heavy body as I stroked his white and black fur. He meowed in protest. I set him down, tossed my purse on the couch, and turned on the computer. My phone chirped, announcing an incoming text from Warren. I ignored it. A second chirp, this one from Emma, caught my attention. *r u all right?* Instead of answering, I closed my eyes and walked my fingers over the map above my desk.

"Eeney, meeney, miney moe." An invisible *I'm-fucked* sign scrolled across the laminated surface. "Where in the world should I go?"

The map refused to weigh in. I abandoned my fortune-telling to fix a sandwich and a pot of coffee, replaying the after-school meeting. I still couldn't believe it. Six teachers riffed at the elementary school, ten between the junior and senior highs. Three veterans with twenty years of experience among them. Emma. Sandra. Me. Red sky indeed. All the loyalty I had given the Hopewell school system faded beneath the dismissal. I bit my tongue so hard I was surprised it didn't bleed.

Unable to chew, I abandoned the sandwich. Swallowing back tears and the panic squirming inside me, I Googled teaching jobs in the Carolinas, Pennsylvania, Texas. Next, I checked vacancy postings in cities near Hopewell. If I found a position in the area, my parents would still be close, but Warren updates, and all those curious eyes and clucking tongues would follow me around forever. I'd be stuck in the same old rut, giving up my self-respect to please them all, to

11

fulfill their predictions for poor little Riley. No. That plan for my life no longer existed. My head throbbed. My mind kept returning to Warren's morning pronouncement, to the choice he had made, the one that nagged at me. Although he didn't say it, I heard the words loud and clear. I wasn't good enough for him. I exploded in a sob of self-pity. The sign-in screen leered at me. I swallowed hard, blew my nose, and sat up straighter. The time for crying had come to an end.

"I need to find a place where nobody knows me, a place where I can start over," I informed the cat, scratching his ears. "Nowheresville in Nothing County. That's where I belong."

Emptying the mug in the sink, I returned to the Internet. Smokey reclaimed his window perch. An hour and a half later, I gave up the search for teaching jobs and switched to ads for summer employment. I pulled up a resumé document from the word-processing file. How best, I mused, to sell myself to an invisible employer. What, after all, set me apart from the other job seekers out there? After several awkward attempts, I crafted a letter I could live with, pasted in my credentials and references, substituting my high school math teacher's name in place of Assistant High School Principal Warren 'Butthead' Carstairs. I highlighted my teenage jobs at Costco and the local laundromat. *Good with money*, I typed in under Special Talents. As an afterthought, I added juggling. It didn't have to be true. It just had to grab their attention. Then I deleted it. No need to scream crazy when what I needed was a job.

"I do have people skills," I protested to Smokey, who yawned, rolled over, and almost slipped off the ledge. "I do."

I stared out the window, then at the calendar. Four days until the first of June, and here I sat, jilted, jobless, and utterly alone. No bridal showers in my future. Old maid was the only card I held. My resolve began to dissolve. Before I caved under the pressure of going off on my own, I emailed the query to five potential Help Wanted postings, printed out three copies for snail mail requests, and addressed the envelopes. The numbness that had accompanied me since Warren's announcement had worn off. In the bathroom, I frowned at the reflection of a foamy-mouthed almost thirty-year-old with no prospects for success in life or love. "It isn't that I have to have Warren," I mumbled around the brush, "but I don't want to go through life alone." Smokey blinked and licked his butt.

So far, the search for a man hadn't worked out well for me. Not that that was my sole reason for living. I loved being a teacher. I didn't remember ever wanting to be anything else. But, in my romantic heart, the one that didn't skip beats on occasion, I harbored a dream of finding a love that would last a lifetime. My college dating record consisted of once-a-week dinners with Andy Fallon that ended before he graduated, received his ROTC commission, and shipped out to Afghanistan, where he fell in love with a helicopter pilot. A brief fling with the talented, vain Blaine Crosley, chef at the chi-chi Rue Fontaine, ended abruptly the night he attempted to tie me to the bedposts and smear chocolate cream all over my body. The police are still howling over that emergency call. And now Warren. If he preferred being single to being with me, what did that say about my future? My eyes blurred. I rubbed them, remembering the lesson plans I still had to type up. I pulled out my plan book and studied the rest of the week. Four more days and the school year would be over. Life as I knew it would change forever. I slipped to the floor and leaned my head against the wall. Smokey hopped into my lap. I ran my hand over his tail, set him down, and crawled to the kitchen to fill his food dish. Standing seemed to involve more effort than I could muster.

J.E. Irvin

I sat beside him as he ate, humming a few bars of an old Sinatra tune about an ant and a rubber tree plant.

"What's wrong with me, Smokey?" The cat meowed twice, an undecipherable response. I stumbled up and made my way to the couch. Pulling the blue and white afghan my grandmother had crocheted for my hope chest up to my chin, I struggled to turn off my mind. Warren was gone. My job was going. What bottomless pit had I fallen into? More importantly, how would I ever crawl back out? I drifted in and out of sleep, unaware of the giant black and purple bruise circling my heart.

Chapter 3

...oh, no, you don't...

Rain pounded the windshield. I hunched forward to peer through the cascading water until the turnoff to Shady Acres Trailer Park loomed on the right. I bumped over the stones at the foot of my parents' driveway, switched off the engine, and gathered my purse. The eco-friendly shopping bag I carried banged against my knees. Gusts of rain punched at me. I hustled along the weedy sidewalk, hopped up onto the concrete block step, and practically fell into the trailer. My father didn't bother to look up from his solitaire hand.

"That you, Riley?" he mumbled.

"Yeah, Pop, it's me. Where's Mom?"

My mother peeked around the door that separated the living area from the bedroom and nodded at the bag I carried. "Hey, Ri, can you put them groceries away? Then come sit. Your dad and I have something to tell you."

"I have something to tell you, too." I squeezed the water from my hair. Droplets dappled the linoleum floor. Several landed on the cards spread across the table.

"Damn, child, can't you do that before you come inside?" Dad grumbled at the two he turned up.

"In case you hadn't noticed," I tapped his bald head with a box of whole-grain spaghetti, "there's a major storm going on."

My mother eased onto the sagging couch and patted the cushion next to her. "Sit, Riley Marie. How's Warren?"

"He's not." I stood beside the sink, gazing at the storm-driven rain lashing the window. My father threw down his cards and swore.

"I thought he was a standup guy. What's he gone and done now?"

"He doesn't want to marry me, Pop. He'd rather stay single."

My father cleared his throat. Mom and I waited, like journalists at a press conference, for his next pronouncement. Harrison Finn had a propensity, like my heart, of jumping out of rhythm. He might spout baseball statistics or discuss the need for unions, but his reasoning always seemed to connect the dots in a peculiar, timely way. We waited, but Dad didn't speak. Instead, he shuffled the deck and laid out seven new stacks of cards.

"Well, that don't make things impossible, does it?" My mother readjusted her position among the cushions. "I mean, he treats you nice, and he's got a good job."

"Mom." My hand jerked. A bag of chips slid off the edge of the counter and burped open, spraying wedges of fried corn all over the floor. The smell tickled my nose, reminding me I hadn't eaten since breakfast.

My mother sniffed. "Hope you're going to clean that up."

On my knees, sweeping handfuls of chips into a dustpan, I almost missed her next words.

"Maybe you two can just move in together before the end of June 'cause that's when your father and I are heading to Florida."

"Wait. What? What's in Florida?"

"A trailer. Nice one, too."

"But," I hesitated, "you've never been to Florida, not even for vacation. What are you going to do there?"

"Live. Permanently." My father cleared his throat. "We're tired of the cold."

"And you have Warren, dear." Mom reached back to pat my head. "You don't need us anymore."

"No. You can't go now." I sounded childish and petty, but their news hit like the final nail in Riley Finn's downer of a life. I threw the spoiled chips in the trash.

"I don't understand, dear. You're a grown woman, living on your own. You have a good job and friends." She sniffed. "Your father and I have the right to a life, you know. Besides, you'll get married and have your own family."

"What don't you understand, Mom? There's not going to be a wedding. Warren and I are over."

My father sprang to his feet. Cards scattered, like pigeons taking flight. "Riley, I don't want to think of you being alone. Can't you fix this?"

"There is no fix for this, Dad." I clenched my fists. "Why can't you just support me?"

"Well, maybe you can change his mind, honey. 'Cause we're not changing ours. We've already sold this trailer. It's all arranged." My mother bustled over, her mules click-clacking over the floor. She ran a hand over my hair. "You're such a pretty little thing, Riley, still thin and firm. Some might even call you sexy. And your hair's that shiny black it always was. If only you didn't frown so much."

"Mom," I shoved her hand away. "I don't want to change his mind. He doesn't want me. Period. End of story. And the truth is, I don't love Warren either. Right this minute, I don't love anybody. And nobody loves me."

"We do, honey." My father's hand trembled as he raised it to my face, a reminder of the Parkinson's creeping its way through his body, "But your mother and I won't be around forever. Who's going to take care of you when we're gone?"

"I'm going to take care of me, Dad."

"Riley, I hear you, but the truth is you've never been a leader. All these years, you seemed content to go along with everyone else's ideas. That's why we didn't think you'd object to ours."

"That's not fair." My voice trembled with the lie. I had always been a compromiser, giving in to keep the peace. I had put my needs and desires last. "This time's different."

"Well, lah-di-dah." Anger crackled through my mother's words, "I hope so 'cause we're not going to change our plans, missy."

"I didn't ask you to."

"No need to shout," she said.

I took two deep breaths and switched on my best teacher voice. "I'll be fine. No reason to change your plans for me. You just go on and move to Florida."

My mother jabbed a finger in my face, her voice whisper-soft and flinty. "Your dad deserves a few good years, and we thought to have a grandchild or two before now. Children are supposed to take care of their parents when they get old. So, you just better rethink this, Riley Marie Finn. Hopewell's a good place to live, but once people find out about this, Warren'll be one of them persons non grata. And you with him."

"I'm not going to be here." I pushed my way around them and plopped down in the recliner.

My parents shared a look before they moved toward me. My father spoke first. "Where are you going to be?"

I had no real idea at that exact moment, but I decided another small lie would serve the higher cause. I did a quick mental review of the map on my wall and picked a state. "I've accepted a job in New York." I didn't elaborate. No need for a full-blown falsehood at this point.

"You've gone crazy, Riley." My mother threw up her hands and returned to the kitchen. Her indictment of me trailed after her. "You're usually such an agreeable child, but you always did have that stubborn streak. I tried to coax it out of you. Guess I failed."

Dad flipped on the TV. The local news featured a crawler detailing flood watches for the surrounding counties and videos of lightning bringing down electric lines, one of them very close to the complex where I lived. I wondered if the power was still on at my apartment. Smokey would be so frightened. Afraid of saying something I would regret, I cowered in the chair, biting my nails while my mother slapped plates on the table and set out a bowl of potato salad. On the screen, a local reporter opined over the downsizing in Hopewell Schools.

"C'mon, Pop, let's eat." I grabbed the remote, muted the reporter's words, and hustled my father to dinner.

"Hot dogs again?" He slathered mustard onto a bun before forking an all-beef wiener from the serving platter.

"Don't know why you have to be so particular, dear." My mother scraped her chair forward until her chest bumped the table. "Plenty of people live together these days. Why, your father and I--"

"That's enough, Wanda." Dad tapped Mom on the back of a hand with the butter knife. "Children don't need to know some things."

"I'm just saying there's more to a marriage than a ring and a ceremony."

I pushed my plate away. "I know, but I don't want that kind of arrangement."

"Seems like you don't know what you want. There was that Andy fellow and that guy who talked through his nose and-"

"He was French, Mom. And he wanted to baste me like a turkey."

"Humph, well, Warren's not like that." My mother prepared to fill another bun. "Here, you're too thin as it is.

You keep not eating, and you might blow away. And what about your doctor? Can't just find a cardiologist in every town. Where'd you say you were going?"

"New York, Mom." I accepted the offered dog, but not the reminder of my heart problem. I had forgotten about the appointment for a routine EKG scheduled next week. One more item to cancel. "The truth is I'm tired of worrying about palpitations."

"You have a condition, Riley." My mother's voice got higher as she wound up her scare speech. "What if you have to have the paddles?"

"They only had to do that one time, Mom. Now that I'm on meds, it never happens." Almost never. Only when my stress level hits two to the tenth power. Like now. But I didn't say that. I crossed my arms over my chest and waited for the fluttering to stop. One, two, three. Cough. Deep breaths. The palpitations settled.

"Eat, Riley." She shoved the bowl of potato salad across the table.

"I'm not hungry, and I'm not going to blow away, and I'm not going to have an attack of arrhythmia and die. I'm through waiting for life to happen to me. I'm going to drive, alone, to my new job, all the way to New York State. I'll call you when I get there." I snatched up the straps of my purse and stepped toward the door.

My father leaned against his plate as he stood up, smearing the front of his shirt with mustard. He patted my back and tousled my hair. "Sorry about Warren, honey. I know you always wanted a family."

I squeezed his trembling hand and gave my mother a quick peck on the cheek.

"This isn't over, Riley," my mother said, patting my shoulder.

"There's just this one thing." I hesitated. I wanted to tell them about losing my job, but that information would spark a whole new confrontation, and I didn't have the heart for it.

Mom folded her arms across her chest. "I knew there was more, knew you'd be wanting something from us."

"Hush, Wanda," my father scolded.

I turned toward Dad and laid my palm on his chest. "Will you take Smokey?"

My mother shook her head, but my father ignored her. "Why, Riley, we'd be glad to take that cat of yours. He'll be a good companion. When are you leaving?"

I turned away from my mother's hard stare. "School's out the end of the week. I thought I'd leave early Saturday. It's a long drive. Do you want any of my things before I put them in storage?"

"You go call that Warren and tell him to reconsider," my mother said. "And you're not going to New York."

"No need to yell, Mom. I got your message long ago." I pulled up the collar of my blouse and closed the door.

"Don't you dare go to New York!" she called through the screen.

The rain had tapered off, but the gutters, clogged by leaves, dripped water in long streams beside the door. I looked back. My parents stood behind the glass, my father's face a sad frown, my mother scowling in her attempt to cope with my failure. She turned away before I reached the car.

"Oh, yes," I whispered into the lull in the storm, "I dare."

Chapter 4

...what have I gotten myself into...

For the rest of the week, anxiety rode me like a second skin. I forced myself to get up in the morning, took a double dose of meds to help me sleep at night. What can I say? I'm part of the drug generation. Nothing dulled the pain of Warren's rejection. Or the shock of losing the one constant I thought I'd always have: my job. The school board met one more time, then officially announced the reductions in force twenty-four hours before school ended for the summer. I tried to stay upbeat. After all, I wasn't the only one shuffled out of a job. Emma lost hers, too.

On the last day of school, she staggered into my room, swiped at her mouth with a tissue, and plopped into one of the chairs around the half-moon-shaped reading table. Her long legs stuck out like insect feelers. I had the oddest feeling that the room was receding, sucking me out of this world into one more alien than anything I had ever known. Emma's frown brought me back to the moment.

"Brought you this." She laid the envelope containing my sabbatical request on the table and placed her hand over it. "You want it back?"

I picked at a fingernail, doubts swirling inside me. She tapped the letter again.

"Here," I deflected. "Chocolate cures all ills, temporarily." I offered her a Hershey's kiss before sneaking a glance at my emails. No replies from the job queries I'd sent. I slipped the cell phone back in my pocket and tugged at my ponytail. Job or no job, I was determined to leave Hopewell. "Pitch it, Em. The Board of Education took care of that avenue for me. How come every plan I have backfires?"

Emma's eyes filled with tears. She covered her mouth, mumbled an abbreviated excuse, and headed for the restroom. I followed, holding her hair back while she puked. Afterward, I wiped her face with a wet paper towel and patted her shoulder.

"Oh, Riley." She held on to me as I straightened her blouse. "What are we going to do if they don't call us back?"

"You'll be fine. Your husband's police consulting job is a good one. Besides, you were going on maternity leave anyway."

Sending me a sheepish grin, she fiddled with the ties on her sweat pants. "Why don't you stay here? You could work on the levy campaign. And you can move in with us to save on rent."

"You're a good friend, Em, and I thank you for the offer, but I can't do that. You and Gary need your space, and you need that second bedroom for the baby." I placed my hand gently on her stomach, then let her go.

"But your furniture, your cat, me!" Emma burst into a second fit of sobbing.

"My parents are taking Smokey," I said.

"At least come over for dinner tomorrow." She wiped her eyes on her sleeve. "Hubs is in Kansas until Sunday. We can have one last girl talk."

"I'd like to come over, but I can't." I put my arm around Emma's expanding waist and walked her back to her room. I couldn't let her see how the idea of leaving everything I knew filled me with ice-cold panic. "This is hard enough as it is. If I stay with you, I might lose my nerve."

"You think?" Emma sniffed. "I think you're gorgeous and crazy and courageous and..." Her outburst trailed off.

"Fragile?"

"No, but delicate maybe. I don't want you to self-destruct a thousand miles away from all your friends."

"I'm not going to self-destruct." I swallowed the angry words threatening to spill free. Why did even my best friend see me as weak?

Emma pushed me away and slammed the door, shutting me out in the hall. Surprised by her intensity, I jumped back, stepped on a brown wingtip shoe, and flailed my arms to catch my balance. When I righted myself, I turned to confront Warren Carstairs. The pinstripe shirt and blue tie complimented his tanned and toned body, which managed, as always, to emphasize my petite stature. His brown eyes looked puzzled.

"Won't return my texts, Riley? That's a little childish, isn't it? I expected more of you."

I fumbled with the lanyard around my neck. "Don't know what to tell you, Warren."

He took me by the elbow and guided me to my room. Settling me into one of the student desks, he crossed his arms and perched on the edge of mine. "I thought I owed you honesty. I thought we were friends, good friends, the kind who could tell each other the truth."

"Well, color me dumb." Rising, I snatched my crystal apple paperweight, stowed it in a canvas bag, and looked around for more stuff to pack. Soft stuff that I wouldn't be tempted to throw at his handsome, frowning face. "I thought we were something more."

The hum of the computer monitor filled the room. Neither of us moved. Finally, Warren stood up. He brushed at the creases in his chinos. "You tell anyone?"

"Only my parents. And Emma."

He fingered the pack of sticky notes on the desk. "I'd hoped to keep this between us."

"Do you really think no one will find out?"

"It doesn't look good, you know."

"For you or me?" I snatched the notes and added them to the bag, then reached out to straighten his tie, sliding the fabric between my fingers. "Don't worry, Warren. I'm leaving Hopewell. My parents are, too. They're going off to Florida to live in the sun. And Emma? She won't say anything. So, if you like, you can tell everyone I broke up with you. You'll look like the injured party. Yeah for you."

Warren jingled the coins in his pockets. "Where are you going?"

I started to spin my new job story one more time when my phone chimed. I picked it up and swept the screen straight to an email from Principal Lord asking if I'd be willing to put my name on the substitute list for next year. I scrolled through two more. A polite rejection from the Cincinnati School District and a note from Emma: *Please, Riley. Take a few weeks to think this through.* I placed the phone face down on my desk and tried to speak around the bubble of insecurity threatening to blow up my resolve.

"Into the wilderness," I said, leaving Warren Carstairs with the most astonished, quizzical look I'd ever seen on his perfectly poised, ruthless face. Before he could respond, I escorted him out of the room and watched until he reached the end of the hall. When I was sure he'd gone, I finished packing away my classroom.

Taking leave of familiar places carves little marks on your soul. At least, it did for me. I wandered the school corridors, drifted by the cafeteria, ran my fingers over the picture books in the library. I pushed through the gym door and sat on a swing in the playground. I searched my memory for moments of happiness to tide me over the next few months, the next year. Every time I stopped moving, panic swelled. I had to do deep breathing exercises at lunch and again when I got home. Sleep refused to come Friday night, no matter how many sheep I counted. Okay, not sheep. Bare-chested Chippendales all giving me a come-on look. Abandoning the sex theme, I gave in to sorrow and sobbed for an hour. Then I rolled up my sleeping bag, made one final pass through the apartment, and dropped the key off in the slot on the Management door. Before the sun began to paint the sky, I reached Columbus and headed north on Interstate 71. I followed Route 76 to Route 80, then turned north on the far side of Sharon, Pennsylvania, always heading north and east.

I drove eight hours that first day, feeding CDs into the slot on the dash and singing along to stop the replay of goodbyes scrolling through my head. When I couldn't keep my eyes open any longer, I pulled into an Express Inn just west of Erie, Pennsylvania. They only had one vacancy, a king-sized room with a view of a vineyard. Wishing I'd brought along a bottle of Cabernet forgetfulness, I lugged my laptop into the room, plopped down on the bed, and checked for messages. Twenty-seven spams and thirteen offers of genital enhancement later, I found two messages from Emma, one sad, the other a fierce rant against stupid asshole Warren.

"Maybe he'll lose his looks and his job and die alone!" she wrote. "We can put a hex on him, okay, Ri?"

Alone in the hotel room, missing Smokey, missing Emma, I turned on the TV, buried myself beneath a mound of pillows, and sobbed again, the news of the world blaring in the background. Images of war and famine and stock market jitters merged with feel-good stories about firefighters rescuing puppies and little girls selling lemonade to raise money for cancer research. Each one made me cry harder, thinking how that wavy Dow Jones line matched my life. I dialed Emma's number only to hang up three times. Then I punched in Warren on speed dial, canceling the call before he could answer. What could I say that would matter?

Besides, what I missed was the comfort and security I believed our relationship had provided, the familiarity, the tame sameness of known things. I considered turning back. Perhaps I could substitute teach after all. Principal Lord liked me, had already asked me to reconsider. There was precedent. Monica Adderley had taken maternity leave and, unable to leave her newborn, decided not to return. When she changed her mind a month later, the Board took her back. At ten p.m., I packed up my overnight bag and went as far as the car before I gave in to the realization that I'd already burned my bridges. I wiped my face with the hem of my cotton tee and made a bargain with myself. One month. I'd give it a month. Then, if I still felt lost, no matter the personal shame and humiliation, I'd crawl back to Hopewell and accept Sarah Lord's offer. Only God knew how I'd survive on sub pay, but at least I'd know my way around town.

The early Sunday morning traffic was light, but the stream of campers and out-of-state vehicles picked up as I followed the highway through Buffalo. Fighting sadness and fatigue, I sipped a Mickey D's large coffee and tried to imagine a new beginning in some small town or a big northern city. The winters in upstate New York were brutal. Buffalo was famous for its piles of roof-high snow. Shivering despite the eighty-degree temps, I experienced a floating sense of horror. The farther I got from Hopewell, the stronger the sense of disconnection. My old life consisted of manicured, climate-controlled suburban vistas. The long stretches of unkempt woods along the side of the road screamed chaos.

A construction detour at Watertown forced me to turn east on Route 3. The landscape shifted from city to suburban to rural. Forested areas, some boggy and impenetrable, crept closer to the side of the road. Huge rocks, granite and sandstone and basalt, appeared like warts, abandoned in the middle of a field or crowded by pines. I hunched forward, looking for the detour signs that would guide me back to the interstate. Every few miles, I checked the bars on my cell phone. Service ran out somewhere east of Carthage. Glancing in the side mirror, I noticed a growing number of houses in need of paint or siding, storefronts with boarded-up windows, gas stations shuttered, their pumps removed. Panic gnawed a hole in my decision. I kept glancing at the fuel gauge, thankful I'd filled the tank before I left the motel. The wall-to-wall traffic had disappeared.

Uncertain of my destination, I pulled over to check the atlas. Route 3 wound its way to Saranac and eventually into Lake Placid. Those names sounded familiar from my job search. Touristy. Friendly. I could find a hotel for the night, check with the locals, and search for work. My heart skipped once, twice, settled back into rhythm. Dark clouds filled the sky behind me. I slowed, hesitant to drive into the unknown with a storm on the horizon. Behind me, a black SUV roared up, tailgating, the occupants hidden from view behind tinted windows. The driver crowded the double-yellow line, roared closer, then backed away. Thunder rumbled. Intimidated, I took the next right turn. Bad idea.

The turnoff proved to be a scant ten yards of paved road that branched into two separate lanes of dirt tracks. The left-hand fork disappeared into a forest. I turned right, my red compact bumping along in the ruts. Twenty minutes later, the lane flared out into a grassy clearing. Off to the right, two trailers leaned beneath the overhanging branches of tall pines, some of their windows covered in brown paper, the others bearing tattered curtains. An old pickup sat on cinder blocks, the tires missing. I surveyed the area, trying to decide what to do. Phone service didn't exist this far away from the main road. Then it occurred to me. No one knew where I was. I glanced at my phone. Maybe I couldn't call anyone, but I could still take pictures. That way, if Bigfoot claimed me, at least there would be a record. I aimed the phone at the trailers. One of the curtains fluttered. Was someone inside? My hands shook.

I peered through the windshield, blinking to clear my tired eyes, then snapped two shots and saved them to my photo gallery. When I put the car in reverse, I narrowly missed backing into the first double-wide. Spooked by the stillness, I gunned the engine and raced back to the paved road. When I stopped, unsure whether to continue east or turn back the way I had come, a huge bird with black feathers landed on the hood. I punched the horn, which uttered a pathetic peep. The bird cocked its head, cawed, and took off. Unsure of my direction, I pounded my hands on the steering wheel. That didn't help, so I rolled down the window.

"What," I shouted into the wind, "have I gotten myself into?"

Chapter 5

...if you don't want an answer, don't ask the question...

I clapped my hands over my mouth. Maybe I shouldn't have shouted. A bear might come charging at me. A wolf could be lurking among the trees. Perhaps the people who lived in the trailers had followed me down the road. When a voice shouted back, I screamed again. Well, I intended to scream. What came out sounded more like a squeak.

"You should've stayed on three." The voice, deep and compelling, carried in the early dusk. I checked the mirrors but saw no one. I opened the door, stretching the seat belt. My hands were sweaty. I released the belt and, balancing half in and half out of the car, looked around. Was I talking to a spirit of the forest? Nerves took over. I giggled.

"Come out, come out, wherever you are." The chant sounded ridiculous and small as it sprang into the wind. Something rustled in the brush along the side of the road. Bear? Bear! Hopping back inside, I dug around in my overnight bag in search of a weapon. When my hand closed around the hairdryer, I pulled it free and held it beneath my chin. Then I pushed the door lock button. Unfortunately, I forgot to close the window. When I looked up, a hairy forearm rested along the seam of the open window. Bigfoot! I bobbled the dryer as I followed the arm up to a shoulder and then to a face hidden behind a beard. The man had a cap pulled down to shade his eyes.

"Really?" He tipped his head. His lips twitched as though he were trying not to laugh. "You planning to blow me away with that?"

I don't know what shade I turned, probably blood-red. Embarrassment made my heart skip. I lowered the dryer and

31

sat up as tall as I could before facing the stranger. He tilted the cap back. A pair of x-ray blue eyes confronted me, the kind that see through your clothes, even the denim jacket I'd slipped on when I stopped for lunch.

"Unless you want to drive in this storm," the man hooked a thumb over his shoulder, "you might think about stopping in Wanakena."

The name, like Saranac and Placid, sounded familiar. As I stared into those intense blues, my heart lurched in an entirely different way. What the hell was wrong with me? I could be looking at a pervert, and I was rating his looks on my personal hotness meter? I coughed twice and cleared my throat. "Wanakena? Is that a town?"

"Nope. Not big enough. It's a hamlet. Just turn right out of this road, drive about three miles. You'll see a SUNY Ranger School sign. Turn right again and follow that road into town. At the general store, ask for Carl." The man settled the cap more firmly on his head. The brim carried an official-looking logo, but I couldn't read what it said before he stepped back.

"Are you a forest ranger?" I said. He didn't answer. Maybe he didn't hear me. I debated whether to repeat the question. After all, he could be a serial killer. My mother's paranoia sounded in my head. I decided not to push my luck. Luck? That was the joke of the millennium. Lost, lonely, and acting like a loon, I might as well tattoo a capital L on my forehead. I shifted the car into drive. The ranger banged on the fender as I pulled ahead.

"Better hurry," he said. "Tell Carl I sent you."

At the stop sign, I checked both ways three times until my hands stopped shaking. Then I pushed the gas pedal and peeled away, scattering gravel and regret behind me. Who was this Carl, I wondered, and how did he and that dark-haired stranger, whose name I didn't even get, know each other? The storm rumbled closer. Under a bolt of lightning, the trees swayed while the memory of that intense stare accompanied me all the way down the road.

Chapter 6

...what's done is done...

"Breathe, Riley," I chanted until the panicky feeling passed. Hunched over the steering wheel, I peered through the storm. The Ranger School sign that identified the next turnoff, County Route 61, sprang up like a giant mushroom. When I saw it, I turned the wheel hard. The tires squealed. Heavy rain splattered the windshield, reducing visibility and increasing my stress. The two-lane road tunneled on. I anticipated passing a new landmark or another fork in the road, but I saw nothing except more forest. My stomach rolled. My head throbbed. Even my goosebumps had goosebumps. I had almost decided to turn around when I spotted a wooden billboard declaring Wanakena the "Gateway to the Wilderness." A wooden placard off to the right, smaller and less conspicuous but equally daunting, announced *Cemetery*.

"Oh, the irony." I wished Emma were here. I could use her calming voice and steady counsel right now. I clenched the wheel so tight my fingers turned numb as I considered my options. Right or left, branches drooped over the road. Lights winked off and on through the trees, suggesting buildings ahead, but I couldn't be sure. The rain pounded. Screw it. I swerved to the right. In less than ten yards, I came to another crossroads bearing another Ranger School sign. I opted to go right again and found myself on a street lined with modest two-story homes that reflected a hodge-podge of styles and historical periods. The road curved before dipping down a hill.

At the bottom, a brick and clapboard structure bore a sign above the porch that read **General Store**. A second, smaller notice shaped like a pointing finger indicated that the hamlet's post office shared the space at the far end. The beam of light I had followed spilled from the store. I parked as close to the building as I could and hurried onto the porch. Unable to stop shivering, I banged on the door. No one answered. I pressed a hand to the glass and peered inside, hoping to catch a glimpse of a clerk or other customers. The wind loosened a note taped to the door and blew it to the ground. I picked it up, only to read that the store was open from six-thirty a.m. until eight p.m. I checked my watch. Seven-thirty. Then I spied a second, hand-lettered notice stuck between the door and the jamb. CLOSED EARLY. COME BACK TOMORROW.

Dashing back to the car, I dropped my head onto the steering wheel and groaned. I didn't have a clue what to do next. The storm rattled the Civic, rocking it enough to make me queasy. I squinted into the night until my eyes adjusted to the darkness. Opposite the store, an expanse of lawn graced by a gazebo spread toward a body of water. At the point where the land and water met, I detected movement. Waves sloshed over rocks lining the shoreline. *Excellent planning, Riley.* I had no place to go, no phone or Internet connection, and I desperately needed to use the bathroom. Maybe I could just blow the horn until someone came to investigate. Or I could curl up and die here, in a place called Wanakena, with my pride wrapped around me like a shroud. I sniffed back a sob, half-hoping weird Mr. Blue-eyes would show up and rescue me again.

A fist rapped on the window. I jumped. The fist, attached to a large, muscled arm, rapped a second time. "Hello? You all right in there?"

I reached for the hairdryer again, snorted at the idea of repeating that foolish gesture, and rolled down my window. Rain hustled in. A man in a yellow slicker held up a lantern and rubbed his chin.

"You're not..." He paused, blinked twice, and started again. "Do you need help?"

"I...yes. I was told to stop here to pick up some groceries. I didn't know the place would be closed." I sounded a touch whiny. *God, Riley, pull it together.*

"Carl Beamish is expecting you is my guess." He bobbed his head beneath a wide-brimmed hat that obscured the upper half of his face, but from what I could see, he was not my mysterious forest man. "Probably set everything out for you. No use letting you wander around lost any longer."

A thousand questions pulsed behind my now-damp eyelashes, but I shook them off. I might not be the person he thought I was, but I wasn't turning down the offer of help. I followed him up the stairs, unable to see past the spread of his broad shoulders. He was taller than me, but then almost everyone was, and, from the back, it looked like he was built sturdy. I shuffled my feet as he bent to retrieve a key beneath a flowerpot, then unlocked the door. He grabbed the notice of closing before it blew away and flipped on the lights. The interior resembled every Vermont Store catalog page I'd ever perused. Shelves and tables groaned beneath stacks of t-shirts and hoodies while souvenirs of carved moose and bear roared at me from rotating stands. The room stretched on, crowded with pantry items for vacationing families.

"Anton Storms." The man offered his hand. He was younger than I first thought, perhaps my age, with dark eyes, a full mouth, and the late afternoon bristle of a beard shading his cheeks.

"Riley Finn." I wiped my sweaty hand on my wet jeans and shook. His grip was rough, callused, and strong. I winced, then pulled free. He slapped his hat against his leg, spraying water in all directions. When I looked up, his gaze narrowed in the lamplight. He had sized me up, it seemed, and found me wanting.

"Well, nice to meet you, Miss Finn. Everything you need is in these bags." He waved at the sacks sitting next to the cash register. "You want me to call Carl and tell her you're on your way?"

I hoisted the canvas totes, staggering under the load. A phone call would reveal me as an imposter. I'd be out in the rain again, alone. That thought made me squirm. Rain drummed against the tin roof. "Oh, that's not necessary. Here's the thing, Mr. Storms. Where exactly am I going?"

"I can help you there." He shot me a look that was part mischief and part mistrust. Of course, if I had been the one Mr. Beamish was expecting, I would know the way, right? Storms slipped behind the counter, took out a pad and pencil, and printed directions in large block letters. I felt like a kindergartner on the first day of school. He tucked the note into my hand and escorted me back to the car. My fingers tingled at the rasp of his palm against mine. He replaced his hat, lifted the lantern, and strode off into the night. When I could no longer see him, I turned on the dash light and studied the directions. Whoever Carl was, I hoped he wouldn't turn me away. I had left the world I knew behind, had no choice but to forge ahead. I glanced at the store. The porch light splayed out, casting that same gauzy beacon that had drawn me to it. Shifting into reverse and then drive, I sped as fast as I dared, unable to shake the notion that the miniature carvings of moose and bear were chasing me down the road.

Chapter 7

...when all else fails, punt...

"Left turn at the wilderness sign. Cross the steel bridge. Take an immediate right. Follow the road until it dead-ends." Storms' instructions stopped there. I repeated them as I peered through the cascade of water covering the windshield. I should have changed the wiper blades before I started this adventure. Or misadventure. My mind conjured a vision of me parking, walking through the stand of pines, and disappearing into the forest, never to be seen again. No, that last part was my insecurity talking. "Buck up, Riley," I ordered. "You can do this."

The tires clanged against the slats of a metal bridge. After I made it across without falling through the openings, I turned left. A stretch of log homes sat scattered down the right side of the road. Most of them perched at the end of long driveways. One, closer to the road, bore a sign advertising Backpacker Adventures. Beyond the house and cabins, I passed a two-story white clapboard, lit by flood lamps, with a separate garage, followed by a long stretch of darkness. Then the road ended. The suggestion of a trail veered off into dense woods. I clicked the headlights from bright to dim and back again, but it was impossible to see anything beyond the trees. Hoisting my overnight bag over my shoulder, I pulled up the hood of my windbreaker, grabbed the groceries, and staggered down the trail. Twenty yards along, I spied another log cabin.

In contrast to the newer structures on the first section of the road, this one had weathered, its gray-green siding causing it to blend into the trees surrounding it. An older woman, tall, with a frizz of white hair haloed by light shining out from the open door, stood waiting on the porch. She waved as I approached, pushed the door open with one hand, and called out.

"So, missy, you found it all right?"

"A Mr. Storms gave me directions." I cleared my throat, unsure of what to say next. "I'm looking for Carl."

"You found her. Carl Partlowe Beamish. Ms. Beamish. Used to be Carole, but I prefer Carl. But, gosh, I already told all the applicants that in the email." She offered her hand. I leaned forward, extended two fingers, and shook. "Which one are you?"

"Riley Finn," I said. "Riley Marie to my mother, especially when she's angry with me. My friends just call me Ri."

Carl wrestled one of the bags from me. Her face scrunched up in a frown. "Well, you're not tall, and you're not blonde, so you sure as pudding aren't LeeAnne McMasters, from Albany, right?"

"Um, no. I'm from Hopewell, actually?'

"Maine?"

"Ohio." I juggled the remaining groceries. My overnight bag slipped off my shoulder. Setting both down, I rubbed my hands on my jeans. "I'm guessing I'm not who you were expecting."

Carl cocked her head, closed one eye, and harrumphed. "Appears you're not, but then you're the one who's made it here. The universe has a way of placing us where we need to be. Well, don't stand there shiverating. Come on in out of the weather."

I refused to move before I cleared the confusion. "I don't want to be in the way. What if this LeeAnne shows up?"

"We'll deal with that when it happens. Fact is, I expected the girl sooner. LeeAnne knows her way around Wanakena. Not like her to be late, but maybe the storm's delayed her, or maybe she lost her way. Suppose you might have gotten lost, too. Easy to do if you're a stranger. Not the best idea to be roaming around on your own here at night."

"What do you mean?"

Ignoring my question, Carl motioned me closer, grabbed both bags, and, chattering on, led me deeper into the house. "I imagine you met Mr. Storms at the store. He called soon as you left. Man turns up in all kinds of weather. Good Lord, you're no bigger than a minute. Don't know if you'll be strong enough to do the shelf stocking and such. Oh, well, what's done is done. If LeeAnne doesn't show up and you don't work out, I'll find someone else. That your real hair color? I've never seen such black tresses. Mine used to be blonde till I got old, and it used to be straight. Look at this frizzy mess. What did you say you do for a living?"

"I'm a teacher. At least I was." I said the last so low I was sure Carl didn't catch it. I was wrong.

"You're a teacher, are you? Maybe I remember that from your application. You did send an application from my Craigslist ad, didn't you? Well, that's a bonus. You can help out with some tutoring up at Star Lake. God knows we got some folks around here as need it. Your cabin's out back. You hungry? Course you are. We'll eat after you settle in."

Beamish's abrupt shifts of topic and her non-stop comments overwhelmed me. I caught myself breathing for her. She set the bags on the counter, then pinned me with a watery stare.

"We need to fatten you up, Miss Riley."

I shifted from foot to foot, flailing like a bug caught in a net, and wondered if Carl Partlowe Beamish was preparing to swat at me. When she finally paused, I said the only thing that sprang to mind.

"Is it all right if I pee first?"

Ms. Beamish hitched up her jeans. "Follow me."

She banged through the back door, hatless, coatless, and determined. I raised the hood of my jacket and hurried after her. She hustled down a path that wound past a plowed garden bed. Ahead, in a clearing surrounded by a stand of hemlocks, sat a newer, smaller cabin. Ms. Beamish led me onto a screened-in porch just big enough for a bistro table and two chairs. A second, sturdier door opened into a kitchen, and beyond that, a separate sleeping area. Between the rooms was a bathroom. She hummed as she fiddled with the radio on one of the end tables until I, much relieved, returned.

"Feeling better?" Ms. Beamish asked. Without waiting for a reply, she began to point out the appliances. "Refrigerator. It's small, but you'll be eating breakfast and dinner with me. Microwave and a coffee maker. Washer. Dryer. Small but efficient. Extra bedding in the cabinet in the loo. Towels and such. Radio. Here are your dishes and glassware. Ever slept on a futon? I'll show you how to open it up later. Your cell phone won't work well up here. Service is spotty, but there are plans to put in a tower at Star Lake this fall. I wish they wouldn't. If you need to make a call, you can use the phone at my place. Just record the particulars on the notepad by the answering machine. Same thing with the Internet. All anyone's got up here's dial-up or satellite service. I have satellite. It's slow. During thunderstorms, it won't work at all. Appreciate it if you don't try to download movies or TV shows. Oh." Ms. Beamish gulped air and opened an accordion door in the lower kitchen cabinet. "If you feel the need for nighttime entertainment, this little TV works. Only gets three channels, all the commercial ones. Or you can come up to the house and watch with me."

Overwhelmed at the blitz of information, I sank into a kitchen chair and folded my hands to keep from displaying my dismay. The smell of fresh-cut wood filled the air. I identified the rumble of a stream or river through the open door as it stuttered and growled over the channel, its rush blending with the wind racing through the pines. Ms. Beamish rattled on. I zoned out, fighting an increasing sense of panic. When she placed one large, work-worn hand on my shoulder and squeezed, my whole body jerked.

"Ever been in the Northwoods before, Ms. Finn?"

Dazed and close to exhaustion, I shook my head.

"Know how to hunt?"

"Um, no."

"Fish? Canoe? Camp? Hike?"

My heart jumped twice. I reminded myself to breathe and summoned up my best teacher voice. "I've hiked in Clifton Gorge," I said. "That's pretty dangerous. People have been injured falling off cliffs there, and I hiked parts of the Buckeye Trail with my friend Emma before she got pregnant. In Ohio. Around the cities."

"Cities." She snorted the word. "City walks don't count."

My head drooped lower. "I'm sorry."

"You saw that sign by the fork in the road?" Ms. Beamish crossed her arms, waiting for my reply.

"Gateway to the Wilderness," I said.

"That's where you are. Now the question is, Ms. Finn, are you going to step through that gateway or turn around and head back with your tail between your legs? 'Cause this country doesn't forgive weakness. Are you weak, Ms. Finn?" Ms. Beamish slid open one of the drawers next to the sink. She took out a flashlight and placed it on the table. Then she turned to go. "Dinner's ready and waiting. Come over when you are. And you can call me Carl if you like."

After she left, I locked myself in the bathroom, stuffed a washcloth in my mouth, and screamed. The feeling of being abandoned and alone intensified. Removing the cloth, I pounded my thighs, muttering aloud all the fears I had failed to embrace earlier. What a weak, soft, pampered idiot I was. Warren's betrayal had gutted me. No matter how I tried to spin it, I had failed at every relationship, even the one I thought the strongest. And now I had jumped headfirst into unfamiliar waters where I knew nothing about the place or the people who inhabited it.

"What am I doing here?" I looked in the mirror, noting the pitiful state of my hair, the droop of my mouth, my bloodshot eyes. "This is, like, Deliverance country. It's so dark under the trees. What if there are wolves? Is there anyone here my age? How did that Storms man know to wait for me?"

The woman in the mirror bared her teeth. *Grow up, Riley.* My stomach growled. Carl had mentioned dinner. Motivated by the emptiness in my gut, I retrieved my overnight case, stowed the toiletries on the shelf above the sink, and shrugged back into my jacket. If a maniac was going to attack me during the night, I wanted to eat first. Shoving the flashlight in a pocket, I left the cabin. I didn't even remember to lock the door.

Chapter 8

...here's to new beginnings...

Carl's house resembled a specialty shop dedicated to *Alces alces*, the largest member of the New World deer family. How I remembered that arcane bit of information escaped me as I looked around the room. A stuffed moose head hung on the wall above the oversize fireplace in the great room. Afghans decorated with the giant deer draped themselves over the sofa and side chairs, and moose-themed placemats graced the table, set with plates and mugs bearing the image of a moose cow and calf. Tiles featuring the animal in various poses covered the surface. The aroma of fresh-baked bread and berries and maple syrup permeated the air. Thank goodness Carl wasn't serving mooseburgers. I suppressed a giggle, but I couldn't contain my hunger as my stomach protested again.

"So, there you are, then," Carl said, the oven mitts covering her hands decorated with antlers. "Riley? All right if I call you Riley? Sit. The muffins are almost done. I'm making granola for breakfast. Got a pot of turkey chili and fresh blueberry cobbler for dessert."

"This looks so...homey." I settled into a chair and ran my hands over the embroidered moose on the napkin.

"Oh, it's too much for most folks," Carl said, "but it suits me, and that's all I care about. I've loved moose since I was a little girl. Not many left around here. We get an occasional one passing through. I have to travel to Canada for my photographs." She raised her chin to a display on the wall. I got up to look closer.

"You took these?" The pictures were the most amazing close-ups of wildlife I had ever seen. Half of the photos featured a bull moose or a cow with her calves. The others displayed various forest denizens: a wolf, a black bear, otters, coyotes.

"After university, I worked in wildlife conservation for thirty years. Have a look through my books. There, on the shelf." Carl gestured with one of the mitts. The timer buzzed. She hurried into the kitchen to take the muffins out of the oven, her knees cracking when she bent down.

I ran a finger over the titles on the shelf, counting seven collections of photographs by C. P. Beamish before she called me to the table. Between mouthfuls of chili and muffin, I asked about the town and the people and the job. Carl seemed happy to share her knowledge of Wanakena. She rattled on about the hamlet's history, although she appeared reluctant to discuss particular inhabitants, and she waved off all my questions about the store.

"I'll go over that tomorrow, and then I'll leave you to it."

"Fine." I helped myself to another muffin, but beneath the table, my leg jittered. A new wave of anxiety joined the one that had accompanied me from Hopewell. This woman expected me to master the art of running a store in a single day? The tremors spread upward until my hands shook. Ms. Beamish went right on talking.

"Only seventy-five townsfolk live here year-round, Riley. Tomorrow I'll introduce you to the ones you're most likely to encounter regularly. In two days, everyone will know who you are anyway. A few more weeks and there'll be lots of tourists, too. Some stay all summer. Some come and go throughout the season. Then there are the students. Suppose you noticed the SUNY Ranger School sign when you turned onto sixty-one? If you came here to meet a man, there'll be students and fishermen, although ranger types are solitary sorts, generally. Have to enjoy being alone to do the work they do."

Being alone appealed to me at the moment. Maybe I should have applied to be a student. I sniffed. "I didn't come here to meet a man, Carl," I said. Muffin crumbs tumbled from my mouth. "That's the last thing I want or need."

"Oh," Carl got up to pour herself another beer, "you're running away from one. Mending a broken heart? Or a cheated one? Been there, done that, decided not to repeat those mistakes. No man, or woman, is going to rule my life ever again. Thing is, you think you'll die, honey, but you don't."

Carl's casual dissection of my private life angered me. "I don't suppose that's any of your business, really, is it? I came for the job, and I intend to see it through." Although I hadn't meant to issue a commitment, I couldn't stop myself. What happened to the give-it-a-month resolution?

"All I'm saying," Carl ignored my outburst, "is rangers are hard men, and strong, but solitary. Normally, it won't do to get involved with one of them. But you can still have a good time. It won't hurt to flirt a little, given the opportunity. Life's too short to spend it on regrets."

When she winked at me, I swallowed hard before broaching the subject uppermost on my mind. "Speaking of men and regrets, I did take a wrong turn. Down the road at Inlet, maybe? And some man who looked like a ranger, he was wearing a cap and a shirt with the forestry service logo, gave me directions to the town. He did seem a little prickly. Should I be afraid?"

Carl set down her spoon and steepled her fingers. "Goatee? About sixty? Potbelly?"

I shook my head.

"Not Gus Jornigen then. Medium height with pockmarks on his cheeks and a voice like sandpaper on wood?"

"No," I said, thinking hard about the man who had stepped out of the brush. "This guy was over six feet. Rugged but handsome behind the beard, I think. He had the bluest eyes I've ever seen. Like laser beams. Felt like he was peering into my soul."

"Oh? Oh, now that's interesting. Hadn't thought to see him working back here this summer. He's an enigma, that one, deep, dark, and mysterious."

She didn't address my concern about him being dangerous. I turned my attention to the cobbler so Carl wouldn't see me blush. The embarrassment of the moment in the car flooded back. I threatened him with a hairdryer. Really? What an idiot I was. Ms. Beamish chatted on.

"I believe you ran into Josh Waylon. He's worked St. Lawrence County, especially the Oswegatchie River, in the past, but things got a little dicey for him last year. I heard he volunteered for fire duty up around Saranac. Not a big talker, our Josh," Carl looked up in time to catch me yawning. "Now, you go on and get your things put away. I'll stop by and show you how to turn on the heater and such, and then you can go right to bed."

I only protested a little as I carried my dishes to the sink, ashamed not to help clean up after dinner. My mother would be appalled. Carl waved me off. I slipped out the front to retrieve my suitcase from the trunk and wheeled it back through the house. With a final rumble, the storm retreated. We walked to my cabin through the solemn dark. The trees dripped moisture, raising a new chorus of plops as we passed beneath them. A mosquito whined above my right ear. I reminded myself to get out the insect repellent. And tomorrow, I'd stick on one of the deer fly patches Emma had left in my mailbox.

Carl made up the bed and left. I was too frazzled to do more than brush my teeth, although I did wonder what she meant by things getting dicey for the ranger. Wandering onto the screened porch, I marveled at the impenetrable blackness of the forest. I wrapped my arms around my waist and recited the prayer my father insisted I say throughout my childhood. *Now I lay me down to sleep...* Then I made my way to the futon, climbed under the blankets, and wiggled into a comfortable position. I left the cabin door open to the sounds of the wind and the river, the song of the wilderness easing me to sleep.

Sometime during the night, I woke to the sound of huffing behind the cabin. Maybe a wolf had ventured close, nosing for entry. Or a bear prowled the perimeter, sniffing for the apples I'd placed in a bowl on the table. I even fantasized about a stranger, with eyes the color of eternity, climbing into my bed. My feet bare, blanket wrapped around me to control the shivers, I got up and closed the door. Then I crawled back onto the lumpy bed, huddled with my pillow, and repeated the only mantra I believed in: what's done is done.

Chapter 9

...what doesn't kill you...

The ravens woke me, their raucous gossip intruding on the pre-dawn stillness. Soon, light leaned through the eastern-facing windows. Groggy and disoriented, I stamped my feet to warm them. I hadn't realized how cold it would be in the mornings here. I hurried through my bathroom routine, moisturizer, sunscreen, a dab of blush, then plodded up to Carl's house. The back door stood open. The smell of fresh-brewed coffee drew me in. I glanced at the clock on the stove and groaned. 6:45 a.m.

"Too early for you, Riley?" Carl greeted me with a pat on the back and a coughing fit.

"If it's summer," I said, accepting the mug she offered. "I should still be sleeping."

"Fresh air and new surroundings make for good alarm clocks." Carl winked. "Have a bowl of granola, and then let's be off. First, we'll walk to the store. Later, I have to drive to Watertown to pick up supplies. Once you learn the routine, that'll be your job."

Carl paced, anxious to get going, so I waved off the offer of breakfast, certain I'd regret it later. My stomach clenched, reminding me of the annual first-day-of-school jitters I always suffered. Performance anxiety, Emma called it, giggling as she ticked off all the occasions when it occurred. Doctor's office. Tests. Trying on bathing suits. First-time sex with a new guy. Like I knew about that. My experience with one lukewarm lover who rationed sex and affection allowed me to claim almost-virgin status, thank you very much. Thinking of Emma reminded me of how homesick I already was. If I ate now, I might throw up, and my friend wasn't here to hold my hair back. Somehow, I couldn't imagine Carl would be sympathetic to a puking employee. But thinking about sex reminded me of Warren's perfidy and the men I'd already encountered here, the ranger Josh Waylon and Anton Storms. Mystery men with hidden pasts and no reason to think kindly of me. Either one could have carted me off in a heartbeat, and no one would have known. Shrugging off that unsettling image, I followed my new boss down the path to where I'd parked my car. As we hiked past, I brushed a handful of pine needles off the hood.

At the end of Reed Road, we passed the sign for Backpacker Adventures. I wanted to ask about the place, but Carl plowed on. We followed the curve of South Shore Road, our hiking boots crunching over sand and gravel and debris left by last night's storm. Along the way, I spotted a board nailed high up on one of the pines. It bore a yellow arrow and the words Janack's Landing.

"What's that place?" I asked.

"Parking lot for one of our trail hikes. Leads to Cat Mountain. The course is about eleven miles. If you want to try it, I've got a map at the store you can use as a guide. Trails abound around here. They look easy on paper, but don't underestimate the difficulty." Carl stood still, her gaze focused on some distant object. Then she shivered, shoved her hands in her vest pockets, and hurried on. "Last year, a hiker died on the Cat."

That sounded ominous. I glanced back at the sign and kept walking. We passed a playground and a basketball court, an outbuilding whose purpose wasn't clear, and several residences. Just beyond a stand of maples and spruce, Carl gestured toward a bridge that spanned the river. The sway of planks hung suspended from cables of thick wire that arched across the Oswegatchie River like a swan's neck. Shading my eyes from the morning glare, I stopped to admire the unexpected grace of the setting.

"Pedestrian bridge." Carl waved a hand at the structure, pride evident in the gesture. "On the National Register of Historic Places."

"It's beautiful," I breathed. "How old is it?"

"Not very, but the original, now that was something. It'd been here since the town was founded in1902. The Rich Lumber Company built it so their employees could reach the lumber mills more easily. None of them loggers left now. The footbridge is one of the longest in the States, about 171 feet end to end."

"The original, it's gone?" I admired the structure. "What happened to it?"

"Ice dam took it down. 'Bout near broke our hearts, but we decided, come hell or high water, we were rebuilding. And we did. Raised the money through raffles and food sales and all manner of creative activities. Don't ever underestimate the people who live here, Riley. They're a tough, determined group. Come on, then. A little tour before work won't hurt a thing." I followed Carl onto the bridge.

The structure swayed as we crossed. Beneath our feet, the river rushed along, heading for Cranberry Lake and beyond, continuing its constant journey east. We stopped to gaze at the water before retracing our steps. When we reached the end, Ms. Beamish put one hand on the support column and chuckled.

"Last winter, a herd of deer used this very bridge to cross the water. Damnedest thing you ever saw. Got a picture of it on the display board." She headed back toward the town. We left the bridge and the history behind. A few yards beyond the historical marker, we reached a four-sided wooden kiosk. Carl pointed out the photographs of lumber workers, early settlers, animals, and celebrations mounted beneath protective plastic. Across the short stretch of road called Hamele Street sat the two-story building that housed the grocery and the Post Office. Red, white, and blue bunting festooned the railed porch. An ice machine crowded next to the store's entrance. A blue mailbox sat out front beside the steps, its slot high enough to accommodate any driver intent on making a quick drop-off. I couldn't shake the compulsion to glance behind me, expecting some woodland creature to stalk out of the bushes or a bearded forestry officer to tap my shoulder and ask for my wilderness credentials. *Like I have any.* I felt like the poster girl for despair.

Carl twisted around. "You say something?"

"Nothing worth repeating." I swallowed the last of my coffee as Carl unlocked the door. Inside, I stopped to orient myself to the new surroundings. The main room boasted a counter to the left. Aided by the overhead lights, I inspected the souvenir sweats and tee-shirts, suspension bridge earrings, postcards, and coasters that dominated the front window display. To the right, I noted the dry goods and fresh fruit bins. Coolers stocked with milk, ice cream, and local beers lined the rear wall. At the very back on the right, I spotted a door marked STOREROOM. Farther left, Carl had added a restroom. Beyond that lay another display room. I wandered back to take a look. The shelves there bulged with fishing lures, books, maps, and other outdoor gear. Returning to the main room, I leaned on the counter and watched Carl open the register and count the money.

"Ever run one of these?"

"I worked retail my senior year of high school," I said.

"Then you'll know how to work the card machine, right?"

I shrugged. That high school job ended ten years ago. "Every store operates a little differently. Please demonstrate how you do it."

Carl spent the next hour tutoring me on my role and my responsibilities of running the store. She showed me a notebook to record purchases in, so their inventory didn't drop too low. "I go into Watertown Mondays, pick up what I can in the truck. Beer and soft drinks are delivered on Fridays. If we get a run on alcohol, you just head over to the Pine Cone and ask Michas if he'll sell you a few cases."

"The Pinecone?" My coffee was long gone, and, as I suspected, my stomach was complaining about not being fed. This city girl didn't like missing meals.

"The Pine Cone, two words. Our local restaurant just up the road. Tomorrow I'll drive you around and show you that and the Ranger School, too. I have a chamber of commerce meeting in Star Lake tonight, so you're on your own for dinner. I left a chicken pot pie in the fridge. Count the money, leave the opening amount in the register, same as today, and bring the rest with you. I'll show you where to stash it when I get home tonight. You have any questions while you're working, just call me." She rested her hand on the old-fashioned landline.

"What if you're not home?"

"Guess you'll be on your own, then, but you're a smart college girl, right? You know how to solve problems when they arise." She cocked her head and waited for my reply.

"Yes, ma'am."

Carl Beamish nodded, although I got the feeling I hadn't convinced her. I squared my shoulders.

"Now." She jabbed a finger at my chest. "I hired you because I need someone reliable. You can have Thursdays off and one other half-day of your choice during the week. The hours are demanding, and the pay's terrible, and there are long spells when no one comes by. So, tell me now if you have the fortitudedeness to do this job."

Fortitudedeness. I bit my lip to hide a grin and my unease. Maybe the time had come to admit that I was not the person for this job. Besides, what if LeeAnne McMasters, the original hire, showed up? Playing for time, I spun in a circle, taking in the racks of snack food, the packages of gummy bears, and beef jerky. I remembered the email want ad written with the word trepidatious, the one I answered, for the job I didn't get. Or did I? Had some trickster god decided to work things out for me without letting me in on the joke? Whatever the reason, I was here now, and Ms. Carl Partlowe Beamish, inventor of words, photographer of wild animals, formidable businesswoman of Wanakena, wanted a commitment. Placing one hand on the counter, I scooped the key to the front door out of the open register. I hoped a fair spell of loneliness and solitude might bring me the clarity I needed to take the next step in my life. The work wouldn't kill me, although the boredom might. Still, I couldn't, wouldn't return to Hopewell, and I had no idea where I'd go if I left this place. Whatever the future held, I decided not to waste the summer searching for it.

"I do, Ms. Beamish." I shook her hand. "And I'll stay, at least through the summer, on one condition."

Carl crossed her arms and frowned. "A condition? What would that be?"

"You have to teach me how to paddle a canoe."

Chapter 10

...working hard for the money...

My first day at the store passed without incident, except for the covert glances tossed my way by locals who came in to browse, speculate, and move on. Well, not all were covert. Several of the townspeople who did stop by stared pointedly and whispered behind their hands. A few ladies greeted my friendly overtures with tight lips and frowns. One started to ask me about LeeAnne, coughed, and left without purchasing a thing. I couldn't blame them for their hesitance. I wasn't what I would have expected. How could they view me with anything but suspicion? Their scrutiny was a test, like the ones I'd experienced in my classroom over the years. I had to earn their trust and respect first. Then, maybe, friendship and affection would follow.

That evening, I demolished the pot pie, poured a shot of Crown Royal from Ms. Beamish's liquor cabinet, and slept like the dead. The following day, I was in the bathroom, toweling off from a shower, when Carl's voice floated through the open window.

"Got an appointment in Watertown today, Riley. Left your breakfast on the table. Don't forget your hat. Deer flies are fierce this time of year." Then, she was gone.

I laced up my hiking boots, pulled on a fleece jacket, and slipped on a ball cap, pulling my ponytail through the opening at the back. As I headed for the house, I mulled over Carl's abrupt departure. She must have forgotten her promise to show me the town. Too bad. I had counted on her introduction to smooth over any missteps in my entry into Wanakenan society. Finding my place here was turning out to be as complicated as it had been back in Hopewell.

The coffee maker beeped as I entered the kitchen. Hot oatmeal steamed in a moose-decorated bowl. Brown sugar and honey and a pitcher of milk sat on the table. After yesterday's experience of no breakfast and a late lunch, I was beyond grateful for the food. I had almost finished cleaning up when I spied a note taped to the refrigerator next to a business card from John Haroldson, M.D. Cardiology. *Oven,* the scrawl read. *Muffins. Please take to the store.*

Settling the cap more firmly on my head, I shoved my hands into moose mittens, wrapped the muffin tins in several towels, and stepped briskly down the path. A cloud of deer flies hovered above the roadway as I reached the end of Reed. I dodged to the left and lumbered across the bridge, the steel spans ringing with each step. Below, through the open flooring, the river winked and flirted. Beyond the bridge, two men walked ahead of me, accompanied by a boisterous, red-coated retriever. Neither man noticed me, but the dog paused. It circled the lot, then rolled its head to glance back.

The guy in front, tall and thicker through the shoulders, disappeared into the trees that edged the gravel parking lot. A marker near the entrance identified this as the beginning of the Moore Trail. The second man, also tall but leaner and more muscled, followed the first into the forest. From the back, I couldn't be certain, but something in the way he carried himself reminded me of the ranger who had directed me to the hamlet. Josh Waylon. I conjured up the memory of blue eyes, a scowl, the hint of a smirk at the corners of his lips. And I, idiot extraordinaire, brandishing a hairdryer like a weapon. My neck and ears burned all over again. I shook off the picture of me attempting to scare him off and trudged on, grateful for the early hour and the lack of vehicles on the road. I rounded the bend only to spot a third man leaning against a truck parked on the berm. He was studying a map spread out across the hood while carving a small block of wood with a penknife. I couldn't see his face, but I noticed the potbelly pushing the front of his shirt. Tufts of gray hair jutted from beneath the cap he wore. Carl's description of the other ranger, Gus Jornigen, came to mind. The man didn't look up as I hurried past him.

When I reached the store, another older male wearing a fisherman's jacket and rubber boots reared up from his perch on the steps. He brandished a walking stick, dipped his head, and spoke in a cultured, scholarly tone.

"Ah, Miss Riley Finn." He followed me up the steps, waited as I unlocked the door, then pressed in behind me. "I see Carl Beamish has settled you right in. She's a stickler for schedules, am I right?"

"Yes, she's rather dictatorial." He waggled his eyebrows. I laughed. "May I get you something?"

"I'm Jesse Livetree. Ms. Finn, and I'm here for several of Carl's famous morning delights." Livetree tamped his cane on the floor with one freckled hand. "Officially, I am the elected mayor of our fair hamlet. I am also an excellent trout fisherman and a teller of tales, true and otherwise. Anything you want to know about our lovely Wanakena, I'm the one to ask."

"I'll remember that, Mr. Livetree." I set the tins down, found a basket beneath the register, and proceeded to fill it with Carl's goodies. The aroma of fresh-baked muffins rose around us. I stood behind the counter, my mouth watering, as Jesse Livetree wandered up and down the rows, tapping as he strolled. When he finally returned to the counter, he brought his dark brown, bloodshot eyes down to mine and grinned.

"I would like these picnic supplies and three of those delicious treats. Raspberry, I hope. Carl knows they're my favorite." He winked.

Lifting the towel off the basket, I gestured at the muffins. "I think they're blueberry today. However, you can take your pick, Mr. Mayor. I don't think they'll last long. What doesn't sell--"

"You'll eat." Livetree finished my sentence. We laughed again. "I need a few more fishing lures, too."

He helped himself to a muffin, then thumped his way into the back room. When he returned, he laid a twenty-dollar bill on the counter, wiped crumbs off his chin, and punctuated the completion of his shopping with a tap of the cane. As I totaled the purchases and bagged them, he waved away the change.

"Just put the excess on my tab, young lady. I'll be back sooner than you think. For sure, tomorrow, when the goodies are just out of the oven." He selected another muffin, tucked the bag under his arm, and stomped his way out.

After the mayor's visit, I waited on a steady stream of people who had two reasons for visiting the store: buying Carl's muffins and checking up on Carl's new employee a second time. Today's group acted friendlier. They responded to my greetings, introduced me to their children, and asked where I was from. Still, I detected wariness in the way they chose their words. I wondered what it was they weren't saying.

The baked goods were gone by ten o'clock, but the shoppers kept coming, First the Colberts, Penny and Martin, followed by the Jacquerry family with their twin girls and a little boy, all under the age of ten, then several people who owned houses on 5th and 6th Streets but only visited on weekends during the summer. A half dozen teenage boys hung around on the porch until noon, estimating their chances of impressing the new clerk by the difference between their height and hers. I shot them my sternest teacher look. All but one mounted a skateboard and drifted away. Gavin Torvald stayed. He introduced himself by dropping an arm around my shoulders to say hi. When I managed to disengage his unwanted embrace, he draped his lanky body halfway across the counter and stared at me. After I failed to pay him any attention, he bought an orange Gatorade and two packages of Oreos. When he finished his snack, he shuffled his way to the back, where he inspected each lure and commented on the pros and cons of individual brands. Since I had never fished in my life, I didn't understand much of what he called out. But I recognized his attempt to capture my attention.

"Gavin, what grade are you in?"

Flattered by my interest, he stood to his full height and preened. "I'll be a junior in the fall. I have my own car now. Maybe you'd like—"

I cut him off as gently as I could. Then I upgraded my classroom credentials from elementary to high school. That should end the flirtation without too much embarrassment. "Many of the students I taught got their driver's licenses as sophomores, too."

"Wait, you're a teacher? But, you're so short."

"I am," I patted his hand, "but I'm lots older than you. I appreciate talking with you, but I need to do some work now. Ms. Beamish expects me to take inventory of the stock. Maybe you can come back another day. Tell me about your school."

Gavin fingered the thread bracelet around his sunburned wrist and hurried out the door. I sighed as I bent to retrieve the notebook that had fallen on the floor. Figures that a teenager would see me as available. How pathetic. On my knees, I searched for the elusive pad, my body in the downward dog position. The door squeaked open. Hushed footsteps padded across the wooden floor.

"Now, Gavin," I stuttered as I rose to my knees, determined to be sterner this time. A reddish-gold head woofed at me. Startled, I fell backward, cracking my tailbone on the floor. The dog I had spotted on the road earlier bounded forward, licked my hand, then turned toward the stocked shelves. His tail wagged, sweeping potato chip bags and cereal boxes onto the floor.

"Hey, stop that!" I reached for the broom stashed in the corner and struggled up. Weapon in hand, I chased after the dog, who decided we were playing. It barked and bounded around the store, nipping at packages as it passed each shelf. Preoccupied with the chase, I didn't hear the door open again or the whistle that recalled the dog, now munching cheerfully on a mooshiepie, a granola and moose jerky local conglomeration, it had liberated from the wrapping. My hair had worked loose from the scrunchie holding it back. Flushed and sweaty and unaware that the top button on my blouse had come undone, I lowered the broom and plowed headfirst into whoever had come in. The impact bounced me backward. I landed back on the floor, spraddle-legged and out of breath. Above me, Josh Waylon crossed his arms and shook his head.

"What's going on in here?" I didn't recognize the daunting baritone with just a hint of southern accent, but the fierceness in the question caused me to scoot backward. I drew my knees under me, staggered upright, and brushed at the back of my khakis. I blinked into the face of the ranger, fisted one hand on my hip, and pointed the broom at the dog panting at his feet.

"Your dog," I intoned, "just ate all our mooshiepies."

"Are you planning to hit me with that?" the ranger asked, rubbing his beard. "I admit, it's a lot more impressive than a hairdryer."

His voice was softer than the one I just heard. The cadence of the east inflected each vowel. If Josh hadn't spoken before, who had? The other man I'd seen on the trail, apparently the one with the southern drawl, pushed his way around Josh Waylon to crouch by the dog.

"Ike," the man held on to the dog's collar with one hand and petted the animal's head with the other, "have you been misbehavin'?"

I remained in place, holding the broom like a club. Shifting my gaze from one man to the other, I resisted the urge to scream. My second day on the job and the store looked like a tornado had passed through. "Look at this mess."

The man petting the dog stood, wiped his hands on his jeans, and winked at me. "I'm Benson Torvald. I teach at the Ranger School. This is Ike. He's just a pup, and, like his master, he doesn't always behave himself, but he's harmless."

The dog barked twice before flopping down. His tail whisked across the wooden floor.

"Torvald?" I lowered the broom and frowned. "I think I just met someone with that name."

"My sister's boy, Gavin, is spending the summer with me," Torvald said. He used his thumb to point over his shoulder. "This Neanderthal is Josh Waylon. He's the strong, silent type. Pay him no mind. He spends too much time in the woods to be good company. Now, Ike, apologize to the lady and ask her how much you owe."

Ike lowered his head and whined. His whole body wagged as he inched closer. Despite my misgivings, I couldn't help but respond to the dog's overture and Torvald's insistent charm. I reached down to pat Ike's head. The dog licked my hand, his tail racing faster than ever. Waylon remained by the door, arms folded, his blue eyes darting between Torvald and the dog. He didn't look at me.

"Josh!" Torvald smacked him in the chest. "Mind your manners or the lady will think you're a serial killer."

"No, I won't, I wouldn't." I looked up in time to catch Waylon's blue eyes looking straight at me, their corners crinkled in disdain. I blushed. Would I always sound like a fool when this man came around? "I mean, ax murderer maybe, but not a serial killer."

Torvald's laugh was as contagious as his smile. He rubbed the stubble of sandy-colored beard that covered his cheeks and chin and took my elbow. "What," he asked as he escorted me back behind the counter, "brings a young, beautiful lady like you to Wanakena?"

"Ben." Josh's rebuke settled on Torvald like a splash of cold water. "I have to call it in."

I thanked the stars I had the counter strategically placed between myself and the men. I had no intention of disclosing my reasons for coming to Wanakena with either of them. I definitely was not sharing them with the charming Ben Torvald, who struck me as a player, or the mysterious, frowning Waylon, whose gaze made every nerve in my body stand on alert. But I couldn't antagonize a customer. I stowed the broom in the corner and searched for an appropriate response. Something in Torvald's speech pattern sounded familiar. I decided to distract both men from my unfriendly reaction. Recalling the sign at the entrance to Wanakena, I leaned on the counter.

"How did a gentleman from South Carolina end up in the wilderness of New York?"

"Nailed my accent, did you? Well, a teaching job beckoned. But maybe it was fate." Torvald reached for a strand of my hair that had fallen forward. As he tucked it behind my ear, his eyes fell to my chest. I looked down. Holy mother of heaven, the tops of my breasts, aided by my push-up bra, rose above the opening of the blouse.

Uneasy with the stranger's fingers on my skin and embarrassed by my wardrobe malfunction, I turned away. I refastened the buttons, smoothed back my hair, and faced the men again, conscious of Torvald's proximity and the wave of disapproval flowing toward me from Josh Waylon.

"Ms. Finn," Waylon stepped to the counter. His fingers wrapped around my wrist, sending shivers up my arm. "I need to use the phone. May I?"

I nodded and wriggled free. I shoved my way around the men to scoop up the discarded mooshiepie wrapper Ike had left behind during his raid. A trail of crumbled pies snaked between the rows of shelves. Ike noticed my frown. With a whine, he dropped to a crouch and laid his head on his paws. Josh grabbed the phone, turned his back, and spoke softly to someone on the other end. He sounded tense. Ben followed after me while Ike remained by the counter. When he finished with the call, the ranger ran a hand through his hair, then gazed at me like someone caught in a memory.

Returning to the register, I totaled up the cost of the dog's rampage while Torvald rattled on about his classes - forestry ecology and invasive insects and plant diseases- and inquired again about my reasons for being in Wanakena. When I mentioned I was a teacher, he immediately expounded on the current state of public schools. Soon, we were discussing the differences in the age groups we taught and the inevitable politics at every level.

Meanwhile, Josh Waylon wandered through the store, balancing an armful of intended purchases while we talked. Ike scooted close to plop down by my feet. When he rested his head on my boots, I knew I'd have to forgive him. Both men noticed the dog's maneuver, but only Ben spoke.

"Ike," Torvald said, "is an excellent judge of character."

I directed a hesitant smile at the dog. "It's nice to know I have one friend in Wanakena."

Waylon paid for his purchases as well as the dog's depredations and moved toward the door. Ike followed at his heels. Torvald handed me two muffins, brushing my palm with his fingers as he did so. "Got a bag for these?"

I reached for one of the wax-coated bakery bags and stashed the muffins inside.

Torvald leaned closer. "Would you be interested in seeing the Ranger School?"

"My boss Carl, Ms. Beamish, planned to show me where it is today." I didn't mention that she seemed to have forgotten the offer. I handed over his change and wrote down the sale items in the notebook by the register.

"Oh, well, your loss." His face clouded over.

"It's kind of you, Mr. Torvald, but I'm a teacher." I smiled to soften the rejection. "I've seen lots of schools." Which wasn't quite true as I'd spent all my years except for the first one at Hopewell Elementary. What a mistake that was. I held out the receipt. "Will there be anything else?"

Torvald rubbed his chin again. "Call me Ben, Riley. I've enjoyed our conversation, wouldn't mind doing it again. I'll call you in a few days. Okay?"

"I'm quite busy, Mr. Torvald, with so much to learn about the store." I fiddled with the pencil I'd used to record the number of mooshiepies Ike had devoured, disturbed about the fact that a stranger had just hit on me. Both Emma and Carl had advised me to flirt a little, but my bruised self-esteem didn't want another round of technical knockouts.

Torvald shoved his wallet into the front pocket of his fishing vest and winked. "I'll call, Riley Finn. We'll work something out."

Behind the professor, the ranger, solid and immovable as stone, shook his head.

"Ms. Finn," Waylon spoke up, "when the police arrive, send them over to Mayor Livetree's house."

"Why? Has something happened?"

"You could say that." Torvald motioned Ike through the door, then twisted to look at the ranger. "Guess that car we found has a driver to go with it, right?"

"It looks like it." Waylon glanced at me, suspicion masking some other emotion in those penetrating blue eyes. "Last night, Gus and I found a body lodged in the rocks by that wide curve in the Oswegatchie not far from the canoe put-in."

"A body?" I clutched the edge of the counter, afraid to let go in case I fainted.

"Yes, ma'am. A woman. The one Carl Beamish was expecting when you showed up."

"LeeAnne McMasters?" I blurted out the name of the woman whose job I'd taken.

Both Torvald and Waylon increased their scrutiny of me.

"How do you know her name? Did you know her? Did you see her when you made that wrong turn?" Waylon stepped closer.

"Carl, Ms. Beamish, told me. I don't, didn't know her. And I never saw anyone on that road, just those two abandoned trailers." The impression of a watcher in the window of one of them came to mind, but I wasn't about to bring that up. They would think I was lying or crazy. Maybe both.

Waylon's gaze traveled down my body, pausing ever so slightly at my mouth and again at my hips. Goosebumps broke out on my forearms. I rubbed them to keep from shaking.

"You're too petite to harm anyone," the ranger said, reaching for the notebook and pen where I kept a record of sales. "Just be careful, Miss Finn. And don't forget to send the police over as soon as they get here. I wrote the directions down for you."

He tore off a sheet of paper, handed it to me, then picked up his groceries and slipped out the door. I followed them onto the porch, watching as he and Torvald stashed their purchases in an official Forest Service truck, then headed up the street on foot. Ike trailed behind, tail wagging as he bounded away. The dog looked back and barked once. Josh Waylon looked at me, too, his face unreadable. Overhead, two black crows wheeled, cawing out the news about the dead woman as they flew.

Chapter 11

... rumors, speculation, and the call of the wild...

A State Highway Patrol car pulled in front of the store ten minutes after noon. I stood by the window as a trooper got out, scanned the street and the lawn area beyond, then bent to retrieve something from inside the vehicle. A long, brown braid hung down her back. I held the door as she strode inside. The woman removed her hat and introduced herself.

"Officer Sandra Kellerman, New York State Police, stationed at Gouverneur. I'm on my way to the home of," she consulted her cell phone, "Jesse Livetree. You must be Riley Finn, Ms. Beamish's summer hire. I understand you are new to the area?"

"Yes. I arrived the same night LeeAnne, er, the victim did, I think." I twisted a rubber band around my finger. Kellerman resettled her hat, glanced around the store, and turned to face me.

"You seem upset, Miss Finn."

"I am, yes. Nervous, actually, Officer. I mean, LeeAnne's fate might have been mine. I don't know how to feel about that."

Kellerman hooked her thumbs in her belt. "I'm sure that is unsettling. It's not every day a person ends up in the middle of a murder investigation, and with all this talk about a wilderness strangler, it's bound to make you uneasy."

"Wilderness Strangler?"

She cocked her head. "Guess no one's shared all the local gossip with you yet. According to Wanakena's newspaper, a killer's stalking the wilderness, strangling young women."

I hid my hands beneath the counter so she couldn't see them tremble.

"That is unsettling." I used her term, although I might have added upsetting, alarming, or downright horrifying. I wondered if I'd ever be able to resume my early morning runs while I was working here. I needed to look up those newspaper articles ASAP. Curious that Carl hadn't mentioned them. "Should I be afraid?"

"Honestly, I don't know. Wanakena's crimes tend more toward drunk and disorderlies at the Pine Cone or speed violations on the highway. The folks who live here are generally well-behaved." She narrowed her eyes. "It's unusual to have two murders roughly a year apart. Tell me, do you recall anything special about the night you arrived? See anything out-of-the-ordinary or strange that might assist in the investigation?"

I shook my head. "I had no idea where I was going, and I got lost. I drove down a road that led into the forest, where I saw two abandoned trailers. I drove back to the main route as fast as I could. Then a ranger found me."

"That ranger was Josh Waylon?"

"Yes, and he sent me here, to the store, and Anton helped me get in."

"Anton Storms?" Kellerman consulted her phone. "He's a fisherman guide."

"I believe so. He let me into the store and told me to take Ms. Beamish's groceries with me. I thought she was a man. Because of her name." The rubber band tightened around my index finger. I yanked it off and stuffed it into my pocket. "Anyway, Anton also gave me directions to her place. When I got there, she offered me the job in the store."

"Ms. Beamish would be Carole Beamish, who goes by Carl and is the owner of the Wanakena General Store,

Wanakena Boat Rentals, and the Marina on Cranberry Lake?"

"I guess." I smoothed a hand over the counter, then looked up. "I didn't know she owned all those businesses."

"Ms. Beamish is a local entrepreneur, a native Wanakenan with influence, political and otherwise. She's well-known in the area."

"Are you from here?"

Kellerman pursed her lips, why I wasn't sure. "I grew up in the Bronx. This place feels like outer space to me."

That explained the accent and the attitude. Still, Kellerman smiled as she handed me a card. "I can't stop long today, but I'll be back to talk with you again, Miss Finn. In the meantime, call me if you remember anything important about that night."

I handed over the paper on which Josh had written the mayor's address, unable to hide my nervousness. As she exited the store, I shivered. Officer Kellerman might not be a native, but the woman had that bird dog look I recognized. Someone was going to pay for this crime, and she intended to be the one to make that happen.

Later that night, Carl returned from her appointment moody and distracted. She didn't mention the Pine Cone or the Ranger School, and I didn't feel comfortable asking about the now-postponed plans. When I shared the news about LeeAnne's car and body, she slumped into the recliner and clawed at the armrests.

"That must be what Jesse called to tell me." She glanced at the phone. "He left a message, but I haven't played it yet. Would you?"

I pressed the button. Jesse's stentorian voice roared at us. He didn't offer details, just explained that the police had recovered LeeAnne's body and that it didn't look like an accident. I shivered again as I burrowed into the couch. Now was the time to push for more information.

"Ms. Beamish, do you believe in the Wilderness Strangler?"

"How did you find out about that?"

"Officer Kellerman told me." I fiddled with the fringe on a moose pillow. "Why didn't you tell me?"

"Didn't see the need to frighten off the help." Carl frowned. "Would you have come here if I had?"

"I don't know. Probably not." We sat in silence until I decided to go on. "How does Mr. Livetree know so much about the investigation? Back home, the police don't give out many details until a suspect is in custody. Sometimes not even then. At least, that's how it seems."

Carl shifted in the chair. "Jesse's a terrible busybody and knows everyone. But that's beside the point. He has a professional connection that serves him well. He served on the force in Star Lake until he accepted a job with the Syracuse police department. While he was there, he made detective. His colleagues keep him in the loop. And he's darn good at figuring things out."

"Maybe he can help find out who did this."

"Riley, don't go fretting over crazy news theories meant to sell papers. You're here, safe and surrounded by good people."

"You don't think I was the one who was supposed to die, do you?" A chill settled over me. When Carl tut-tutted, I got up to turn the fire on under the kettle. "Would you like a cup of tea?"

Carl acknowledged my offer with a nod. "Now, don't you going stewing about something that has nothing to do with you. I agree this is a bad business and the last thing Wanakena needs, but you've got absolutely no reason to think it's about you. No one even knew you were coming here. And there is no sense in spreading silly, sensationalistic rumors. Our little hamlet's been working its way out of that recession that hit years ago, and we still haven't recovered. Talk of a dead body or some imagined wilderness strangler is not conducive to attracting tourists, unless it's the ghoulish kind. I do feel bad for Josh. The last thing he needed was to find another one."

"What do you mean?" I leaned forward. Carl glanced at me, then looked away.

"He found the other one, too. Last year." She fisted a hand over her heart and reached for my help to stand. Then, pleading a headache, she shuffled her way down the hall and into her bedroom. Alone with the cat and the stuffed moose over the fireplace, I abandoned the tea idea and played back the mayor's message on the answering machine, hoping to ferret out more details from his terse statement. No luck there. Annoyed by Carl's dismissal of my concerns, I warmed up some leftover meatloaf and carried it back to my cabin. Once inside, I checked my phone. No messages from Emma or my parents. Exhausted, I slipped into my pajamas, snuggled under the comforter, and looked out the window at the stars visible through the pines. Then I got up and walked through the cabin again. This time, I locked every door and window.

Over the next few days, Carl and the locals skirted around the news of LeeAnne McMasters' death. Everyone wanted to know what I saw the night I arrived, but no one came right out and asked. Instead, they circled the issue as they shopped. Have you been to the put-in yet? Did you see any wildlife on your way into town? Pass any strange cars on your way while you were driving here? How, I wondered, would I know they didn't belong?

It wasn't twenty-four hours before Officer Kellerman returned to the hamlet. She took a statement from Carl, then came by the store for mine. I had nothing more to offer than what I had already told her, and since Josh Waylon could vouch for my demeanor and location, she appeared to dismiss me as a suspect. Still, the suspicion I'd noted in the ranger's eyes rankled. How dare he think, even for a moment, that I could do something like that? However, he did seem to discount it as quickly as the thought occurred. Which also made me mad. All my life, I'd been judged too small to do so many things. Too tiny to play ball and too weak to serve as team manager. Not strong enough to carry a flag with the drill team or set up a booth at the international fair. I was tired of being dismissed due to my size. Even though I had reason to be glad of my diminutive stature this time, it made me furious. Maybe I was going crazy after all. Or maybe Josh Waylon would call to apologize. I banished that thought, but it kept sneaking back. However, nothing happened. The ranger didn't call and ask forgiveness for being rude. Benson Torvald didn't call either, although his nephew Gavin became a constant presence at the store.

The teenager established a routine almost as predictable as my own. Every morning he greeted me as I arrived, then followed me inside, grabbed the broom, and swept the porch. After a pause to load up on snacks, he hung around, looking lonely. He always bought the same things, a fruity drink and mini chocolate chip cookies. He ate them standing in front of the counter, then wandered around, fingering whatever souvenirs caught his eye. Unable to discourage his presence, I decided to enlist his help. Soon, I had him stacking wood, wheeling in the cases of soft drinks and beer, and keeping the shelves in good order.

At the end of the first week, Gavin slumped against the counter, pushed back his shock of sandy hair, and grinned at me. "We're a good team, aren't we?"

It was impossible not to return the smile. "Yes, we are. And that's all we are."

"I know." A faint blush stained his cheeks. His hair flopped forward again, hiding his eyes. "Ben already told me I'm too young for you."

"Ben?" I dusted the jars of tomato sauce lined up along the side shelves. "Oh, your uncle Ben."

"Yeah, but we can still be friends, right?"

I recognized the plea in his eyes. I'd felt the same way with he-who-shall-forevermore-be-nameless once, for a nano-second. "Yes, of course, we can be friends."

"So, who do you think killed that lady who was supposed to be Ms. Beamish's assistant?"

"I have absolutely no idea, Gavin. And I'm trying not to dwell on it."

"Yeah, I'd be pretty spooked, too, if I was you."

"Were."

Gavin's face turned the color of cooked lobster, but he didn't stop talking. "Okay, if I were you. After last year's mysterious death, we sure don't need another one. Hey, maybe a serial killer is living right here in Wanakena."

"You've been watching too many creepy movies." I wanted to find out more about the first murder, but he was already moving toward the door. "Hey! You still have a few chores to finish. Time to empty the trash, young man."

Disappointed, he stashed his skateboard behind the counter and scuffed his way to the outside bins. When he came back, he rushed to help me lift a bag of ice into the cooler.

"Thanks, Gavin. Your parents must be very proud of you."

He ducked his head and reached for another bag. "I doubt that."

Oops. I had touched a nerve. I tried to smooth things over. "Well, I bet your uncle's glad to have you. He told me so."

"Ben did? He never says that to me, but, hey, I almost forgot." Gavin wrestled a note out of the side pocket of his shorts. "He gave me something for you."

I took the crumpled paper from him and turned away to read it.

Miss Riley (notice my respectful tone), I've been busier than expected. If you're free next Sunday evening, may I have the pleasure of showing you my school? We can also have dinner at The Pine Cone. Ben 315 674-1189 Please say yes :)

"This can't be happening," I murmured.

"My uncle do something wrong?" Gavin moved around the counter.

"No." I slipped the note into my pocket and managed a smile. "He did something right. It's just--"

"Hey, you don't have to tell me what a tool he is." Gavin threw up his hands and hooted.

"If he's such a tool," I said, "how come you're spending the summer with him?"

He crossed his arms and kicked at a dent in the floorboard. "My mother thinks it'll be good for me. Says my friends in Syracuse are a bad influence."

"Is Syracuse where you live?"

"No." Gavin picked up a package of Twizzlers and tossed it from hand to hand. "My father took a job there a year ago. I didn't want to move from Buffalo."

Anger crackled in his words. I recognized the homesickness that crouched beneath the surface of his statement. Still, he needed to consider his mom's point of view. "Is she right? Gavin? About your friends?"

"Maybe. I don't know." He threw his arms up in the air. Before I could respond, he flung open the screen door. "Hey, Miss Finn, do you fish? Hunt? Canoe? 'Cause we could go sometime if you like."

I accepted his offer for what it was, a way to move past the moment. "No, I don't. Sorry. I've only fished off a dock once, when I was five. And I don't know how to canoe. I asked Carl to teach me, but I think she forgot. She's been preoccupied these past few days, and I hate to nag her."

With a furtive look, Gavin closed the door and crept closer. "Don't tell anybody here, but I'm working on my eagle scout award. I'm a good paddler. I could teach you to canoe and kayak and count it as one of my service projects. I think." He bit his thumb, waiting for my reaction.

I scratched a mosquito bite on my neck, wondering how I'd become so entangled with the flirtatious Torvald men in such a short time

Chapter 12

...plagued by coincidence and things that prowl the night...

Travel-weary campers looking for easy meals to fix kept me from closing the store on time, and I arrived late for dinner. Carl had already sat down to eat when I slipped, exhausted, onto a chair and shook out my napkin.

"Last-minute..." she paused to stir the bowl of stew between us, "customers?"

"A boatload of fishermen." I filled my plate, tore off a hunk of fresh-baked bread, and held it to my nose. "This smells wonderful."

Pleased by my accolade, she scooped a second helping onto her plate and shrugged. "Probably heading out with Anton Storms or up the Ausable with Ron Dugas early tomorrow. He and his wife Amy run that adventure lodge two doors down. Did the latecomers buy much?"

"Cleaned us out of Rapallo lures, deer jerky, and that craft beer from Saranac. Should I make a run to Watertown tomorrow?"

Carl swallowed before waving her spoon in the air. "I'll come down early and look over your list. Could be we have more of what we need in the storeroom. I'll check the attic storage, too. Anything interesting happen today?"

I poured her a second cup of tea. "One of the professors at the Ranger School sent me a note, offered to show me around."

Carl slapped her forehead. "Oh, Riley, I forgot my promise to take you up there. And to the Pine Cone, too. Damn, I'm just getting so old and feeble-minded."

"It's fine, Carl. I understand."

"No, you don't understand. This doctor's got me all anxieated with his tests and recommendations."

"What kind of tests?"

Carl brushed off the crumbs on the front of her plaid shirt. I waited for her to elaborate, but she avoided my gaze.

"Are you going to tell me what's going on?"

"All in good time, missy. There's no need for you to know now. It's personal stuff." She reached down to pet the cat twining around her ankles. When she looked up, the anxious expression in her eyes gave way to curiosity. "Anyway, who's the professor?"

"Ben Torvald. He came in earlier this week. Well, it's almost last week now. He and Josh Waylon stopped by."

"When?"

"The day after they found LeeAnne's body, the same day they found her car." I sopped up gravy with the bread. Carl drummed her fingers on the table.

"Torvald? Big man? Lots of hair, and one of them model beards? You know, just enough to make you think he forgot to shave? The rest of the family's been coming here for years, but Ben only shows up sporadically. He did teach at the school last year, so I guess they hired him back, although I don't know why. Bit of a philanderer, our Ben. He and Josh roomed together during their student days, about ten, no, fourteen years ago. That explains so many Josh Waylon sightings lately. Normally, the man doesn't come out of the woods until the tourists leave. Do you trust him?"

I choked on the bread. Carl pounded my back until the fit passed.

"Who?" I croaked.

"Torvald. Waylon is solid as they come. He's just heartsore, honey, and sad and bitter and lonely." She sipped her tea and sniffed. "I wish he'd offered to show you around. Or, better still, asked you for a date."

Now I really was confused. "Who?"

"Why, Josh, of course. Can't recommend the Torvald character, seeing as how I don't know him well at all."

"I don't think Josh likes me," I said. "He scowls every time we meet."

"Scowl or not, Waylon's the man to call if you need help. He's a fine woodsman and an even finer father."

Father? I choked again. Maybe Carl was experiencing some senior insanity. How could Josh Waylon ask me for a date when he was married? And what was going on with me? I reacted to Waylon sightings like a schoolgirl with a rock star crush. When he accidentally touched me, every last nerve went on alert. I blamed it on the eyes. What a sap I was. I wasn't keen on going out with Ben either. I didn't trust my heart to make good choices.

Carl glanced at me but didn't say anything more about the men. We finished dinner in a flurry of work-related plans. After I carried the dishes to the kitchen and cleaned up, I returned to the great room. Carl had already settled in the recliner. Her head slumped against the moose headrest, eyes closed, mouth open, her snoring a signal our conversation was over.

I wrapped an afghan around me to guard against the cool night air and hurried down the path to my cabin. Loneliness dogged every step. I missed Emma and my other friends. I missed Smokey. I even missed my dad's goofy smile and my mother's frown. Everything familiar had vanished along with the plan I had for my life. I choked down a huge gulp of self-pity and jogged on.

Thin clouds raced southward, shifting to hide and then reveal the moon that hung like a Cheshire smile above the clearing. The darkness under the trees beckoned, promising to disclose secrets if only I would step into the shadows. I lingered on the screened-in porch, the note from Ben Torvald clutched in my fist, peering through the pines at a tumble of rocks that edged the shore beyond the path. The river, silvered by moonlight, gurgled by. On the opposite bank, a darker presence shifted out of the forest. I pressed my nose to the screen, peering at the suggestion of something large and predatory that seemed to stare with peculiar intent at my cabin. I calmed my breathing and listened for huffing or snorts, anything that would help me identify the shadow. I blinked once, twice, and the image faded as though the creature had never been there at all.

Chapter 13

...boy friends, bagels, and bears...

A cold front moved in overnight, dropping temperatures under the average fifty-four-degree lows typical of the area in June. Unable to dispel the thought of a watcher on the riverbank, I stuffed manicure scissors into the back pocket of my jeans and practiced pulling them out in one quick move. Then I returned to my morning ritual. "If I run into anything," I mumbled around the toothpaste coating my mouth, "I'll either kill it or give it a cuticle trim." The woman in the mirror, eyes slightly bloodshot from an uneasy sleep, ignored my threat. Wishing that I'd packed the gloves currently residing in Emma's attic storage, I bundled up in a floral cardigan beneath the navy-blue fleece pullover that Warren had given me two Christmases ago. Last year, my present was a Dustbuster. Yeah, not the most romantic of gifts. That should have tipped me off, right? I can be so clueless sometimes. I pushed that memory away as I stepped out of the cabin into a steady rain. Carl beckoned from the house.

"Got an umbrella, Riley? 'Course you don't. Probably didn't think to bring one. Persnickitous rains come and go as they please. You'll soon learn that about our Adirondacks. And the mist." Carl scanned the clouds. "Wait until you see the haze that drifts over the mountains. Looks like a bridal veil or a shroud. It can be beautiful or sinister, depending on your inclination. Well, hurry up, hop on in here now. Eat. We got things to do."

Last night's awkward conversation forgotten, Carl rambled on as she bustled about the kitchen. I helped myself to orange juice and a mug of her home-ground coffee. Then I noticed the camera equipment waiting near the door.

"You planning to take pictures today?" I snagged an orange cranberry bagel and a napkin before picking up one of Carl's camera bags. "What's in here anyway? It weighs a ton."

"I had planned to go up to Lake Placid, but that'll have to wait another day unless the weather clears. In the meantime, I thought we'd run into Star Lake. It's time," Carl looked down her nose at me, "to get you a fishing license."

I swallowed a mouthful of bagel and winced. "Why exactly do I need a fishing license?"

Carl rapped me on the head with a potholder. "When you're hanging out with rangers, you have to be prepared. Fishing is what we do here. Well, one of the things most of the men and a great many women do here. Don't you know that the trout is New York's state fish?" She winked at me as she sipped her coffee. Neither of us said anything, just stared at each other like the moose that populated her cabin, imaginary antlers waving in the heated air.

"I didn't come here to meet men," I finally offered.

"Oh, I know you didn't. And I don't blame you for running away from that man, whoever he is, who hurt you. Thing is, Riley Finn, you don't have to look for a man to have one find you."

"I think..." I abandoned my thought to finish my breakfast and threw the napkin in the recycling bin, thus avoiding Carl's critical eye. My employer was a stickler for not placing anything in the trash that could be repurposed. "Maybe you're right, but I don't think marriage is in the cards for me. Ever. There's some ingredient missing in my finding-a-mate genes. Maybe I'm just not cut out for it."

"You sound like a woman who's given up." Carl pulled out the chair next to me and sat. "You think because all your friends are married and you're nearing your thirtieth birthday that your life is over? To hell with that. I spent the first forty years of my life doing exactly what I wanted to do, traveling, working for the causes I believed in, setting my own rules. I followed my own path. Then I met Glenn Beamish at an ecology conference at The Grail in Maineville, Ohio, and bam! I was hooked. We shared a life for five years before he decided to take a job in Alaska. I didn't want to go that far from my beloved Adirondacks, and that was that. I went back to living life my way. And I'm richer for it, all of it."

I waited for her to say more. She didn't. "So, he left you?"

"No, hon." Carl rolled down the sleeves of her blouse and buttoned the cuffs. "I left him. The thing is, you have the power to choose how you'll live. You're young enough to make the choice. Be happy. Be sad. But be your own person. Live your life on your terms, not the bloody world's. Or some man's. Now, it's time to open the store. I'll come for you around noon, and you can put up the closed sign. We'll only be gone for an hour. Bring money. They don't take checks or cards in Star Lake. Carry down the rest of the bagels. They're in the picnic basket. And don't forget the umbrella."

I hurried across the steel bridge, watching the river speed along beneath my boots, and wondered about Carl's story and her advice. Was I strong enough to set my own course, which is what I was trying to do this summer, for the rest of my life? Screw it. I had until Labor Day to make up my mind. By that time, Warren's betrayal wouldn't hurt so much, I hoped. Perhaps I should expand my knowledge of the male species. Ben's note still rested in my pocket. I could call him from the store.

With my head down and the umbrella angled against the rain, I failed to notice the mayor until he called my name.

"Morning, Miss Riley." Jesse Livetree followed me into the store. "What has Ms. Beamish prepared for us today?"

I smiled at his covetous glance at the basket. "Bagels, Mr. Livetree, and they are dee-licious. I'm sure you'll want more than one."

The mayor waited while I turned on the lights, fired up the space heater, and returned the umbrella to the porch. I used tongs to lift out his selections, then placed them in a bag.

"Suppose you heard?" He counted out his change on the counter. "Black bear spotted up at the cemetery this morning. The biggest one so far this season. Probably a male."

Goosebumps rose on my arms. "Maybe that's what I saw last night."

"You saw a bear last night? Where?"

"I'm not sure. It might have been nothing more than my imagination, but I swear I saw a shadow standing on the riverbank across the river from my cabin."

Livetree cocked his head to one side. "Did it seem to be watching you?"

"I thought so." I scooped up his change and sorted it into the drawer. "I'm sure that was just fanciful thinking."

The mayor laid his cane on the counter and harrumphed. "Bears are curious creatures, Miss Riley. He may have taken a liking to you, or it could be you saw one of the human bears around Wanakena. Looking at you, it's easy to see why."

A blush crept over my cheeks. Livetree tipped his broad-brimmed fishing hat and shook his head.

"Walk softly, Miss Riley, as Theodore Roosevelt said, and always carry a big stick." He retrieved his cane and started for the door. Before he reached it, Gavin Torvald banged through. When the mayor staggered back, Gavin caught him by the elbows.

"Sorry. Sorry. I didn't mean to." The boy steadied the mayor, clapped his hands, and looked at me. "Miss Finn, did you hear about the bear?"

Recovered from the near fall, Livetree settled his hat more firmly on his head and winked again. "Big stick, remember?"

Gavin leaned on the counter. "It was creeping around up at the cemetery. Biggest one I've ever seen."

I patted the scissors in my pocket. Fat lot of good they'd do. "Have you seen many bears?"

Gavin blushed. "No, not a lot, but everyone's saying the one I saw was huge, for a bear, I mean. It must be a male. It stood on its hind legs when Ben and Josh and I drove up. Then it went crashing through the bushes and disappeared."

"I hope that's the last anyone sees of it. So," I dusted crumbs off the counter, then pointed to the calendar on the wall, "when do my lessons begin?"

Gavin rested his forearms on the counter. Water dripped from his head to splatter over the clean surface. "You're sure you want me to teach you?"

"Of course, I do." I crossed my arms. "Not today, but soon. If I'm going to spend the summer here, I'd better learn something."

"Great! Ms. Beamish will probably let you use one of the rental kayaks, and one of the canoes, too. I'll bring mine down to the beach."

"Beach?" I frowned, trying to remember everything Carl had shown me that first day. "I don't remember seeing a beach."

Gavin pointed across the road. "Well, there's a rocky strip right past the green and a sandy one a little farther down the shore, just beyond the path to the footbridge. The sand beach is easier for beginners."

As soon as he said it, I recalled the layout. I stepped outside to gauge the distance from the bandstand, now sporting an open-sided tent in the center of the lawn, to the crescent strip of shoreline.

"What's the tent for?"

"Music." Gavin strummed an air guitar. "Every other Friday, musicians come to town to play. This week, it's a rock and roll tribute band. Next week some jazz combo is booked. And Uncle Ben says there'll be two bands and tons of fireworks on the Fourth."

The fourth. Of July. Less than a month away. I felt queasy. The last time I'd watched fireworks, Warren and I and Warren's mother had sat on the bleachers at the stadium at Hopewell High. While the air filled with bursts of color, I dreamed of a future where the holiday outing became a familiar ritual in our lives. Thinking about Warren got me thinking about school and Emma. I'd been in Wanakena more than a week and hadn't spoken to anyone back home yet. The need to check email, use my cell phone, and contact the outside world grew into one of those itches you can't quite reach. Carl had offered the use of her computer, but the first time I tried, the connection took so long to establish, I'd given up. The time had come to try again.

"Gavin." He jumped at my command. "Do you have a laptop?"

His cheeks reddened again. Uh-oh, I realized teenage boys and computers might mean violent video games or forbidden porn. He gave me a puzzled look. "Ye-es."

I checked the dial-up connection below the counter. "Can you bring it here?"

He looked outside. "But it's raining."

I pointed at the umbrella, folded my arms, and nodded. "And bring your video games."

He hesitated for a moment, then grabbed the umbrella and ran into the rain. "If I'm not back in ten minutes, call the rangers," he shouted.

"Oh, great." I had forgotten about the bear prowling around the outskirts of Wanakena. I shook off my unease and addressed the image of a moose on the mug I was dusting. "Now I'm a bully, too."

*

Gavin and I had reached level thirteen on Masterminds of the Universe when Carl rushed in. She shook out her rain hat and tossed her car keys on the counter.

"I've decided to stay behind and watch the store, Finn," Carl announced. "You go on over to Star Lake and get your fishing license."

I looked up from the computer and frowned. "Where's Star Lake?"

"It's right off Route 3. Easy to find." Gavin hitched up his jean shorts. "I can show you."

Carl grabbed him by the collar and propelled him toward the door. "Gavin Torvald, you go on home for lunch. Now. Miss Finn is working." She pushed him out and down the steps.

"But, but--" Gavin sputtered as he tried to stop his downward fall, "my laptop!"

I hurried to close the game and typed in my email address. I barely had time to read the first of what appeared to be twenty messages from Emma. *BIG NEWS! CALL ME!* And in smaller letters, *where r u, Riley? Please call.* I closed the laptop, gathered up all Gavin's games, and grabbed the keys.

"Here, Gav," I called after him. When he turned, I handed him the laptop. "We'll finish our game tomorrow."

He rolled his eyes, stuck his tongue out at Carl's back, and flipped his skateboard down from its perch next to the stairs. Pushing with one foot, he raised the umbrella over his head and rumbled toward Third Street, where the Torvalds owned a house.

"That boy needs a job," Carl muttered.

"He has one." I brushed past her. "He's been helping me stock the shelves in exchange for tutoring." I spotted her van parked in the side lot and checked my pockets for cash. The two fifties I'd shoved in this morning coiled around Ben's note. Ben! I still hadn't called him. I punched in the first four numbers. Did I really want to do this? Okay, first things first. Star Lake and the license. Then phone calls, a whole raft of phone calls. I waved goodbye over my shoulder.

"Gavin Torvald's working with you?" Carl called after me.

"Ayuh." I delivered my interpretation of a Downeast yes with batted eyes. She rolled hers. "He's my assistant. And, he's going to teach me to paddle a canoe and a kayak."

"That might be a problem," Carl said. I glanced over my shoulder. Ms. Beamish stood on the steps, rain sluicing off her hunter's cap, her face scrunched up in a scowl. I wondered which part – Gavin working for me or the kid teaching me to paddle – she saw as a problem. Her disapproval left me with a raft of unanswered questions.

Chapter 14

...more instructions from the universe...

Last night's rain had basted the landscape in silver.
Iridescent puddles rippled in the ditches lining the paved
road. I drove from the cabin back to Route 3, turned right,
and followed the winding road to Star Lake. I hadn't asked
Carl for directions or more information about where to go.
She needed to believe I was competent to handle whatever
came up. Besides, I was tired of depending on others to get
around. I had spent too much of my previous life allowing
someone else to lead the way. I wanted to forge my own path
now. The farther I traveled from Wanakena, the more
intense the urge to keep driving. Lake Placid lay farther
along the route. I could play tourist there, explore the former
Olympic site by myself. The impulse not to return to the
hamlet grew. Then reality set in. Running away would negate
all my efforts to prove myself responsible. *Don't be an ass,
Riley Finn*, I whispered. I clenched my teeth when I passed a
sign announcing Star Lake's boundaries. I reduced my speed,
scanning both sides of the road until I spotted a red brick
building bearing the sign Town of Star Lake Administrative
Offices.

As I pulled in, I passed a van with *St. Lawrence
Handicapped Services* painted on the side. A stout woman,
dark hair caught up in a ponytail, was unloading children in
wheelchairs. After she arranged them in a circle, she
tightened the elastic band around her ponytail and wiped an
arm across her forehead. She gazed back and forth from the
children to the front door of the building as though expecting
help. No one came outside. I pocketed Carl's keys and
approached the group.

"Hello. Do you need some help?" When she frowned, I offered my hand. "Riley Finn. I work in Wanakena."

The woman returned my greeting, then scowled. "Don't know what's keeping them. I'm only the driver. Supposed to be teachers here from the summer rec program."

"Well, I'm here, and I'm a teacher during the school year." I grabbed the handles of a wheelchair. "You stay with the group. I'll take them inside one at a time. Who should I ask for?"

The woman fanned her face with one hand and shrugged. "I'm just supposed to drop them off."

"That's all right. I'll find out." I pushed the little girl in the first chair up the ramp and into the building.

"Hello?" My call echoed down the hall. "Anyone here?" I listened for doors to slam or a phone to ring. The window to the licensing area was closed. I parked the girl next to the wall and locked the wheels for safety. Then I knocked on the doors leading down the hall from the waiting area. No one answered. I returned to my charge to examine the lanyard around her neck. Calinda. I crouched down until she and I were at eye level, took her hand, and shook it gently. Calinda blinked, but she didn't make eye contact.

"I'll go get the others, Calinda. You wait here, okay?" I raced down the ramp toward the woman in the lot and reached for the second wheelchair. The boy's tag read Johnny Joe in bold red marker. He smiled when I said his name. Above our heads, thunder rumbled. I hurried to wheel him inside. Twice more, I returned, for Marie and then DeSales, who wore a helmet and rocked back and forth as I escorted him along. Eyes shifting between the building and the sky, the driver relented and pushed the last boy, Timmy, up the ramp. Her distress was frightening her charge. I slowed to speak to him.

"I'm here for a fishing license, Timmy. Do you like to fish?" I didn't expect the child to reply. After all, I was a stranger. He wrung his hands and peeked up at me, his eyes a deep and vibrant brown.

"I. Like. Fish." His words were halting, but his meaning was clear. I set the lock on DeSales's chair and hurried to take Timmy from the driver.

"Well," I said, "I don't know how to fish, but I'm here to get a fishing license. Silly, huh?"

He giggled. I laughed with him. Once they were all inside, I spoke to the children while the driver jiggled door handles and yelled down the hall. Finally, a woman in a patterned smock carrying an open container of yogurt scurried out from a room at the very back of the building.

"Oh, dear, Bertha, I'm so, so sorry. You're early, and I'm all alone here today. Our volunteers have both called off. Well, let's just take the children into the break room. We'll watch a movie this afternoon." Flustered and twitching like a rabbit, she waved toward one of the closed doors before turning to me. "Who are you?"

I introduced myself, explained my intention to buy a fishing permit, and moved to the licensing window just as an unseen hand slid it open. Bertha nodded her thanks to me, then offered to come back an hour earlier than usual, to which the woman in the smock, Mary Lou Haines, according to her badge, nodded with relief. I filled out the paperwork and handed over the seventy-dollar fee for a non-resident license, frowning at the rapid decline of my limited funds. I had no way to access my bank account back home yet, and I hadn't received any wages from Carl, a lapse I needed to clarify soon. As I walked past the wheelchairs, Timmy's hand flopped out, his fingers twining themselves in the pocket of my jeans. When I reached to disengage him, he squeezed my hand. Mary Lou Haines hurried over.

"Now, Tim." She released me from his grip. "You have to let the lady go. There you are, Miss--? I'm sorry. I forgot your name."

"Finn. Riley Finn. I'm working for Carl Beamish in Wanakena."

"Say thank you, Timmy, for Miss Finn's help." She set off, then hesitated. "Wait here."

Timmy twisted to watch me as she steered him toward the break room. When all the children were settled, she returned.

"Sorry about that," she said. "But, you know, I've never seen Timmy react that way to a stranger. That boy doesn't take to just anyone."

I waved off her apology. "It's okay, Ms. Haines. I'm a teacher. And I'm curious. Why are these children here?"

"We offer a summer recreation program for special needs children. It's the least we can do for their families." Ms. Haines lowered her voice. "We rely on volunteers to help. Most of the time, it's not a problem. This summer, however, has been challenging. As you can see, these children have cerebral palsy or more severe conditions. Having a few hours free from their care can be a godsend for their parents."

"That's an admirable thing to do."

Ms. Haines raised a predatory eyebrow. "You said you're a teacher. Perhaps you could help us out."

I stepped through the door of the recreation room. Timmy turned in his chair, his eyes following me as I spoke with Ms. Haines.

"I'm afraid," I said, "I can't come every day."

Ms. Haines's shoulders drooped. "I was so hoping you could help us."

I blundered on. "Well, perhaps I could do one afternoon a week. I'd have to speak to my employer."

"That," Ms. Haines clasped her hands in front of her chest, "would be wonderful. Which day do you prefer?"

We decided on Tuesday, the extra half-day off from my store duties Carl had promised. Back in the boss's van, I headed toward Wanakena, pondering the speed with which I was being submersed into this Adirondack world.

As soon as I returned, Carl left, but not before taking a parting shot at my most recent purchase. "I expect you to use that license, Riley. Sooner rather than later. Make that Torvald man take you to his favorite fishing spot. I'm sure he has one."

Ben. Once more, I had forgotten about him. To call or not to call? *Don't be a wimp, Riley.* I squared my shoulders, marched to the counter, and, despite the way my hand trembled, dialed the number on the note. I tapped my foot as I counted the rings. Half of me wanted Ben to pick up. The other half prayed the call would go to voice mail. Instead, after ring number ten, a woman answered, a Scandinavian accent clear in her greeting. I almost hung up. After her third hello, more abrupt than the first two, I forced myself to speak.

"This is Riley Finn, from the General Store. Is Professor Ben Torvald there?"

The woman laughed, a sound half-flirty and half-amused. "Nowhere else."

"May I speak with him?"

Her voice grew distant, as though she had turned away from the receiver. "Professor Torvald? Professor? Hey, Ben! Phone."

While I waited, I wandered the length of the phone cord, rearranging products on the shelves and wondering what was taking so long. The woman had muffled the phone somehow. I heard a rumble of raised voices, followed by a thud as she slammed the phone down.

"Don't be a bitch, Bir," Ben said. When he spoke to me, the honeyed southern tones returned, a direct contrast to the recent snarky command. "That you, Riley? I'm so glad you called."

"Who is that?" the woman asked. He mumbled something I couldn't make out. Footsteps receded in the background.

"Riley?"

"I'm still here," I said, wishing I weren't.

"I thought you might decide not to," Ben said.

"Is this a bad time? Because I can call back."

"No, it's fine. I'm holding a study session before a big test tomorrow, and everyone's a bit on edge. We'll be at it all night. I'm taking the students on a ten-day campout following the exam. We'll be sleeping under the stars, foraging for edible roots, the whole wilderness experience. Experiential learning, I believe it's called. Here, it's just routine training."

"I didn't know there were women enrolled in the program."

"Why, Miss Riley, do I detect a hint of jealousy? And here I thought y'all didn't like me."

"No." I cursed my stupidity as I rubbed the spray of saliva off with my sleeve. "It surprised me, that's all. I didn't think about women taking the course. All the rangers I know are men."

"I guess that's true. Josh. Gus. Me." He rustled papers while I tried to think of a way to end the conversation. Before I could, he shifted into a more professional demeanor. "Not a high percentage of women take the summer program, but the overall numbers are growing. It turns out that females make excellent foresters. Isn't that right, Birgit?"

The woman who answered the phone must have returned. I heard her laugh.

"Can you get everyone back now? Thank you." More shuffling of papers.

"I can tell," I said, "this is a bad time."

"No, it's fine. Birgit's gone to the classroom, and you and I have a date to arrange." Ben's voice became more seductive. "Are we on for a week from Sunday? You'll be able to close the store early, won't you?"

"Sunday?" I hesitated. Clearly, my fragile ego had not decided how to feel about rejoining the dating pool. But I had called him. And Sunday evening was the least busy time at the store. How did he know that? I gave myself a mental smack on the forehead. Duh. The Torvald family came here every summer. I'm sure Gavin told him about my schedule. Then I wondered if he tried to date all the newbies in town. Or all the students.

"Come on, darlin', don't make me beg. I want to see you."

He was laying it on a bit thick. I rolled my eyes. Then I heard Emma urging me to live a little, remembered Carl saying it wouldn't hurt to flirt. Persuaded but still cautious, I agreed.

"Fine. And I would like to see the school."

"Great. I'll make reservations at the Pine Cone for a week from Sunday and pick you up around seven. Will that work?"

"It will."

"Great. And I'm sorry, Riley, but I have to get back to my students. Until next Sunday."

I ignored the hysterical voice chanting *no, no, no, it's too soon* in my ear, ignored the way my heart jumped twice. What had I done? Voices from the porch announced the arrival of customers. I rang them up and finished tallying the morning's receipts. Fifteen minutes later, the store got busy again. It wasn't until after five that I recalled the all-caps email message from Emma. While I waited for the call to go through, I scribbled the children's names on the pad next to the register. Calinda. Timmy. DeSales. Who had I forgotten? When Emma answered, I broke into tears.

"Riley! You're alive, thank God," Emma said. "How are you? What's happening? Tell me all about Wanakena. Have you met any men yet?"

"Fine. More than you can imagine. It'll take way too long to tell you about this place. And, yes, I've met men." The comfort of our friendship soothed me. At the same time, guilt prickled. I missed Emma more than I had anticipated, yet I hadn't called her for two weeks. "Now, what's the big news?"

"You're not going to believe this. I'm so mad I could kill him."

"Kill who?"

"Carstairs, of course. He's the new principal of Hopewell Elementary. The School Board voted on it last night."

"I don't understand." I leaned against the wall. "He never said anything about applying for that position. But I guess it's not unexpected. He always did want to be an alpha dog."

"Yes. No, but Riley, that's not the worst thing." Emma took a deep breath. "Are you sitting down?"

"What is it?"

"Are you sitting down?"

"Yes." I slid onto the stool and gripped the edge of the counter, steeling myself against whatever Emma would share next. "Now tell me."

"Don't hate the messenger." She inhaled audibly. I waited, ready to hear anything, except for the one thing she did say.

"Warren," she whispered, "is engaged to be married."

"What?" I cradled the phone to my ear. I must have misheard her.

"Oh, Riley, it's true. Can you believe it? Warren Carstairs, that prick, is going to marry some woman he met on the Internet."

Chapter 15

...keeping my options open...

"Are you sure," I gulped back the tears streaming down my face, "it's an actual woman?"

Emma choked out a laugh before bursting into tears herself. We cried in companionable silence until I gathered my shattered self-esteem and stuffed it back where it belonged, next to my bruised and aching heart.

"Riley, are you all right?"

"Do I have a choice?' I scrubbed my face with a tissue, blew my nose, and slumped over the counter. "Besides, I have a date."

"You do? You really do? Well, see, you don't need that asshole. Carstairs did nothing but drag you down. Tell me, is this date gorgeous?"

"He's a looker. And probably a player. I think he considers me a likely new conquest."

"Well, don't make it easy on him, sister-friend. Listen, I have to go. My stomach isn't liking the tuna salad I ate for lunch. Promise you'll call me soon, okay?"

"I promise." I broke off the connection before I could hurl the phone against the wall. Warren was a jerk. What a fool I'd been, pining over someone who forgot me the moment he stepped out of my life. I finished the day in a haze of doubt, anger, and frustration. The how-could-he's morphed into how-didn't-I-know's, then what-did-she-have-that-I-didn't's. By the time I closed for the night, all the tears I'd stifled erupted on the walk back to Carl's place. When the sobbing stopped, I probed my heart like a sore tooth, trying to find the truth about our relationship. To my surprise, at the bottom of all the anguish, I found relief. The life I imagined with Warren had been a mirage conjured by the desire to escape becoming an old maid. But my employer lived alone, and she was doing quite well for herself. Other women survived the extinguishing of marriage hopes. I could, too. Instead of going into Carl's, I ran straight to my cabin. I washed my face and hands and tried to cover up my swollen eyes and pale cheeks with a little makeup and a lot of fury. By the time I stepped into the boss's kitchen, I was convinced nothing showed. Foolish to think that. Carl took one look, tossed down the ladle she was holding, and folded me into her arms.

"Oh, honey," she soothed, "what's that damnable man done now?"

I hiccupped out the story of Warren Carstairs and the idiot Riley Finn. Oddly enough, laying it out for Carl removed much of the sting. My pride suffered the most. The knowledge that I'd invested so much time and emotion in a man who didn't harbor the same feelings stung like a bitch.

"Just you sit right down, Riley." Carl hustled me to her recliner and pressed me into the comforting leather. "I'll have dinner on the table in a minute. Then you and I can figure out a way forward. Which begins, I might add, with you dating other men. You're the prettiest little thing to grace our wilderness in a span of years. I mean, with all that hair of yours and those violet eyes, why, you're a modern Elizabeth Taylor, honey. Lord knows the town's been talking about who's going to win your heart."

"They have?"

Carl chatted on, her words muffled as she turned to lift her latest batch of corn muffins from the oven. She set them next to the bowls of chili and returned to pat my shoulder.

"There's even a bet going. Who will be the first to ask you on a date? My money's on that pushy Torvald man. 'Course, lots of people are betting on him, so the odds aren't good. Had to qualify it with an actual calendar day for the date to decide a winner."

Still flushed from the crying jag, I didn't think my face could turn any redder, but it did. "What day did you pick?"

Carl pursed her lips. "He already did, didn't he? That rascal. Saturday. I believe Amy Dugas put her money on Sunday, says it makes more sense to choose a day when most people don't work."

I sampled the stew before shrugging. "Yum. This is tasty. And Amy wins."

Carl plopped onto a chair, covered my free hand with her hot-padded one, and grimaced. "I can see as how you'd say yes to Ben. He's a charmer, for sure. Still, I wish Josh Waylon'd wake up. Man needs a reason to keep going, for him and for his son."

"Carl," I blew air over the spoon to cool the next bite, "I know you mean well, but I can't date a married man. I won't do that, ever."

"Honey, who said anything about Josh being married?"

I leaned forward to look her in the eye. "You said as much when you said he had a son."

Carl removed the moose hot pads and settled across from me. She helped herself to a muffin. "Josh was married, Riley, to that hiker who died last year. Well, that's not the whole truth of it. Amanda Waylon was murdered, strangled, it seems. But she had moved on from him way before that. Walked out on him and their son. That bitch carried on with anyone who showed any spark of interest."

I sat back, stunned by her revelation. No wonder he looked so sad--and so angry. Not difficult to see why he'd hate women. Carl dabbed at her eyes with a handkerchief, then shoved it up her sleeve. "Man's plenty bitter at the way life's turned out for him. But I've known Josh since he was a youngster. He's a good man, Riley, better'n many others here in Wanakena. Not his fault, all this gossip."

"Gossip? About what?"

"Poor man. He's the one found his own wife's body on the trail. Had to hike back just to tell the news and get help. Some believe he was the one who killed her. Not without cause, mind you. If anyone had a reason to murder Amanda, Josh did. Still, I know he would never do such a thing, God help him. And now, he's found another one."

Chapter 16

when it rains, it pours...

Saturday started with a downpour that shifted to a misty drizzle by midmorning. But that didn't deter the weekend fishermen or the few confused travelers asking for directions or looking for a restaurant. I welcomed them all, sold the fishermen cartons of beer, sacksful of camping meals, and most of the new lures Carl had picked up on her restocking trip after visiting the doctor's office. I had spent the last few nights studying local maps, so I felt rather confident in directing the tourists toward Saranac or Lake Placid. Gavin ended up being quite helpful, too, carrying purchases to cars, re-shelving depleted supplies, and talking with the anglers about the best spots for catching trout and bass. He took the pressure off me to respond to all those specific questions, which was just as well. I couldn't stop thinking about Emma's revelations. Or Carl's.

Humiliated by Warren's deception and embarrassed by the knowledge that everyone in town was placing bets on my dating status, I longed to barricade myself in the cabin and wait for the world to forget I ever existed. When I wasn't stewing about my unlovable past, I fretted about the unnerving interest I felt in Josh Waylon and those piercing eyes of his. He could be a killer, I told myself. Then there was Ben. For better or worse, I had accepted a date with Wanakena's most notorious Romeo. What was I thinking? I knew he fancied himself a ladies' man. And that Birgit woman who'd answered his phone sounded like she knew him better than any student should. The bigger puzzle was why I even cared. It's not like I wanted to hook up with Ben Torvald. I simply wanted to believe that I had worth, that I could appeal to a man like him. Handsome, educated, with a good job, he epitomized the dream date of many single ladies my age. Other than adding me to his conquest list, I couldn't imagine why he was interested in me. The cloud of self-doubt that had pursued me from Hopewell grew until I imagined myself smothered beneath it.

As the influx of shoppers dwindled, I made a mental tally of how many I'd waited on that day. I paid special attention to the growing number of regulars. Their initial misgivings had given way to a grudging acceptance of my role at the store, although the longer LeeAnne's murder remained unsolved, the more rumors circulated. Of course, after Carl, Gavin Torvald placed high on the list of those I counted as friends. He was proving to be a reliable assistant and a willing confidante. Not that I shared my deeper concerns with him, but I did enjoy our conversations about school and the wilderness. The mayor, Jesse Livetree, made it a point to stop by every morning for his regular pastry fix. To my surprise, Anton Storms, who'd rescued me that first night in Wanakena, had also taken to dropping by, usually in the late afternoons. Returning from day trips to popular fishing spots, he managed to catch me alone most of the time. He'd prop his arms on the counter, gaze at me with those intense brown eyes of his, and ask about my life. Which was a little flattering and a little intrusive. Why did he care about my favorite sandwich or color? To be fair, he also shared a lot about his own background. Anton was younger than I first thought, in his early thirties. He'd grown up the fifth son of a Portuguese mother and SAR father whose roots went back to the Mayflower. He had the rugged build of a lobsterman, which jibed with his story of migrating inland from coastal Maine to cater to amateurs hoping for a fish tale to take home at the end of their vacation. The man was funny and ruggedly charming and, except for all those questions about my favorite things, respectful of my personal space.

Then there were the rangers. Their visits became more frequent, too. Josh and his partner Gus Jornigen generally filed in right after the mayor left. They carried their coffee and Carl's daily baking treats to the Adirondack chairs on the porch. Propping their feet on the railing, they savored the scones or muffins in quiet contemplation of the day to come. They were typical of the breed, according to Carl, when I told her how they ignored me.

"Those guys," she said, winking at me, "taciturn but observant. Don't dismiss them too quickly. They're hanging around for a reason." No matter the rumors, Carl remained firmly on my side. She shared local gossip and refused to accept my evaluation of Wanakenans as suspicious. But something had changed with her, too. In the beginning, we spent the nights in front of a toasty fire, making lists and going over store receipts. Now, she barely favored me with a curt goodnight before she wandered down the hall to her room. Ever since her visit to the cardiologist, she'd become more like a phantom presence, withdrawing into herself despite my efforts to engage her. After my sobbing confession of Warren's perfidy, she stopped communicating except in short bursts. All her promises to teach me about the area evaporated. Our morning conversations had dwindled to occasional comments on the weather or practical discussions regarding supplies for the store.

Last night, leaving the after-dinner cleanup to me, she wrapped herself in a baggy cardigan and, carrying her Bible, retreated to the recliner, where she passed the hours until bedtime engrossed in the books of the Old Testament. As far as I could tell, in Carl's present circumstance, suffering and tribulation had overtaken redemption. When I tried to draw her out about what was troubling her, she insisted I mind the store and let her be.

Bear sightings had died down, too. I spent the evenings in my cabin, scrutinizing the opposite bank of the river, searching for the shadow I'd seen that first week. And I pondered the prospect of a stalker hanging out in the woods. Someone had murdered LeeAnne McMasters on the very road I had driven down my first night here. Her death could have as easily been mine.

Sunday, the skies cleared, gifting us with a gorgeous but windy day. When I made my way to the big cabin, Carl was staring blankly at the range hood above the stove.

"You'll have to manage without me this week." She eased into one of the kitchen chairs, cupped the mug of coffee in her hands, and perused the dark liquid. "I'll be gone."

The abruptness of the announcement drew me from my own thoughts. "Carl, I don't think I'm ready to go this alone."

"You have to, Riley." Carl snatched my hand and gripped it so hard my fingers grew numb. "I know I haven't been myself these past few days, but I trust you."

"If you trust me," I pulled a chair next to her, "tell me what's going on."

Carl studied our clenched hands. "I have to have surgery. Doc's going to place three stents in my heart. He says it's minimally invasive."

"Oh." All the air left my lungs. A dozen platitudes came to mind. I only managed one of them. "Well, that's not so bad. Lots of people have that done."

"That's not all." Carl moved away from the table. She brushed her hand over the moose tiles, curled the edge of a placemat with her fingers, then flattened it out again. "They found a spot on my left lung. It might be cancer. It probably is. While they've got me on the table, they're going to do a biopsy."

I moved to her side to wrap an arm around her waist. She leaned into me. Together we gazed at the stand of wildflowers blooming in the garden, listened to the river with its constant song of passage. I slipped my other arm around her and held her tight.

"You don't know it's cancer, Carl. Not yet. Sometimes what we imagine is worse than the actual fact." And sometimes it's the reverse. Like my expectations before meeting Warren at the coffee shop.

The timer buzzed. Carl wriggled free and took out the rolls she'd prepared for the morning. I returned to the table, the scent of cinnamon overriding the taste of disaster.

"I'm not ready to go on without you, Ms. Beamish, so you'll just have to come back healed."

Carl managed a weak smile. "For such a little bitty thing, you sure have a big voice."

I lowered my head and reclaimed my chair. When I reached across the table, she let me take her hand. "We'll get through this together, okay?"

She scooped scrambled eggs from the platter to her plate and sighed. When she looked up, I saw how frightened she was.

"When's the surgery?"

"I have to go for pre-op tests tomorrow. The procedures are scheduled for Wednesday."

"Okay." I chewed a fingernail. "Can I still have Tuesday afternoon off? Remember, you said I could have a half-day in addition to Thursday."

"You got something to do Tuesday?"

I gulped down my orange juice and shoveled in the eggs. If I didn't hurry, I'd arrive late to the store. Mr. Livetree and Gus and Josh Waylon would be waiting. Or maybe they'd give up and leave. I didn't parse out why that thought disturbed me.

"Mm-hm. I promised to help tutor the special needs kids at Star Lake on Tuesdays."

"Really?" Carl rocked back as though the announcement pleased her.

"Well, I am a teacher, and I like to think I'm a good one." I hoped that boast was true. "It's the least I can do."

"Indeed. Well." She wiped her mouth with her napkin. "I think that's a fine idea."

"And I can close the store Wednesday and go with you to the hospital. Which is where, by the way?"

Carl shook her head. "Fifty miles from here. Canton Potsdam Hospital. I don't want you to come with me, Riley. I need to keep the store open, and I don't want you to watch me die."

"You're not going to die." I hugged her fiercely. She waved me off and returned her attention to breakfast. Cinnamon rolls tucked under my arm, I darted out the door. I waited until the screen door banged shut before I wiped the tears trickling down my face. Disaster, it seemed, accompanied Riley Finn no matter how far she ran.

I jogged all the way to Reed Avenue, fighting the urge to scream. In the short time I'd been in Wanakena, Carl Beamish had become an important person in my life. Her rambling conversations, delicious meals, and comforting support restored my shattered ego. She couldn't die now. She just couldn't. I crossed the steel bridge, stopping when I noticed the solitary man standing by the store's front door, Ike at his side. Josh Waylon, a beardless and impossibly handsomer Josh Waylon, had come alone.

Patting down my wind-blown hair, I slipped several loose strands behind my ears. Why did the man unravel me so? Now that I knew about his wife, I fought the desire to offer comfort and empathy. He didn't like me, had made it clear he disapproved of my arrival in the town for some reason. And I certainly couldn't reveal Carl's confidence about his past. So, why was he here this morning, all by himself? I glanced toward Hamele Street, wondering where Jesse had gotten to. The mayor wasn't a hard-core churchgoer, although he might turn up occasionally if he thought it would benefit any future re-election campaign. I had spotted signs in the storeroom touting *a Livetree was better than a dead Courtney Elm*, his first and only rival for the position in the fall. I shrugged off my disquiet, striding with what I hoped was confidence toward the store. Ike leaped down the steps, barked a greeting, and bounded over to nose my elbow. I scratched his ears and told him what a good dog he was. Tail wagging furiously, he herded me toward Josh.

"Good morning, Mr. Waylon." I petted Ike's head, slipped by the ranger, and put the key in the lock.

Waylon crossed his arms. "Morning, Miss Finn."

The corner of his mouth twitched the same way it did when I threatened him with the hair dryer. I blushed and flipped the lights on. He held the door for Ike, then stepped inside.

"I thought Ike was Ben's dog. Are you taking him for the day?" I placed the rolls on the counter and lifted the cover. The aroma of fresh-baked goodness enveloped us. "Where is Gus this morning?"

Waylon frowned. "Just so there's no mistake," he said, "Ike is my dog. I let Ben borrow him to pick up women, something Torvald's fond of doing. And Gus is doing campsite checks. We're keeping a closer eye since last week's discovery."

He gazed above my head, his look faraway and sad. Unable to resist the urge to soothe, I touched his hand. "What happened isn't your fault, Josh."

He shifted his eyes to mine, but he didn't remove his hand. "How can you be so sure of that, Riley?"

I shivered. The way he said my name coupled with the contact of our hands made my heart skip. Not now, I ordered, surprised that I'd had no significant fibrillation episode since I'd made my way into this mountain wilderness. Except when Ben asked me out. "Because I'm a good judge of character, Mister Waylon." Like that was true. "And because you had me cornered down that empty road, and you sent me here."

"That's true." The shadows in his eyes lifted. The corners of his mouth did, too. His smile transformed his rugged attractiveness into full-blown gorgeous. I stepped back, freeing his hand with some reluctance. The ache in me to be cherished and loved cried out for more, please. I cursed the flush spreading over my face. Josh eyed the cinnamon rolls.

"I hope some of those are for me."

"Since Mayor Livetree's not here to contest it, you can have as many as you want." The bell above the door tinkled. Three fishermen strolled in, accompanied by Anton Storms. Gavin tripped in behind them.

"Morning, Miss Finn." The boy peered down at the threshold. "Sorry I'm late."

Anton caught Gavin's elbow to balance him. The other men ignored us as they chatted about who was going to catch the most fish. Josh leaned closer.

"Pick out four for me, please, and add a mooshiepie for Ike." Eager to inspect the newcomers, the dog sniffed everyone's boots. He huffed at Gavin and Storms, then trotted over to sit by my feet. I packed the rolls into a bag and accepted Josh's money. He rubbed his hand over Ike's back. "Come on, boy, we have work to do. On the way out, he glanced at the men in the store and then at me. "Be safe, Riley."

Chapter 17

...taking the bitter with the sweet...

I watched Josh and Ike cross to the ranger's truck.
When he looked up and caught me staring, I retreated from
the window, unnerved. What the hell was wrong with me?
The way he'd said my name earlier had sent my pulse racing.
I held on to the moment, then shook it off. What good could
possibly come from a such a visceral reaction? I didn't
understand why, but the woman parts of me had an intense
desire to find out what else those lips could do besides say
my name so seductively. Anton Storms tromped around the
store, interrupting my ruminations. So did the fishermen's
wives, who straggled in after their husbands, complaining of
wine headaches from last night's revels at the Pine Cone and
the lack of shopping in Wanakena while the men satisfied
their need to play woodsmen. One or two cast sly glances at
Anton. A blonde with her hair in a high ponytail and a pouty
mouth whispered in his ear and giggled. He was polite but
not encouraging. The guide probably got hit on a lot. When
he saw me watching, he winked. I gave him a thumbs up and
hurried to assist the newcomers.

I sold out of rolls before ten, then spent the rest of the
morning fielding complaints about early risers buying all the
goodies and the lack of church-going believers among the
tourist folk.

Gavin approached me at noon, his chores complete.
Outside, several of his summer friends milled about.

"Miss Finn?" He shuffled his feet. "Okay if I go now?"

I nodded, too busy with the receipts to pay more
attention until he stepped closer. "Um, do you think you'd
like to have your first lesson next week?"

"Lesson?" It took me a moment to process his request. Then I remembered. "Fishing or paddling?"

"Both. Tuesday's supposed to be a mild wind day, better for going out on the lake. I can get all the equipment we'll need as long as you have your license."

"I do." I patted my back pocket. "But Tuesday's not good for me."

"Oh." His face registered his disappointment. I hurried to clarify.

"I promised to help tutor the summer kids at the Star Lake town hall on Tuesdays. Will Thursday morning work?" Even as I said it, I realized I'd have little time to attend to my own laundry and shopping. Hard to believe how busy my life had become in such a short time. That reminded me that I hadn't brought many clothes to Wanakena, which meant I needed to come up with something to wear Sunday for my date with Professor Torvald. I snorted at the thought. Shouldn't I be more excited about going out? After all, Ben was handsome, charismatic, smart, and very good at flattery. Shades of Warren Carstairs. Maybe that's why I was reluctant to begin a relationship with him. I could call and cancel in a voice message. I wouldn't even have to talk to him. Then Emma's voice nagged in my ear. *It's only one date, Riley. He asked you. No one else did.* I shushed my best friend's eerie commentary and waited for Gavin's answer.

"Yeah, that's cool. So, you're gonna help the crippled kids?"

"We use the words special needs now, Gav."

"Sure, I get it. No prob. Their folks'll really like that. Josh, too. See you at the beach at eight Thursday."

Before I could ask why Josh Waylon would be pleased about my tutoring the kids in Star Lake, Gavin skipped out the door. I chalked my confusion up to being an outsider and set to work dragging cartons of canned goods out of the storeroom and re-stocking the cooler with soft drinks. I closed at six, taped a note on the door with a phone number in case of an emergency like the one I had two weeks ago, and headed back to the cabin. Carl was in no shape to cook tonight, and I wanted my favorite Italian comfort food in the worst way. After a shower and a change of clothes, I packed the ingredients I'd bought into my backpack and headed over to the main house. It wasn't long before the aroma of ground beef, tomato sauce, and cheese wafted around the kitchen. I slathered garlic butter on half a loaf of ciabatta, grated more parmesan, and set the table. When the timer went off, I woke Carl, settled her in her favorite chair, and ladled out a generous helping of lasagna. The day's conversations continued to play in the back of my mind. Carl noticed.

"Something wrong, Riley?"

I smiled sheepishly. "No, ma'am. Just thinking about the day's events."

"Well, let's hear it. I could use some good news."

"Don't know how good it is. Gavin agreed to teach me how to fish and paddle." My heart chose that moment to skip beats, which caused me to question whether I had taken my meds that morning and wonder where I could refill my prescription, when needed. I took two deep breaths, coughed, and the palpitations stopped.

"You all right?" Carl grabbed my wrist. "Your pulse is all fluttery."

I coughed again just to make certain everything fell back into rhythm and grinned at her. "Just a hiccup. No worries." I forked some lasagna into my mouth, playing for time. "I also re-connected with a gorgeous golden retriever named Ike, who, I found out, belongs to Josh Waylon, not Ben Torvald."

Carl harrumphed loud enough to cause the plates to rattle. "Just like Ben to pretend to something that wasn't his. What else happened?"

"I don't know if it qualifies as interesting, but Anton Storms brought a large party into the store. He's quite the popular guy. The wives were hanging all over him, but he winked at me. Not sure how I feel about that."

"Me, neither. He's a hunk, for sure, but he keeps to himself more than most. A bit of a mystery, our Anton, but basically harmless." Carl chugged her water and held out the glass for more. "Any more gossip about our newest murder victim?"

"I don't think so." I detected a note of hesitancy in Carl's question. "Did you know her well? LeeAnne McMasters?"

Kneading the hem of her shirt, Carl shrugged. "Well enough, I thought. I promised to hire her for this summer. She worked at the Pine Cone last year, so I didn't know her more than casually, but she seemed eager to return to Wanakena and I needed the help. Except then I got your application, and I figured I'd wait to see which one of you showed up first."

"That sounds a little manipulative, Carl."

She looked away. "Yeah, maybe, but I got the better deal in the end. I'm no saint, Riley, best you know that. I do things the way I want, and that usually means someone objects. I'm not apologizing for it. And you're avoiding my question. Do they know anything more about her murder?"

I gnawed my lower lip, confused and feeling guilty about the circumstances that led me to take the place of a dead woman. "No, honest, nobody said anything, not even Josh."

"Josh?" At the mention of the ranger, Carl perked up. "He came to see you?"

"I don't think so. He needed some supplies and a snack for Ike, but he did buy four cinnamon rolls. He shaved his beard, too." I felt the warmth creeping up my neck and changed the subject. "Strange that Jesse Livetree never showed up today. Maybe his absence means the police have found something out. Yesterday he mentioned that the sheriff over at Gouverneur had scheduled a press conference on the autopsy, but I don't know where or when."

"I'll make a few calls later, see what I can find out." She finished her helping of lasagna and held the plate up for seconds. I settled deeper into my chair, happy to have brightened the gloom of the past weeks. All in all, except for LeeAnne's murder, I felt better about my place in Wanakena. I didn't feel as lost in its wilderness. After dinner, while I cleaned up and stowed the leftovers for later in the week, I contemplated the one encounter that stood out the most, the one I had almost dismissed. Josh Waylon making no move to free his hand from mine. And his parting words:

Be safe, Riley. Safe. But from whom, Ben Torvald, Anton Storms, or Josh himself?

Chapter 18

...stretching the boundaries...

Monday morning, Carl left before I could ask what she found out from her phone calls, but not before preparing her usual treats. A trail of animal tracks accompanied me down the path from her cabin to the road. The deer prints I identified easily enough... two impressions resembling an inverted heart, trampled, like mine, beneath larger, deeper indentations. I didn't know what had made those. I clutched the basket of pastries tighter. My neck itched. I turned in a circle, wary of making eye contact with a predator. When nothing looked back, I picked up my pace, determined to display a confidence I didn't quite feel. When I met up with Gavin Thursday, I was going to ask about shooting lessons, too.

Mayor Livetree was waiting in his usual spot, carefully groomed and smelling of Old Spice, a fragrance I associated with my dad. Gus and Josh, however, failed to show. Anton Storms brought his normal contingent of chatty city dwellers. While they shopped, he flirted with me. I didn't mind the distraction. Carl thought he was harmless. I wasn't so sure, but he didn't say or do anything I could misconstrue. The banana nut muffins were gone earlier than usual, and the rest of the day passed without incident...or additional visits from a certain enigmatic ranger. The steady influx of locals and tourists kept me from worrying about my boss. When I returned home that night, she had already gone to bed. I read her note on the refrigerator.

I'm all right, Riley. Just tired, Help yourself to the roast chicken.

I slipped down the hall to listen at her door. The absence of snoring told me she was still awake. I considered knocking, then abandoned the idea. My loneliness didn't give me the right to disturb her. I checked that all the doors were locked and scurried to my cabin. Rustling noises outside kept me awake until well after midnight. Although I tried to dismiss them as the antics of skunks or raccoons, my mind insisted on conjuring up the form of a burly shadow creeping out of the forest to prowl around the yard. When I finally fell asleep, the bear shadowed my dreams, morphing from Ben to Anton to Josh. I woke around four to a thumping outside the bedroom window. My heart skipped a beat. I retreated to the bathroom and pulled out the bottle containing my afib pills. Only three left. Tomorrow, while I was in Star Lake, I would ask about the nearest pharmacy. Back in bed, I closed my eyes and counted pine trees until the faces of the children I had met last week intruded, their bright eyes and eagerness to please replacing killer wildlife and wilderness stranglers. This time when I fell asleep, only cute little chipmunks invaded my dreams.

The next day, Carl acted more like herself. She was up and moving confidently, and she had prepared a mountain of baked goods. When I raised my eyebrows, she waved a pair of tongs and laughed heartily. "Can't have my customers neglected while I'm recuperating."

"You know, boss," I grabbed the tongs from her to layer the scones in a basket, "I am actually quite capable in the kitchen. Remember my lasagna? I enjoy cooking, and I make a pretty mean lemon pound cake."

She placed her hot-pad covered hands on her hips. "Why didn't you say so earlier?"

"You never asked." I looked over the remaining items and shrugged. "We freezing these for later?"

She nodded as she pulled out storage containers. When we started on the brownies, I hesitated. "Do you mind if I take some of these to the kids in Star Lake?"

Carl wrapped her arms around me and kissed my cheek. "I knew you were the right one for the job, Riley. Now, if only certain other residents will come to their senses when it comes to you."

I waved her attempt to play matchmaker. "Did you find out any more details about LeeAnne's death?"

She counted out seven brownies and stowed them in a moose tin. "According to Jesse, the autopsy corroborates the initial suspicions. LeeAnne was strangled the same as the hiker last year. And this is just between you and me, but the cord used to do the deed on her is missing. As in nowhere to be found. And here's more weirdness. Forensics discovered fish scales on both women's necks."

"Which means what?"

"Which means all our local men are primary suspects. Ben. Anton. Gus. Josh. Even Gavin and Jesse Livetree. Anyone who cleans fish is bound to have remnants on their clothing."

"Oh, that's not good." I thought about the men she mentioned. I couldn't imagine any of them doing such a thing. "But the clients that Anton brings to Wanakena, wouldn't they be suspects, too? And the people who camp and fish?"

"You're right, honey, they could be, but the police believe both women were killed by someone they knew."

"Why do they think that?"

"Neither of the victims showed any sign of fighting back. None. So the more likely explanation is they were killed by somebody who knew them and was familiar with the territory around here. He knew how to get away. Anyway," Carl glanced at the clock, "better hurry or your customers will be getting restless."

I settled the basket on my hip, stuck my hand in my pocket, and gripped the handle of the fish knife I'd borrowed from the store to replace the cuticle scissors. No bear better try stalking me. Then I headed downtown. By the time I arrived, Jesse was pacing the porch, his walking stick tapping an impatient rhythm on the boards. He raised it over his head when he saw me coming.

"Hurry up, girl. My mouth is watering already." He stepped aside to let me unlock the store. Once I set the basket down, he selected his usual complement of treats, laid his money on the counter, and hurried back outside. I checked the register, watered the spider fern hanging by the window, and slipped back to the storeroom. I was wrestling a carton of mooshiepies off a shelf when I sensed someone come into the room. Before I could turn, Josh Waylon moved up behind me.

"Looks like you could use some help, Riley." His arms guided mine to help balance the box. My entire body tensed. He brushed against me as we lifted the carton, the muscles in his forearms exposed below the rolled-up cuffs of his shirtsleeves, his beardless mouth close enough to tickle the hairs on my neck.

"Hey, Waylon, everything all right?" Gus called from the front of the store, his normally quiet voice loud, his tone confrontational. I shivered.

Josh shifted his weight. His thigh brushed my backside and an entirely different tremor passed through me. He smelled like the outdoors, piney and fresh. I wanted to bury my face in his shirt. I scooted beneath his arm, scrubbed my face with my sleeve until the heat subsided from my flaming cheeks, and escaped into the store. Ike padded over to lick my hand. Josh followed, the box of mooshiepies perched on his shoulder. Gus had already packaged their selected pastries and laid two bills on the counter.

"Where do you want me," Josh said, "to put these?"

I stuttered at his request, my mind caught on the first part of his question, then pointed toward the shelves where Ike now waited expectantly. Josh and I exchanged a look, the dog's anticipation easing any awkwardness between us. I opened the carton and handed over one of the treats. Ike did a happy dance and looked up at his master. Josh nodded, then dusted his hands and headed for the door.

"Everyone's in a hurry today," I opened the register and placed the money inside. "Must be a busy time."

Gus frowned. "We're headed up the Oswegatchie," he said, "looking for something to help us solve this latest crime."

I could see he didn't want to say more. The idea of a murderer on the loose in their territory didn't sit well with either ranger. When I glanced up, Josh was standing by the door, the frown he usually wore replaced by a steady stare that left me feeling naked and exposed.

Carl came by at noon. She settled into the chair behind the counter and pulled knitting needles and a ball of yarn from the moose-embroidered bag she carried. "Run along, Riley," she said, "but don't you forget to eat lunch. Need to put some meat on those skinny bones of yours."

"Yes, boss." I grabbed an apple from the produce bin, a bottle of water from the cooler, and added a package of beef jerky before I jogged back to the cabin. I triple-checked to be sure the door was locked, then headed toward Star Lake, a little concerned that my natural need for security was morphing into obsessiveness. The tin of brownies rode shotgun beside me.

When I pulled into the lot, the children were lined up and waiting outside the building. Bertie, the driver I met last week, tapped her foot as she flicked a lighter from hand to hand. Her frown turned into a grin as I got out of the car.

"Glad to see you, Ms. Finn. The kids are, too."

Calinda smiled up at me. Johnny Joe and DeSales looked at my shoes, but Marie raised her hand for a high five. Timmy grabbed my arm.

"Here. Miss. Miss Finn." He opened his fingers to reveal an origami swan in his palm.

I crouched beside his chair. "Did you make this for me?"

He bobbed his head, then waited for me to accept the delicate paper creation. I didn't know how he had managed to create such a beautiful piece of art. My eyes watered. I blinked and put on my sunglasses.

"You can... keep it... forever," he said. "Dad. Helped me."

"Thank you." I kissed the top of his head and returned to my car. I placed the swan on the dash before wheeling him up the ramp. Miss Haines greeted me as she waved everyone into the activity room. I left Timmy with her and hurried back to help bring in the others. Once the children were settled, I began the lesson. Three hours passed faster than I expected. The brownies were the highlight of the afternoon, the messy trays and chocolate mouths convincing proof. I'd have to bring treats more often.

Miss Haines interrupted our last song to announce that the bus was waiting. She wheeled the children out while I put away the art supplies. It felt good to be back in a classroom. It wasn't until I stepped outside that I realized not all the children had gone. Timmy's wheelchair was waiting next to a vehicle that looked familiar.

"Miss Finn." The boy paused between each word, but after only one lesson, his speech was improving. Maybe all he needed was a little confidence. "Come. Meet my dad."

My heart jumped like a fish when Josh Waylon climbed down from the driver's seat. He leaned against the door, pinning me with another of those startling blue gazes. I pounded my chest and coughed, hoping to arrest the coming arrhythmia. Josh placed a hand on Timmy's shoulder.

"I'll just be a minute, son." The ranger stalked toward me, thumbs hooked in his pockets, t-shirt stretched tight across his chest. Ike slipped out the open door to lay down next to Timmy, his eyes as riveting as his master's.

"Riley?" Josh stopped me before I could escape. He grabbed my shoulders and pulled me toward him. "Are you all right?"

"Yes." I forced a cough. "It's just my crazy heart."

He slipped an arm around my waist. An electric charge raced through me. "Do you need water? Do you need to sit down?"

"No. No." I pushed away, embarrassed at my weakness and aware, in a way I hadn't been before, of how tall he was. "It happens sometimes. No worries." And I was right. My traitor palpitations had stopped as suddenly as they began. Josh's hand lingered at my waist.

"Timmy said he had a really cool teacher."

"But," I searched for something relevant to say, then blurted out the first thing that came to mind, "you don't like me."

"Miss Finn." His thumb traced circles on my lower back, "I don't think you know me well enough to say that. However, my son adores you, so thank you for that." Before I knew it, Josh Waylon pulled me into a one-armed hug, then walked away. I stood frozen, watching as he loaded his son and then the wheelchair into the truck. The jeans he wore stretched tight across his backside, emphasizing his slender hips and amazing ass. Ike circled the lot, then raced over to drop at my feet. His gaze shifted from Josh to me as though he expected me to climb in the truck with them. Part of me wanted to do just that. The other part fought to gain perspective. The desire Josh Waylon stirred refused to settle, but I didn't need another Warren Carstairs. And I definitely didn't need a man who might have murdered his wife.

Chapter 19

...the trouble with theories...

I hated watching Carl drive off to the hospital alone. She headed into the pre-dawn darkness before I had a chance to remind her to be careful on the road. It seemed wrong to send her off to surgery without a friend. Last night she finally admitted she was scared and anxious, so I promised myself to close the store early and drive to Potsdam that evening. I could get there while it was still light, but I'd have to drive back in the dark, something I was dreading, what with wilderness stranglers and bears on the loose. I gathered the morning breakfast pastries and began my daily trek into the hamlet.

As I neared Backpacker's Lodge, a woman called out from the side herb garden. She had scissors in one hand and a howling baby in the other.

"Riley? Riley Finn?"

"Yes. And you're Amy, right? Carl told me about you and your husband and your business. I'm sorry we haven't had a chance to get acquainted yet."

"Well, there's no time like the present, is there? Can you give me a hand?" She held out the baby. I set the muffins on the porch and gathered the wriggling infant into my arms.

"You're a little fuss budget this morning, aren't you?" I cooed in the baby's ear, bouncing her up and down. She stopped crying long enough to latch on to one of my earrings and tug. Laughing, I freed my ear. "No, you can't have everything you see, sweetie. What's her name?"

Amy finished snipping rosemary, thyme, and sage leaves, stuffed them in the front pocket of her apron, and sighed.

"This is Annie, and she is not co-operating this morning. I'm glad you remembered me. Ron and I stopped in your first day and introduced ourselves, and I intended to come by before now, but, well, life's complicated sometimes." She rescued me from another Annie earring grab just as two boys tumbled through the front door. "See what I mean?"

I reached over to smooth down the baby's fine blonde hair and felt that familiar tug inside, the one that reminded me I wasn't getting any younger and neither were my eggs. "I envy you. All these complications mean you love and are loved."

She smiled and started up the steps. "By the way, if you and Carl are free tomorrow, Ron and I would love to have you come for dinner. Our next group of lodgers won't be here until Friday. And I make a mean meat loaf."

"Meat loaf!" The boys shouted in unison as they raced around the yard. "Dad, Mom's making meat loaf!"

"I, we'd, love to, Amy, but Carl's gone to the hospital and won't be home until Saturday at the earliest." At least, that's what I inferred from eavesdropping on her latest phone call. My employer tended not to share important details with me.

"Oh, dear, I didn't know about that. Is it serious?"

"It could be. She's having heart surgery today. I'm driving to Potsdam after work to check on her."

"Heart surgery?" Amy stepped closer. "If it wouldn't be an imposition, I'd like to go with you. Would you mind?"

"Mind? You just made my day. I've been dreading the drive alone."

"Great." She shifted the baby to her other hip. "I'll be ready by seven if that works for you."

I was so happy to have someone to ride with me that I skipped all the way to the store. Even across the steel bridge, which clanged beneath my feet and made my ponytail flip wildly across my shoulders, which explains why I missed seeing Anton and Gus until I literally stumbled over them. They were squared off like two bull moose. Anton stood face to face with the older ranger, fists clenched, a look of fury on his face. Gus had one hand on his belt. The other rested on Anton's chest.

"I better not find you're lying to me." Gus's shout carried across the green.

"I told you where I was, Jornigen, so you and that asshole partner of yours best not spread stupid lies about me."

"You explain how your best fishing knife got abandoned all the way up the Oswegatchie and I'll back off."

"Seems to me it's you who has explaining to do. You're the navy vet. You know all about tying knots."

Gus stalked closer. Anton backed away. They spotted me at the same time. I slowed my approach, nervous about intruding. Each man attempted to hide his animosity, but I practically burned in the flame of their anger. I waved as I mounted the steps to unlock the door. "Morning, Gus. Anton. Nice day today."

Gus scrubbed a hand over his mouth. Then, hustling over, he offered to carry the muffins. I shook my head. Inside, I took refuge behind the counter. When I dared look up, I saw Anton make a fist at Gus's back and steam off toward the docks.

"Sorry you had to see that, Miss Riley. That LeeAnne girl's murder has everyone seeing plots where there are none."

I shrugged off his explanation. "You buying for two this morning?" I kept my eyes down so he wouldn't see the interest with which I awaited his answer.

"No, just for me. Josh took a sick day today."

"Oh." I pressed a hand against my chest, the ache not one of my palpitations but something far more unexpected and surprising. "Is he ill?"

"No, but his boy is. Timmy suffers seizures from time to time. He had one this morning. They're on their way to the hospital now."

"I'm sorry to hear that." I busied myself with his change before I asked the question uppermost in my mind. "Do you know where Josh is taking him?"

Gus shrugged. "Not sure. Got other things on my mind."

After what I'd overheard between him and Anton, I risked another question. "How's the investigation going? Have you found any evidence?"

The ranger shot me a calculating look. I busied myself with filling out the receipt book until he reached over the counter to grab my wrist.

"Best you mind the store, Miss Finn, and leave the detective work to those of us trained for it." He snatched the muffins and strode for the door, stopping before he reached the threshold. "Could be Josh has taken Timmy to Potsdam."

The screen door banged behind him, then opened again as Gavin bounced in. He called out a greeting, then began stocking the shelves. I stuffed my hands in the pockets of my vest. For the first time since I arrived in Wanakena, I couldn't wait to close up shop.

Business was brisk all day. Everybody took their time making their selections, including the family that staggered in ten minutes before seven. I did my best impersonation of Carl as I hurried them along. Some people just can't make up their minds about which junk food they really need. Finally, they dumped their items on the counter, paid, and strolled out. I locked the door, made mental notes about what I would need to replenish tomorrow, and raced down the road.

Amy waited outside the eco-lodge, a picnic basket by her feet. I greeted her as I ran by.

"Be right back!" Brushing pine needles off the windshield, I counseled my heart to remain steady before I drove back to pick her up.

"Here." Amy passed me a sandwich and asked about my day. I mumbled an appropriate word or two, then concentrated on the road. Neither of us spoke much as we dug into the steak sandwiches, one of Ron's specialties. And the coconut squares begged to be eaten. After we finished, Amy lifted my spirits with stories about her kids and the guests who returned to their lodge year after year. By the time we pulled into the hospital, the tenuous bond that existed between us had strengthened into a strong cord of shared views and love for children.

A volunteer at the front desk directed us to the ICU, which caused my heart to skip a beat. But the gentleman explained it was standard procedure after stent and biopsy surgery. I swallowed hard before asking about Timmy Waylon, but the receptionist only cocked his head and checked the computer screen.

"Are you a family member?"

"No, but I am his teacher." Well, that was a stretch, but Amy didn't blink.

"Ah," he said, "guess that makes you a special case." He handed me a slip of paper with the room number and pointed us down the corridor. Amy and I followed directions to the intensive care unit, checked in with a nurse, and waited to be allowed in to see Carl.

"One at a time," the nurse cautioned as he directed us to the room where Carl lay staring at the wall. Her hands, rarely still, clutched at the blanket. When she spotted me, she gestured wildly.

Muttering about cranky patients, the nurse propped the door open. He checked the monitor, made sure the oxygen tube was in place, and shook a finger at Carl. "Now, Miss Beamish, no excitement. You're going to be moved to a regular room shortly, provided you follow the doctor's orders."

"Just wish you'd let me get up and move around."

"Ms. Beamish." He folded his arms and tapped his foot. "Behave."

"All right, I'll be good." Carl steepled her hands under her chin and vamped. "But only if you let me see my friends. Both of them."

The nurse wrote something on a clipboard and motioned us over. "She's a real ballbuster, isn't she? You can visit, but don't stay more than ten minutes. She's doing well, but she really should rest."

Amy dropped back. "You go on, Riley. Then you can go find Timmy while I'm with Carl."

There was logic in her suggestion. I smoothed my hair and went in. When Carl reached for my hand, I felt the tension in her grip. "How are you feeling, boss?"

She blinked against the glare of the overhead light before pulling me close.

"Get me out of here, Finn. Now."

I patted her cheek. "You know I can't do that, Carl. But if you do what they tell you to do, they'll let you come home sooner. Now, say you're glad to see me."

She took a deep breath and settled back against the pillows. "I do thank you for coming, dear. I'm actually feeling pretty good. Doc Richardson's just being cautious. Now, tell me about your day."

I entertained her with an account of the day's customers, especially the junk food crowd. That subject exhausted, I moved on to the gossip shared by locals, the fish tales and wildlife sightings of the tourists. Carl never let go of my hand. When I finished, she patted my cheek, squeezed my fingers for the hundredth time, and let me go. "You're like the daughter I always wanted, Riley. Now send that precious Amy Dugas in here. Best neighbor ever, to my mind."

I kissed her, tucked the blanket tighter, and returned to the waiting area. After Amy sat down by the bed, I wrestled free the slip of paper with Timmy's room number and headed to the elevator, the stuffed moose I had brought for him nestled in the crook of my arm. The closer I got to Room 231, the more nervous I grew. What if he was seriously ill? Although we'd only had two afternoons together, I already felt attached to the boy and responsible for him. I didn't understand why. I just knew he meant more to me than the other students. I lifted my hand to knock when the door opened and a man backed into the hall.

"I'll be right back, Tim." Josh said. "I'm just going to check with the nurse."

Timmy's words floated after him. "Okay, Daddy."

I skipped backward, the stuffed animal cradled to my chest. Josh heard me gasp and turned around. There was such sadness in his eyes, and yearning, and beneath it all, a hunger I recognized as kin to my own. My heart skipped, but not with palpitations. I almost reached for him.

"Riley." He touched my shoulder. I stumbled, and he caught me. Once again, I wanted to drown in that clean, earthy scent. Forever. He briefly tightened his arms around me but then pushed away. I bit my lip, unable to speak amid the emotions he awakened in me. He ran a hand through his hair, looked over his shoulder at the boy lying so still in the bed. "I can use your help. I need to talk to the doctor and find out when Timmy can go home. Will you stay with my son?"

"Of course," I said, unable to stop the thoughts flooding through me. How good it felt to be in his arms. How good it would feel to be cared for and cherished by this man. I slid one foot forward. The other followed as I made my way toward the boy in the bed. As Josh hurried down the hall, I claimed his spot. "Hey, Timmy, I hear you've had an exciting day."

"Miss Finn."

I tucked the stuffed animal beside him. "Thought you might want a companion to share this adventure with you."

He pressed the moose to his chest. His eyes sparkled.

"Th-thank you. I love it."

"I'm glad, but you know what? Mr. Moose is here to see that you get better real soon because I expect you in class next Tuesday. Will you promise to do that?"

"Pro-mise." Timmy wriggled closer to the side rail. He touched the hand I had rested there and pulled it toward him.

"Story?" he asked. I sorted through the ones I could recite by heart and the ones I'd have to improvise. "Goodnight, Moon" seemed the best choice. As I began, he sighed. Before I reached the end, Timmy Waylon had fallen asleep, the moose nearly invisible under the blanket. When his hand dropped from mine, I looked up. Josh was watching me, his arms crossed, his look inscrutable. Everything I thought I saw before was now buried beneath a stern, unblinking stare. Maybe I had imagined it all. He waited for me to rise, then steered me into the hall.

When we stepped out of the room, he glanced over his shoulder and closed the door. He grabbed me and pushed me back against the wall. "Why are you here, Riley?"

I met his blue-eyed glare with a frown. "I came to see Carl. When I learned Timmy had been admitted, I wanted to see him, too."

"Carl Beamish? She's here at the hospital?"

"She had stent surgery today." I paused. "Gus told me Timmy was here."

"You brought him a gift." His tone rattled me down to my toes.

"Your boy deserves to be cared for. Don't push everyone away just because you're angry."

"You don't know what you're talking about."

I considered what to say next. He didn't know that Carl had told me about his past. Maybe I should tell him. The pain he carried was eating away at the man he could be. "I know enough. Don't punish me for being kind, Josh Waylon. It's the only way I know how to be."

Instead of answering, he traced a thumb down my cheek, then ran it over my lips, sending new messages through my body.

"I bring grief to everyone around me, Riley. Don't become one of my casualties." He didn't wait for a reply, just turned and disappeared into Timmy's room. I remained rooted in place, afflicted by the certainty that Josh Waylon wanted to kiss me as much as I wanted to kiss him. Which was crazy stupid. I struggled to control the emotions churning inside as I made my way back to the ICU. Amy had fallen asleep in a chair. Carl was arguing with the nurse. I stuck my head in to say goodbye.

"Riley," Carl said. "Take me with you."

"Saturday, boss. You have to wait until Saturday." I ignored the pout, said good-bye, and thanked the nurse. Then Amy and I hurried back to the car. We had an hour's drive to Wanakena. Neither of us talked much on the way back. I couldn't wait to be alone in my cabin. I needed to ponder what the hell was going on between me and the troubled ranger.

Chapter 20

... wild hearts and calm winds...

Thursday, the sound of rattling outside my cabin roused me from a restless sleep. Gavin stood outside the screen door, fishing gear slung on his back and paddles balanced on his shoulder. I yelled a greeting, then wiggled into my only pair of knee-length leggings, donned a camisole, a flannel shirt, and a hoodie, and collected the backpack filled with snacks I'd prepared the night before. I held up my hiking boots, decided they didn't suit the morning's activities, and reached for a pair of water shoes Carl had left for me. I strapped them on and went out to greet my instructor. The boy appeared to have grown taller over the past few weeks. He hunched forward to hide the fact that he, too, now towered over me.

"Ready, Miss Finn?" He glanced at me from beneath the fringe of hair that shaded his eyes.

"Not yet, Mr. Torvald." I gestured for him to follow as I skipped up the path toward Carl's cabin. "First, we eat."

Gavin hummed tunelessly as he stacked the paddles and the fishing rod case against the outside wall. I sat him at the table, poured coffee into our mugs, and moved to the stove. By the time the hash browns were sizzling and the eggs ready to serve, I had learned all about his best friend's new girlfriend, the latest escapade of the Dugas boys, and the most recent bear sightings. We ate breakfast to the accompaniment of the weather forecast from the satellite radio he carried.

"It's important to know the conditions before you set out on the water," he said. "Especially if you're a beginner."

"You sound very serious, Gavin."

"I mean..." He blushed. I patted his hand.

139

"I didn't mean to tease you. That sounds like good advice." I dumped the dirty dishes in the sink and clapped my hands. "Ready when you are, professor."

The flush on his cheeks faded as he led the way down the path. Above us, ravens circled the pines. The wilderness yawned its way into morning. I stopped at the store to hand Jesse the day's muffins and make sure he was comfortable with the arrangement for the day. Afterward, I jogged to the beach where Gavin had unpacked the fishing rods and laid out the lures. He turned out to be an excellent teacher, patient, enthusiastic, and willing to repeat instructions until I truly understood what I was doing. By ten o'clock, I had more or less mastered simple casting without snagging the hook in the trees, the dock, or my clothing. I even caught a smallmouth bass, a two-pounder that I had to cut the hook out of before releasing it back into the lake. Of course, I didn't know it was a bass, which is when Gavin told me about The Wild Center, located down the highway in Star Lake.

"You really should visit there, Miss Finn." Gavin wiped down the rods and stowed them in the case. "The place has these storyboards that tell the history of the Adirondacks and the animals that live here. There's lots of fish from the area."

"It's really called The Wild Center?"

Gavin nodded. The longer he spoke, the more estranged I felt from Hopewell and the Riley Finn who wanted a dull, routine, unsurprising life. Wanakena and its people were unraveling all my preconceptions about myself and the world beyond my hometown. This wilderness was erasing my self-imposed boundaries and forcing me into uncharted territory. I had encountered elusive rangers, unselfish teachers, and legendary fishermen. I had bonded with loveable little kids, intense teens, and unconventional adults. I had also become a suspect, if only temporarily, in the murder of one woman and intrigued by the mystery surrounding her death and Amanda Waylon's. This tiny hamlet, this gateway to the Adirondack wilderness, had taken me in, then encouraged me to push beyond the limited life I once envisioned. Caught up in my job and my boss's troubles, I had stopped dwelling on Warren Carstairs and my lost teaching job. I realized, with a jolt, that my heart was moving on.

"Miss Finn? Can you hand me the tackle box?" Gavin asked. As I handed it over, I put the Wild Center on my list of places to go during my time in Wanakena.

"You're good at this." I buckled the life jacket he handed over. "You should think about being a teacher."

He flipped his hair off his forehead and stared at me. "You serious, Miss Finn?"

"Yes, Gavin, I am." I picked up a paddle. "Now, teach me how to use this thing."

"Canoe or kayak?"

"Which is easier for a rank beginner?"

He pointed to a kayak. "No sense in putting off the inevitable."

He helped me settle in and pushed me away from shore before hopping into his own craft. In seconds we were midstream. He paddled with sure strokes over the calm water. I struggled to keep my boat going straight.

"Watch me." Gavin demonstrated the stroke again and again. Frustrated but determined, I kept at it, anxious to master the basics without making a fool of myself. My instructor circled back to help. I twisted to the left, overcompensated, and felt the kayak shift. I heard Gavin shout, but I didn't understand the instruction. With no idea how to regain my balance, my hips slipped sideways. I yelled and held the paddle above my head as I floundered and went under. I came up sputtering. All the clothes I'd worn, now soaked, dragged at me, but the life jacket kept my head above water.

"Miss Finn!" Gavin guided his kayak toward me. "Hold still. I'll tow you back to shore."

"No." I shook my head. "I'm not done yet. Teach me how to get back in."

"Okay." Gavin paddled closer. "Flip your boat over. Good. Now, grab both sides of the kayak and pull yourself up until your bellybutton is over the center. Steady. Don't lose your paddle!"

It took three tries before I heaved my shivering body up and into the boat. The sound of clapping echoed over the water. I glanced toward the shore, only to see half of Wanakena gathered on the lawn, watching me. I groaned.

"Don't pay any attention to them," Gavin said. Easier to say than to do. Heat raced up my neck and over my cheeks. I had to look like a drowned rat with third-degree burns. Gavin steered closer. "Everyone has to learn that skill sooner or later, Miss Finn. But you got right back in. I'm proud of you."

I looked into his earnest face and sputtered a thank you. I'd been humiliated by a master when Warren dumped me. I could handle this. The sun came out, warming my skin where it wasn't covered by drenched cloth. I unzipped the life jacket, peeled off two layers, and refastened the personal flotation device. Gavin waited until I was ready, and we began again. He never raised his voice or expressed exasperation. Grateful for his patience, I persevered. By noon, my arms shook like noodles and I had splashed myself with enough lake water to fill a bathtub. But the exercise dulled the chill from the dunking and eased my embarrassment. A sense of accomplishment accompanied me to shore. The onlookers had mostly drifted away. I made a deliberate effort not to look at those who remained. Back on the beach, I staggered from the kayak, removed my vest, and tossed it in the boat.

"You did good, Miss Finn," he said. "You didn't even panic when you dumped the kayak. Don't worry about the gear. I'll take care of returning it." He grabbed the paddles and started up the bank.

"Gavin?" When he looked over his shoulder, I held out my hand. "Can I keep a paddle? I'd like to practice before next week's lesson."

He handed it back and nodded toward the store. "Want to get something to eat?"

"Actually, I have a better idea. How about I fix lunch before I head to the hospital to see Carl. Does tuna salad and a brownie sound good?"

I didn't have to ask twice. We jogged up the road, the familiar routine easing my worries over Jesse Livetree taking care of the store. Since I'd arrived in Wanakena, I'd given up my daily runs, unsure whether it was safe to go out alone and too tired each night to ask. I matched Gavin stride for stride, the breeze warm against my face. It wasn't until we turned onto Reed that I noticed the park service truck at the entrance to the trailhead. Josh was sitting in the bed, Ike beside him, watching Gavin and me. He wore that same unreadable look he'd given me at the hospital. I lifted my head and ran faster, letting the wild fill me with its untamed spirit and unbridled courage. That will show him, I thought, but deep inside, a different chord sounded, one that wished he were running beside me instead of a sixteen-year old boy on the cusp of becoming a man. Ike barked once when we passed. Gavin waved. Josh waved back, but he never took his eyes off me. I felt his gaze all the way to the cabin.

*

The drive into Canton/Potsdam Hospital was lonelier without Amy, but at least I didn't have to drive in the dark.

The hospital had transferred Carl to a regular room. I entered just as she concluded an argument in which she insisted on ordering a mooseburger and fries. The nurse, a different one from the ICU staff, stood her ground.

"No, Ms. Beamish. You're on a low salt, low-fat diet. Doctor's orders."

"Riley! Tell this person that I'm hungry and need my protein."

I tossed my purse in a chair, grabbed the hand not hooked up to an IV, and shushed her. "You want to go home sooner rather than later, don't you?"

Carl nodded, but she wasn't happy. She snatched her hand back, folded her arms, and pouted. The nurse whispered her thanks and scurried away before Carl could yell again. I filled the boss in on the latest news about Wanakena and my introductory lesson in flipping a kayak.

"What about all your men callers?" She winked at me.

"They're around." I turned away before she could comment on the red creeping over my cheeks. "I haven't seen Anton though. Seems strange for him not to be hanging around."

"Oh," Carl said. "He's probably gone in to Saranac or Lake Placid to drum up more business. That man has an uncanny knack for finding gullible townies to buy his stories about knowing the best fishing spots."

"You mean he doesn't?"

"Well, sure, but Gavin Torvald knows more about the fish in our lake than that transplant from the coast. Still, Storms does bring in a fair amount of tourist traffic. Despite his mysterious past, he charms folks into renting his boat and his expertise. I expect he'll be back with new recruits before you know it."

We discussed her recovery, went over store orders for the following week, and solidified the arrangements for Jesse to bring her home Saturday.

"Even after I get back, the doctor says I have to take it easy." She sniffed. "You have to keep the store going, Riley. Wanakena depends on us. And I know you will."

Touched by her faith in me, I promised to take care of everything, then waited for her to fall asleep before I hurried over to Timmy's room. He was sleeping, too, the moose snuggled next to his chin. Josh wasn't there. I pulled a chair closer and watched the boy's narrow chest rise and fall, my heart twisting at the fate that had left him with such formidable challenges. I kissed his forehead and sneaked out before he woke. Somewhere between the elevator and the parking lot, I made a promise to myself to do whatever it took to help him grow stronger. On the drive home, I wondered why I felt so drawn to the Waylon men. Emma would blame it on my compulsion to make everything better for everyone else. I, however, attributed it to the chaos creeping into my once-tame heart. Sometimes, one had to take that unexpected leap into the unknown.

I stopped for a sandwich in Canton before getting back on the road. The evening light lasted until the final twenty miles back to Wanakena. When I pulled in next to Carl's truck, something large and dark scuttled down the path between our cabins. I froze, waiting for the thing to return. Nothing moved in the darkness. I scrabbled in the glove compartment for a flashlight, but I was afraid to get out of the car. All those teenage sleep-over tales of men with hooks and attacks on lovers in parked cars jostled for attention in my memory. I strained to see through the mist swirling up from the river. It curled and grew in the shadows cast by the porch light. My hands shook as I shifted into reverse and zigzagged back down the lane to the Dugas's house. Thankfully, Amy had put her number in my contacts list. I called her, my voice only a little shaky.

"Stay in the car, Riley," she said "Ron and I will be right out. Then you can come inside with me."

"No, Amy. You stay with the kids. I need to be sure whatever it was is gone." I paused to check my pulse. I waited for my heart to jump. Nothing happened. Grateful for that respite, I asked what was uppermost in my mind. "Do you think it was the bear?"

"Probably." Her calmness reassured me. "Here's Ron now."

The front door of the lodge opened. Ron Dugas, his chef's apron still tied around his waist, carried his rifle. He plodded down the steps, opened the passenger door, and climbed in.

"Drive, Riley. Let's see if it's still there." I inched the car forward. We rolled into Carl's spot in front of the cabin and stopped. Ron scanned the clearing, then hopped out and motioned me to follow. We crept onto the porch and let ourselves in. Nothing inside Carl's cabin had been disturbed. I secured the front door, and we exited through the kitchen. I clung to Ron's jacket as he led the way down the path from Carl's. He flashed the light and searched the ground for tracks. When we reached my cabin, he handed over the torch and nudged the screen door open. It banged loose and sagged from the hinges.

"That wasn't broken when I left this afternoon," I said. In the kitchen, the apples I had stored in a bowl on the table lay scattered across the floor. Someone or something had smashed every one. The odor of rotting fruit permeated the room. Ron crouched to poke at the remains of one with a pocketknife. When he rose, an iridescent speck balanced on the tip of the blade.

"I think you should stay at our place tonight, Riley."

I circled the mess on the floor. Anger roared in my ears. This cabin was supposed to be my safe space.

"Did a bear do this?"

Ron looked at me, his expression puzzled. "No," he said. "A human animal made this mess. I'm calling the state police at Gouverneur."

We waited for twenty minutes until headlights flashed across the clearing, followed by the light from a powerful torch illuminating the path. Ron pushed me behind him as boots crunched over the pine needles and clomped through the broken screen door. I recognized Officer Kellerman as soon as she stepped into the kitchen. She acknowledged both of us before examining the mess on the floor. After she photographed the destruction, she pulled on gloves, squatted, and extracted another sparkling shard from the floor. Placing it in an evidence bag along with the one Ron found, she took out a notebook. Her braid slipped over one shoulder as she bent to write.

"Let's start with where you both were prior to coming here."

While Ron gave his account, I wrapped an afghan around me to stop the shakes. When Kellerman turned my way, I recounted the day's activities. I ended with a description of the shadowy form I spotted running from the cabin as I pulled in.

"So, the last time you were in here before returning tonight was around one p.m.?"

"Yes. Gavin and I had lunch. Then I cleaned up the kitchen, stuck a load of laundry in the washer, and checked that the windows and doors were locked."

"And you left the apples on the table?"

"Yes."

"How many apples?"

I closed my eyes. Did I count them as I took them from the grocery bag and placed them in the bowl? "I'm not sure, maybe eight."

"Well, there are only six on the floor now, and these." Kellerman held up the bag with the shiny objects.

"What are those?" I asked, leaning closer.

"Shards of glass, from beads," Kellerman said, "like the ones in these photographs." She scrolled through her phone, stopping to show me a closeup of a neck with something embedded in the skin. When I'd had a good look, she moved on to a second photograph. In this one, a string of beads mounted on what appeared to be a strand of leather or rope was laid out next to a tape measure. The strip measured eight inches. I grabbed my neck and swallowed, hard.

"Was that used..." I stopped.

"To choke someone? Yes." Kellerman tapped the first picture. "We believe LeeAnne McMasters was strangled with the same type of necklace used on last year's victim, Amanda Waylon. However, the one used to harm LeeAnne is missing. You don't have a necklace like this, do you, Miss Finn?"

"What?" I touched my neck again. "No. You don't think...no."

"I'm just interested in establishing the facts," She cocked her head and waited for me to speak. I looked at the pieces of glass in the evidence bag.

"You think these beads are like the ones in Amanda's necklace?"

"Could be. We'll let the forensic guys do the comparisons to be sure. But I'm almost positive they're the same. My sister has a strand just like the one in the picture. They've been popular souvenir items at Lake Placid for the past five years."

"But not now?" Ron frowned.

"No." Kellerman closed her notebook, scrolled through the photos one more time, then closed the screen. "The woman who made and sold them is no longer in business."

I knew I shouldn't ask, but I did anyway. "And who was that?"

"Amanda Waylon," she said. "Ranger Waylon's deceased wife."

Chapter 21

...coming up for air...

Officer Kellerman remained with us until a second officer arrived and began to process the cabin for fingerprints and other clues that might help identify the intruder. After she left, Ron rode with me back to the Lodge. Amy waited on the porch, clutching a sweater around her to ward off the night chill. I lifted my overnight bag from the back seat and locked the car. I had reached the steps when a truck came racing toward us. The driver spun the vehicle to a stop. Dirt and gravel sprayed out, fanning over the roadway. I jumped back as Josh Waylon barreled from the truck. He greeted Ron and Amy, then swung toward me.

"Are you all right?" He moved closer, the frown back on his face.

I tried to swallow the fear, but the night's terrors won out. A single sob escaped, followed by tears. Without a word, Josh wrapped his arms around me and pulled me close. The strength of his grip promised protection. I rested my head against his chest, grateful for this short suspension of his disapproval. When I stopped crying, he stepped away. I shivered at the loss of contact.

"What are you doing here?" I wiped my eyes and waited for his reply. Ron and Amy retreated to the porch, not quite out of earshot.

Josh ran a hand through his hair. He was dressed in jeans that hugged his long, muscled thighs, and a plaid shirt with the cuffs rolled up. A tattoo of pine trees snaked up his left forearm. When I looked up, concern and something else loomed in his eyes.

"I just got back from the hospital and heard what happened. Timmy would never forgive me if I didn't check and make sure you were okay."

"Timmy? Is he better?"

"The doc says I can bring him home tomorrow."

"That's good to hear. But I still don't know how you learned about—" I motioned in the direction of Carl's house.

Josh glanced at Ron and Amy. His mouth curled up at the corners. "Word gets around in Wanakena."

"Not at midnight, it doesn't."

"Not to worry, Riley." Amy came down the steps and put an arm around me. "I called him. I thought he should know."

"You?"

A look passed between them. "Waylons stick together," she said. "Right, Joshua?"

"Wait. You and Josh are related?"

Amy punched him on the arm. "We're cousins. My mother and his father, sister and brother."

The disconnect between what I thought I knew about the people in Wanakena and the truth made me dizzy. "Why didn't you say something before?"

"Didn't think about it." She turned toward the house and tugged me along beside her. "You coming, cousin? I've got blueberry pie left over from dinner and enough coffee to give everyone a midnight caffeine high."

Instead of answering, Josh looked at me and waited. Over all my rational objections, my body went on high alert. The man was a magnet I couldn't resist. And I should. His silence meant the choice was mine to make. I considered the possibility that he was the mysterious intruder and discarded it. I still tingled from his embrace. If I sent him away tonight, I might seal off all possibilities of a relationship. This time my head and my heart agreed to a detente.

"You might as well come in," I said. "I think we could all use a little blueberry pie."

"Will you give me a raincheck, Riley?" Josh backtracked to his truck. "It's been a long day, and I have to meet Gus earlier than usual tomorrow."

I clenched my fists. Rejected. Again. I should have known.

"Riley?" he repeated. I exhaled and nodded. Could I be more pathetic? Amy and Ron said goodnight and went inside. I stayed on the porch, watching as he drove away. But the plea in his voice stayed with me. What did he want me to understand? After Amy showed me to one of the recently vacated guest rooms, I lay awake, listening to the wind rattle screens and sigh a path through the restless pines, wondering what demons kept the ranger up at night.

Chapter 22

...fish tales...

By morning, all of Wanakena buzzed with the news of a possible bear prowler at the Finn cabin. It seemed like the entire local population stopped by to purchase a drink or snack and ask about the sighting. Officer Kellerman had warned me not to say anything about what she found inside, so I stuck to my story of a ransacked kitchen and the sight of a dark, lumbering shape sneaking away into the forest. It was past noon when Gavin and Anton came in together, sharing fish stories and making jokes at the expense of the tourists.

"Haven't seen you in a while, Mr. Storms," I said. He was wearing a new fishing vest. "Been to the big city?"

"Does that mean you missed me?" He leaned on the counter and winked. The dimple in his chin deepened.

"Just keeping the local gossip machine well oiled," I said, wondering where this new smart-mouthed Riley had come from.

Anton grabbed my hand and held it, palm up. He traced the line below my little finger all the way across my palm. "You have a very sensitive and loving heart, Miss Finn."

"You can tell that from looking at my hand?" I slipped free of his grasp. "I didn't know you had psychic abilities."

"Of course, I do. That's how I find all the big fish. By the way, Gavin says you're developing a talent for catching bass." He reached for my hand again. I gave it to him with some reluctance. He ran his thumb across it. "But I don't detect any callouses. And no slices from hooks."

I gave Gavin the evil eye. "One lesson does not a great fisherman make."

"Not true, Miss Finn." Gavin tugged on his ear. "You're a natural. You caught a fish with your first cast."

Anton held up a finger to silence us. "No matter. When you're ready," somehow he made it sound like a promise of more than fishing, "I'll take you out on my boat."

"Can I come, too, Mr. Storms?" The boy hurried to stand behind me. "Miss Finn and I are a good team. She's even learning to kayak."

Anton pursed his lips, blew out air. His gaze lingered on my mouth. "You're turning into a regular wild thing, aren't you?"

That made my transformation sound sexy, but I brushed off the insinuation along with the crumbs from the morning's pastries. "This is the gateway to the wilderness, Mr. Storms. When in Rome…"

"This, Miss Riley Finn, is not Rome, and you are a babe," he looked me up and down, "in the woods. Be careful or that bear prowling around might just find you."

"Hey, Anton," Gavin poked the fisherman in the chest. Although as tall as the older man, the teenager had fewer muscles. His thin frame vibrated from the contact. "You shouldn't go scaring her like that."

"Not trying to scare her, Gav. Just being practical." The dimple flashed again. "I apologize if I upset either of you. I spend too much time alone with the fish and not enough around civilized people. Listen, I have a new group coming in at two. Maybe I can make it up to you another day, Riley, by taking you to lunch. The Harborview in Cranberry serves a mean cheeseburger. I'll even let the kid come along as chaperone."

Gavin rolled his eyes. I almost did, too, but the prospect of a boat trip into the lake town appealed to my newly discovered sense of adventure.

"Perfect." I nodded to Jesse Livetree, who passed under the entrance sign and tapped his cane on the floorboards. "How about next Thursday? First, Mr. Torvald will give me my lessons. Then we'll meet you at the dock. Around noon?"

The mayor stomped closer. He scowled at Anton as the guide backed his way out the door. More shoppers entered behind the mayor. Soon I was too busy to worry over this strange version of myself who flirted with abandon, accepted dates at the drop of a hint, and forgot about being the target of a night stalker. When the memory of Josh Waylon saying goodbye the night before hit me, I bit my lip in frustration. The he-likes-me, he-likes-me-not pattern of our developing relationship, if it could even be called a relationship, made my head hurt. And I had other things to think about besides the tension between us.

Ron and Amy had convinced me to move in with Carl when she came home. Until then, I was staying at the Lodge with them. I must admit that I loved playing hide and seek with the rambunctious Dugas boys, and little Annie had stolen my heart. Still, as I rearranged the potato chip bags on the shelf, I contemplated my morning and the upcoming weekend. I had now accepted two dates with perfect strangers. The ever-charming Ben Torvald would return from his campout tomorrow, and I had agreed to go with him to the Pine Cone Sunday. I cringed as I thought of how the rumor mill would churn around all my activities. And what would Warren think of this changed Riley? That I'd gone crazy? Who, I asked myself, cares? Emma would cheer. Emma. I hadn't called her as I promised. I had to remedy that soon. I wondered what Josh Waylon would think, too, when he found out I was going out with Ben and Anton. Perhaps it didn't matter to him, after all. My heart did a lazy flip-flop, then corrected itself. Apparently, the cowering woman I used to be and the wild creature now invading my body didn't particularly agree. Josh Waylon might not care about me, but I definitely felt something for him.

Chapter 23

...sharing secrets in the night...

By the time I closed the store Saturday, Carl had called five times to ask when I was coming home. She sounded querulous, and a little lonely. Amy had checked in on her every hour, and Jesse Livetree had insisted she call if she needed anything, but I had become her go-fer girl. Flattering as it was, I had a lot of work to do. Carl insisted that the store stay open and functioning, especially as we approached the Fourth of July. That, Carl had reminded me at least twenty times, was our prime money-maker. The tourist crowd was growing more numerous every day. All the Backpacker Lodge rooms were rented through the month of July and half of August. When I moved back to Carl's cabin, Amy was sad to see me go, but she was also relieved. So was the boss.

It was almost nine-thirty by the time I staggered into the great room, arms filled with a week's-worth of groceries. Amy had been kind enough to leave a tuna casserole in the oven. Along with the aroma of fresh-baked bread, Carl's cabin smelled heavenly. Seated by the table with Mutzi, the inside-outside cat, purring on her lap, she waited to hear about the past few days.

"Jesse hinted at some goings-on at your place," Carl said, waving a fork in the air. I placed the plates on the table. She tucked in like she was starving. How she managed to speak around the mouthful of noodles, I'll never know. "Come on, Riley. Spill."

"Take it easy, Carl. Please. There'll be time enough for stories after dinner." She grumped at me, then cocked her head as I recited the sales numbers for the days she'd been gone. "Last week was very profitable. The coming ones should be better, no?"

"Long as everybody keeps quiet about that murdered girl," Carl murmured.

I pretended not to hear as I helped her back to the recliner. The cat purred around my ankles, anticipating a taste of tuna. I fished out a few chunks for her, then washed and dried all the dishes before making myself comfortable on the sofa. Carl patted her lap. Mutzi hopped up, circled five or six times, then plopped down to wash her paws like a proper cat.

"So, tell me the good stuff. You still going out with Ben Torvald tomorrow?"

The question caught me by surprise. "How did you remember that?"

She pointed at her chest and laughed. "Just because my ticker has problems doesn't mean there's a thing wrong with my mind. I keep track of everything going on in our hamlet, Riley, and don't you forget it. Now, answer my question so I can ask the next one."

"I guess I am. He's been gone all week, so, unless he calls to cancel, we still have a date." I chewed the inside of my cheek. Did I feel good or bad about that? After spending last night with Amy, Ron, and Josh, I felt conflicted. The ranger had shown up around nine, shared dessert and coffee with us, and listened as Ron described the clients coming in next week. Although he hadn't touched me again after an obligatory one-armed hug, he did spend most of the evening staring at my mouth. I heated up just thinking about it.

"It's good for you to get out, girl. You should mingle. Date." Carl tapped her chin, "That way you'll have a chance to compare candidates."

"Candidates for what?"

"Lover, of course. Can't have you coming all this way for a summer fling just to go home empty-handed."

"I didn't come here for any kind of fling." When I saw her smirk, I realized she was teasing. I decided to come clean about my other inappropriate decision. "Anton Storms asked me to lunch in Cranberry next week."

"Did he now?" She stroked the cat, who stretched and yawned. "And you accepted?"

I removed my hair tie and fluffed my hair, hoping to distract her from the blush staining my cheeks. "I did."

"Well, aren't you the sly one, Miss Finn. Mr. Waylon better up his game or lose the match."

"Josh?" Saying his name sent a tremor down my spine. I shook my head. "He doesn't like me that much."

"He showed up the other night, didn't he?"

"Which night?"

"Riley." Carl put up a hand to forestall my protest. "I know you've spent the last two nights at the Dugas place. And I know Mr. Josh Waylon, who doesn't go anywhere where there are people, visited last night. What I don't know is why you were there to begin with. No one's saying. Time to spill the beans, kiddo."

I worried a thread on the cuff of my shirt before I spoke. "When I came home Thursday, I saw something cutting across the clearing. I went to get Ron, and he came back with me. Something or someone had been in my cabin. Smashed all the apples. We thought it might have been a bear."

"But it wasn't, was it?" Her eyes gleamed. The possibility of real gossip perked her right up.

"No. Officer Kellerman checked it out and found something on the floor, something that proved it wasn't a bear."

"Did she now? What was it?"

I tore the thread off with a loud snap. "A bead. Or, rather, shards of a glass bead. Like those in the necklace that strangled Amanda Waylon. Kellerman indicated that the coroner believes the same kind of necklace was used to kill LeeAnne McMasters."

Carl gnawed her lower lip. She stroked the cat's ears before looking up. "Do me a favor. Go in the bedroom and bring me the jewelry box from the dresser."

I did as she asked. The mahogany box had an inlaid top made of cedar and cherry wood strips and a polished brass clasp. I ran my fingers over the beautiful craftsmanship before I handed her the box. "Who made this for you?"

Carl squeezed my hand before settling the box next to the cat, who meowed and jumped down. "Josh made this. Among other things, the ranger has a talent for woodworking."

I crouched beside the recliner, fitting this new information into what I already knew about the man. Carl lifted the lid and searched among the items within. She pulled out a string of amber-colored beads, each separated by a carved wooden one. "Did the necklaces look like this?"

I held the strand up to the light, watching the way it reflected through the beads. "Yes and no. The one in Kellerman's pictures didn't have wooden beads. All the ones I saw were amber or silver."

"Huh." She pinched her nose and closed her eyes. "I'm guessing Amanda made those, then. She and Josh made this one together."

I ran my thumb over the individual beads, traced the delicate etching on each wooden one. Why did something so beautiful end up so deadly? I handed the necklace back to Carl, trying to understand how the Waylons' jewelry ended up strangling two women.

Chapter 24

...the heart is a fey creature, given to wild and reckless play...

It took exactly ten minutes to jog from the store to Carl's place, two more to go from there to the cabin she had designated as mine. I loved the freedom of having my own space, but the violation by the unknown intruder had soured me on staying there alone. Still, I had yet to relocate my things to Carl's spare bedroom, so I stood in front of the closet in my cabin, staring at the few date-worthy items before me, unable to shake my reluctance to go out with Ben.

I shoved the hangers back and forth, evaluating and discarding the same pieces of clothing one after the other. Emma would have selected the sexy, black, off-the-shoulder blouse and paired it with tight jeans. Amy, whom I had consulted, had recommended a sundress and a shawl. Sometimes, she said, the air conditioning in the Pine Cone blew too cold for her taste. Carl urged me to wear my favorite plaid shirt and khakis, a suggestion I did not take seriously. Despite my hesitance toward Ben, I wanted to look like a woman, not a lumberjack. I checked the clock. Ten minutes to seven and I couldn't decide. I slipped my only sundress, a navy-blue crinkle cotton number, off the hanger and held it up to the mirror over the dresser. The pale-cheeked Riley who used to wear it had morphed into a tanned and freckled outdoor woman. The sundress no longer looked like me. I hung it back in the closet and sorted through the remaining pieces. Slacks and a pullover? Too teacherish. Denim skirt and tee? I resembled a teenager. I finally selected a pair of tan-colored pants that hugged my rear, a brown camisole just low enough to show a teensy bit of cleavage, and a green cardigan that brought out the hazel in my brown eyes. I could roll the sleeves up if I got too warm, turn them down if I got cold. I had just finished applying a few strokes of blush when the screen door banged. Ron and Josh had repaired it while I was at work yesterday, and the new hinges squeaked. I hurried to close the bedroom door before Ben saw the mess I'd made. When he stepped into the kitchen, I had to cough to keep my heart from jumping.

Ben Torvald had shaved off his beard, too. His chin bore the same cleft as Gavin's and when he smiled, revealing his straight, white teeth, I recalled a line from Little Red Riding Hood. Why, Grandma, what big teeth you have! I pushed away the wolf's response. My date wasn't a creature from a fairy tale, although his size conjured up the fleeting shadow of the night prowler. I shoved that thought down as well and ignored Carl's advice that I compare all my dates to the blue-eyed ranger. Josh Waylon, I determined, was not going to be a spectator, real or imagined, on my first date in Wanakena.

"For you, Miss Riley." Ben handed over a clutch of wildflowers, columbine and daisies, an orange tiger lily buried among them.

I blushed when he said my name. His accent turned it into an invitation, an echo of Rhett Butler priming Scarlett for a kiss. I took the bouquet and rooted under the sink for a vase. When none surfaced, I rescued an empty coffee can from the recycling bin and filled it with water. Then I offered Ben a drink. He declined. He took my hand and lifted it to his lips, smirking when I tugged it free.

"Nervous, Miss Riley? I assure you, darlin', I do not bite." His declaration made me shiver. "They're holding a table for us, but I wanted to show you the school first. Shall we go?"

I recoiled when he led me to his Jeep, doorless and piled high with camping gear. Mud spattered the tires and hood, proof of last week's outdoor adventures in the forest. He spread a towel over the passenger seat, fastened my seat belt, and climbed in. The car rattled down the road, headed toward the Pine Cone. I searched for topics of conversation, ended up sharing local gossip and store trivia. Running out of root beer when suddenly, everyone wanted one. One of Gavin's friends shoplifting a box of snack crackers, which slid out from beneath his tee as he passed the register. Busted! Ben laughed, then listened intently as I chattered on about my fishing and paddling lessons. I skipped the part about me dumping the kayak, gushing instead about how good an instructor Gavin was. Just as I was about to ask him about his week of camping, he braked suddenly to avoid a squirrel darting in front of us, and a pair of women's panties slid out from under my seat. That ended my curiosity and strengthened the belief that Professor Torvald was indeed a player. I shoved the underwear out of sight with the heel of my sandal, remarked on the song playing on the radio, and turned up the volume, ending the conversation. We bumped across the bridge, turned right, then left, and followed Ranger School Road to the campus.

The school faced the water, its cream and green exterior lined with the windows of the classrooms and dormitories. The grounds appeared neatly manicured. A line of small white houses sprouted like mushrooms up the hill beyond the central structure. When Ben pulled in behind the main building, two boys and a girl exited and headed toward the soccer field. Each of the males carried a ball. The girl, tall, blonde, and stunning, wore cutoff jeans and a tank top that emphasized her ample chest. When she spotted the Jeep, she halted and, shading her eyes from the setting sun, glared at me. The boys waved and kept walking. The blonde jogged over, breasts swaying as she ran.

"Torvald!" She put her hands on her hips and cocked her head. The movement thrust her chest forward and bared her throat, which held several strands of beads that caught the evening light. "Come play. I promise not to beat you too badly."

"Can't, Birgit," Ben called. He shoved the keys in his pocket, swung around the Jeep and helped me out of the passenger seat. "Maybe next time."

At the back entrance, he held the door until I stepped inside. I glanced over my shoulder. Birgit had not moved. She watched until the door closed, her face carefully blank while her eyes sparked with malice.

Ben's tour lasted half an hour. I was impressed by the way his professionalism replaced the playboy persona. He showed me the maps he used, the locations of campsites, and the towers that allowed the rangers to spot forest fires. He didn't stop until my stomach growled in the middle of a minilecture on the ecology of the Oswegatchie.

"I need to feed you, don't I?" He flashed an apologetic grin and led me back to the Jeep.

South of the Ranger School, the Pine Cone Restaurant squatted on the bank of Cranberry Lake, its red-sided sprawl of cabins, attached rooms, and the restaurant itself all fronted by an outdoor picnic area and a boat dock offering rental space. We arrived just after eight. Most of the tables had been claimed by local families, many of whom I recognized from the store. A few tourists sat scattered among them. The barstools were also filled, although Ben spotted two empty ones tucked away near the wall-mounted TV and steered me toward them.

Shouts of "Torvald" greeted us. I heard Jesse Livetree call my name, as did a few others at his table. A waitress balancing a tray wished us good evening and nodded at a six-top where two customers were beginning to stand up.

"Gimme a minute, Ben, and I'll let you have that table." Without waiting for a reply, she continued on with her load of orders. While we sat at the bar amid the confusion of friendly conversation and mouth-watering aromas, Ben directed my attention to Cranberry Lake, explaining its creation in 1865 when the state authorized the building of a dam. I found the information interesting, nerd that I was, which encouraged him to continue. He placed an arm around my waist and pulled me closer, an intimacy that staked a claim I wasn't willing to acknowledge. Still, I paid attention as he spoke, filing each piece of information away for later reflection. When another instructor from the school came over to speak to Ben, my mind wandered back to the tour and the woman called Birgit. I recognized her voice from the one time I had phoned there. She had to be one of his students, a ranger-in-training, and one of the campers on the week-long outdoor trip. Did the underwear in his vehicle belong to her? If so, what was that about? Did I even want to know? Eew.

The waitress returned. She wiped down the table, set out utensils and napkins, and invited us to sit. We had just opened the menus when Jesse popped up, like a genie from a bottle, over my right shoulder, which he patted as he pulled out a chair and sat down.

"Evening, Torvald. Didn't expect to see you back here in Wanakena after last year's kerfuffle."

Ben half rose from his seat to shake Livetree's hand. "Funny how things work out, isn't it? Like they say, it was an offer too good to refuse. Nice to see you again, Mayor."

The men chatted about old acquaintances. I was determined to ignore them as I pored over the menu choices, but when the mayor mentioned Ike, I laid the menu down.

"Saw you and Waylon taking the Moore Trail last week. How's Ike doing?" Jesse cracked his knuckles and folded his hands on the table. "That dog was the pick of the litter for sure. I regret letting him get away from me."

Ben closed his menu, too, and, shrugging, steepled his fingers before speaking. "He's fine, I guess. Josh took him up to the fire camp on Grass River. Don't know when they'll be back."

"Well, that's interesting." I looked from Jesse to Ben, who had no idea I already knew the dog belonged to Josh. What bothered me most was his intention. If a man lied about such a simple thing as a dog, what else would he lie about? The image of Warren Carstairs intruded. I looked at Ben, curious to know how he'd explain the ruse. "You led me to believe Ike belonged to you."

Jesse chuckled. Ben quirked an eyebrow.

"Can't blame a man for using any means necessary to capture your attention, Riley." He reached for my hand.

"Torvald," Jesse said, "you're still up to your old tricks. Looks like they worked, too."

Heat rose up my cheeks. I pulled my hand free and turned to the mayor. "Tell me about Ike."

Livetree settled into the chair, pausing for effect as he rubbed his chin. He was enjoying Ben's discomfort. "Nothing I like better than talking dogs. My Maggie, she's the best bitch I've ever had, and I've had a lot of them. She had her last litter nine months ago."

Ben snorted as if to say, *here we go again.* Livetree cut his eyes toward me and shook his head. "After all the turmoil last year, I thought as how Josh could use a companion. I let him take his pick before I sold the others. He got the best of that deal, for sure."

"What turmoil?" I avoided looking at Ben.

Livetree hummed a little under his breath.

"I don't really know what happened. Police kept the details to themselves. But the way I heard it," Ben said, "a hiker slipped off the edge up on the trail to Cat Mountain. Her head got tangled up in vines or something. She died right there on the trail. Josh found the body."

Surprised by Ben's muddled account of the murder, I sipped from my water glass. The mayor nodded. "Strange way to die, strangled by a vine ...or something," he said. I decided to dig a little deeper.

"It wasn't just any hiker, was it?"

"No." Ben drew back, exchanged a glance with Livetree, and opened his menu. "It was Amanda Waylon, Josh's wife."

I waited for more, but the conversation died away. We sat in silence as the restaurant hummed around us. Finally, Jesse signaled for a drink refill and continued talking about Ike and the rest of the pups. When the waitress arrived to take our order, we resumed talking. Neither man returned to the subject of Amanda Waylon. Despite hints from Ben, the mayor remained at our table. He ordered a third round of drinks and shared tales of the ranger school, regaling us with interminable sagas of lost tourists. Ben grew quieter as the evening dragged on. I enjoyed the fish and chips and a piece of strawberry pie until a yawn sneaked past my defenses.

"I'm sorry, Miss Finn." Standing to stretch, Jesse leaned across the table to pat my arm. "Didn't mean to spend your evening talking about myself."

Ben glared at the mayor, but he didn't say a word. Just shook hands and wished Jesse a good evening. A second yawn escaped as Ben turned back to me.

"Sorry," I said, "I've got an early day tomorrow." Carl had agreed to stay at the Lodge with Amy while I worked at the store. I would be up earlier than usual to get her settled there.

We said little on the drive back to town. The night sky glowed with stars. The panties had slipped into view again, a reminder that whatever else Ben Torvald was, he wasn't a one-woman man. I shoved them back under the seat. When we arrived at Carl's, he held my hand all the way to the door. Before I could step inside, he leaned down to kiss me, his lips soft as they settled on mine.

"I had a nice time tonight, Miss Riley," he said, "despite Mr. Livetree's monopoly of the conversation. Next time I'll take you someplace farther away from Wanakena and its denizens, someplace where we can get to know each other better."

I pulled away and backed onto the porch. "Thank you, Ben, for an interesting evening." As the screen door banged, I flicked the lock into place and moved farther inside. I leaned against the wall, listening for the scrape of his footsteps down the path, the distant crunch of the tires over the gravel road. Jesse's intrusion seemed more calculated than random. What revelations, I wondered, was the old man trying to incite? Or prevent? When I was certain Ben had gone, I stepped back outside and faced the river, pondering the actions of the woman named Birgit, a man who preferred conquest over commitment, and a dog who belonged to a sad and bitter ranger. My blue-eyed ranger, I almost whispered, but he wasn't mine and never would be.

An owl swooped low and whooshed around the corner of the cabin, reminding me that predators prefer the night. I shivered, haunted by the tales of a woman who had died in the forest a year ago and of another woman killed the night I arrived, one who might have been me. I pondered the coincidence of amber beads and necklaces used to choke and kill. Before I went in, my thoughts turned once more to Josh Waylon, alone and lonely, watching for forest fires in the deep Adirondack woods.

Chapter 25

...treading water and hoping for the best...

The calendar above the ice cream freezer announced, in bold red, white, and blue, that the Fourth of July wasn't that far off. I circled the date in black marker and returned to the inventory. Carl had asked me to bring the file home tonight. She was worried about running out of supplies, especially since she and Jesse and several other locals were in charge of Wanakena's annual celebration – an all-day picnic on the green followed by a jazz concert and the obligatory fireworks out over the water. I tried to convince her to relinquish her duties to others, but she was adamant about her role as chief enforcer of tradition.

"But, Carl," I reminded her, "the doctor told you to take it easy."

"I will, Riley, I will. It's just that everybody," she had insisted as I deposited her in Amy's sitting room that morning, "will be there. I have to make sure they have a good time."

With a sigh, I left for the store, reminding myself to speak to Jesse about keeping her calm. I was sweeping out the stockroom when Gavin showed up fifteen minutes late, sporting a peach-sized bruise on his forehead. More cuts and scrapes covered his arms. He looked exhausted. He scuffed his way in, leaned against the doorjamb, and sputtered an apology.

"What," I hurried over to inspect the damage, "happened?"

He collapsed onto a packing crate and shook off my concern, his teenage desire to appear tough warring with the little boy still trapped inside.

"Gavin." I took him by the arm and led him back to the register. He winced as he eased onto the stool. "Did you get into a fight?"

He dipped his head. "I don't want to talk about it," he said.

"Sorry, kid. That excuse won't work with me." I folded my arms and tapped my foot.

He hung his head. "You have to promise," he said. "No lecture."

"Hold on." I scurried back to the ice chest and ripped open one of the smaller bags. Wrapping a handful of cubes in a towel, I returned to press the makeshift bag over his eye. He grabbed my arm and squeezed until I looked at him.

"And, Miss Finn, you have to promise," he glanced out the window, "you won't tell Uncle Ben."

"Why not? He's your guardian while you're up here, Gav. He has a right to know."

"Please, or I won't tell you." He stuck out his lower lip.

"All right," I said, certain that it wasn't. "You have my word. Now, look at me. I need to check your pupils for signs of a concussion." Before I could finish the examination, the Morganstern kids trooped in, followed by their mother. Gavin huddled on the stool for fifteen minutes until, cloth sacks bulging, they filed out again. The mother gave Gavin a quick once-over, shook her head, and murmured, "Boys."

By the time I finished recording the recent purchases, Gavin had retreated to the storage room, where I found him napping on the floor, several packages of toilet paper bunched under his head. I shook him awake and guided him out front where I could keep an eye on him.

"You have to stay awake a little longer, just in case." He nodded. I re-crossed my arms and gave him my best teacher stare. "Tell me what happened."

"We went into the woods last night."

"Who's we?"

"Perry and Cal and me. After we heard about what happened at your cabin, we thought we might find the bear or the person pretending to be a bear. It was dark. We hid behind some rocks, told ghost stories. Then we heard thrashing in the woods about twenty yards up the river from your cabin, but on the opposite bank, you know, the side where we were."

"Was that wise? Going out at night with a predator on the loose? And I'm presuming you didn't tell Ben where you were going."

Gavin shook his head. "My friends, they got scared. And—"

"And?" I shook his arm. He refused to look at me. "Gavin. Tell me what happened after that."

"I stayed up the tree."

"You were in a tree?"

"Yeah. I mean, after the noises, when my friends took off, I climbed one. I was safe."

"Gavin, bears can climb trees."

"Oh." He flushed. "I didn't think of that."

"Do you think what you heard was a bear?"

He shook his head. I waited. Fear flitted across his face.

"Don't hold back. Tell me everything."

"Well, the branch broke, and I fell. That's why my arms are all messed up. And when I tried to get up, something hit me. On the head." He repositioned the icepack over the lump on the back of his head. "I'm pretty sure I passed out. When I came to, all I could think to do was run. I'm a coward."

He teared up. I handed him a tissue. "You're not a coward, Gavin. You are young and very brave, and, yes, very foolish. What if you'd been more seriously hurt? What if you'd broken a bone?"

"There's something else."

The catch in his voice made me bite my lip and scoot closer. "What else?"

He reached into the pocket of his cargo shorts and pulled out a handful of stones. No, not stones. Beads. "When I came to, I was scrabbling around trying to stand, and I found this."

"It was on the ground?"

"Yeah, just lying in the dirt." He dropped the necklace in my palm. The strand slipped loose. I tightened my grip and examined it until I realized something. The clasp was broken, and the beads looked just like the ones in the photograph of the necklace used to strangle Amanda Waylon and probably LeeAnne McMasters. I'm sure it was my imagination, but I swear the thing shifted in my hand. I dropped it on the counter and jumped back. The screen door banged open.

"Where did you get that?" Josh Waylon loomed in the doorway, his eyes on the necklace. Darting from the counter to the door, I checked to see if anyone was coming, then flipped the OPEN sign to CLOSED and pulled down the blind. I grabbed Josh and dragged him over to Gavin.

"Tell him, Gavin." I pointed at the ranger. "Tell him what you told me. All of it."

The boy stared at his feet. "He'll tell Ben. I'll be grounded."

"No. You can trust Mr. Waylon." I didn't know if that was the truth or simply my desire to believe in someone. I looked at the ranger. He clenched his fists but kept very still. "I trust him," I repeated. "You can, too. Tell him."

Josh's eyes widened at my declaration, but he didn't say anything. Gavin stumbled through his tale one more time while I poked at the beads. The necklace really did resemble the one Officer Kellerman had shown me. Amber and silver beads strung on a leather cord. And it closely resembled the strands Birgit sported last night. Lost in possibilities, I snatched the necklace and wandered off, trying to make sense of the boy's strange story. Who was prowling the forest at night? Why would they want to hurt a teenager? I didn't hear Josh approach until he stood right behind me.

"Riley."

I looked up, unable to keep my hand from trembling as I held out the necklace. "The attacker must have lost this. Why would they hurt a boy?"

"To stop him from identifying them. To send a message."

"Well, it worked." I clutched the beads tighter. Josh wrapped my hand in both of his.

"I want you to give this to me, Riley. I don't want you to have it in your possession."

Gavin stomped over. He grabbed for the necklace, but Josh was quicker. He worked the strand free from my grasp and stowed it in his pocket.

"Why don't you want me to have it?" I didn't know what I wanted him to say, but right then I needed reassurance. Wanakena's small town charm had suddenly been tarnished by the attack on Gavin. Two women were dead. I didn't want either of us to become a third victim.

Josh cupped my cheek. I shivered at his touch. His eyes sent a message I couldn't interpret. Gavin shoved between us. "Yeah, why?"

Josh stirred like a man shouldering a heavy burden. "Because women who own one of these tend to wind up dead. I don't want that to happen to Riley. Do you?"

Gavin gaped at him. "Why didn't they kill me then?'

"I don't think that was the intent. You were simply in the wrong place at the wrong time, and they didn't want you to see who they were."

"Who do you think did this?" I rubbed my arms against the chill his words created.

"That's the real question, isn't it?"

Outside, along the ridge across the river, thunder crackled. The sky grew thick with clouds. No one said it, but we all knew. A storm was coming.

After Josh left, I helped Gavin concoct a skateboarding accident to account for his injuries. The boy was spooked enough. He didn't need to deal with more trouble from his uncle. I also gave him the following day off to help him recover from his adventure in the woods. The next morning, I dropped Carl off at the Dugas place as usual, then hurried to the store. When Jesse showed up for his pastry fix, I asked him to mind the place while I made a run into Saranac. That put me behind schedule for the day. I didn't know the roads or the local police well enough to exceed the speed limit, although I did think it might be fun to drive a sports car around some of the curves.

By the time I arrived at the Star Lake town hall that afternoon, all the children were waiting inside the classroom. Their enthusiasm eased my anxiety. However, Timmy barely raised his hand to acknowledge me. My heart ached. I suspected his recent hospital stay had unsettled him. Determined to bolster his spirits, I sang "Jeremiah was a bullfrog," making up my own lyrics as I danced my way around the room. My silly antics soon had even Timmy smiling. I spent one-on-one time with each child but reserved the bulk of my attention for Josh's son. When I finally flopped down beside him, he bobbed forward and swiped at his mouth with the back of a hand.

"Thank...thank you, Miss Finn." The stuffed moose peeked out from the neck of his shirt. I rubbed my nose against the moose's and smiled at Timmy.

"Looks like you have a special friend with you today. Does Mr. Moose have a name?"

"Fi-fi-finnegan." His gaze captured mine. I leaned back on my heels.

"That's a swell name. Thank you for taking such good care of Finnegan." My voice rasped with unshed tears. What was it about these Waylons that made me so emotional? At that moment, I would have killed a bear to keep Timmy safe. So why hadn't his mother felt the same way? The boy's lips curved in a smile so genuine that my heart skipped a beat. I thumped my chest until it returned to normal rhythm, reigning in my anger at the woman who had birthed and then abandoned him. I didn't know anything about Amanda Waylon, as a woman, as a wife, as a mother. All I had to go on were rumors and gossip, mainly from Carl. My boss's account of a female who chafed at the restrictions of her life and welcomed any man into her bed had spared no details. If the stories were even half-true, I hated what she had done to Timmy and to Josh. They deserved better. Determined to do what I could to make this time with the boy count, I took a deep breath and pulled out the flashcards I had prepared. While the others watched a Disney movie, Timmy and I worked on his enunciation.

The afternoon sun hid behind a bank of clouds as we exited the building. The other children had left half an hour ago. Josh had called Ms. Haines to say he was running late. I wheeled Timmy down the ramp, scowling at the hint of rain. When I neared the bottom, I was so intent on watching the ground for rocks that I almost ran over Josh. He reached forward to grab the wheelchair, his muscled forearms drawing my eye and leading once again, despite my best intentions, to speculation about the rest of his body. Desire coiled through me. Impossible, Riley, I chastised myself. Josh hugged the boy and lifted him up.

"Riley. Can you get the chair?"

I followed them to the van. Josh handled Timmy with such gentleness. A man that good to children and dogs had to be good to women, too. I couldn't square this picture with one where he strangled two women. I folded the wheelchair in anticipation of stowing it in the back of the truck. I had lifted it when the ranger reached around and took it from me. Caught between the tailgate and his body, I flushed bright red from the contact. I swallowed hard, ducked beneath his outstretched arms, and hustled toward my car.

"Riley." He checked over his shoulder, stalked closer, lowered his voice. "My kid adores you, you know. You have to stop giving him so much attention."

"I adore him, too." I saw anger in his eyes. "I won't do anything to hurt him, Josh. I promise."

"You'll leave," he said. "You'll go away, and that will destroy him."

I wanted to tell him I wouldn't leave, that I would always be around, but I couldn't make that statement. The summer would end, and I had no idea where I'd be after that. I stood there, gazing into those come-hither eyes, when he leaned closer. I wanted him to kiss me. Instead, he lifted my chin the way he had in the store and rubbed a thumb across my lower lip. "You're already destroying me."

Before I could catch my breath, he was striding back to the truck. I watched him drive away, my heart thumping and my thoughts running wild. My thighs were wet, my breasts ached. His touch had aroused every part of me. Damn. I didn't need this wild and dangerous attraction, but I couldn't deny that it was there.

*

The following day flew by in a flurry of orders, deliveries, tourist questions, and more requests to snap photos than I ever had before. Gus and Josh stopped by in the morning. I avoided looking at the ranger until he took me aside and handed me a note from his son. I shivered when his fingertips grazed mine. He glanced at Gus over by the cooler, then brushed a knuckle down my cheek.

"You've got dirt on your face. Have you been working in the storeroom?" Unable to speak, I nodded. He tapped the note. "You better read this. My son heard me snap at you yesterday. He insisted that I apologize and thank you properly for Finnegan. I'm sorry, and thank you."

His words made my stomach clench. He and Gus strolled out, leaving me with an urgent need to use the bathroom. I scurried toward the back of the store, the wild notion of dragging the man with me floating in my head. In the cramped confines of the room, I gazed at the woman in the mirror, wondering who had replaced timid and sedate Riley with this lust-crazed female. "Settle down, Finn," I cautioned. "He's just being nice because his son likes you." But I didn't know how to turn off my feelings. When the note rustled in my pocket, I took it out.

Thank you, Miss Finn, for the baby moose. Please come visit us soon.

Each letter had been meticulously printed on the lined paper. The signature read *Timmy and Timmy's father*, under which the boy had penciled *Josh*. The invitation brought tears to my eyes. I heard the shop bell tinkle. I'd been gone too long. I hurried out, but the store was empty.

Anton Storms showed up that same afternoon, smelling of wind and fish. He related a story about one of his clients almost falling overboard before reminding me of our lunch run to Cranberry. Reluctant to curtail my Thursday lesson and distracted by the latest encounter with Josh, I begged off until the following week. Storms wasn't about to give up.

"We'll make it a late one then. How about we leave after you're finished for the morning?" His insistence wore me down. "Remind Gavin not to tire you out too much."

That puzzled me. Storms had a good-sized boat with an outboard motor. Surely, we were taking that to Cranberry and not kayaks. Or did he have some other action in mind? I shrugged off that thought. The only man insinuating himself into my dreams was the blue-eyed ranger and those fantasies kept waking me up at night.

"Steady, Riley," I mumbled. Anton gave me a quizzical smile, but he didn't comment. I stayed behind the counter, nodding at his stories and laughing at his jokes until he picked up his sack of supplies and said good-bye.

More visitors ambled in, examining the produce, loading up on beer and snacks. I shook off my man problems and concentrated on serving their needs. To my surprise, Ben dropped by toward closing. He handed me another bouquet of wildflowers and issued an invitation to picnic at the fire tower later in the week. I couldn't think fast enough to deflect him, so we ended up agreeing on a late afternoon hike up the mountain to eat dinner and watch the sun set Thursday evening. By the time I closed the store, I felt completely numb. Somehow, I had agreed to dates with Anton and Ben on the same day, when the only man I wanted to spend time with teased and intrigued me but kept his distance physically and emotionally. Maybe, as Carl suggested, I would have to make the first move. My heart did a quick two-step at the thought. I took several deep breaths and coughed until it settled back into rhythm. I reminded myself to stop in Star Lake after the children left next Tuesday and make sure my heart prescription was on file. Then I locked up and headed back to Carl's cabin. I had just passed the Lodge when my phone chimed. Emma. Guilt nagged as I answered the call.

"Hey, girlfriend," she cooed, "you ignoring me or what?"

"I'm so, so sorry, Emma. This job keeps me really busy, and my boss was in the hospital, so I had to work extra hours."

Immediately, her tone changed from accusatory to concerned. "Oh, Riley, I'm sorry. What happened?"

"Carl, Ms. Beamish, has a heart condition. She had stents put in a week ago." I took a deep breath and plunged ahead. "So, I went to visit every day after work. I'm also teaching kids on my half-day off. Oh, and, I had a date."

She cut me off with a whoop. "Okay, crazy woman, you are holding out on me. C'mon, my friend, spill. I've been stuck in the house with nothing to do except puke and sleep since school let out."

"Is everything all right with the baby?"

"Better than all right. My grandma says the sicker you are, the stronger and hairier the baby." She giggled. I laughed with her. "Now, please tell me what's going on. Did you have a good time on the date? Is he cute or sexy or both? Did you, you know, do more than kiss?"

"That, Miss Emma, is none of your business. But the answer is maybe, yes, yes, and no."

We both groaned. Then Emma switched to her serious voice. "You don't like him, do you?"

"Not like that. I—"

"You're not still pining over Carstairs, are you?"

"No." I took another cleansing breath. "Not him."

"Not him." I couldn't keep anything from Emma. We knew each other too well. And she deserved the truth, at least as much as I understood it. Still, I hesitated until she asked. "Who's the other guy, Riley?"

"Well." I didn't know if I wanted to discuss Josh with her. It felt premature to bring him up. "Someone else asked me out, too. Sort of."

"Someone else. Sort of. Whatever that means. Okay. Let's see if I have this right. You have two guys sniffing after you, and the one you want is unavailable?"

Emma exuded sympathy and understanding. What did I have to lose by telling her about Josh Waylon and Timmy? But the murders? Once I told her, she'd begin lobbying for my return to Hopewell, and that was the last thing I wanted. I had changed since I'd been in the wilderness. I actually enjoyed being a part of Wanakena's quirky collection of eccentrics and misfits and genuine human beings. And a very curious part of me, the one who read every Sherlock Holmes story I could find and devoured my mother's ancient Nancy Drew books, wanted to find out who had murdered Amanda and LeeAnne. So, I shared a little about Josh, how we met, his sad marital history, Timmy's difficulties. That fact sent Emma in a completely different direction.

"Wait, you're helping kids with disabilities? Why didn't you call me sooner?"

"I should have. But we're talking now, and I could use your help. Can you give me some tips on how to plan lessons for him and the other children?"

Emma's love of her subject area took over. She rattled off a number of ideas and activities and promised to send more in an email that very night, as long as I promised to call at least once a week. We hung up before I reached Carl's back door. I shot a wistful look at my cabin, then kicked the dust off my boots and went inside.

Later, after putting the dishes away and tucking Carl in for the night, I stretched out on the recliner and opened my notebook. I drew two circles, one with Amanda's name in the middle and one with LeeAnne's. Right now, the only connection between them was the necklace used to strangle them. There had to be something more. Carl had given me the only useful information I had about Josh's ex, and Carl herself had hired LeeAnne. What had she said about McMasters? Closing my eyes, I dredged up that initial conversation, something about LeeAnne working in Wanakena last year. The women must have had more in common, some point of overlap. Maybe they knew each other. All the townspeople would have known Amanda – Jesse Livetree, Ron, Amy, Ben, Anton, Josh. Gavin? I wasn't sure. Had the boy been here last year? After I yawned three times in succession, I decided to call it a night. I tucked my pencil in to save the page and checked all the doors and windows. Better to be locked up than violated. Or dead. On that cheery thought, I turned out the lights and settled in bed, a plan for finding out more about the dead women already forming.

Chapter 26

... dip your paddle in the water and go...

The timer on the stove buzzed at five-thirty a.m. I groaned and buried my head in the pillow to block out the rattle of baking pans. Bunking at the boss's place had some definite disadvantages. When I finally stumbled into the kitchen, Carl insisted that, with Jesse's help, she could look after the store today. Despite my protests, she refused to back down. I checked my cell for messages, sent Emma a brief thank-you text, and helped myself to oatmeal. Before I had a chance to finish my coffee, Gavin knocked on the door, fishing poles and paddles strapped to his back. I poured the coffee into a travel mug and laced up my boots. The three of us strolled into town together. I worried about Carl's stamina, but she relished being up and about. She barely broke a sweat on the walk, although she did collapse onto the stool as soon as I unlocked the door. Gavin and I discussed the plan for the morning while Carl fanned herself with one of the brochures announcing the Fourth of July Celebration in Wanakena.

Morning sun rayed through the pines, gilding the Oswegatchie River in gold. I inhaled the scent of pine as I followed Gavin down to the shore. For this lesson, we settled into a canoe and headed east toward Cranberry Lake. The wind had not yet picked up. River song greeted us, the lap of waves against the shore, the chortles as it eddied around a rock or a submerged fallen tree. Ravens croaked out the daily gossip above our heads. Gavin steered into a small cove just off the point and handed me a rod. The next two hours passed in quiet contemplation and minimal chatter as I cast my line and reeled it in. I hooked two small bass. Gav snapped a photo each time, then helped me unhook the catch and slip it back into the water. A larger smallmouth spit out the lure and got away. I didn't mind. I felt pride in my achievements and a little more confidence in my ability to adapt in this wilderness environment. My instructor gave me a thumbs up, then directed the boat toward another cove farther around the spit of land. I decided I'd had enough silence for one morning. Besides, I had a plan to implement.

"I bet you know just about everybody around here," I said over my shoulder, "don't you, Gavin?"

"I guess. I've been coming up here since I was born."

"Were you here last year?"

"Keep us steady, Miss Finn." He rested his paddle in the boat and picked up his fishing pole. "I want to test the water here."

I followed his instructions, careful not to push too hard. The canoe barely drifted in the windless morning sun. Gavin sent his line zinging over the water before he answered me. "Last year we only came up for the big holidays. My sister made the high school volleyball team, but the coach said if she missed even one practice, she'd be cut. So, I had to stay home, too."

"I didn't know you had a sister." With Gavin's permission, I stowed my paddle. My line sailed toward the shallow water.

"Yeah. Kirsty. She hates it here, said it's too backwoods for her."

"Well, some people might think that, but I kind of like it. By the way, Carl told me that LeeAnne McMasters worked here for a while last year."

"Really?"

He reeled in and cast again. When he didn't say anything, I tried another approach. "Wouldn't that be strange, though, that you might have seen her?"

"I don't think so. I mean, I don't think she was here when we visited, but maybe. I didn't spend as much time in town as I am this summer." He blushed when he cut his eyes at me. "You should ask Uncle Ben. He always knows all the women. No offense."

"None taken. I know exactly who your uncle is."

"Don't get me wrong, Miss Finn, Uncle Ben's okay. For me, anyway. But he hits on all the good-looking women no matter where he is. He never dates anyone for long. I don't think he'll ever get married."

"Good to know."

"I mean," he set down his rod, picked up his paddle, and steered us away from the shore, "you just seem like a lady who wants to, you know, get married and have a family."

"Is that what you think?" I smiled to soften the hint of nasty in my words. If even a teenage boy could discern that, I must give off some kind of desperate vibe. To certain perceptive men. Was that why Josh wasn't interested? I wasn't the summer fling he was looking for? I faced forward. "Pathetic, Riley."

"Did you say something?"

"Just talking to the fish." I stared at my line. "Isn't it about time for my paddling lesson?"

"Yeah. Let's go back and get the kayaks. You need to practice on your own."

We headed toward the beach. As my thoughts snagged on the desire to find someone to share my life with, movement on the hillside caught my attention. I shaded my eyes against a flash of red among the trees. A figure appeared, then disappeared too quickly for me to discern if it was a man or a woman. Or a bear. When I stopped paddling, Gavin noted the tension in my shoulders.

"What's wrong?"

I pointed at the disturbance in the forest.

"Probably a day hiker," he said.

"Is there a trail up there?" I concentrated on the spot where I last saw movement.

"Yeah."

I turned at the slight tremor in his words. "What's wrong?"

Gavin sighed. "That's the trail where Mrs. Waylon died."

Chapter 27

...a lot of digging for a little bit of truth...

I spent the next hour paddling back and forth in front of the hamlet. I should have felt silly, especially when Carl and Jesse and a handful of shoppers came out to observe my progress. The account of my first clumsy attempt had circulated fast as a raven's caw. I'd endured several days-worth of jokes at my expense, so I should have been embarrassed to keep demonstrating my inexperience. Instead, I decided to finish what I started, to prove to everyone, especially myself, that I could do this. A warm glow settled in as I executed each of Gavin's instructions without incident. When he noticed my arms quivering, he waved me in. After I pulled the kayak onto shore, he clapped me on the back. This time, the onlookers cheered. I exaggerated a bow and skipped toward the store, unable to stop smiling. Perhaps I could master this outdoor-woman thing by summer's end.

Carl was waiting on the porch. She handed over a bottle of water and motioned me into the store. The mayor clomped in after us, his cane thumping on the floor. He limped toward a second stool someone had pulled out of the storeroom and helped himself to the last muffin in the basket. I wanted to ask about his leg when I recalled the night he joined Ben and me at the Pine Cone. He hadn't carried the cane then, and his stride was as strong and true as mine.

"You going home for lunch, Riley?" Carl settled herself behind the counter, wincing as she sat. Guilt replaced suspicion.

"Maybe you should let Jesse take you home, Carl. You can rest this afternoon. I'll stay here and take care of customers."

She frowned. "Don't think I don't see what you're trying to do. You promised no cododdling."

I opened my mouth to argue when the mayor spoke up. "Our Ms. Beamish is not the type to be fussed over, Riley. Best you go on enjoying your day off and let her learn the hard way."

A curious look passed between them. I opened my mouth to ask what they were planning when Gavin tapped my shoulder.

"Thanks for a great morning, Miss Finn." He peeked out the window at the gazebo and the teens gathered there. In addition to the three boys with him from the other day, two girls had joined the group. One, a freckle-faced redhead, stared back, hands on her hips and a saucy pout on her pretty face. When he hesitated, I gave him a shove. "Go. Be a teenager. Have fun."

"But," the boy turned beet red, "I'm supposed to go to Cranberry with you and Mr. Storms."

"I'm old enough to handle things, Gavin. Now, go." I nudged him down the steps. He had reached the middle of the street when a battered pickup with Maine license plates squealed into a parking spot, sputtered twice, and died. Anton Storms climbed out, his red vest and waders evidence of a morning spent cleaning fish after squiring tourists to hidden coves around the lake. He peeled off the waders, revealing jeans and a long-sleeved tee emblazoned with the words *Gateway to the Wilderness* above a sketch of the forest. Around his neck he wore a leather strand with a single amber bead that nested in the hollow of his throat. When he caught me staring, he sketched a bow and grinned.

"Your chariot awaits, Miss Finn."

His actions were so at odds with the Anton of the past few weeks, I wondered if he'd been drinking. But when he approached, I didn't smell alcohol or marijuana. Instead, I inhaled the scent of eau de lake masked by the fragrance of Tom Ford Noir.

"We're going to Cranberry in the truck?"

"No, ma'am." He pointed toward the dock and an antique woodcraft moored there, the name *Mystère* painted on the bow.

"That's yours? I thought you owned a fishing boat."

He took my elbow and steered me across the street. Gavin and his friends had moved on, their skateboards rattling over the uneven pavement. "A man can have more than one boat, Riley. As it happens, I inherited this one from my grandfather. He used to ferry people around this particular lake before he and my grandmother moved to Maine."

I stuttered through an apology, totally beguiled by this version of the enigmatic fisherman. "I thought you weren't from around here."

"Been checking me out, Miss Finn?" He handed me into the boat.

"No, but the people in Wanakena have a habit of sharing gossip whenever they come shopping."

He climbed in after me. "I don't doubt it. Bunch of busybodies, if you ask me. In fact, I'll bet Ms. Beamish has shared all kinds of stories with you."

"Nothing bad," I hurried to clarify. "She just said you moved here from the east coast."

"I did. Last year. I wanted to see where my mother's family came from." He handed me a lifejacket and waited until I fastened it. "I liked the scenery and the people, decided to stay awhile."

191

He started the engine, eased away from the dock, and headed out into the lake. The sky, the cerulean blue of a Renaissance painting, promised a perfect summer day. I didn't mind the breeze ruffling my hair or the sheen of sweat along my arms. Gliding across the water, awash in sunshine, I felt free, and daring. If Anton was around last summer, perhaps he could tell me more about Amanda and LeeAnne. The boat sped on. It wasn't long before I spotted the clutch of buildings that made up the town of Cranberry on the lake of the same name. Over the noise from the engine, Anton chatted about his clients, pointed out landmarks, and explained how the wind in this part of the Adirondacks could be a fickle beast.

"Best to always be prepared when you venture onto the water."

"Gavin told me the same thing."

He angled the boat toward the shoreline and slowed. "In the woods, too. Don't go walking alone, Riley, and don't go without a weapon."

I shivered. His words sounded half warning and half threat. He must have sensed my unease. Reaching over, he tugged me closer to his side. He placed one of my hands on the wheel and the other on the throttle. His arms encircled me, his mouth resting next to my ear. He pointed out the location of a swimming beach as we cruised to the dock-restaurant that leaned out over the lake. Although our bodies didn't touch, I sensed the tension in his arms where they rested next to mine. He seemed keyed up, eager to make a good impression. I dismissed the thought that it might have been him I saw on the hillside trail. A man couldn't be in two places at once, and he had been with clients all morning. When we neared shore, he nudged me aside and steered us in.

The burgers were juicy and hot, the fries crisp. I ate like a starving cat. Our conversation centered on my fishing and paddling adventures to date. He teased about my dumping the kayak. I insisted I was training in the event of a real accident. Once or twice, I brought up the mysterious deaths, but Anton evaded my overtures. Finally, hunger satisfied and curiosity at full tilt, I simply asked him straight out.

"Anton, will you tell me something if I ask?"

He eyed me over the top of his soda, his dark eyes unreadable. "If I can."

He was setting parameters, although I didn't know why nor where they lay. I decided to be more direct. "Before, in the boat, were you warning me specifically about going out on the water or into the woods?"

He wiped his mouth. "You're not from here, Finn. You don't know how quick weather conditions can change. The Oswegatchie twists and turns for a long way. You get lost up there, you might die before anyone found you. As for the woods, there are animals."

In his pause, I heard echoes of Josh. "I know about bears, Anton."

He gazed at me. "Human animals, Riley."

I saw an opening and plunged in. "You mean like the wilderness strangler who killed Amanda Waylon and LeeAnne McMasters?"

He focused his gaze on a photo of fishermen on the wall above the booth. "Maybe."

"Did you know those women? Amanda and LeeAnne?"

He turned back to me, his expression suspicious. "Why is that important to you?"

"Because half the town still suspects I had something to do with LeeAnne's death. The other half believes I might be the next victim. I'm tired of not knowing what I'm up against."

He cracked his knuckles. "For such a tiny thing, you sure do get worked up."

"Stop calling me tiny. It's not all about size, you know."

"So they say."

I ducked my head at the smirk on his face. He rapped the table, then crossed his arms and sighed. "Does anybody ever deny you anything, Miss Finn?"

"All the time, Mr. Storms." I sipped the rest of my soda until the straw made that bubbly sucking sound.

"I don't believe you." He lowered his voice and leaned toward me. "Most everyone within a hundred miles of Wanakena knew Amanda. That other girl, LeeAnne, she showed up in early July, looking for work and thrills. She waitressed at the Pine Cone on the weekends. The rest of the time she clerked in a souvenir shop here in Cranberry. Anyone who spent time in those two places was probably acquainted with her."

"Gavin says he didn't know her."

Anton tossed his napkin on the table and reached for my hand. "Gavin is a hormonal teenager who barely remembers what he ate for breakfast. For the record, I don't think he was here much last summer. Now, Amanda and LeeAnne, they weren't teenagers. They were women on the hunt for men. Is that what you are?"

"What I am?" Flustered, I tugged free of his grip and hurried for the door. He pulled me up short to face him.

"Are you a tease, one like those two bitches, only interested in toying with guys? Because if you are, you'll invite danger just like they did."

"Are you saying they deserved what happened to them?"

He touched the bead at his neck, twisted it until the cord pulled tight. "I'm saying they were looking for fire, and they got burned."

The venom in his statement startled me. Was he angry at my questions or at the women who, as he seemed to suggest, invited their own destruction? I wasn't certain I should ride back with him, but I had no other way to get home. Home. I stumbled over the thought of Wanakena as home. Anton didn't seem to notice or care what I was feeling. Back on the dock, I buckled on my personal flotation device and huddled against the seatback as Anton undid the mooring ropes and backed away from the shore. The lake had developed an afternoon chop. We were in for a bumpy ride. The bead around his neck caught the sunlight and flashed, reminding me of other questions I had forgotten to ask. In an effort to re-establish the pleasant mood, I rose to stand by him.

"I really like your…" I fingered my neck as I searched for the right word to describe what he was wearing. Necklace seemed too girly, but it wasn't a chain. He lifted it, then allowed the bead to settle back against his skin.

"It was a gift, one that serves as a reminder that life is fragile and time only a construct designed to fool us into thinking we have more of it than we do."

I lowered my gaze. I hadn't expected the fisherman from Maine to turn philosopher on the water. "I'm sorry. I didn't mean to pry."

He flung an arm around me. "I'm sorry, too, for my outburst back there. For what it's worth, I don't think you're at all like Amanda or LeeAnne, or I wouldn't have asked you to come with me."

The sadness in his eyes surprised me. There was more to his story, details he hadn't shared. One thing he had revealed, however, was that, like Ben and Josh and most of the men in the area, he had been acquainted with the dead women. The last of my questions, unasked and gut-wrenching, remained. Which of Wanakena's inhabitants hated Amanda and LeeAnne enough to kill them?

Chapter 28

...when it rains cats and dogs, you can expect to get bit by one of them...

As the summer crept closer to the Fourth of July, Carl and I established a routine that suited us. She continued the morning baking and took over in the store on Thursdays. Tuesdays, she and Jesse shared the afternoon shift, with Gavin filling in any time Carl "felt tuckered." With fewer than ten days until the Independence Day celebration, frenzy gripped the hamlet. Locals gathered in groups of two or three throughout the day to discuss everything from who was bringing folding chairs to who was in charge of the barges for the fireworks display. Ben phoned again. I was too tired to do more than acknowledge the stream of consciousness he employed to bring me up to date on the affairs of the ranger school. He didn't mention the picnic date and I didn't bring it up, but he did say something about stopping by Sunday. I pleaded a customer and hung up just as Josh strolled in with Ike to tell me about the fire watch being set, his gaze as intense as ever. I asked about Timmy and he handed over another note.

When are you coming to dinner?

The boy was determined to bring us together no matter how much his father disapproved. I caught Josh staring at me when he thought I wasn't looking. His eyes conveyed a message I couldn't decipher. I toyed with the idea of making that first bold move. Only the ghost of Warren Carstairs held me back. I wouldn't survive another rejection. But at night, in my fantasies, Ranger Josh did a whole lot more than stare. I chided myself for my stupid daydreams, but I didn't abandon them.

The twenty-ninth of June a hailstorm launched itself over the lake, drumming furiously against the bandstand and the store roof. The resulting drop in temperature ushered in a steady drizzle that kept most patrons away. Those who did venture out didn't linger, filling their cloth sacks with staples and scurrying back home. Eager to fill the time, I finished restocking the beer cooler when the bell above the door announced the arrival of a hardier soul. When I looked up, the woman named Birgit confronted me, lips pursed, eyes narrowed.

"May I help you?" I took a cautious step backward, mindful of her reach. As attractive as she was, she had muscles that spoke of time spent in the gym. If she wanted to hurt me, I'd be powerless to stop her.

"I just don't see it." Scorn laced her words. She crossed her arms and looked down at me. I moved behind the counter.

"Maybe if you tell me what you need, I can get it for you."

"Oh, I don't need anything. I decided to come by and judge for myself why Ben is interested in you." She looked me over and smirked. "Nice hair, but no real tits to speak of. You're built like a girl, well, except you're short. Really short."

Stung by her assessment, I rose to the bait. "For a young woman attending training school, Birgit, your name is Birgit, isn't it? You're already overblown. Your looks will be gone by thirty, and your body will turn to fat after one child. Instead of harassing me, I suggest you spend your time and energy studying for your career. You're going to need it. And, you really should leave Professor Torvald alone. After all, there are rules against teachers fraternizing with students."

Her face mottled a deep red. She placed her hands on the counter and loomed over me. "Listen, you twit. Ben

Torvald belongs to me. I beat out that girl last summer and I'll win this time, too. No one understands him better or knows how to please him more."

She ran her tongue over her bottom lip to suggest how much she had done to please him. Nausea filled me. Whether Ben felt the same or whether he was just playing games, her unspoken threat cooled any interest I had in Benson Torvald. However, it did make me curious.

"Who did you bully last year, Birgit?"

She paused, thinking I was jealous, to savor the moment. I held her eyes as she backed away. She swung the heavy braid of hair off her shoulder. "Oh, there were many women who wanted him. A former student who followed him here. That stupid waitress at the Pine Cone. The woman who offered herself to any guy wearing pants, except the man she had. But, in the end, Ben chose me, and that's the way it's going to stay."

A car pulled into the lot, lights spearing through the drizzle. Birgit launched herself toward the door. "Stick to teenagers, Finn, and leave the real men alone."

She rushed out, brushing shoulders with Gus Jornigen as they passed on the porch. Gus removed his hat and pounded it against his thigh. Water dripped onto the floor.

"What was that bitch doing here?" he groused.

"Warning me to stay away from Ben Torvald."

"She's one to talk." Surprised at his tone, I busied myself with counting the meager receipts of the day while the rush of anger cooled. Gus scowled. "Ben's always stirring up the ladies. Does he have you in his sights?"

When I glanced up, the grizzled ranger had clenched his fists. I hurried to reassure him. "No one has me in their sights, Gus, I promise. One Sunday night was my first and last date with that man. Still, I wonder about her and the women who died."

Gus shuffled closer. He slapped his hat on the counter and pointed at my nose. "Don't you be thinking about turning sleuth, Riley Finn. Whoever killed those women is a force to be reckoned with."

"By force, you mean man."

"Ayuh," he mumbled.

"What if a woman did it? Killed them, I mean."

He turned to watch Birgit head up the road toward the Ranger School. I watched with him as she unrolled a yellow slicker, shrugged it on, and slogged through the puddles pooling along the berm. For as long as we watched, she never once looked back.

Chapter 29

...and then the sun comes out...

I couldn't wait to see Timmy the following Tuesday. Emma's teaching suggestions had added substance to our weekly sessions. Even in the short time I'd been working with the children, each one had improved. Timmy had made the most strides. Although he still worked hard to pronounce some words, the consonant sounds came out clearer. But it wasn't his speech that won my heart. It was the boy himself, who seemed happier and more confident. His whole demeanor brightened when he saw me. I found it impossible not to care about this child whose mother had left him and then been so cruelly murdered and whose father was so obviously in pain. I also realized that as much as I looked forward to seeing the child, I anticipated seeing his father even more.

The afternoon passed more quickly than I expected. Before I knew it, Ms. Haines came in to announce the bus had arrived. Timmy and I hung back until the corridor cleared. I said good-bye to the staff and wheeled him down the ramp and across the gravel drive. And there he was, Josh Waylon, leaning up against the truck. His arms were crossed over a white tee that displayed his muscular chest. I enjoyed a moment of unabashed lusting from behind my sunglasses as I pushed the wheelchair toward him. Josh's own aviator glasses didn't reveal what he was thinking. Birgit's words echoed in my mind. *I just don't see it.* I bit my lip. Early on, based on my stature, Josh had dismissed me as a serious candidate for the murder of LeeAnne. Did he also judge me too insignificant to qualify as a romantic partner? I had almost reached him when he smiled, slow and careful, like I was a wild bird he had flushed up from the brush.

"Mr. Waylon."

"Miss Finn." Seconds ticked by. I held my breath. Squatting, he gathered his son in his arms and kissed him. "How'd it go today, buddy?"

Timmy squirmed in the embrace and whispered something in his father's ear. Josh nodded. The boy glanced at me and proceeded to explain what he'd learned about frogs today, how he got to pet the one I'd rescued from the shower in my cabin. When he imitated a bullfrog croak, neither of us could keep from laughing. While Josh settled the boy in the cab and loaded the chair into the truck bed, I checked Timmy's backpack When Josh turned to me, I held it out.

"Be careful." I giggled. "There's a frog inside."

"Why," Josh said, "am I not surprised?" He lifted out the glass jar holding the frog and stowed it on Timmy's lap before rolling down the window so his son could feel the breeze. Then he approached me.

"I was wondering." He shoved his hands in his pockets. I glanced over his body, blinked, and looked away. "Timmy's grandparents are coming to stay for the Fourth of July picnic and fireworks. They'd like to meet you."

I fisted a hand to my heart, begging it not to act up. "I have to work."

One corner of his mouth twitched. I wanted to press my lips there to see what he would do. At that thought, my heart did flip a little. "Not all night." He stepped closer. "You have to eat sometime. And, in case you forgot, my son has issued several formal invitations."

"I haven't forgotten." I pressed my hand over the pocket where I kept the messages.

Josh eased forward another step. I lifted my gaze to meet his. "Have dinner with us," he said.

"Yes! Yes!" Timmy pumped his fist out the window. The frog croaked.

Before I could reply, Josh leaned down. His breath stirred the hair on my neck. I shivered. "Don't overthink this, Miss Finn. Say yes. My mother makes the best damn fried chicken known to man."

Timmy continued to lobby out the window for my answer. Josh waited, hands tucked beneath his armpits, eyes unreadable behind the tinted lenses. These two impossible men were weaving some kind of magic that turned me into a scrum of emotions.

Timmy leaned out the window, the seatbelt strap straining. "Fireworks!"

Josh motioned for him to sit back against the seat. When he turned to me, I opened my arms, capitulating. "Of course, fireworks," I said.

"Is that a yes, Miss Finn?" He brushed a strand of hair off my cheek.

"Yes. I accept. It's easy to see I have no chance against this united front. Besides, who could resist fried chicken and fireworks?"

"Good choice, Miss Finn. I'd hate to disappoint my son."

"What about you, Mr. Waylon?" The question skittered out and floated between us. I wanted to disappear.

"What about me?"

"Would you be disappointed?" I held my breath, afraid of what he'd say next. He didn't say anything, just cupped my cheek and ran his thumb over my bottom lip. Before I could react, he crossed to the truck and started the engine. Timmy waved as they pulled away. I clasped both hands over my chest, probing the unanswered question like a sore tooth. Josh's touch ignited a yearning for more touches, for that unconditional love of fairytales and happy-everafters. When the dust of the truck's passing settled, I drove to Wanakena, the touch of Josh's thumb lingering on my mouth.

Chapter 30

...fireworks, part one...

I spent the afternoon of my next day off in the storeroom, rearranging stock and gloating over the success of the morning lessons. Gavin had let me paddle my own kayak to the selected fishing spot, where I caught and released three nice-sized bass. Afterward, we journeyed all the way to Cranberry and back. My arms were sore, but I experienced a new confidence in my ability to belong here in the wilderness. I didn't mind giving up part of my free time, so when Carl asked me to take over while she went home for a nap, I didn't protest. She left Jesse in charge of the register. I'm pretty sure he forgot I was there, which made it all the more surprising when a voice I recognized as Anton Storms rose above the hum of the coolers. The men had left the front of the store, moving closer to where I was working. I didn't intend to eavesdrop, but the anger in their voices made me curious.

"I warned you to stay away from her," Jesse said. "You'll jeopardize everything."

"You're not in charge of this operation, Livetree. I only brought you in as a favor to your old boss."

"Wanakena's my territory, son. You best be sure to remember that."

"If it all blows up in your face, pops," Anton hissed the word, "I'll be sure and pass that info along."

"Leave the girl out of it." The sound of a hand slapping against the cooler glass punctuated Jesse's command.

"She's not a girl. She's a woman, and a smart one." Anton blew out a loud breath. "She'll figure it out on her own unless we distract her."

"No." The shout echoed throughout the store. I crouched behind a stack of pallets, hoping Jesse wouldn't remember my presence. I didn't know if they were talking about me, but one thing was clear. Anton and Jesse were involved in something secretive, and they didn't want me to find out about it.

I stayed hidden, listening to the angry stomp of Anton's fishing boots recede toward the register, followed by the slower shuffle of the mayor. Funny how he only used the cane when I was around. I waited for the screen door to bang before checking the clock above the rack of snack chips. How long was long enough to allay any suspicions that I had heard them? I grabbed several packages of napkins and arranged them like a pillow under my head. Then, lying down, I pretended to be napping, only I dozed off for real. I woke to Jesse shaking my shoulder and calling my name.

"Forgot you were back here, Riley. Maybe you ought to go on back to Carl's and rest in your own bed."

"Oh, wow, I guess this morning's paddle really tired me out." I gathered the gear Gavin had left with me and headed home. As soon as I reached the cabin, I checked on Carl, who was still asleep but breathing comfortably. I fed Mutzi, who whined outside the back door until I relented and let her in. Then I set the table, placed chicken breasts in a bag to marinate, and prepped green beans for dinner. After one more peek at the boss, I retreated to my room and pulled out my murder book. It had been a few days since I'd updated the pages, and I was eager to add the new information I'd acquired. Birgit Sandsdottor had risen from the periphery to occupy a more prominent place on the suspect list. She had admitted to knowing both Amanda Waylon and LeeAnne McMasters, and she despised them for their interest in Ben Torvald. All the men I knew also had reasons to dislike the two women. But would their antipathy necessarily lead to murder? The bead necklaces added another layer to the diagram. Even Gavin, hit on the head by an unknown person, ended up a part of the picture. Was his attack a warning as well, or only someone's idea of a sick joke? Josh certainly didn't think so. He didn't even want me to have one of the necklaces in my possession. In my mind, I replayed the conversation I'd overheard from the storeroom. I wrote it down almost verbatim. As I looked over the notes, I realized that everyone in Wanakena looked guilty.

I spent the hour before dinner imagining one scenario after another to explain the facts, only quitting when my head began to throb. I needed to discuss this with somebody unbiased and logical. Of course, I dialed Emma's number. The phone rang ten times while I paced the room, then sat and worried the fringe on the pillow sham. As soon as her voice mail kicked in, I left a message. Still anxious, I searched through the pockets of the clothes piled on my bed until I located Sandra Kellerman's card. The policewoman was clearly competent, committed to enforcing the law, and seemed trustworthy, although she did treat me like a suspect at times. I hemmed and hawed before punching in the number, only to have it answered by a dispatcher who explained that Officer Kellerman had been temporarily reassigned to Saranac. Would I like to speak to someone else? I declined to leave my name, hung up, and fell back on the bed, the pillow clutched to my stomach as I contemplated talking to Josh. Suspect or not, he might be the only one I could trust to listen to my theories and convince me I wasn't crazy. *But*, that nagging inner voice pinged, *what if he's the killer*? Several connections pointed that way, but in the deepest part of my heart, I refused to believe he could do something so chilling. Besides, he had invited me to meet his parents. A murderer wouldn't do that, would he? I played our conversation over and over, reliving the pleasure his invitation sent to all parts of my body.

In the kitchen, the timer buzzed. I heard Carl stirring. When I joined her, she had already set the double boiler to steam the green beans. Soon, we were enjoying a hot meal, savoring the last of the herbed scones. and reexamining the store schedule for the next three days. Gavin had agreed to work a full eight hours on the second, third, and fourth of July, which would free Carl up to work with the celebration committee.

"I saw the fireworks in the storeroom." I finished the last bite of chicken and rose to clear the table. "Is it really safe to keep them there?"

Carl drained her glass of iced tea and held it out for a refill. "What we've always done. Safest place in Wanakena, locked up tighter than a virgin's —" Her voice trailed off. "Are you worried?"

"No, I guess not. I just wondered." I shook the placemats over the sink and set them back on the table. Carl traced the moose's head as she watched me.

"Something bothering you, Finn?"

"No." I loosened my ponytail, replaced the hair tie. "Maybe. How well do you know Anton Storms?"

"You had lunch with him last Thursday, right?" I nodded, and she continued to run her hands over the table. "He's a bit of a puzzle. Keeps to himself, mostly, but he sure knows a lot about everyone. He and Jesse butt heads at times."

"I suspected that."

"Someone talking about them?"

"Not exactly. I heard them arguing in the store."

"What about?"

"That's just it." I didn't want to share my suspicions with her. "I couldn't really tell. I only heard raised voices and threats."

"Well, that's certainly peculiarous. Did Anton do anything to frighten you?"

I turned on the dishwasher and began to scour the pans. "No, but he seems sad. Disillusioned. A little angry, like most of the men in town. He wears a necklace with one bead. It looks like the ones the Waylons made"

Carl finished drying the baking pan and handed it to me to put away. "I remember now. Amanda made a big fuss about him when he first arrived. Petty way to bait your ex-husband, but by then, she was beyond caring. Played up to Anton real bold one day right in front of Josh. Thought she could make him jealous enough to want her back. Fat chance of that after she whored around with anything that wore trousers. Still, it hurt him, anyone could see that. And everyone did. Later, when she tired of Anton, she did the same thing to him. Humiliated that man in the worst way by leading him to think she was serious and then dumping him in public at the restaurant. Don't you worry none about all that old news, Riley."

I promised not to put too much stock in speculation, but I refused to ignore the facts. What happened with Amanda Waylon and probably with LeeAnne, had affected everyone in the hamlet. Now I, too, was caught in Amanda's sticky web.

The following days trickled by, slow as molasses, one drip at a time. Children straggled in for popsicles, then stampeded out again, their tanned and smiling faces a welcome break from my dark ponderings. None of the men in my life stopped by Saturday. Not even Mayor Livetree, which, of all the strange things going on in Wanakena, seemed the strangest of all. The mayor never missed a morning treat. I mentioned his absence to Carl over dinner, but, preoccupied, she did nothing more than mumble at me. I spent the evening re-reading my murder notes, searching for the thread that bound all this together. I also wondered why Emma hadn't returned my call.

The third of July turned out positively frenetic. The residents of Wanakena wandered onto the green, stood together in groups pointing and nodding their heads, then wandered off. By noon, Carl and Jesse had taken charge of decorating the bandstand. Every time I looked out the window, one or the other of them was directing someone to set up chairs or ordering someone else to take them down. By late afternoon, the noise of hammering had dissipated. Flags were installed, trash bins set out, and strands of twinkling lights hung from pole to pole. Meanwhile, out on the water, a professional crew from Saranac was attending to the fireworks display. A knot settled in my chest. Tomorrow I would meet Josh's parents.

Around four, during a momentary lull, I decided to tidy the shelves below the register when the bell above the door tinkled. I spoke without standing. Even to me, I sounded like I was buried in a well. "Good afternoon. I'll be right with you."

"I certainly hope so, darlin'" Ben Torvald peeked down from above. I crawled out from under the counter, banging my head on the top shelf. When I rose to my knees, my face was even with his crotch. I blushed. He extended a hand.

"I'd be glad to help you stand, Riley, but I think I like you better on your knees."

The blatant sexual overtone changed my embarrassment to fury. Ignoring his hand, I pulled myself up, using the stool for balance, and stepped away.

"Did you come in to buy something or just to harass me?" The words no sooner left my mouth when the door banged open again. Ike scampered in, followed by Josh.

"What's going on?" Josh was wearing his uniform, so I knew he was still on duty. Ben raised his hands and backed off.

"Just having a little fun with our Miss Riley." Ben's drawl grew thicker. He feigned repentance. Josh looked at me. Whatever he saw made him frown.

"Why are you here, Ben?" He called Ike to his side.

"Peace, y'all," Torvald said, turning back to me. "I just came by to invite you to watch the fireworks tomorrow. Assuming you're free, that is."

I glanced at Josh. My cheeks heated again, but the reason was completely different. "I thought you got the message earlier. I won't be going out with you again, Ben."

That rocked him. He placed his hands on the counter and shook his head. "You can't mean that, Riley. I'm sorry I forgot about the picnic, but we had such a good time that night at the Pine Cone."

From the corner of my eye, I watched Josh frown and tap his leg. A nervous tic or something more? "This has nothing to do with the picnic invitation. Your girlfriend paid me a visit."

"My girlfriend?" Ben scratched his forehead. Then his eyes went dark. "Birgit. She's not my girlfriend. She's my student."

"Apparently, she thinks differently. She warned me to stay away from you."

Josh pushed past Ben to stand beside me. "Did she threaten you?"

I looked up, captivated once again by those blue eyes. "Not exactly. She did make it clear that she has first claim on Ben."

Torvald cursed too quietly for me to hear, then swept his gaze between Josh and me. "I'll clear things up with her, darlin'. Then I'll come back to talk with you. If you'll give me a second chance."

I bit my lip. I did not want another date with him. I especially didn't want to give Josh the impression that I was interested in the man. So, I said the first stupid, silly thing that came to mind.

"I've already filled out my dance card, Mr. Torvald. Your name's not on it." I stood as tall as I could. Josh moved close enough that I could feel his leg pressing against mine. Neither of us moved until Ben Torvald stomped down the steps. I held my breath when Josh bent down and whispered in my ear. "I hope you put my name on that card, Miss Finn."

He and Ike moved then, strolling down the aisle toward the mooshiepies. My whole body was humming a song I'd never heard before. Beneath the drumbeat of my wayward heart, I detected a strong chord of desire. When they reached the dog's favorite snack, Josh offered one, ruffling Ike's fur with his long, strong fingers. I imagined those hands stroking my body. When he stood to look back, he must have seen the arousal in my eyes. I turned away, busying myself with rearranging cigarette packs. Back at the register, Josh laid a dollar on the counter, unwrapped the mooshiepie, and fed it to Ike.

"Tomorrow." He tipped his hat. After he left, I ran to the bathroom to wipe the drool off my chin. There was nothing I could do about the wetness between my legs.

Chapter 31

...fireworks, part two...

Independence Day ticked every box on the perfect summer day chart. The air sizzled as the temperature rose. A light breeze ruffled the waters of the river out into the lake. A giddy sense of celebration suffused Wanakena. Amy raced into the store three times that morning to purchase a missing but necessary ingredient and to chat with me about the evening's plans. The last time she appeared, right before noon, I mustered the courage to ask about Josh's parents. She simply patted my arm and said, "No worries, Riley. They're going to love you." I didn't say it was Josh I was hoping would express those sentiments, but before I could coax more details out of her, she scooted out the door. Then Anton strolled in. He was wearing jeans and a shirt that highlighted his significant abs and shoulders. Twin tattoos of anchors decorated his forearms. He handed over a bouquet of tiger lilies.

"Got a vase?" He propped an elbow on the counter and waited for my reply. I had nothing to say. Not only had we parted on strained terms, but the conversation I overheard between him and Jesse made me wary. I shifted from foot to foot.

"It's all right," he said, misinterpreting my hesitation. "We can just use a can."

He handed over the flowers and ambled toward the coffee stand, where he searched among the jumble of containers. When he found one that was mostly empty, he poured the remaining grounds into a cup and returned to the counter. The scent of lilies reminded me of florist shops and funeral homes. When I poked one of the blooms, pollen dusted the counter.

"They are beautiful," I said. He opened a bottle of water and emptied it into the can. Reclaiming the flowers, he took out a knife, and with precision, snipped the stems until they fit into the container.

"I apologize for my behavior on the trip back from Cranberry." He waited for me to make eye contact. "Wanakena has a lot of secrets, Riley. Maybe it's best you don't peek too far beneath the surface."

Leave the girl out of it, Jesse had demanded. Was this Anton's way of doing just that? I rotated the flowers, looking for the prettiest side to present to customers as I wondered what to say next.

"The question is," Anton touched my arm, "will you forgive me?"

"Of course. I didn't mean to upset you, so maybe it's partly my fault." I waited to see if he would ask, as Ben did, for another date. He didn't.

"So, see you at the lawn party?" He had already moved away. A muscle in his cheek ticked when he looked at me.

"I'll be there."

"That's good, that you'll be there. I have a late charter, but I should make it back for the fireworks." He turned and crashed into Gavin hurrying back from his lunch break. The two did that stutter dance, both moving the same way twice until one gave up. Anton left. Gavin stared after him.

"What did he want?"

"Brought me flowers. Did you have a good lunch?" His mussed hair and a trace of lipstick on one cheek gave me a pretty good idea of what he and the redheaded girl had been doing. I feigned thirst and picked up my water bottle. He blushed beneath his fringe of hair, stacked his skateboard behind the door, and scurried toward the fishing section, mumbling about straightening the lures. I settled on the stool and thought about the coincidence of Ben, Josh, and

Anton all stopping by within a half-hour of each other. It almost felt like they were checking up on me. Had my not-so-subtle inquiries worried them? And what did Birgit have to do with the murders? I shuddered, recalling her clenched fists and the way she towered over me. The woman raised all my hackles. She could simply be a bully and a jealous girlfriend, but my gut wanted to transform her into something more ominous. Was that assessment fair? I busied myself tidying up, trying to reset my overactive imagination to summer idle.

By five o'clock, people had already gathered on the lawn. Each family staked off their territory with caution tape, erected tents to keep the sun off, and set up tables for food. Carl came for me at six.

"Go on home, Riley, and freshen up if you want. I understand you're dining with the Waylons tonight."

"Amy told you." I tried to act angry, but nerves took over. Carl wrapped an arm around my shoulder and squeezed until I wriggled free.

"They're gonna love you, Miss Finn." She glanced at the counter. "Who brought the flowers?"

"Amy told you to say that." I finished tallying the receipts and handed her the notebook. "The lilies are from Anton. To apologize, he said, for his bad temper. I think it's a form of a dear John letter."

Carl threw back her head and howled. "Not likely. Nothing scares that man off once he's made up his mind. Just remember what I told you. Josh Waylon's the better choice."

"Oh, I know that now, ma'am. I think my body does, too. But I'm pretty sure he's not as interested as I am."

Carl peered at my frowning face. "Lah-de-da, Missy. After tonight, you'll see. Fireworks, you know."

Chapter 32

...fireworks, part three...

The pink tank top I'd ordered online showed off my newly acquired tan, and the knee-length jeans were modest enough not to offend parental sensibilities. I stood on the edge of the lawn, shading my eyes as I searched for the Waylon gang. I spotted Amy first, standing next to a tall woman with hair the same color as Josh's. I threaded my way through the crowd, acknowledging the greetings of Wanakena's inhabitants as I passed. Most of those who had their suspicions about me appeared to have relented. I only caught a few dubious stares. A number of tourists did one-eighties to look my way. Several, recognizing me from the store, waved. I had almost reached the two women when Timmy squealed my name. Before I could brace myself, two small hands gripped my shoulders as he launched himself from Josh's arms onto my back. I reached behind to keep from falling, lifted him higher, and planted my feet. Josh held on to his son's frail form, the three of us smooshed together. Josh's hands settled at my waist.

"I. Am. A sandwich," Timmy crowed.

"We're all a sandwich," I said. Josh released me and waved his parents over. His mother didn't wait for a formal introduction.

"Riley." She leaned in to give me a hug, then kissed Timmy's cheek. "I'm so very glad you're joining us this evening. I don't think my grandson would be too happy if you didn't. Neither would we. Come over and sit."

Josh extricated Timmy from the stranglehold he had on my neck. His father stepped into view. Extending a hand, Mr. Waylon gripped mine between both of his and repeated his wife's greeting. In their faces, I saw the traits that had

217

blended to create their son. A handsome family, the Waylons, with a touch of grief in their eyes.

Music filled the air as the quartet on the bandstand began to play. We crowded around the table Mrs. Waylon and Amy had set and shared the food. Timmy insisted on sitting next to me, which meant Josh installed himself on the other side of the boy. His parents and Ron and Amy sat opposite us. The Dugas boys demanded to sit next to Uncle Josh, and so we ate, joined together by a love for good food and the children who chattered among us. I envied them their easy laughter. Try as I might, I couldn't see my parents welcoming a stranger with such ease and affection.

After dinner, Josh's mom and I packed the leftovers into coolers and carried everything to their car. Ron and Josh set up a game of corn hole. Timmy, riding Josh's back, wrapped his arms around his father's. Together they tossed the bean bags toward the goal. Amy and Ron's two boys were more interested in scoring than tossing. They inched closer and closer to the plywood gameboards, dropped the bags in, and ran, giggling, to hide behind Ron while Amy fed and diapered Annie. I must have had a wistful look on my face. Amy held the baby out.

"Would you like to hold her?" Before I could respond, Josh's mother tapped my shoulder.

"Riley, let's take a walk." She took my arm and walked us over to the cable bridge. I watched the water flowing beneath our feet. She stood beside me, silent for a long while, before startling me with another hug.

"You like my son, don't you, Riley?"

"Is it that obvious?" I edged away, desperate to hide the blush in my cheeks, but she kept pace. Finally, I met her gaze, speared by the same blue eyes that her son had. I shrugged. "I didn't expect to, Mrs. Waylon."

"Please, honey, call me Julia. We never expect it, you know. Love."

"It's way to early to—" I stopped, "I mean, I can't be in love."

She shrugged. "No? Love often comes unannounced, taking root in the most unlikely soil at the most inopportune moments."

I smiled at the winsomeness in her words. "Is that how it happened for you?"

She strolled past me, almost to the far end of the bridge. When I caught up, she leaned on the railing. "I had big plans for my life. I intended to ski in the Olympics. One can't grow up in Lake Placid without imbibing some of that magic potion. I worked all through high school, saved my money, and practiced every chance I could. When I turned eighteen, I found a coach and a sponsor, and I went out on the circuit. I was doing pretty well, even got a call to try out for the national team, when I ran into this boy working at a lodge outside of Calgary. He took my breath away, literally. He was working the top of the ski lift when the braking mechanism failed. The lift was speeding toward the end pole, taking me with it. He pulled me from the seat before the thing crashed, but the bar conked me in the head. Knocked me out cold. When I came to, he was holding my hand. He hasn't let go of it since."

"Did you mind? Giving up your dream?"

"Not for a minute. We had Josh and his brother and sister, taught them all to ski. I became an instructor. Oh, I'll admit I sometimes wonder if I might have been good enough to make it to an Olympic run, but not often, and not with regret." She took my hand. "My son needs a woman who will care for him in a way his first wife never did. If you can be that woman, Riley Finn, I will cherish you forever."

Tears threatened. I blinked faster. "I'm not sure your son even likes me."

"Oh, my dear, that man is pining for you. All he needs is a little nudge." She slipped her arm into mine, and we strolled back. At the end of the bridge, Anton Storms blocked our way.

"Mrs. Waylon." His greeting seemed very formal. "Riley. Can I talk to you?"

Julia hiked one eyebrow and pursed her lips. "It'll be dark soon."

"I won't be long." I crossed my arms and waited for him to explain.

"You look really nice." His gaze swept over me. "You with the Waylons?"

I nodded and stepped off the bridge. He followed. "And Amy and Ron. I don't want to be rude, Anton, but they're expecting me to sit with them."

He grabbed my arm, glanced over his shoulder, moved closer. "Be careful tonight, Riley. What I mean is, don't go walking by yourself."

"What's that supposed to mean, Anton? Is it another threat?"

"No, not a threat. A warning." He rubbed his chin. "There's things going on. A person could end up in the wrong place at the wrong time."

"Could you be more mysterious? Just say it plain."

He brushed a lock of hair behind my ear. "Some of these tourists aren't the most upstanding citizens, Riley. I don't want you to get hurt."

I shrugged off his words, but the argument between him and Jesse nagged at me. Somehow, his advice was related to their disagreement. Plus, there was all this melodramatic reference to evil out-of-towners. I looked up to see Josh watching me as I crossed the green. The tension in him eased when I neared the group.

"Miss Finn!" Timmy squirmed in his wheelchair. "I want to sit by Miss Finn."

"Don't fuss, Timmy," Julia said. "Miss Finn will make room for you."

I sat on the blanket next to Amy and the baby. Josh carried Timmy over and settled him in front of me. When I wrapped my arms around the boy, I felt his heart beating beneath the thin cotton tee. By that time, Jesse Livetree had climbed onto the bandstand. He blew into the microphone. His muttered *testing-testing* caused a frenzy of giggles among the teenagers in the crowd. The sun had set. Long reddish-purple streaks swirled above our heads. I inhaled the odor of boy sweat and kissed the top of Timmy's head. Someone dropped to the ground behind me. Two long legs stretched out on either side of mine as Josh braced himself against my back. I stiffened, all too aware of the proximity of my behind to his formidable front.

"Thought you could use something to lean on." His whisper stirred my hair. Sandwiched between the two Waylons once again, I struggled to separate the comfort of the child from the allure of the man. What would Emma tell me to do? Relax, of course. Go with it. I caught Julia looking over. She gave a not-so-subtle thumbs up. Heat spread through me, pooling between my legs. I looked down. Timmy's head pressed against my chest, the pressure pulling the tank top lower to expose the tops of my breasts. When I turned to thank Josh, I saw that he had noticed, too. His hands rested at my waist, then slipped around to pull me closer. I relaxed against him, aware of his arousal the moment I did so.

"Look!" Timmy pointed to the sky as the mayor finished his speech, none of which I heard. Above the water, a starburst of silver filled the sky. The Dugas boys shouted. The night resounded with the excited screams of children and the oohs and aahs of adults as Wanakena's Fourth of July fireworks exploded. We shared the excitement as the twins and Timmy debated their favorites. Josh leaned around to answer his son's questions, his body enveloping mine with his familiar scent of fresh air and pine. Drawn by his presence, I snuggled closer until his grip tightened, and he pressed his mouth to my ear.

"You're driving me crazy, Riley Finn." He rested his chin on my shoulder and kissed my neck. I was glad of the darkness that enveloped us. It hid the flush spreading across my chest. The few streetlights on Hamele Street had been extinguished to enhance the viewing. I laid a hand on Josh's thigh, felt him tense. Every nerve in my body went on high alert.

His parents shifted in their chairs. Annie stirred, and Ron took her from Amy. The final cannonade of explosions shook the ground. Soon the lights strung around the lawn came back on, causing the crowd to squint and laugh and rustle as they returned to the present and headed home. Josh drew away from me. The separation jarred me back to reality. Timmy had fallen asleep, his body now heavy in my arms. Josh came around to lift him when a shout rang out.

"Bear!" A woman screamed from the far edge of the crowd. Arms above her head, she came charging toward us, panic in her voice. "There's a bear!"

Chapter 33

...stolen kisses and secret suspicions...

The rustling turned into panic. Parents rushed their children past us, heading for the beach. Josh handed Timmy to his father and pushed me toward Julia. "Go to the bridge. Amy, take the kids and go with them. Ron, come with me."

I watched Josh shift into ranger mode. All business, he yelled for Gus. Across the picnic area, his partner acknowledged the call. Ron and Josh pushed through the mob of panicked citizens. Gus caught up to them at the edge of the green. I stood on one of the camp chairs to follow their progress. Suddenly, all the lights in town flashed on, causing me to wobble. I steadied the chair and followed the rangers. At the western edge of the seating area, a dark form tore at a trash bin. The wind picked up. Paper plates and napkins scattered across the roadway. Julia tugged me down.

"Come on, Riley." She dragged me along after her and Amy. "Josh knows what to do."

Over the shrieks of the crowd, I heard his voice. "Gus!" He gestured toward the forestry truck parked in front of the store. "Bring the tranquilizer darts."

His mother continued to pull me with her. By the time we reached the bridge, others had noticed where we were going. They swerved from the roadway to run with us.

"No." I stared at the cable bridge, calculating the weight it might hold. "There are too many people. It might break."

Amy and Mrs. Waylon stopped beside me. Ahead, Mr. Waylon had reached the center of the structure. He cradled Timmy against his chest and shouted for us to keep running. Below, along the narrow strip of beach, kayaks and canoes rested, ready to be rented in the morning. I slipped down the incline and turned over the largest canoe.

"Get in. Hurry." Amy climbed aboard, Annie snuggled in the carrier against her chest. I handed the boys to her and helped Julia climb in. I ran back to the accessories locker, grabbed life jackets, and tossed them into the boat. The two smallest would fit the boys, but there was none for the baby.

"Tuck her inside yours, Amy. We don't have to go far." I strained to shove the canoe into the water, then roped it to the kayak I had chosen.

"Bears can swim, you know." Amy's words rang across the water.

"Never mind," I answered. "Paddle."

She and Julia matched my strokes, their expertise greater than mine. We floated from shore, then turned to look back at the lawn roiling with anxious patrons. More people followed us onto the water until the crafts formed a flotilla. I searched for Josh but no longer saw him.

"Riley," Julia called. "Relax. Josh knows the right thing to do."

I have no clear idea of how much time passed. Thirty minutes, maybe an hour. My arms shook from the effort to keep the boat steady in the current. The wind increased, pushing us farther from land. Amy used the rope to pull the kayak closer to their craft. We waited in silence- - even the children. When two shots rang out, followed by a shout, everyone jumped. There was a pause, then a third shot. Someone leaned on a car horn. When the cheers started, I knew we were safe. Amy and I paddled back to shore. I jumped into the water and dragged us over the sand. Then I helped the others out. Ron ran down the bank toward us. He gathered Amy and the children in his arms and hugged them before ushering his family toward home. Mr. Waylon reached us just as Josh appeared. When he tried to take Timmy, his father demurred.

"Your mom and I will take care of Timmy. You see to Riley."

"I'm all right. I just need to sit down." My legs buckled and I collapsed onto my knees. Josh removed his shirt and, crouching, helped me put it on. I buried my head in my arms and waited for the shaking to subside. When I lifted my head, Josh was looking back at me.

"Let's get you home." He helped me stand, his arm at my waist firm and supportive. We walked across the lawn, passing Gus and a group of students from the Ranger School.

"What are they doing?"

"Their job." Josh tightened his hold as we made a wide circle around the sedated bear. "They'll relocate him deeper in the forest. See the tag on his ear?"

"What if he comes back?"

"Then we'll have to put him down, for everyone's safety."

We were almost past the trainees when I spotted Ben. He held a gun, prepared to shoot again if the sedation wore off. He paused when he saw us, wiped a hand over his mouth, and turned back to the work. I had made an enemy, but I was too exhausted to care.

Cars were jockeying to leave the area as we followed the path across the steel bridge and headed down Reed Road. My strength returned, but Josh didn't let go. When we reached Carl's cabin, he helped me up the steps.

"Will you be okay?"

"For now." My voice wobbled. He cupped my cheek.

"I forgot to thank you."

"For what?"

"For a very special evening, and for saving my family." Even in the dark, I felt his eyes looking into me, aware of the attraction I felt for him. *All he needs is a nudge*, his mother had suggested. From the top step, I could almost look him in the eye. So that's what I did, snaked my arms around his waist, rested my head on his chest, thought of all that had happened this evening. I pushed aside the questions I had about the murders of Amanda and LeeAnne. Every suspicion faded away, crowded out by my growing feelings. With his arms around me, I felt protected, safe. I needed to trust someone, so I decided to trust him.

"Will you come inside?" When he hesitated, I sighed. "Please. I want to show you something."

"You sure we won't disturb Carl?"

"I'm positive. My boss sleeps hard. If we're quiet, we won't disturb her."

"All right." His hands slipped lower, cradling me against him. "But first, I want to kiss you."

He waited for my answer. I gathered my courage and touched his cheek. "I'd like that very much."

He lifted me until we faced each other, our bodies aligned in a way that shook my control. His kiss was slow and sweet and inviting. I didn't want it to end, and when it did, I wanted more, so much more. When he set me down, I took his hand and, moving quietly, led him through the rec room into the kitchen. I opened the refrigerator and took out two bottles.

"I think we deserve a beer, don't you?"

He pulled out a chair, then tugged me closer, planting a kiss on my cheek. "Woman, you just made my night."

I set the bottles down and emptied a bag of corn chips into a bowl. "Do you want a glass?"

"No." He took a long swallow, but his eyes never left mine. "What did you want to show me?"

I held up a finger. "Wait here." Tiptoeing down the hall to my bedroom, I gathered the notebook with the crime diagrams, checked my hair in the mirror, and straightened my top. Behind me, reflected in the glass, the bed waited. The thought of Josh lying there pinked my cheeks. I took a deep breath and returned to the kitchen.

"Before the fireworks, Anton stopped me."

"I saw." His eyes narrowed. "What did he want?"

"He warned me not to walk alone tonight." I held up my hand to stop him from interrupting. With the notebook clutched to my chest, I recounted the argument I overheard between Storms and Jesse Livetree. Then I spread my notes across the table. "These circles represent LeeAnne and Amanda, um, the two women victims. Where the circles overlap indicates how they are connected."

"Their murders, you mean. How their murders are connected." When I nodded, he rested a hand on my knee. "You don't have to worry, Riley, about hurting my feelings."

"Okay." I sipped my beer, debating how best to go on. "This circle lists all the suspects, everyone who knew both women and interacted with them."

Josh studied the drawing, then read down the assumptions I had made regarding each suspect. When he paused, it was impossible to ignore the shadow in his eyes. "Do you really believe I could have done this?"

I scooted my chair closer to rest my hands on his forearms and shook my head. "No, Josh, I don't believe that."

"Why not?" His need, naked and tortured, shone in his eyes. All the hurt and loneliness of the past rippled between us.

"Because you are a good man. I have seen how you treat your son. I have watched you with your parents. And with Ike. You try to hide who you are, but I see you."

The silence expanded until he lifted me onto his lap and kissed me with an intensity I'd never suspected. I surrendered, breathless and trembling, to my own need. His tongue explored mine, waking in me a carnal yearning. He whispered my name, shifted me to straddle him, buried his hands in my hair.

"They think I did this," he said.

"I know you didn't." I rested my forehead against his.

"You have no idea what that means to me." He kissed me again, leaving me stunned and aching for more. Then he settled me back in my chair. The separation felt like a blow. He cradled my face as he spoke.

"You haven't seen how they look at me. The police have questioned me more times than I can count. I almost lost my job because of it."

"I know who you really are." I covered his hands with my own. "You have to help me prove they're wrong."

"I've been trying, Riley." He looked away. I forced his gaze back to mine.

"You don't have to do this alone." The clock on the stove ticked. Outside, an owl hooted. "I have so many questions. What do you think is going on between the mayor and Anton? Was Ben involved with both women? Is it possible Birgit did this? She has a necklace like the ones they wore. So does Storms. And, there's the one Gavin found on the ground the night he was attacked in the woods. The killer probably lost it there. Is that why Anton warned me? Does he know something we don't?"

Josh picked at the beer label, then lifted the bottle to his lips. We drank in silence, thinking through the possibilities each of the scenarios presented, while our hands roamed. I couldn't get enough of touching him. When he spoke again, all the anger and despair were gone. "I don't want you poking around in this, Riley. It's dangerous. And you're—"

"I'm what? Too small to count? Don't underestimate me, Josh Waylon, and what I'll do for the people I care about."

I cursed my runaway mouth and stopped talking to prevent any more stupid revelations from spilling free. But I refused to back down. I meant what I said, even if it revealed more than I intended to. I shifted my attention back to the notes, searched for a starting point. Finally, it hit me.

"We should begin with the necklaces," I said.

Josh rested his elbows on his knees and steepled his hands. "I saved all of Amanda's inventory papers. I'll pull them out again. Kellerman confiscated the originals after they found LeeAnne's body, but I made copies of everything."

"I don't want you to reopen old wounds."

He reached for the notebook. I moved it away. He drained his beer, wiped his mouth, signaled for another. I shook my head.

"Riley."

"Josh." We stared at each other, the test of wills morphing into something more profound. He leaned forward and pressed his mouth to mine. This time his kiss was pure desire, an intrusion and an exploration that sent a message to my core. When he pulled away, I sighed.

"What was that?"

"An IOU, Miss Finn," he said. "For later, after this cloud is lifted, when I can breathe again without looking over my shoulder."

"I hope it doesn't take too long." I lifted my bottle with a shaky hand and swallowed the contents before I carried the empties to the sink. "I don't think my heart could stand that."

He followed me, placed his hands on my shoulders, then wrapped me in an embrace. "Neither could mine, Riley Finn."

"Then you have to let me help."

Releasing me, he returned to the table. He tapped the notebook before sliding it over. "Let me see what I can find out about these connections. You stay safe and keep doing your job."

"What...what's," I stuttered around the ache to have him hold me again, "my job?"

"Fighting for the people you care about. And running Carl's store. Now see me to the door and lock up."

As I led him out, I thought about my empty bed and wished he would ask to go there. But I knew he wouldn't, couldn't. Until we cleared his name, Josh Waylon would hold himself back from any commitment. He didn't kiss me again, just touched my cheek and moved off into the night, desire and suspicion trailing behind him like a cloud.

Chapter 34

...plunging into deeper water...

The next day, none of the men came by the store, not even Jesse. I caught sight of Birgit lurking on the road into town during my morning jog around Wanakena. I had missed running these past weeks and decided to rise even earlier to fit in a half hour of exercise before work, but I was careful to stay on the main roads.

The holiday had depleted much of our display stock. After my run, I used the morning to replenish the empty shelves and tidy up the souvenir bins. By noon, I was ready to leave. The stockroom, piled with boxes, had grown claustrophobic and the itch to see Josh overwhelming. Had he reconsidered last night's encounter? Had he dismissed my notebook notes as more foolish than promising? I pushed back my apprehensions and squared my shoulders, anticipating four hours free from the drama of the past few weeks. I was looking forward to working with the children at Star Lake, and I was eager to see Timmy, to hear what he thought about the picnic and the fireworks. I wouldn't mention the bear.

When I arrived at the town hall, the minibus was unloading. Only three of the students were in attendance. DeSales, the driver told me, was on vacation with his foster family. Marie had suffered an asthma attack and was recovering at home. Despite missing them, I realized their absence meant I could concentrate my efforts on Calinda, Jimmy Joe, and Timmy. Together, we played an alphabet bingo game and worked on hand-eye coordination. Afterward, I gave each child a large, easy-to-manipulate puzzle board and had them work separately while I addressed their individual speech needs. As usual, I saved

Timmy for last, knowing once I sat next to him, I wouldn't want to leave.

"Did you enjoy the picnic yesterday?" I replaced the puzzle board with the word cards and waited for his reply.

He bobbed his head, inspected the cards, and tapped the one with the word amazing.

"You have to say it for me." I tickled the back of his hand. On the first try, he managed the word without stuttering. Thrilled at his success, I shuffled the cards and thought about my next question, but before I could pose it, he tugged at my arm.

"I saw the bear, Miss Riley." His words were halting but clear. "I saw who chased it."

"I thought you were asleep, Tim." I lifted his chin. "Are you telling me you were faking?"

His sly grin made me laugh. "Why, you sneaky little guy. Why did you do that?"

He scooted forward in the chair. "My daddy likes you. I heard him tell my grandma. Do you like him?"

I was so surprised, I lurched forward, scattering several of the cards onto the floor.

"Do you?"

"Maybe." I dipped my head. "Why don't you tell me more about the bear."

"A shadow chased it."

I shuddered. "A shadow?"

Timmy nodded. "Uh-huh. With a long stick."

"Are you sure that's what you saw? A stick wouldn't be much good against a bear, honey." I tried to imagine a person beating a bear with a piece of wood. Wouldn't the bear turn on him?

"A fire stick." Timmy raised his voice, one small fist banging the tray. More word cards fluttered off the tray.

"Did you tell your father?"

He shook his head. "He was sad this morning."

"Sad? Does he seem sad a lot?"

Again, the boy nodded. "Grandma say he's lonely, Miss Riley. I am, too."

I wrapped my arms around him and rocked us both, ignoring the tray pushing against my ribs. When he calmed, I sat back and picked up the fallen cards. "I'm glad you told me, Tim. Now, your speech is getting so much better. Let's keep working."

At the end of the session, I hurried to tidy up, eager to pass along to Josh what Timmy had revealed about the bear. To be honest, I wanted to see him, to judge for myself if last night had changed him as much as it did me. I wheeled Timmy down the ramp and looked over the lot. Josh's truck was not there. I spotted Julia waving me over to a silver SUV. Disappointed but determined not to show it, I pushed the chair over and waited as Mr. Waylon loaded Timmy into the car. While he folded the chair and stowed it in the back, Julia gave me a hug.

"I know you were expecting Josh, dear. He said to tell you he's working on the IOU. Does that mean anything?"

Heat rushed through me, coloring my cheeks. "Can you give him a message back?" When she nodded, I bit my lip, thinking how best to convey the information without raising anxiety. "Tell him to ask Timmy for the story about the bear."

"The bear?" Julia frowned. "Last night's bear?"

"This is very important, Julia. Timmy saw something that might help Josh. And, thank you for coming to get your grandson. He's doing so well."

"No, dear." She patted my hand. "Thank you for bringing them both back to life. Keep up the good work."

She hurried to the passenger side and climbed in. As they pulled away, sun sparked off the mirror of a truck idling at the far end of the lot. I glanced up as it bumped over the berm, fishtailing gravel across the road. The vehicle looked familiar. It was down the road before I could be sure, but it reminded me of the one Anton Storms drove.

That night, still disappointed at not seeing Josh, I stowed the leftovers from dinner and wiped the table while Carl fell asleep in the recliner. The cabin creaked and, outside, the pines soughed every time the wind blew. Down the hall, my phone chimed. I hurried to the bedroom to pick up before it went to voice mail.

"Josh?" I held my breath.

"So, hey, girlfriend," Emma chirped, "expecting a call from a guy?"

"Emma!" I flopped on the bed and switched the phone to my left hand. "I tried calling a million times last week. Is everything all right?"

"Sorry, Ri. We've had a few things to process."

"Then I repeat my question. What's going on?"

In the background, I heard Gary yell at the dog to sit. He sounded a bit frantic. Emma blew her nose. "You remember we had that ultrasound scheduled?"

"Yes. You said you didn't want to know the sex of the baby. You wanted to be surprised."

"We were surprised, all right." I waited through a huge pause and three heavy sighs. "And before I tell you anything, you have to promise to come home at the end of the summer."

"Emma, what's going on?"

"Prepare for a shock, girlfriend." Half laughing, half crying, she stammered out the news. "We're having twins. Like, I don't know whether to be happy or terrified. Two babies, Riley. We're so excited and scared. How am I ever going to manage? How will I ever go back to teaching?" She burst into sobs. I murmured every soothing platitude I knew until she calmed down.

"Listen to me, Emma Evans. You and Gary have large, involved families and a boatload of friends. Plenty of help. And, they won't be babies forever. Don't fret, Em. You can handle this."

"Only if you're here. Please say you'll come back to Hopewell."

I sat up. The thought of leaving Wanakena made my heart skip. I pounded my chest and coughed. I considered taking an extra pill to calm the flutters that hadn't bothered me until my friend mentioned returning to Ohio.

"I don't have a job anymore, Emma. I have to support myself somehow. Besides, I don't even have a place to live. I gave up my apartment. My parents are going to live in Florida. They're probably there now."

"You haven't talked to them since you left?"

"No. And I probably won't. Look, you know I love you, and I'd do anything for you. But there are six more weeks of summer. You're not due until October."

"The doctor says I might deliver early. They have to watch me more closely, in case of, you know, premature—"

"Stop, Em. You're going to be fine. Your babies will be fine. And we'll talk about my return closer to Labor Day, okay?" I promised to call in two days and hung up. When I caught a glimpse of myself in the mirror, all the old insecurities rushed back. My best friend in the world was having two children and I wasn't even married yet. The longing to have what she had spread through me. I grabbed a pillow and closed my eyes, fighting the panic and self-pity. When the phone chimed again, I checked the caller ID. *Unknown.*

Punching *Answer,* I offered a tentative hello. There was a pause. I repeated my greeting. An electronic voice growled, "Stop poking the bear or end up like Amanda and LeeAnne."

Chapter 35

...lost on a river of doubt...

I didn't sleep well the next two nights. My mind kept imagining attacks by the unknown caller. When I did doze off, a brown bear chased me through the store, claws grazing my heels as I fled. Each time it lashed out, I jerked awake, convinced that my pursuer was hiding in the shadowed corners of my room. By Thursday, I was exhausted and looking forward to quiet time and the serenity of being on the water, out of the reach of scary dreams and phantom bears.

Gavin appeared right after dawn, as usual, lugging our fishing gear and eager for breakfast. He loved Carl's daily treats as much as everyone else in Wanakena. That day she had baked cheese biscuits. The easy banter between the two of them soon lifted my anxiety over the threatening call. I hadn't told anyone about it yet. Perhaps it was nothing more than a prank, but I didn't believe that. However, I determined to say nothing that would spoil the moment. Carl raised her eyebrows.

"You all right, Riley?" She cradled her favorite moose cup in her hands. "You're frowning."

I forced a smile. "Nothing's wrong, boss, just bear dreams." She harrumphed but didn't push the issue. I filled travel mugs with hot chocolate, then relieved Gavin of half the gear. We took our time walking to the beach, where we loaded the kayaks and headed out to open water. A heron rose from the near shore and flew overhead, squawking at our intrusion. Ducks floated in our wake, diving or preening. Only a few cirrus clouds marred the lightening sky.

The hours we spent fishing restored some of the equilibrium I had lost. I shook off the feeling of inferiority that always haunted me. I was an outdoor woman now, eager to stand on my own. I refused to be intimidated by an anonymous voice. I would share my concern about Timmy's story with Josh and tell him about the strange call. We had spoken only briefly yesterday morning when he stopped by the store with Gus. Ike had demanded more attention than either of the men. Before I finished petting him, they had to leave. Josh paid for the dog's usual treat, then lingered by the register until Gus stepped outside.

"Can I see you tonight?" His eyes settled on my mouth.

When I handed over his change, my fingers grazed his. Even that brief touch set me tingling. Clearly, he saw my reaction. He trapped my hand in his, tracing the lines on my palm, then brought it to his lips.

"Tonight, Riley." Releasing me, he stuffed the change in his pocket and left. Ike panted after him, the dog's gaze fixed on the snack his master was unwrapping.

The memory of that conversation had me eager for the day to end. I secured my fishing pole and followed Gavin back to shore. We carried the kayaks up the beach. When I stumbled, he caught me. "You all right, Miss Finn?"

"I'm fine, Gav, just thinking too hard. Hey, am I ready to try this on my own?"

"Well, you're doing better, but I don't think you should go out alone. Why?"

"I want to explore a little farther up the river this afternoon. You could come, too, make sure I do things right."

He shook his head. "I'd like to, Miss Finn, but I'm going to the airport with Uncle Ben. My parents are flying in for a visit."

"I didn't know there was an airport close to Wanakena."

"Yeah. Adirondack Regional. It's about an hour and ten minutes away. I'm sorry."

"No problem. I promise I won't take any chances. Just tell me how to get on the Oswegatchie." I pointed upriver.

"Are you sure you want to do that?"

"I'll be careful, I promise. I just want to test myself where no one can see." I had tired of the locals gathering to observe my progress, especially after that spectacular dump the first time I tried to paddle on my own. Gavin shrugged.

"Your call, Miss Finn." When we reached the lawn area across from the store, he spread a map out on the floor of the gazebo and pointed out the put-in at the end of the very road I had driven down the night I arrived.

"Is it beyond those two creepy trailers?"

"I don't know about the trailers, but you turn here," he pointed to a spot on the map, "and stay to the left when the road splits. Once you reach the drop-in, you'll know it. There are signs. Anyway, you go down the bank to a small strip of sandy soil. But be careful in the water. There are big rocks off to the left of the put-in, so you have to paddle hard to the right, go upriver. There's a small set of rapids shortly after the put-in. You'll probably have to get out and drag the kayak up the incline, but it's very doable this time of year. After that, the river just winds back and forth for miles. Go as far as you want, then turn around."

I committed all his instructions to memory, folded the map, and stuffed it in my dry bag. We made our way back to Carl's, where I fixed lunch. I asked Gavin about his mom and dad. Since our extended time together, he was more comfortable talking about his family. While we ate, he opened up about their conflicts. The teen was more interested in video games and girls than his father thought he should be. He didn't participate in any team sports, although he loved the outdoor activities he was teaching me. When he left to meet his uncle, I thought about what he'd shared. Why were children so often expected to fulfill the unrealized dreams of their parents? That led me to consider Josh and Timmy, the patience and, indeed, love that Josh displayed for his son. A man shamed by his wife, humiliated by her infidelity, suspected of murder, yet strong enough to continue caring for their boy. I wanted that man, even if only for the summer. I looked forward to seeing him later. But first, I was going paddling.

Tying the kayak on top of the car, I loaded the paddle, dry bag, rope, and a personal flotation device. I also packed a few snacks to power my excursion. I waved to Amy as I passed, but I didn't stop.

"Hey, Riley," she called over the squeals of the boys running through the sprinkler. "Where are you going?"

"Paddling," I shouted. "Up the river."

I assumed it would be easy to retrace that initial wrong turn I had made on my way into Wanakena without being scared, but I was wrong. As soon as I turned down the access road, my legs shook. The deeper into the woods I drove, the more fearful I became. Then the turnoff toward the trailers came into view. I made sure all the doors were locked and increased my speed through the curve to the left. When I checked the rearview mirror, I saw movement in the brush. Was someone hiding there? Was a bear following me? I hadn't forgotten the phone call, just shoved it to the back of my mind. Now I wondered if it was foolish to go out alone. But the new, improved Riley welcomed this bolder and previously unknown side of me.

I drove on, breathing easier as the path to the trailers disappeared from view. Twenty minutes later, I pulled into the parking area. The put-in was as rustic as I expected. No restrooms. No pavement. No other cars. I got out, checked for wildlife in the immediate area, and carried the kayak down the bank. To the left, the river swirled as it met the massive rocks blocking the passage toward Cranberry Lake. Calmer water greeted me on the right. I stowed my gear, dropped the boat in the water, and climbed in. As I pulled away from land, I listened for the call of birds, the whir of insects, human voices. Only the river itself, murmuring as it flowed beneath the boat, greeted my arrival. I searched the water for any rocks lurking beneath the surface.

Not long after I put in, the rumble of the rapids reminded me to get ready to wade through rushing water. Gavin had told me true. The water wasn't deep. Still, I struggled against the current, nagged by Anton's previous warning to stay safe and Josh's entreaty to be careful. When I reached the top of the incline, I sagged against the marshy shore and tugged the kayak closer. I stumbled farther from the cascading water, climbed in again, and paddled hard to avoid being swept back toward the rocks. Soon I was winding back and forth through high banks framed by thick growths of grass and underbrush. Now I heard birdsong, a mix of familiar and foreign that swelled and ebbed around me. Entranced by the chirping and whirling above, I strained to spot and identify as many species as I could. Chickadees flitted above my head. Herons, angry at my intrusion, protested along the banks. In the distance, a woodpecker pounded away. I took my phone from the dry bag to check the time, noting that I had no cell coverage. I'd been out on the water for an hour.

Unaccustomed to such steady effort, my arms protested. When I located a tree branch hanging over the water, I tied up the kayak and ate my snacks. After the break, I felt energized and ready to continue, so I decided to paddle a half hour more before turning around. I had maneuvered two more wide bends when I heard men's voices. Their words carried over the water, the tone menacing. I couldn't tell if they were upstream or downriver. I paddled slower, straining to hear something that would help me place their location. The only word I recognized was *car*. They must mean mine. No other vehicles were parked at the drop-off point when I arrived, which meant the men were paddling upstream. Were they chasing me? The riverbanks, choked by grasses, provided no hiding places. I had no choice but to continue upriver. Soon my lungs were burning, and my arm muscles quivered. Overhead, clouds built into thunderheads. Even if I turned around now, I'd be caught in the storm. I paused long enough to struggle into my raincape and take several swallows of water.

Raindrops speckled the front of the kayak. I caught my breath as I hauled on the paddle, lost control, and careened into a marshy bank. The voices had faded, but I was afraid to stop. I pressed on until, exhausted, I found a narrow inlet. I shoved through the overhang of reed grass, curled over the bow, and huddled beneath the cape as thunder crashed overhead. Lightning crackled in the distance, then repeated, closer to me. I closed my eyes and prayed.

By the time the storm rolled on, I was shivering from the cold and the damp. I bailed water with my hands, cursing my thoughtlessness in not bringing even a cup with me. Dusk crept over the river as darker clouds massed in the west, promising more rain. Caution kept me from moving. If the strangers were waiting for me at the put-in, maybe I should remain where I was. Stay or go? The sedge hanging over the river rustled. A heron croaked, its throaty outrage reminding me I didn't belong here. I drank the rest of my water and started back.

The heavy downpour had swollen the current. As soon as I re-entered the main stream, I felt the tug. I backpaddled to slow my progress, unable to see each turning until it was upon me. If I wasn't careful, I would upend the kayak and find myself in the water. I didn't even want to consider that. I squinted into the gloom. Tendrils of fog slithered among the grasses, spreading themselves over the Oswegatchie. It grew harder to make out the route ahead. I pushed on, losing track of time as I paddled the twists and turns of the streambed. Thunder rumbled behind me. Suddenly, the river fanned out in a rush. The rapids galloped ahead, their swollen flanks waiting to throw me over. Water roiled against the banks, covering even the narrow strip of land I might have used to walk my way down. I had to run the rushing cascade in the dark, the now-invisible rocks waiting to batter me beneath the boil and froth.

I clenched my teeth and stroked harder. The current grabbed the kayak and sent it racing. I maneuvered the paddle like a pole, shifting from side to side to stay upright. At the top of the falls, the boat tipped forward, righted, and swept down the incline. I screamed as it sped over the watercourse. The prow hit a rock, bounced, made a half-turn, then shifted left. I leaned hard on the paddle and shot forward into a deeper pool. I had made it through, but now the swift-running water surged. Caught in the flow, the kayak headed straight past the put-in, aimed dead center for the hulking granite barrier anchored in the stream ahead. I cursed, loudly, and backpaddled, my frantic efforts dwarfed by the turbulence around me.

Chapter 36

...adding fuel to the fire...

People say, in moments of confronting death, that we relive our past. In that moment of desperation, all that flashed through my mind was the accusation Josh had made, that I would leave him and Timmy alone. I gripped the paddle harder, vowing that if I made it out of this, I'd let them both know that I wasn't going anywhere, not yet. I blinked the rain from my eyes. My fingers cramped. Every muscle burned. I screamed my frustration and fought harder to keep the kayak from the rocks.

"Riley!" Above the roar of the river, I heard my name.

I strained against the current, my arms heavy, my legs trembling.

"Riley! Grab the rope." I risked a glance toward the put-in. A light blazed from the shore, its rays shattered into pinpoints by the fog. I strained to hold the paddle upright and peered into the night. Off to my left, Josh stood in waist-high water, a coil of rope dangling from his hands. On the shore, Gus Jornigen held a lantern.

"Hold the light steady, Gus," Josh said, his voice low and calm, as though this were a training exercise.

The kayak rocked. I backpaddled. For every foot I retreated, I slipped forward two. Josh launched the rope in my direction. I planted the paddle in the rocky stream bed and lunged. I missed. The paddle wrenched free. The kayak rocked and swung around. Now I was facing upstream with my back toward the rocks.

"Turn the boat, Riley." Josh called out. "Nice and steady." I sobbed as I swept the paddle in wide circles, fighting fatigue. Twice I managed to turn, only to have the water push me back. I made one more sweep. The kayak bounced and tilted, but now it faced the bank. Josh gathered the rope and tossed it out again. I anchored my feet below the gunnels and propelled my body upward, snatching the line as it sailed over my head. I wrenched the paddle out of the water and twisted the rope around it. Then I hung on as Josh reeled me in. Three big hauls and the kayak settled into the quiet water near the sandy put-in. I dropped my head and sobbed, but I didn't let go of the rope. Josh dragged the boat onto the shore. He untangled the paddle and tapped my fingers.

"Riley," he said, "you can let go now. It's all right. You're safe."

My hands were numb. I willed myself to stand, but my legs failed to obey. "I can't move," I said.

"I've got you." He pried my grip free and lifted me out of the boat. Water dripped off us. Gus slid down the bank to collect the kayak.

"My house," Josh said. "It's closer."

"Wait." I tried to raise my head and failed. "My car."

Josh smoothed the wet hair back from my face. "Gus will bring it. Where are your keys?"

"Dry bag," I rasped. With my head cradled against him, Josh strode up the muddy path to his truck. He settled me into the passenger seat, tucked a blanket around my legs, and buckled the seat belt. My body shook. My teeth chattered. We had gone only a few yards when I reached for him. "Josh." My throat spasmed. "I'm going to be sick."

He threw the clutch into park, hauled me out of the seatbelt, and held me as I threw up the remnants of the snack bars. By the time we reached his house, I could barely move. His mother took one look and shook her head.

"Explanations later. Right now, get her into the bathroom, Josh. Timmy's watching TV. Make sure he stays there." She patted my arm. "Let's get you warm, dear."

I dozed off, or passed out, as the steam from the bath filled the small space. She shook me awake and handed me a washcloth. The warmth revived me enough to assess the damage. Mud caked my legs. Debris from the river, leaves, grass, petals from an unknown flower, floated in the water. I soaked for a long time before she came back with an armful of clothing.

"These won't fit you, dear, but they're warm and dry. And," she smiled, "they belong to my son, not his ex-wife."

Content to follow orders, I held still, relishing the care with which she dried my shivering limbs and helped me into the long-sleeved Henley, sweatpants, and fleece pullover. They smelled like Josh. I huddled into the hood as she rolled up the pant legs.

"Do I look ridiculous?"

"You look adorable." Julia patted my cheek. "Now, comb your hair, then come have some soup. After that, you are to go straight to bed. You can tell us all about your adventure tomorrow."

Mr. Waylon and Josh were waiting in the kitchen. As soon as we entered, both hurried over to help me sit. Julia exchanged a look with his dad, and they both left the room.

"You sure you need this hood?" Josh said, pushing it back to run a hand over my damp hair. I managed a smile.

"Stop teasing me." I pulled it back on. "I just want to get warm. I've never been so cold."

"I have a better idea." He wrapped his arms around me and pulled me onto his lap. I was very aware of my naked self beneath his borrowed clothing. "Eat, Riley. Then I'm taking you to bed."

That perked up every little part of me. I lost myself in the idea of Josh and me in bed together. He planted a kiss on my forehead and shoved the bowl closer. The aroma of home-made chicken noodle soup elbowed aside any erotic scenario. My hand shook, slopping more than a little onto the table. Josh took the spoon and fed me. I finished it all and nodded for seconds. Laughter filtered in from the living area, Timmy's loudest of all. Soon I heard Julia announce it was time for bed. Josh set me down and moved to the sink. In a minute, his mother brought Timmy in to say goodnight. I held the boy close, reveling in the feel of his little arms around my neck. When she took him away, all the pent-up emotion of the day escaped. Josh scooped me back onto his lap and held me until the tears ebbed.

"I'm sorry." I rubbed my face against my sleeve, wondering how unappealing I looked after a drenching in the river and a prolonged crying fit. Julia and his father called good night from down the hall. The door to their room closed. "Thank you for rescuing me. How did you know I was gone?"

Josh settled me more firmly against him. "Amy. She called to tell me you were heading off somewhere with a kayak on your car. I figured you only knew one place to go."

"Don't yell at me," I whispered.

"I will never yell at you, Riley." He tucked my head against his chest. "I met Gus at the put-in. He had already talked to Gavin. The kid told him your plan."

"I needed to prove I could do something myself."

"I understand that, but why did you stay away so long?"

"That wasn't part of the plan. I thought someone was after me." I wiped my nose on the tissue he handed me and sniffed. "I heard men's voices. They were looking for me, I think, so I kept going. It turned dark before I knew it. Whoever was after me gave up, but then the storm came."

"You did good, babe. I'm proud of you."

248

"Did you just call me babe?" I arched an eyebrow and studied him. At home, he was a different man, relaxed and funny and so damn sexy.

"You are a babe, Riley Finn. Why do you think every guy in Wanakena is chasing after you?"

"They're not." I picked at my wrinkled thumb. "Not every guy."

"Yes, they are. But this guy has you, right here, right now." His lips met mine, soft and sweet, but when I opened to his gentle urging, they became demanding. I responded to him with a demand of my own. I don't know how long we stayed there, exploring with our mouths and our hands. But I couldn't stop the yawn when he let me go.

"Now, it's time for bed." He rose with me still in his arms and walked us to his room. My body was ready to respond to more than kisses until another yawn escaped. Josh tucked me under the covers. He took off his shirt and pants, slipped in behind me, and spooned against my back. I sighed and settled in, rubbing against him. He was instantly hard. I reached back, but he caught my hand. "Not tonight, babe. You need sleep."

I shook my head. "I need you, Josh."

"Not yet, honey. Tonight, you need to sleep." He calmed me with whispers and promises. I closed my eyes and drifted off, the memory of water splashing over my thighs nothing but a murmur amid the safety of his arms.

I woke alone to sunlight and the gossip of ravens in the pines that lined the yard. The smell of bacon frying drifted down the hall. The snick-snick of a wheelchair over the wood floor made me sit up and pat my bed hair. Muscles I didn't know I had screamed at me until I recalled Josh's hand slipping beneath the hoodie to curl possessively around one breast. Gods, but I needed to have that man soon or I was going to spontaneously combust. I had never felt such a rush of desire in my life.

"Hi, Miss Finn." Timmy peeked around the half-open door. "Breaks, breakfast's ready. Want some?"

My stomach growled an answer. I accompanied him to the kitchen where Julia had set out fresh-squeezed orange juice and a jar of maple syrup. She raised tongs in greeting as she layered bacon slices on a paper towel.

"Morning, Riley. You look much better after a good night's sleep."

"I'm so sore!" I ignored the knowing look she gave me. We didn't have sex, I wanted to say, but why should she believe me?

"Josh said to stay until you're ready to go back to the cabin. He'll tell Carl you won't be in until later."

"Oh!" I bumped the table as I rose. "I forgot. I have to go to work."

She steered me back to my seat. "Not until you eat."

Arguing got me nowhere. At her insistence, I devoured six pancakes. Timmy only ate five. We giggled way too much over the blueberry smiley faces Julia had made in his stack. She added a pot of tea, and we drank in companionable silence while the boy finished his milk. After he took his plate to the sink, he wheeled his way to the living room to watch the news with Grandpa.

"I washed your clothes, Riley, but they're not dry yet. You'll have to come back and get them later." A sly grin let me know it was part of her grand plan. I shook my head.

"You're incorrigible."

She set the teacups in the sink. "I know what my boy needs. So will you, when you have children of your own. Nothing worries a mother more than a child who is hurting."

"Thank you, Julia, for everything you've done and are doing. But it's best to let Josh decide, don't you think?" I gathered the dry bag and keys from the top of the microwave and looked back toward the bedroom. "Do you want me to change the sheets?"

She smirked. "Do they need to be changed?"

I blushed. "No."

She laughed and handed me the keys to my car. "Gus dropped it off earlier."

"I guess I have him to thank, too, along with your son. He saved my life."

"Sweetheart, Joshua was broken. You're putting him back together. Don't be afraid. He was desperate to find you. I've never seen him so anxious. Remember, Riley, a man's actions reveal his true self."

All the way back to town, I thought about her words. Actions reveal the man. I believed I knew Josh's heart, but I'd been wrong before, terribly wrong. And what about the others? What had Jesse, Ben, Angus, even Birgit, done that told me who they were and what they were capable of? I wondered if Josh had found out anything about the necklaces. Perhaps that information would provide the clues to stitch this all together. Of course, maybe none of my "suspects" were guilty. Then I'd be back to square one, with no way to erase the suspicions trailing after Josh.

At Carl's house, I took two pain capsules, braided my hair and pinned it up, and dressed. I held Josh's fleece to my face one more time, breathing in his smell. A determined voice checked off chores in my head. Solve the murders. Clear Josh's name. And, most importantly, get Josh Waylon in my bed. Soon. I squared my shoulders against the ache of sore muscles, locked the cabin, and jogged very slowly into Wanakena.

When I arrived at the store, Carl was pacing the porch. She enveloped me in a bear hug, eyes bright with unshed tears. I noticed two new Adirondack chairs in forest green propped up against the front of the building.

"Are we selling those?"

She followed my pointing finger, then scowled. "No. Jesse brought those over for us to use. And don't try to change the subject, Riley. I want to hear all about your paddling accident."

"There was no accident," I said.

"Don't get all huffy, Finn." She marched me inside and practically chained me behind the counter. "Now spill."

"The good news is," I snatched a muffin from the basket, "Gavin is a very good teacher."

While she sat, eager and silent, on the stool, I recounted my river excursion. I blamed myself for over-estimating the weather. I didn't include the voices I had heard or my belief that men were chasing me. Over the summer, I had learned that anything I told Carl she shared with Jesse. Right now, Mayor Livetree remained on the suspect list. I didn't want to chance tipping him off. More than that, maybe I would recognize the voices from the river if I heard them again, and what better spot to spy from than the back of the store. I sent Carl home, intending to carry out my plan when each of my prime suspects came in. If I wasn't at the register, they would call out to me. Stupid, I know, but it seemed like a swell idea when I was plotting it out in my head. The phone call remained another mystery to solve. I hadn't mentioned it to Josh yet. He and I had a lot to discuss. My inner wild woman laughed at that. She knew I wanted more than talk. The old Riley would have waited for the man to make the move. The new Riley was determined not to delay any longer.

I checked the front of the store, then slipped past the snack shelves and stopped by the coolers along the back wall. Up front, the bell jangled.

"Hello?" I waited for a response. No one spoke. "Be with you in a sec."

I straightened the gallons of milk, checked the expiration date on the pints of cream, and hurried toward the register. Birgit blocked my passage. In uniform, she exuded authority, and almost as tall as Josh, the woman intimidated by stature alone. When I took a step back, she smirked. She lifted a soup can from the display and tossed it from hand to hand.

"Heard you had some trouble on the river."

"Word travels fast." I shouldered past her. "Too bad no one knows what happened to Amanda and LeeAnne."

"Yeah. Too bad." She replaced the can and followed me. Something in her tone made me turn around. Birgit looked perplexed, as though she had not thought about the murders that way.

"Look, Birgit." I took my place at the register. "I don't want Ben Torvald. I already told him not to ask me out again. So, you can back off."

"I know. He told me. That's not why I'm here."

Curious, I eased onto the stool. Now at eye level with the tall Scandinavian, I felt more in control. "What else do we have to discuss?"

She leaned on the counter, toying with the necklace that matched the ones Carl had shown me. She was only wearing one today. "Word is that you're interested in clearing Josh Waylon's name."

I fiddled with the order pad, hoping to forestall the blush threatening to color my face.

"How would I do that?"

Birgit checked over her shoulder. We were alone in the store. She continued to twist her necklace. "I heard LeeAnne got one of these chokers like mine last summer when she worked at the gift shop in Cranberry."

"Where'd you hear that?"

"She told me. I thought you'd want to know, but if you don't—"

"All right." I decided to take the bait she offered. After all, I did want to dispel the cloud over Josh and Timmy's heads. "Were they sold there?"

"I'm not sure. It's funny, how it happened." A touch of an accent colored her words. "One day at the restaurant, we were talking about money, our lack of it, actually. And she reached into her purse and pulled out her necklace. I was told, she said, if I wear this, it will bring me luck."

"Did it? Bring her luck?" When she rolled her eyes, I corrected myself. "Before, I mean, before it didn't."

"I guess. The following day, I saw her talking to one of the other professors. Not Ben." It was her turn to blush. "Then that night, I was back at the restaurant and asked her what he wanted."

"Which professor?"

Birgit waved off my question. "Simons. Simmons. Doesn't matter. He's gone now. Anyway, he had asked her to help with his research. All she had to do, she told me, was take a package into Lake Placid once a week."

"What kind of package?"

"Samples," Birgit said, "of trout specimens from various ponds in the area. Apparently, he was working with a conservation group from the museum down the road."

"The money was good?"

Birgit paused. "Better than good. LeeAnne told me that, between waitressing and delivering the packages, she would earn enough to pay for next year's tuition. That's really why she was coming back to Wanakena."

"But she never made it."

"No." Birgit stretched and shoved away from me.

"But if this professor is no longer here, she wouldn't have that job, would she?"

"Don't know. Maybe one of the new instructors continued the research."

"What does any of that have to do with the necklace?"

"That's how the professor knew to offer her the job. Said it marked her as special."

"Is that why you have one?"

She narrowed her eyes. "I don't need a necklace to make me special."

"May I see it?" I held out my hand, wondering if she would allow me to examine the beads. Birgit hesitated, then removed the strand and dropped it in my palm. I recalled the necklaces in the crime photos. Amber and wood beads on a brown cord, and one silver bead in the center bearing the symbol of a crescent moon. Hers was an exact match.

"What does this mean?" I pointed at the intricate carving. The metal caught the light, throwing the symbol in relief. At first, I thought it was a lunar sign, but as I examined it more closely, the marking resolved into a letter C underscored by a short line.

Birgit snatched the necklace from me and peered at the symbol. "I have no idea."

"Maybe," I softened my words as Jesse Livetree stomped up the steps and pushed on the screen, "you shouldn't wear it anymore."

"I don't need your advice, Finn."

"Shouldn't you be telling this to the police?"

She flipped her braid over her shoulder. "Didn't think of it until this morning, actually. You can tell them, can't you? Show them what a good detective you are."

"Are you planning to buy anything?"

Birgit huffed and grabbed a basket to fill with purchases as the mayor greeted me. I noticed he was using the cane again. I wondered, not for the first time, why his affliction came and went. I turned away to check my phone as he moved farther down the aisle. He called my name, asking my opinion on a new brand of cookies we had stocked. That's when it hit me. The voices on the river. One of them belonged to Jesse Livetree.

Chapter 37

...ignition...

Josh knocked on the door of Carl's cabin shortly after nine. The boss was awake, pacing and snorting like a cornered moose. Her latest lab tests had revealed a higher-than-expected cholesterol count, and she was still upset about my escapade on the river. When Josh came in, she enveloped him in a hug.

"Thank you, thank you, for saving Finn."

"It was Gus who found Riley's car. If he hadn't--" Josh gave me a look that set every part of me on alert.

"Gus? I thought you found the car," I said.

He frowned. "No. He caught up to me as I was coming out of town. Said he'd been to the drop-off point and your car was there, but he could find no sign of you."

"Well, that's mighty curious," Carl said. "Isn't that close-lipped man Timmy's godfather?"

Josh sat and rested his forearms on his knees. "He is. That was Amanda's doing, but I agreed. He's not much of a talker. A very private guy. We've worked together for almost ten years, and I still know very little about him."

"I think Gus sees you as the son he never had," Carl said.

"He's different from most of the men I've met here." I shrugged. "He doesn't offer much when he speaks. Just warnings."

"Warnings?" Carl sat beside me and took my hand. "What kind of warnings?"

I closed my eyes, piecing together his words from the few conversations I'd had with him over the last few weeks. "Gus cautioned me about playing detective, told me not to look too deeply into the murders."

257

"Riley." Josh waited for me to look up. "You said you heard two men talking on the river."

"I did." One of them had been Jesse Livetree, I was certain, but I didn't want to reveal that in front of Carl.

"Is it possible Gus was one of them?" Josh asked. I shivered.

"You all right, Riley?" Carl said.

"Just a ghost walking over my grave. My Grandma used to say that every time she got the chills." I blinked at Josh, willing him not to ask more right now.

Carl settled into her recliner. Josh moved to stand by the fireplace. "How's your recovery going, Ms. Beamish?"

"Up and down, Waylon, up and down, but it's going." She inquired about his parents and Timmy. We shared more tidbits of local gossip before she excused herself and went to her room. Soon, the TV began to blare. I think she turned it up on purpose. Josh caught my eye and winked. I blushed. He settled next to me and planted a kiss on my cheek, then one on my lips. We got lost in each other for a time.

"You're making it very hard for me to concentrate, Miss Finn."

"Maybe," I said, my cheeks warming as I headed into the kitchen, "we should talk about what we found out. Want some coffee?"

"I'd rather have a beer."

"I can do that." I handed him one of the local IPAs. "Now, please tell me you found out something about the necklaces."

Josh pulled a wad of notes from his back pocket. He shuffled through the pages until he located what he was looking for. "Contrary to the messy way she lived, my...wife, Amanda, kept precise notes on the jewelry inventory. The police looked over the balance sheets, checked our bank account, but somehow they overlooked this."

"What is it?" I fingered the leather-bound volume the size of a large index card. "It looks like an address book."

"I only realized what it contained two days ago. At first, I thought it was just a collection of addresses for sending Christmas cards. But after you and I talked, I decided to have another look through everything she left behind."

I touched his sleeve. "I'm sorry. I didn't mean to stir up bad memories."

He covered my hand with his. "I'm not sad, babe. I'm angry. What she did to us, to me and to Timmy, it burned away all my feelings for her. But I do want to find out who killed her, and why. Until I do—"

I moved closer, hoping my presence would convey what my words could not. He sipped his beer as he sifted through the pages.

"Here's the thing. Amanda sold her jewelry – necklaces, bracelets, earrings, rings – at most of the tourist shops between Cranberry and Lake Placid. But the curious thing is she had a secondary market for the ones she made that were more distinctive, unique, like the one she was wearing when someone murdered her. Like the one that may have been used to kill LeeAnne McMasters."

"Have they located that one yet?"

"Maybe." He lifted his eyes to mine. "I gave Kellerman the one Gavin found."

"Oh." I touched my neck, remembering Birgit fingering her beads. They resembled the ones in Carl's collection. What could my boss have to do with any of this?

"Birgit wears a necklace," I said, "like Amanda's, and like the one Gavin had. It's funny, though. The first time I saw her, she had three strands around her neck."

"You talked to Birgit again?"

I nodded. "It was so strange. She came by the store today. To apologize, she said. Since I warned Ben off, she doesn't view me as a threat."

"She showed you her necklace?"

"Yes. I thought it was odd, really. She told a story about LeeAnne working for a professor who paid her to deliver fish samples for him." I drummed my fingers on the moose placemat. "I asked her not to wear it."

"Why?"

"I don't think it's a coincidence that both women were strangled by the same type of necklace."

He took another drink. "She didn't buy the necklace? It was a gift? Did she say why?"

"She didn't say anything about her own necklace, just LeeAnne's. The whole story sounded off. A Professor Simmons or Simons asking LeeAnne to deliver research to Placid once a week. Paid well, according to LeeAnne."

"Riley," Josh said, "there was no professor by that name at the school last summer. I would know."

"You think Birgit is lying?"

He rubbed a thumb over his chin. "I think Birgit Sandsdottir is a manipulative bitch capable of almost anything to get what she wants. Why she would spin this tale to you bothers me."

"Carl has several of the necklaces in her jewelry box, although I've never seen her wear one. She wasn't a fan of Amanda."

Josh grimaced. "No, she wasn't. But Ben never mentioned anything about research at the school. Something's not quite right, for sure. Have you told anyone else about her story?"

"No, only you."

He rummaged through the address book again, shaking his head. "There are so many puzzles in here. Lists of initials that don't match anyone I know. Whatever scheme Amanda was running, she didn't want anyone to find out about it. Here. You look. Maybe you'll see something I missed."

After I read through the lines of printed initials and dates, I told Josh about the argument I overheard between Jesse Livetree and Anton Storms, and about the voices on the river. "I'm sure that Jesse was one of the men out there."

"Could the other man have been Storms?"

I shook my head. "I'm positive it wasn't him. I could barely hear the other man, although I can't imagine Jesse being out there with a stranger."

"What possible reason could the mayor have to be out on the river last night?" Carl said.

"Ms. Beamish." Josh offered to help her sit. "Have you been spying on us?"

She waved him off, plodded to the table, and dropped onto a chair. "I came out to get some water and heard Jesse's name. I've known that man since we were toddlers together. Even after he moved on to police work in the big city, we kept in touch. Knew his wife, Laurie, too. Sad she passed so early in their life together. He's an upstanding, bull-headed shark of a man. Never did think he'd retire. But sneak behind people's backs? Frighten young women? That doesn't sound a bit like him."

"Well, someone did." I recalled the weird phone call. "It might have been the mayor on the phone who threatened me."

"What are you talking about?" Carl said.

"What phone call?" Josh leaned across the table. I tried to distract him with an offer of another drink, but he refused to back down. "Riley. Explain."

As I recounted the strange call, I admitted what I had been reluctant to acknowledge. "Okay, it might have been a real threat."

Josh grabbed my arm. "Babe, this isn't a Nancy Drew mystery you're involved in. Two women are dead. You can't keep secrets from me anymore." He scrubbed at his face, then skewered me with a look that conveyed how worried he was. I rubbed my hands to warm them. He looked at Carl. "That goes for you, too, Ms. Beamish. The three of us are a team now."

Carl moved to the chair next to me. "Riley, is there anything else you haven't told us?"

I ticked off what I knew on my fingers. Birgit's information. The mysterious phone call. Gavin's attack. Timmy's observation regarding the bear. The argument between Jesse and Anton. When I mentioned the last again, Josh scooted closer.

"What else do you recall about that argument, Riley?"

I did my best to relate everything I remembered. When I finished, Josh looked at Carl.

"Ms. Beamish, tell me what you know about Anton Storms, especially how he might know the mayor."

Carl chewed her lip. "Maybe it's not coincidental that he turned up last year two months before Amanda was hurt. Brought his boat, posted flyers advertising the fishing charters. She pursued him pretty hard, as I recall. Forgive me, Josh, but it's no secret that Amanda went after anything male. Then she dumped him in a very public way. Storms always seems to be around when something happens, doesn't he? Like the night you arrived, Riley."

"It was weird that he was hanging around the store in the rain." Of course, Josh didn't know about that either, so I had to tell him how Storms approached my car, then sent me on to Carl's place. "But he seemed all right the day we went into Cranberry for lunch. Except when I asked about his necklace."

"What about it?" Those blue eyes pinned me in my chair. I touched my neck again.

"He acted sad, remorseful, maybe. I got the impression it meant more to him than he was willing to say."

We drank as we considered each new piece of information. Ice cubes clunked into the bin in the fridge. Josh glanced at the clock the same time Carl did. With a yawn, she pushed up and headed for the hall.

"Time for bed. I expect you two to make a plan. Let me know tomorrow what I can do to help solve this puzzle, so you," she smirked at me and then Josh," can get on with whatever it is you're intending to do together."

I watched her shuffle away, her back bowed under the weight of the Jesse revelations. I understood her confusion. Mayor Livetree didn't seem like a man capable of evil, but then my experience was limited. Josh still held my hand. When I looked his way, he brought it to his lips.

"I'm going to go, too. I want you to stay safe. You can listen and ask questions," he placed a finger on my lips, "but you are not to go out alone, not on the river and not on the trails."

I started to disagree. He stopped my protest with a kiss. I kissed him back. He lifted me out of the chair and pulled me closer. When I wrapped my legs around his waist, he staggered back, bracing himself against the wall as the kiss deepened. I was gasping when he set me down.

"You have no idea how much I want you, Riley Finn. But I won't ask you to be with me until I clear my name."

I stood as tall as I could to touch his check. "I told you already. I know who you are, Josh Waylon. The rest doesn't matter."

"It does to me, babe." He kissed me again, then led me to the door. "Lock up, and don't answer the phone unless you recognize the caller."

"Aye, aye, boss." I feigned a salute.

He gathered me in and, grinning, whispered, "You'll pay for that, Miss Finn. I'm keeping a list."

"Of what?"

"Of all the ways I'm going to make love to you."

He left me there, aching with desire and the tantalizing prospect of being bedded by a man who knew exactly what he wanted. I hurried to my room, the list of mysteries to solve echoing in my brain. As I washed my face and brushed my teeth, I whispered a prayer that no one else would be hurt before we found the killer.

Chapter 38

...pull one thread and the unraveling begins...

Two days later, Gavin was at work in the storeroom, sorting through boxes for items we needed. I was checking the orders and counting the days left in my summer employment when I heard shouting. I stuck the pencil behind my ear and hurried toward the back. "Gavin?"

No answer. I called again, louder. The ruckus continued. When I entered the room, Jesse Livetree had the boy by the front of his t-shirt and backed against the wall, growling as he demanded an explanation. I hadn't seen the mayor come in. How had he gotten past me?

"Tell me the truth, boy," Jesse said. "What did you hear?"

Gavin flailed at the older man, unwilling to land a punch but desperate to free himself. During the struggle, they upset a carton of paper towels. The rolls bounced across the floor. Several landed beside the mayor's cane, which lay abandoned near the stacks of winter ice melt that had been pushed aside, revealing a back door I had no idea existed.

"I didn't hear anything, Mr. Livetree. Honest. We were just hanging out on the dock and listening to music."

"This isn't a game, son. I need to know. People's lives depend on it."

I kicked my way through the mess and tugged on the mayor's arm. "Let the boy go, Jesse."

Livetree turned, his face drawn and pale. "You don't understand, Riley."

"Why don't you let the boy go? We'll all sit down, and you can explain it so I do understand." When Jesse released his grip, I shooed the boy toward the store. "Gavin, go watch the register. Please."

He shrugged away from the mayor and bulled his way toward the coolers. I rescued the cane from beneath the toppled boxes and used it to close the storeroom door. Then I went to the secret door, slammed it shut, and looked for a deadbolt. There wasn't one, only an inset in the knob itself. I held out my hand. Livetree pressed a key into it, and I secured the lock. I shoved the key in my pocket, dragged pallets over, and motioned him to sit. I didn't relinquish the cane.

"I'm guessing you really don't need this, do you?" I perched on two of the pallets, balancing the mahogany stick with a worn brass handle over my knees, and waited for him to speak.

The mayor blew air between his teeth. "Riley," he said, "I don't want you mixed up in this."

"I already am." I tapped the cane on his arm. "What conversation are you afraid the boy overheard?"

"Nothing for you to worry about."

"Fine." If he wouldn't divulge that, maybe I could shake him another way. "Why don't you tell me what's going on between you and Anton Storms?"

He rubbed his hands together, sighed, and looked over his shoulder. Satisfied that we were alone, he jabbed a finger in my direction. "I knew you were trouble the first time I set eyes on you, young lady. And I was right."

"You have no idea, Jesse, how much trouble I can be. Now, just tell me what's going on."

"Only if you promise not to breathe a word to anyone. And I mean anyone."

I thought about Josh and our recent agreement to share everything we learned. I hated to break that promise, but what the mayor had to say might be the opening we needed. I nodded but crossed my fingers behind my back. A small lie to serve a greater purpose. He cleared his throat.

"Anton Storms is a drug task force agent working undercover to expose an opioid pill mill operation in place somewhere around Wanakena."

I filed that away to discuss with Josh later. "What does that have to do with you?"

"After my Laurie died, I thought I'd escape all those big-city drug nightmares and come back here for some peace and healing. Then I discovered the scourge had made its way to my little piece of the wilderness. The feds had an interest in the area operation and sent in Storms. I met him through my contacts. We decided to pursue the investigation together."

"You both agreed to work undercover."

Livetree cut his eyes away. "I pulled some strings. Storms didn't like it, but he had no choice."

"Let me get this straight. He's not a fisherman, and you're not retired."

"Oh, Anton's a fisherman all right. He's won several bass tournaments over the years, so his skill and reputation provided the perfect cover. Who would question a charter captain who knows all the best fishing holes? And no one wonders why an old townie comes back home after losing the love of his life. We make a good team."

"Except when you argue." He didn't respond. I moved on. "That was you out on the river the night I got lost, wasn't it? But Anton wasn't with you."

"Yes, I was out there, and I was there to protect you, and that's all I'm going to say about that, Riley."

"You aren't going to tell me who was with you." He shook his head. It was my turn to sigh. "You scared the shit out of me."

"I realize that now, and I am sorry. But we are this close," Jesse held his thumb and forefinger up, "to finding what we're looking for. And you, young lady, are not going to spoil it for us."

"Is that why you were fighting with him in the store last week?"

He rubbed his face. "You heard that, too, did you?"

"I did."

He shrugged. "Anton has his suspicions about who killed the women. He's been trying to find a way to draw out the killer. We discussed several schemes that might work. When he said he wanted to use you as bait, I said no."

I opened my mouth to respond. He waved me to silence. "No way are we putting you in danger. End of discussion."

"Do you believe Josh had anything to do with what happened to Amanda and LeeAnne?" I desperately wanted him to say no. He hesitated long enough to raise goosebumps on my arms.

"I'm speaking as a cop now, and the answer is maybe. Josh certainly had a motive to kill his ex-wife, plus means, and, of course, opportunity. The man spends most of his time in the woods. He knows the area better than anyone around. But I can't see why he'd go after the McMasters girl. She was involved with Ben Torvald, not Josh, until she went home last fall. I was surprised to learn she planned to return this season."

A pounding on the storeroom door brought us to our feet. Gavin, breathless and wide-eyed, flung it open so hard it dented the drywall. He pointed back toward the register.

"You have to come out now, Miss Finn. They're waiting to talk to you."

I smoothed the hair off his forehead and shook him gently. "Calm down, Gav. Who's waiting?"

"The McMasters. That dead girl's parents. They're by the front door, and they don't look happy."

Before I made my way through the mess on the storeroom floor, I handed the cane to the mayor. Then I gestured at the fallen towels. "Please clean this up. And push those pallets and boxes up against that secret entrance. I don't want any more unexpected visitors."

Jesse met my gaze with another shrug. "I'm coming with you, Riley. You might need some backup."

I smoothed the hair that had escaped my ponytail and entered the store. When I reached the end of the aisle, I spotted a man with his arm wrapped around the shoulders of a red-haired woman. Gray streaked the sweep of the woman's bangs. Anguish showed in the set of their shoulders, and deep lines carved their once-handsome faces. I thought back to the pictures I'd seen of LeeAnne. She had her mother's pale skin and freckled nose but resembled her father through the eyes and mouth. The pair looked up at my approach, and each stood a little taller. Neither one took my outstretched hand. I snatched it back.

"I'm Riley Finn. I understand you want to talk with me."

Mrs. McMasters looked me over. I watched an opinion form in the purse of her lips. Insignificant. Too small to be of consequence. I drew myself up as far as my five feet two inches would allow and waited for one of them to break the silence. Mr. McMasters released his wife to confront me.

"We need to know how you came to take the job LeeAnne was supposed to have." His tone conveyed anger, dismay, and a loss so profound it robbed him of volume.

"It was a mistake, sir, really," I said. "I had applied for the position but heard nothing from Ms. Beamish. I decided to drive up here anyway, to take a chance on finding some other work. When I arrived, in the middle of a storm, the people I met thought I was expected. They sent me to Carl's place, and she, well, she took me in and hired me."

"You look nothing like our daughter." Mrs. McMasters sniffed loudly. "But perhaps you or this gentleman or someone else in this awful place can tell us why you called her from Wanakena the night she died."

The accusation surprised me. "Mrs. McMasters, I didn't know LeeAnne. I never even met her. I'm not sure why you think I am the person who called, but I assure you I am not."

The couple looked at each other. Mayor Livetree clomped around me, introducing himself as he herded them farther away from the register. "If I may ask, why is this so important to you?"

"Because," Mr. McMasters said, "whoever called warned her that she was about to lose her summer job unless she drove down right then. She refused to say who it was, just packed her things and left as soon as the call ended."

Mrs. McMasters prodded Jesse with the tip of one manicured finger. "Whoever called her must have killed her."

I stood my ground, even though my knees were shaking. LeeAnne's mother was crying. Her father looked at me with haunted eyes.

"I'm curious, Mrs. McMasters," I said, choosing my words with care. "How do you know it was someone from Wanakena who called your daughter?"

The woman folded herself into her husband's embrace. Her hands worked knots in the fringe of the scarf she wore. "We were there when she got the call. I asked who had called and she said a friend from Wanakena. I assumed it was a woman."

"Miss Finn," Mr. McMasters voice cracked with sadness, "We're desperate. If you can tell us anything, please. Help us."

"I'm so very sorry, really, for your loss, but I can't tell you anything more. Maybe you should speak with Carl Beamish."

"LeeAnne was our baby, our only daughter. I don't understand who would do this to her." Mrs. McMasters sagged against her husband, her sobs filling the silence. I reached behind the counter for the tissues when a tremendous boom shook the store. Cans rattled on the shelves. Snack bags slid across the floor. Jesse tossed the cane and raced onto the porch. Gavin darted past me, what-the-fucks trailing behind him. I hurried after them. The McMasters remained inside, frozen by sorrow and unable or unwilling to process what was happening. I couldn't either. I clung to Jesse's sleeve as he and Gavin hurried down the steps. In the east, in the sky above the Waylon property, a fireball raced upward, expanded, and then morphed into a mushroom cloud of black smoke. Releasing my grip on the mayor, I ran past them and down the road.

"Josh? Timmy?" I repeated their names as I forced my way through the crowd of onlookers standing and staring at the smoke in the distance.

"Riley." The mayor's hand landed with force and tugged me back. "That's not over Josh's house. I think it's the trailers in the woods."

Chapter 39

...chaos...

Distant sirens alerted us to the approach of firefighters and emergency personnel. Jesse and Gavin drove off behind Ron, who activated the volunteer beacon on his truck. Other residents hurried to implement what appeared to be a disaster plan. When Carl came down from the cabin, she filled me in on the preparations.

"Fire's always a concern in the wilderness, Riley. We have an evac plan, as well, but unless they send a trooper to order us away, we won't leave. Some of our folks supply medical care. The rest will provide food and drink for those fighting the fire."

I hugged myself against the ache in my chest. Where was Josh? Was Timmy all right? What about Mr. and Mrs. Waylon? Mostly, I thought about the clearing deep in the woods where the trailers sat, that eerie calm I sensed the night I arrived, lost and more than a little afraid. The more I recalled that scene, the more I believed someone had peeked out from one of the tattered curtains. The trailers could be part of the drug ring the mayor and Anton were hunting. The person hiding inside may have caused the explosion or been injured when the trailer blew up. Josh might have been in the area, checking for poachers or fires. I punched on my phone, debating whether to call him. If he was fighting the fire, he wouldn't have time to answer. If he was working elsewhere, he might not have cell service. Even if he could answer, he might resent the interruption, view it as intrusive, the sign of a clingy woman. Well, I had been that once, months ago, but I had changed. I shoved the phone in my pocket and returned to the store.

Carl stayed with me throughout the afternoon and into the evening. When the first group of volunteers straggled in, they used the restroom, accepted the bottled water we offered, then left for one of the feeding stations set up on the lawn. A few slipped into the storeroom to catch a quick nap on the sleeping bags I'd laid out for them. A man with a singed beard leaned on the counter, rubbed his face, and rambled on about what he'd seen. He reeked of smoke.

"One of them trailers was completely destroyed." He fisted his hands, then threw them in the air. "Boom, and it collapsed into a gazillion pieces of burning aluminum."

Carl refilled his empty canteen and set it by him. He lifted his cap, scratched his head, and yawned. "What about the other trailer?" I asked.

"Badly damaged," he said, "but it looked like some of the contents were salvageable. The firemen pulled out a slew of boxes. Looked like medication of some kind. Might be certain folks find that important."

Around nine, a new wave of volunteers arrived, along with two truckloads of students from the Ranger School, Birgit and Ben, faces blackened from soot, among them. Birgit looked excited to be part of a real operation. Ben looked defeated. When he approached the register, Birgit raised an eyebrow and scowled.

"Hey, Riley." He reached for me. "I could use a hug."

I ignored the overture. He did look like he could use comfort, but I had no intention of giving it to him. Carl noticed my discomfort. She put one hand on his shoulder and patted his chest with the other. "Hard day, huh, Ben?"

"Where's Jesse?" He glanced around the store, exhaustion and unease evident in the set of his shoulders, the line of his mouth.

"He and Gavin went to help," Carl said. "You must have seen them."

"I saw Gavin. Right before he got hurt."

"What? Gavin's hurt?" I touched him then, grabbed his arm and shook it until he looked at me. "Why didn't you say something right away?"

Birgit pushed in between us to slip an arm around Ben's waist. "Anton Storms is injured, too. They've both been taken to Star Lake."

"How long ago?" I fished my keys out of my purse and slung it over my shoulder. Birgit stopped me.

"Gavin's injuries are minor. A few burns on his hands and face. Anton's in more serious condition. Somebody shot him."

"Shot him?"

"Take a breath, Riley," Carl said. She held my hand as she turned to Ben. "How serious is it?"

Ben spoke so low I barely heard the words. "He might die. I have to talk to Jesse."

"I'm betting the mayor's with Anton and Gavin," Carl said.

I released her hand and banged out the door, calling over my shoulder, "I'm going there now unless the road is blocked."

Carl hurried after me, wheezing from the exertion. "You're not going alone, dear. Ben, I'm leaving you in charge."

Ben caught the key Carl flung his way. We hurried toward her car. I covered my nose to block the scent of burning. The sky had a charcoal tinge, overlaid with scattered light from the disaster scene. Despite the distance, it was easy to discern the glow of the still-raging fire. I wondered how much toxic smoke it had released, if there were gas tanks or other flammable items still waiting to explode. My heart pounded. Startled by the intensity of the palpitations, I leaned on the hood to catch my breath. Had I taken my meds that morning? I couldn't remember. I coughed three times, the violent outbursts arresting the flutters. Carl took the keys from me.

"You're not driving." She opened the door. Ben slammed it shut.

"Neither of you is fit to drive. I'll take you. I put several cases of water on the porch and locked up. Birgit will go back to the school and phone me with updates."

"No. I want to go with you." Birgit shoved him against the car. Ben shoved back.

"Dammit." He raised a hand, then lowered it. "Go back to the office, Birgit. Contact me from there. Go now."

Birgit clenched her fists, then glowered at me. The truce I'd imagined between us disintegrated. She squared her shoulders and strode in the direction of the Ranger School. I helped Carl climb into the back seat, settled in on the passenger side, and gazed out the window at the food tents set up on the green. Ben held his hand out. Carl dropped the car keys into his palm and huffed.

"Be careful, Ben Torvald. Your chickens are coming home to roost."

He inhaled sharply before steering the car toward the Clifton-Fine Hospital in Star Lake. During the ride, I whispered prayers for all the first responders, for Gavin, for Anton, but mostly I prayed for Josh. When we arrived at the small hospital, the parking lot was full. Ben squeezed into a narrow space between two trucks, issuing commands as soon as he turned off the engine. I let myself out and hurried around the front of the car.

"Keys." I held out my hand. As soon as he placed them there, Carl and I rushed through the emergency entrance. We hadn't taken two steps before I spotted Gavin sandwiched between a man who resembled Ben and a woman with eyes the same shape and color as the boy's.

When he saw us, Gavin shrugged free of his parents and headed toward us. I touched the bandage on his forehead, then carefully took his wrapped hands.

"I'm all right, Miss Finn." He nodded at Carl, then buried his head against my shoulder. Carl moved to hug him, and we rocked the boy between us as he sobbed. His parents reached us before Ben did. Mrs. Torvald shook my hand, then Carl's.

"I understand we have you two to thank for keeping our son occupied and out of trouble this summer." Her smile, so much like Gavin's, won my instant allegiance.

"Gavin's taught me so much this summer, Mrs. Torvald, and he has been invaluable in the store," I assured her. Carl murmured her agreement.

"Alice, please, and this is my husband, Jens. We're very grateful for all you've done for Gav. We hoped Ben would provide more guidance." She glared at her brother-in-law. Ben bristled.

"I offered to keep an eye on him, Alice, not raise him."

I stepped between them. "Gavin has a great future ahead of him. Everyone has had a hand in helping him move toward it. Now, where's Mr. Storms?"

Gavin twisted a lock of his hair. "He's in bad shape, Miss Finn. They're transferring him to Watertown."

"Watertown? That's not a good sign." Carl bit her lip. "Well, Samaritan Medical does offer more services."

The thwack-thwack of a helicopter sounded outside. I left the group and went to the information desk. "I understand Anton Storms is being transferred to another hospital. Is there any way I might see him before he goes?"

"Are you family?"

"No, but we," I gestured to the Torvalds and Carl, "we're his friends. He has no family here. We just wanted to let him know he's not alone."

"I'm sorry, Miss—"

"Finn. Riley." I stuck out my hand. She hesitated before shaking it.

"I'm sorry, Miss Finn. Perhaps the doctor will speak with you. Let me call and see." While she dialed, I watched the Torvalds argue in low voices. Carl caught my eye, raised her eyebrows, and shrugged. I turned back to the receptionist, who shooed me away with a peremptory wave of her manicured fingers. I rejoined Carl just as Alice and Jens cut off Ben's apology with a curt, "We're taking our son home." I stopped them.

"Summer's not over yet, and we still need his help at the store. Are you sure he can't stay a while longer?" Gavin's eyes brimmed with relief and gratitude. Alice patted me on the shoulder.

"We'll talk about it, dear. Right now, we're going back to the house in Wanakena. Everyone's ready for a little downtime."

Grateful for her concession, I walked back to check with the desk once more. I missed Josh marching through the entry and right up to Ben. When I turned back, he had already grabbed the professor by the shirt. Ben swung a punch that landed a glancing blow to Josh's stomach. With a grunt, Josh released Ben's shirt and raised both arms. His right fist connected with Ben's chin. A left hook drove Torvald against the glass door, which shuddered beneath the impact.

"Gods-damned idiot men. Stop this right now." Carl stepped between them.

"Carl, no!" I darted forward, plowing into Ben's back. My attempt to save the boss only succeeded in toppling us all. Carl sat up, stunned.

"Riley." Josh pulled me out from under Ben. I crawled to my knees, accepted Josh's hand, and stood up. Ben staggered to his feet.

"You son of a bitch." Josh nudged me behind him. "You sent Anton to the trailers, didn't you?"

Ben wiped the blood off his chin and snarled. "I had no idea Storms went there."

"Did you plant the tripwire?"

"What fucking trip wire?"

"The one that triggered the bomb."

Ben snorted blood and wiped his hand on his shirt. "Why do you think I know anything about those rat-infested trailers?"

"Because that's where you and Amanda used to hold your little trysts." Pain laced every word Josh spoke. I tried to process the knowledge of Ben and Josh's wife as lovers and that Josh knew about them. I placed a hand on his back, felt the muscles tense. Carl staggered to her feet and, arms akimbo, bulled her way to confront Ben.

"So, it's true. You and Wanakena's tramp were a thing."

"It's not what you think, either of you."

"I think it is." Josh stepped forward. I hauled him back. He looked at my hand on his sleeve, then covered it with his own. His eyes softened. "It's okay, Riley. I'm not going to kill him. Yet."

Ben's nose continued to bleed, dripping down his chin and onto the collar of his shirt. Josh pulled me closer and returned his attention to Ben. "Was Amanda helping you distribute the pills?"

Ben limped over to a chair and collapsed. He wiped his face with his shirt, exposing the once-taut abs now turning flabby. "I didn't kill her, Josh. I swear. I cared for her."

"Not enough to stay faithful to her." Josh spit the words. His scorn reignited Ben's anger.

"She didn't care, Waylon. She wasn't a one-man woman, either. We had an understanding."

"And LeeAnne? Did she understand? Was she okay with your man-whore ways?"

Ben struggled up to snarl at Josh. "LeeAnne was a tadpole swimming with sharks. She offered herself up like a sacrifice."

"Was she one of your mules, too?"

Ben nodded, defeated. "I swear, I never stored any explosives there, never booby-trapped anything. I had no idea those trailers were wired to explode."

They argued back and forth, their voices rising. From the corner of my eye, I spotted a security guard coming down the corridor. Jesse Livetree followed close behind.

"Guys, you better move outside before they get here." I cocked my head in the direction of the guard and Jesse. Josh squeezed my hand and, taking Carl's elbow, escorted us into the night. Even here, this far from the fire, the air carried the odor of burning. Bits of ash sifted over our heads. We stood there, pondering the aftereffects of the explosion, the revelations the disaster had laid bare. I pieced together what I could.

"Josh, are you saying Ben Torvald and Amanda had an opioid distribution network?"

"Yes. I found proof in her book. They were cooking meth, too."

"And LeeAnne was involved in that network?"

He nodded again. His arm tightened around me.

"Do you think Ben killed them?"

He wrapped his other arm around me and kissed my forehead. "No, babe, I don't think he has it in him to be a killer."

"Then who murdered them?" Carl asked, her question rasping in the sooty air. Josh didn't answer, and I couldn't. I had no more proof to go on now than I'd had before the explosion.

"Maybe the same person who shot Storms and wired the trailers to blow," Josh said.

Jesse joined us then. Inside the hospital, the cop guarded Ben. We were still standing on the walkway when Officer Kellerman pulled in, cruiser lights flashing. She placed plastic ties on Torvald's wrists and loaded him into the cruiser. I rested against Josh, inhaling the scent of smoke and ash and sweat. None of it mattered. He was alive, and I was grateful for this answer to my prayer. Jesse tried to hug Carl. She pushed him away.

"You have a lot of explaining to do, Jesse Livetree."

Jesse sighed. "If I tell you everything, will you forgive me?"

Carl harrumphed and crossed her arms. "How's Anton?"

"Not good." Jesse shoved his hands in his pockets. His cane, like his old man persona, was nowhere in sight. The four of us stood in the parking lot, gazing up into the still-glowing sky, which stared back in silent reproach. I shivered, my emotions a mix of glad and sad, unsettled by the thought that, for all we now knew, we were no closer to solving the murders. Amanda Waylon and LeeAnne McMasters remained ghosts in the forest, unable to rest until we caught their killer.

Chapter 40

...with a little help from friends...

Carl and I led the caravan back to Wanakena. I drove. Jesse followed, then the Torvalds, who had witnessed Ben's arrest from the parking lot. Josh's truck brought up the rear. I checked the mirror repeatedly, anxious that I might lose sight of his headlights. When we reached the hamlet, I swerved to avoid plowing into the crush of cars lined up along the road. Carl squeezed my knee before I could turn onto Reed.

"Don't go home, Finn. Take us to the Pine Cone."

I glanced at the clock on the dash. "It's awfully late, Carl. Are you sure they'll still be open?"

"Trust me, kiddo. The rangers and firefighters are still fighting to keep that blaze from spreading into the forest. The Pine Cone will be open."

She was right. The neon sign lit up the night, as well as the vehicles lining the roadway, forcing me to search for a place to park. Behind me, Jesse honked. Josh did a U-turn to squeeze between two vans on the opposite side of the road. I wedged the Civic next to a hearse and laid my head on my hands. Carl massaged my shoulders, murmuring about baking twice the treats tomorrow. Once we had all parked, we joined up and staggered through the door together. Everybody at the bar lifted their beers in a salute, then turned back to their conversations. All the square tables had been pushed against the walls and loaded with trays of barbecue, mac and cheese, scalloped potatoes, and ham. Patrons, devouring food and talking non-stop, crowded in at the remaining tables. The events of the evening and my worry over Josh's safety had trumped all other concerns, but now, inhaling the aromas, I realized I was starving.

283

The Pine Cone's owner waved a towel at the food. "Help yourselves. Plenty to eat. Beer? Or something stronger?"

"Bring a pitcher, Micah," Jesse ordered.

Josh nudged me toward the food with a hand on my waist. My skin warmed at his touch. I grabbed two plates, handed one to him, and lifted the lid off the barbecue. We proceeded down the line, adding whatever looked good to the pulled pork and ham slices we had chosen. A waitress swiped a rag over a table and chairs as we approached, then filled our mugs with beer. Lifting his glass, Jesse waited for the rest of us to join him.

"To the finest group of Wanakenans I've ever known." We clinked glasses and drank. When he caught my eye, he winked, drawing me once again into the closed circle of locals. I was too hungry to consider all that meant. While we ate, I balanced my promise to Josh to stay safe against the need to take more aggressive action. How could Ben Torvald have gotten involved in drug peddling? And, if one of my students had been murdered, would I keep secrets, or would I expose as much truth as I could? Josh noticed my brooding. He pointed his fork at my plate.

"Something taste bad?"

When I looked at him, all my fears burst free. Tears rolled down my cheeks. I scrubbed them away with the backs of my hands and turned to Jesse.

"No more secrets, Mr. Mayor. Cliché or not, it's time to put all our cards on the table. Anton might not live. Ben's been arrested. Gavin's suffered burns that may leave scars, and Josh might have been killed, too." That realization produced a fresh spate of tears. Josh reached for me, but I held him off. "No. It's time to disclose everything and find the killer. None of us will breathe freely until that happens."

Josh relaxed and took my hand. I squeezed his fingers. He squeezed back. Heat raced through me, coiled in my belly, moved lower. The conflict of emotions left me dizzy. Carl topped off our glasses, and Jesse whisked our plates away while I took one more shaky breath and put on my teacher face. Josh brushed a stray lock of hair behind my ear. I forced myself to meet his gaze.

"You're right, Riley," he said. "No more lone wolf investigations. It's time to pool our knowledge. Who goes first?"

I raised my chin at Jesse Livetree. "Tell us about you and Anton and the trailers."

Elbows on the table, fingers steepled, the mayor recounted his undercover work with Anton Storms. How they suspected but could never catch Ben or his supplier at the trailers. Their increasing belief that Amanda Waylon had introduced the distribution of drugs into St. Lawrence County and beyond. However, they lacked proof. Every time they visited the area where the trailers rested, they came up empty. Finally, Storms overheard one of his fishing clients talking about a score in the woods. Anton went to check it out. "The trailer must have been rigged to blow if anyone but those involved attempted to go inside."

"Someone must have been watching the place," I said. "Waiting to shoot whoever turned up."

"I think you're right, Riley." Jesse shook his head.

"And, it could have been me," I said, "the one who got blown up. I mean, that first night, when I was lost, I thought about stopping there for help."

"Why didn't you?" Josh scooted closer.

"I didn't see any sign of people. No cars or trucks. Although I did think one of the curtains twitched. And," I closed my eyes and revisited the clearing, "I might have seen the barrel of a gun, but I'm just not sure. I was so spooked, I turned around and drove back to the highway. That's when I met you."

Carl crossed her arms and snorted. "You might have been killed, Riley. Geezes H. Christopher!" Jesse laid a hand on her arm, and she turned on him. "And you, pretending to be a cripple, leading me to feel sorry for you."

"I'm glad you did, Carl. Made the days tolerable."

We all grew quiet, thinking about what might have been. Then Josh pulled Amanda's notebook from his jacket and laid it on the table. "I've spent the last three nights going over Amanda's coded entries. I also visited all the shops where she sold her jewelry. Only the one in Cranberry, the souvenir shop in Star Lake, and the antique mall in Saranac had the special ones that match the strand Birgit showed Riley. The couriers in the network she and Torvald set up had to be discrete and very loyal. They made a lot of money, and they took a huge risk in doing so. When I showed this book to Kellerman, she made a copy. Then we went to the bank in Tupper Lake."

"What did you find there?' Jesse asked.

"Money, in the branch where Amanda kept her profits."

"If anybody came in with large amounts of money, wouldn't that raise suspicions?" I rubbed at the condensation on my mug. "I thought the law required banks to report deposits over a certain amount."

"Not if you store the bills in a safety deposit box. Boxes, actually. Each of the women in the group had one."

"Did you know about it before you went there?" I fought the suspicions crowding my weary mind.

"I had no idea until I found a key taped behind the headboard of Timmy's bed."

"She used Timmy?"

"She did." He rubbed a thumb over my wrist to calm me. "I had no idea what it was for. Kellerman and an FBI agent from Syracuse figured out that it belonged to a deposit box. They got a warrant, and we went there. When they opened Amanda's box, they found money and the names of all those involved, including Ben."

"Was there a lot of cash?" Carl said.

Josh nodded. "More than I'll make in my lifetime."

I shook my head. "If he and Amanda were making so much money, would Ben jeopardize the action by killing her?"

Jesse drummed his fingers on the table. "About that. I agree with Josh. I don't think Ben Torvald killed Amanda Waylon. She was his golden ticket, and she recruited plenty of eager young women into the fold, so to speak. He was having a grand time spreading his love around."

I cringed. He had planned to add me to his list of conquests. We grew quiet, pondering the revelations. Josh went to the bar to procure a fresh pitcher. I shrugged off the image of myself as a dark-haired sleuth with a Sherlock Holmes hat and magnifying glass before I asked a new question. "Who had the strongest motive?"

"Not only motive, Riley. The killer also had to have the means and the opportunity." Jesse stopped drumming. "Have any of you created a list of possible suspects? Because I did. Three persons of interest are sitting at this table. The rest are spread throughout the population of Wanakena."

My shoulders drooped. Everyone leaned forward, elbows rubbing as we huddled closer. "What we need," I said, "is a plan. But right now, I'm too tired to come up with one."

"What we all need is a good night's sleep." Jesse finished the last of the beer and rose unsteadily to his feet. Carl grabbed his arm and draped it over her shoulder.

"You're coming home with me," she said. "Give me the keys." He only protested a little before handing them over. They made their way toward the door. Jesse glanced back and winked. "See you, Riley. Tomorrow."

Josh swung around to face me. "I'm following you. No arguments. I want to make sure you get back safely."

"What about Timmy?"

"Mom and Dad are staying the night. They'll all be snug in bed by now."

I accepted the offer and jogged to my car. We reached Carl's cabin just after one a.m., but I decided against going inside. Maybe she and Jesse needed some private time. When Josh stepped up beside me, I took his hand and made my way along the path to my place.

"I should go now, Riley. It's late, and you have an early day tomorrow."

I ignored the comment. Our footsteps crunched over the path. At the door, I rested my hands on his chest, relishing the feel of his heartbeat beneath the shirt. When he tipped my chin, his eyes caught the moonlight leaking through the pine branches.

"You, Josh Waylon, reek of smoke and sweat. You need a shower and some clean clothes."

"I suppose," he said, "you have a plan for that, Miss Finn?"

"I do." I tugged him onto the porch and into the kitchen. We shuffled down the hall to the bathroom. I pushed him in and held out my hand. "Towels are on the shelf. Give me your clothes."

His eyes sparked, that piercing blue shifting to a darker hue. "What will I wear in the meantime?"

"We'll figure something out." He handed out his shirt, pants, and t-shirt. I was pretty certain he was wearing underwear, but they weren't in the pile. "Everything, mister."

He peeked around the door, then tossed a pair of boxers at me. "Demanding little wench, aren't you?"

I filled the washing machine with soap, treated several spots with stain remover, and set the timer. Through the thin wallboard separating the rooms, I could hear water splashing against the ceramic, and suddenly, I lost my nerve. I was still standing by the laundry closet when he came down the hall. The towel wrapped around him did nothing to hide the contours of his muscled thighs. He scrubbed at his hair with a hand towel, flicking drops of water against the wall and onto the floor. Tossing it over his shoulder, he smoothed back his wet hair and looked at me.

"Your turn."

I swallowed down a nervous laugh and slipped past him. My chest rubbed against his naked body, sending my nipples on high alert. He caught my chin and brushed his thumb over my lips. I held my breath.

"Where am I," he said, his words a caress, "supposed to stay while my clothes are drying?"

"Um. We'll figure that out. If the timer goes off, toss them into the dryer, okay?" I hurried down the hall and locked myself in the bathroom. My heart banged out a frantic two-step. I undressed to its rhythm, rested my forehead on the pebbled glass door, and waited for the water to heat. The stall had a molded shelf for shampoo bottles and soap. I closed my eyes and stepped in. The rising steam soothed the ache of muscles and rinsed away the odors of smoke and ash. It did nothing to calm the heat coursing through my veins, the throbbing between my legs. I had never wanted any man the way I wanted Josh Waylon. As I dried off, I realized all my clean clothes were in the bedroom. When I opened the door, there he was.

"Riley." He said my name like a prayer. I leaned into him, stood on tiptoe, and pressed my lips against his neck, along the line of his jaw, over his mouth. I was so hungry for him, but he was hungrier. He buried one hand in my hair, locked the other around my waist, and lifted me up until our bodies fit together. My towel slipped free. I wrapped my legs around his waist. He staggered back against the wall. His lips found mine, made demands. I obeyed.

"Riley," he nipped at my bottom lip, groaning when I shifted against his erection, "We should wait. I intended to wait, but I want you so damn bad. Are you sure, babe?"

"Make love to me, Josh Waylon." I curled my fingers in his damp hair. "Please." Any more words were lost in the kiss that carried us into the kitchen. He hoisted me onto the counter and dropped his towel. Suddenly I felt shy. All the insecurities from my past came back to me. My mother urging me to put on weight. Warren telling me I was too skinny. Birgit disparaging my boobs. "I'm not very big."

"Riley," he murmured against my skin. I arched against him. "You're all I need or want." He pressed me back against the counter, ran his tongue over my nipples, sucked and licked until I panted. He kissed the skin beneath my breasts, my belly, trailed his tongue down my body, stopping only to explore my sex with his mouth. I bucked against him. He growled with pleasure before moving back up to my breasts, sucking first one and then the other. Then he was kissing me again, exploring my mouth. He picked me up and stalked his way to the bedroom. He laid me down and settled beside me, his hands molding and caressing as he gathered me in.

I had very little experience with men. Warren was the only one I'd ever had sex with. I'd given a few blow jobs in college and to Warren, too, but he was small, nothing like this man whose erection thickened with every stroke. Warren preferred to finish with all the lights off. I had never seen him fully naked. Josh's body reminded me of ancient gods rising from the sea, his muscles sculpted by the nature of his job and his gene pool. I swept my gaze over him.

"Do you like what you see?"

I inhaled audibly.

"What's wrong, babe?"

"You're incredible." Warmth rushed over my chest, spread to my cheeks. "You're the most beautiful man I've ever seen. And you're very...big."

"I won't hurt you, babe." He caressed my face, planted a kiss in the hollow of my throat. "But if you want me to stop, I will."

I reached down to wrap my hand around him. His cock jumped at my touch. He growled again. "Don't tease me, Riley."

"Never." I slid down and licked the tip, opened my mouth to draw him in, and tasted him. His hands cupped my head while he murmured my name.

"My turn." He knelt between my legs and lifted them over his shoulders. When his tongue moved over me, I moaned.

Josh lifted his head. "You taste like heaven."

I bucked against him again, but he held me tight, licking and sucking until the orgasm swept over me. When I came back to myself, he was cradling me in his arms. "Please, Josh. I want to feel you inside me."

He was gentle and slow, surprised, then even more aroused by my pleas for more. I marveled at the way my body opened for him, how he cried out with pleasure when the urge overtook both of us, and we shared the height together. I never wanted it to end. When he slipped out of me, I felt empty, but not alone.

"Riley." He stroked my hair, ran a hand down the length of my body. "You're so beautiful. Tell me what you're thinking."

"I'm not used to compliments, or pillow talk." I tried not to blush.

"Is that what this is?" He kissed one corner of my mouth, then the other, nibbled my lower lip. "You can trust me, Riley."

I touched his cheek, traced the mouth that had brought me such pleasure.

"You are the first man to give me an orgasm, Josh Waylon, the only one. I don't think I'll ever want anyone else."

His held me closer. "Did I hurt you?"

"No." I traced the lines of his face. "You gave me a gift."

"No, babe," he said, "you are the gift."

I didn't intend to fall asleep in his arms, but I did, slipping into dreams while he stroked my hair and promised to make love to me again in the morning.

Chapter 41

...on the trail...

"Riley." Josh woke me as promised, with kisses and sex. He made me come twice, once with his mouth and then with his cock. My whole body sagged against him as he finished.

"I don't think I can move." I said.

"I know just the thing to get you going." He gathered me up and angled us both into the shower. The water sluiced down, rinsing away the odor of sweat and sex and waking every nerve.

"This is not a good idea," I groused as he lathered his hands and washed me. When he cupped my sex, I arched into him. "How can I want you already?"

He braced me against the wall and continued his ministrations until I gasped his name and welcomed him in. This time I slid to the floor, my arms and legs like jelly. He crouched beside me, soaped my hair with shampoo, and stretched out his long, untanned legs.

"Are you sore?" He kissed me again, then pulled me up.

I nodded, then bit my lip. "But I've never felt so good."

"If you don't stop looking at me like that, Miss Finn, we're going to call in sick and spend the day in bed doing unspeakable things to each other." He stepped out and searched for the towels we'd abandoned last night. Bringing one to me, he left again, returning with his now-dried but wrinkled uniform. I wrapped myself in his regard and went about the business of dressing when his cell rang. "No, don't go," he mouthed, pulling me next to him. "It's Gus."

I listened as his partner filled him in on Anton's condition. The fire brigade was finishing up at the trailers before the arson inspectors took over. Josh arranged to meet him at the store so they could plan the schedule for the day while enjoying Carl's daily pastry choice. When Gus asked where Josh was, he winked at me.

"Keeping an eye on things in Wanakena," he said.

Carl and Jesse were sitting at Carl's kitchen table, trying to pretend nothing happened last night. However, the boss's cheeks were glowing. I wondered if the mayor was as accomplished a lover as my Josh. That thought stopped me cold. He wasn't mine, although my heart seemed to believe otherwise. If we didn't solve the mystery of his wife's murder, the cloud over him would never lift. And where, then, would that leave me? When I looked up, all three of my companions were watching me.

"Where have you gone dawdle-dreaming, Missy?" Carl shoved a chair from the table and pointed. "Sit. I, ahem, trust you spent a restful night."

Jesse snorted the coffee he'd just sipped. Josh massaged the back of my neck and winked at her. "Riley was kind enough to offer me a shower and wash my clothes. Now, it's time to firm up our plans and get on with the day. Gus will be waiting at the store in exactly," he glanced at the clock, "fifteen minutes."

The buzzer chimed on the stove. Carl removed the tins of blueberry muffins and transferred them to the baskets. We helped ourselves, slathering butter and speaking between bites.

"My first order of business is to check on Storms." Jesse rubbed his chin. "After that, Kellerman and I will visit with the FBI fellow. I want to go over the crime scene photos. Now that we know more about Amanda and Ben's connection, we might see something we missed, a detail that didn't stand out before."

Carl agreed with him. "Good idea. I might contact the McMasters, see if they know any more about LeeAnne's mysterious caller. And they must have wondered how a girl selling souvenirs and waiting tables made enough money to pay university tuition. Unless she kept it a secret. Maybe there's more they haven't told us."

"Gus and I will go back to the trailers, check out all the campsites along the river between there and Wanakena." Under the table, Josh laid a hand on my thigh. I blushed. Carl and Jesse pretended not to notice. "It's not clear how anyone could have come and gone unseen the night LeeAnne was murdered."

"You saw me." I didn't realize I spoke aloud.

"Yes, I did, Riley. Maybe you saw something, too, only you didn't know what is was. We'll talk more tonight."

"Wait." They all stood, dumped their plates in the sink, and moved toward the door. "What am I supposed to do?"

"Mind the store," Carl said.

"Keep your ears open," Jesse suggested. "You might hear something interesting, especially after all the excitement yesterday and Ben's arrest."

"Stay safe." Josh handed me the muffins.

"That's not fair." No one paid any attention to my objections as they filed out. So, I made up my mind to do my own investigating. When Gavin came to work, if he showed up today, I had a plan of my own, one he could help me carry out.

Gus was waiting on the porch when we arrived, whittling as he whistled some tuneless ditty. Ten minutes later, they were all gone. I swept the floor, restocked shelves, and rearranged displays. I also spent an ungodly amount of time with my eyes closed, replaying every moment of last night and this morning. The memories left me hungry for

Josh. My nagging voice, the one that always told me what a dolt I was, warned me not to believe he intended more than one-night of bliss. However, my wild heart disagreed. Josh, it insisted, was nothing like Ben Torvald. Or Warren Carstairs. My ranger was a stand-up guy. In more ways than one. There it was, that possessive my again. I cautioned the new Riley not to get carried away, then put on my welcoming face when the bell above the door tinkled. Several locals and a group of tourists filed in, looking for the famous home-made goodies available only in our store. I shuffled my feelings and worries about Josh to the back of my mind and did my job.

It was past noon before Gavin appeared. He looked worse in the daylight than he had last night. His hands were basically useless, swathed as they were in bandages, and the pain medication was wearing off.

"Sorry I can't be more help, Miss Finn." He fumbled a coffee filter into the machine. "I'm leaving all the work for you to do."

"No worries, Gavin." I settled him at the register, "How are your parents this morning?"

"Tired. Angry. Mostly glad I'm okay." He spun the stool around. "They like you, Miss Finn. They think you're a good influence. And, guess what? I'm going to be around a while longer. After what happened yesterday, my dad has to stay to help Uncle Ben. He's in a lot of trouble, isn't he?"

"Yes, he is. But, Gav, you're not him."

"That girl, Birgit, well, I guess she's a woman, she keeps calling and asking if we've heard anything. I think she might be in trouble, too."

When more shoppers filed in, I helped them with their selections while Gavin rang them up. The crowd thinned as the afternoon progressed. By three, we were alone again.

"Listen, Gavin, tomorrow's my Tuesday afternoon with the kids at Star Lake, but I'll be done by four. I was thinking maybe you could show me some of the trails. I mean, it's almost August, and I haven't gone hiking once. And that is something I know how to do."

His face brightened, but I saw the pain in his eyes. "Sure, Miss Finn. We could definitely do that. There's the Moore Trail and the—"

"I really want to go over there." I pointed at the hill rising on the far side of the pedestrian bridge. "I want to climb the one that goes up to the top."

He gulped. "Oh, you mean the trail where Mrs. Waylon died?"

"Yes. Will you show me?"

Glancing over his shoulder, he rubbed his hands together. "I guess. Are you sure you want to go up there?"

I wiped my sweaty palms on my jeans. "Of course, I'm sure. Now, it's time for you to go home and rest. Take your pain pills, and don't come back until tomorrow around 4:30. I want to leave then so I can be back at the cabin before the sun sets."

He frowned. I had badgered him, gently, into agreeing. Now all I had to do was keep it secret from the others. I didn't know what I expected to find, but I needed to see for myself the spot where someone strangled Amanda Waylon.

As the day faded, so did my resolve. That old sense of being alone, unwanted, unloved, resurfaced. So did the memory of Josh. The man had possessed more than my body last night. He had captured my soul. The need to feel him inside me again overpowered me. When he walked into the store, he must have seen it on my face. He checked over his shoulder, then closed the inner door, backed me up against the counter, and ran his hands down my back and up under my top. I tasted yearning in his kiss, hunger, a desire that matched my own.

"Damn, I missed you, Riley. What have you done to me, woman?"

I released a shaky breath. "The same thing you've done to me. Kiss me again."

He did, right before Gus pounded on the locked door. I smoothed my hair and reattached my bra as I scampered toward the storage room. Whatever they had to talk about didn't include me, but that didn't mean I couldn't do more eavesdropping. Maybe I would learn something important.

Chapter 42

...into the wild...

Timmy clung a little tighter as I loaded him into the Waylon's van. Julia hugged me, too, thanking me again for bringing joy back into Josh and Timmy's life. Her admiration only strengthened my desire to find out what happened to Amanda and clear the Waylon name. I drove as fast as I dared back to Wanakena. Gavin met me by the bandstand. With the bandages covering his hands, he could no longer bite his nails, which meant he scuffed the grass until the front of his tennis shoes turned green. I greeted him with a hug and a backpack filled with snacks and drinks.

"We should get going, Miss Finn. It's a long way to the, um, the place where it happened."

"Lead the way, Gav." I followed him across the pedestrian bridge and down to South Shore Road. We straddled the berm until we reached the spot where two trails met. To the right, the High Falls Loop Trail continued in a 50-mile circuit around the lake region. To the left lay the Dead Flow Creek Trail, a hike of several miles that passed by Janack's Landing before meandering on toward Glasby Pond.

"What's beyond Glasby?" I pulled a water bottle from my backpack and drank thirstily.

"We head up the trail to Cat Mountain. That's where they found her."

I noted the tension in his voice. He did not want to take me there. "Gavin, you don't have to go. Just point me in the right direction. There must be markers, as well as campsites along the way. I'll be fine."

"There are a few directional arrows by the Landing and one at Glasby Pond, but the rest of it is pretty isolated and unmarked. This late in the day, you probably won't encounter any other hikers."

"It's all right. You should go back. Just," I bit my knuckle, thinking of my options, "do one thing. Let Ms. Beamish know where I've gone."

"And Mr. Waylon? Should I tell him?"

"I'd rather you didn't. Trust me. I won't get lost." I held up the compass hanging from the zipper of my vest. "I've got bug spray, water, trail bars, and my phone."

"Phones don't work out there." He shifted from foot to foot, thinking through my argument. "Thing is, Miss Finn, I'm kind of in a spot here. If I go with you, my parents will kill me. If I don't, the mayor and the ranger will."

"Not an easy choice. I promise I won't let anyone blame you, okay?" I put a hand on his shoulder. "Go home, Gavin."

He sighed, then took out a map and showed me the trail outlined in yellow marker. I memorized the major turns, stuffed the map in my backpack, and headed off. The path was fairly level at this stage, but I was glad for Carl's hiking stick. I felt safer carrying it, just in case I came across a bear. Gavin had penciled in a number of landmarks, unusual tree trunks, patches of deadfall, the rotting frame of an old shed. There was even a memorial cross by the trail where they discovered Amanda's body. But that was a long way off. I paused to take another drink and walked faster.

It took more than an hour to reach Janack's. I passed the campsites Gavin had circled on the map. They were unoccupied. The trail continued toward Glasby Pond. I set a steady pace, my mind seesawing between thoughts of Josh and the few clues we had discovered as I tried to piece together what had happened to the murdered women. When I reached the pond, I checked the time on my phone. Six o'clock already. If I kept the pace, and if my calculations were correct, I had at least another hour to go, then three more to get back to town. Damn. I stowed the water bottle and increased my stride. Despite my careful planning, I'd be hiking back in the dark. For reassurance, I patted the pocket where the flashlight rested.

The trail marched uphill. When I spotted caution tape blocking the path, I halted. The yellow ribbon ran from a tree to a temporary sign erected to the right of the upslope. *Closed for Maintenance.* Strange that no one had mentioned this. I shrugged off the pack and dug inside for the bug spray. That's when I spotted footprints leading up the hill, the heels planted more deeply than the toes. They didn't appear big enough to match Josh's. I blushed at the reason I knew that, then straightened and ducked under the barrier.

Evening approached, deepening under the trees. The bugs grew more determined. I sprayed my arms and legs as I walked, sipped my water, used the stick to hold back foliage that had grown over the path. It was almost seven o'clock when I spotted the marker. A simple white cross, engraved with Amanda Waylon's name and birth and death dates, rose at the edge of the trail. One of Amanda's necklaces had been draped over the center post, *Good Riddance Bitch* carved into the crossbeam. Someone was glad that the woman was dead. Would Josh have done this? Given his anger and hurt over his ex-wife's betrayals, it was possible, but I doubted that he was responsible, which begged the question of who had left the message. Perhaps it was nothing more than a bit if teenage vandalism, but my gut said no.

I used my cell to snap photos of the memorial, then examined the trail itself. Near the cross, I discovered a perfect boot print in the dirt. I sidestepped around it, recording a video, and continued upward along the trail. I spotted more evidence of a visitor to the site. Maybe the tread on the prints could identify the mystery visitor.

Convinced I had uncovered an important clue, I snapped more pictures. Then, stuffing the phone deep in my pack, I turned back.

I had only gone about twenty feet beyond Amanda's memorial when I heard rustling off to the left. I peered into the gloom. Among the trees, a shadow appeared, matching my strides. I took out the bear spray I carried and flicked the tab to the on position. I forced myself not to run and estimated the distance left until I neared the bottom of the elevated trail. I ducked under the tape and started to jog. The sound of pursuit intensified. Reminding myself not to panic, I kept up a steady run-walk, retracing the route to Glasby Pond, although I knew I'd find no help there. The campsite had been abandoned. I was out here alone.

Evening birdsong lilted through the canopy. I held my breath, listened for other animal noises. To the right, a squirrel scurried through the underbrush. I balanced the stupidity of hiking alone against the elation of finding the prints. Surely, the reward was worth the cost. Above the trees, the sky deepened from orange and purple to gray. I paused for a drink and dug out the phone. No coverage. I secured the flashlight to the shoulder strap of my pack, then listened for more rustling, but the forest had settled into that dusky quiet before night fell. I swatted at mosquitoes whining around my ears and slogged on. If I could make it to Janack's, I could call Carl or hire a boat to take me back to Wanakena. Distracted by the thought of help, I failed to see the raccoon until it scampered across the trail in front of me. I stumbled and fell, skinning my palms as I skidded forward. I caught my breath, struggled upright, and brushed the dust from my jeans. When I looked up, Gus Jornigen blocked the path, his hands curled into fists. He frowned. I backed away.

"Riley." He took a step toward me. "I warned you to let things go. Why did you have to come out here?"

Fear threatened to paralyze me. I squared my shoulders. "Did Josh send you?"

"Josh? No, he doesn't know I'm here. He's a good guy, a talented ranger, but he overlooks the truth right before his eyes. You, on the other hand, never stop looking. If only you had stayed the timid little shopkeeper."

Gus didn't appear to carry a gun, but I couldn't see behind him. The handle of a fishing knife rose from the sheath on his belt. When he raised his hand, one of Amanda's necklaces dangled from his fingers. "I need you to put this on, Riley."

The truth slammed into me. I took another step back. "It was you who killed Amanda. Why?"

He scrubbed at his chin. "Guess it doesn't matter whether I tell you or not. Josh is my friend. More than that, he's the son I never had. He didn't deserve what she did to him. Amanda, well, she was a piece of shit related to me by blood, a stain on the family honor. It was bad enough when she slept with half the town, but then she wanted me to help her with that drug business...that was a step too far. I did it for my friend. I'd do it again."

"Did you kill LeeAnne, too?"

His gaze turned inward for a moment, then snapped back to me. "No. Barely knew her. Had no reason to go after her. Some damn fool copycatted me. Good for me, bad for you. Now, don't make this tougher than it has to be. I can't have you running back to town and telling everybody."

"Josh loves me." I stumbled over the words. Maybe I was going a bit too far, exaggerating the relationship from Josh's point of view, but I needed to keep Gus talking, needed to find a way to convince him to let me go. Then I looked in his eyes, and I knew that was a foolish hope. I reached into my pocket.

"Once upon a time, he loved Amanda, too. He'll be sad, but he'll get over it." As he said the last words, he lunged at me. I drew out the bear spray, closed my eyes, and held my breath. When he grabbed my arm, I unloaded the container into his face. He howled and clawed at his cheeks. "Damn you, Riley!"

I edged to the right, watching as he staggered back, scrubbing at his eyes. Tears dripped onto the front of his uniform. My eyes burned. Ignoring the sting, I stepped closer and swung the walking stick between his legs as hard as I could. The blow brought him to his knees. I gasped, unloaded more of the spray, and sprinted around him. The flashlight wavered as I hurtled down the path, no longer as frightened of bears as of Gus Jornigen, who intended to make me one more victim of the Wilderness Strangler. I skidded around a bend in the trail and headed toward the Landing. My lungs protested. With every stride, my feet grew heavier, the hiking boots a drag on my desperate run. I didn't dare look back. I didn't know how long Gus would be incapacitated, and I needed to cover as much ground as possible. He wasn't young, and he was injured and furious, but he had been a ranger for many years. He knew the forest. I was no match for an accomplished woodsman. I pushed on, driven by self-preservation and the knowledge that if I died here, I would never see Josh and Timmy again.

Even as I ran, I mourned for Josh. Now he would lose his partner, a man he called a friend, one who had stood by him through the last year. Then I grew angry. Gus had kept silent, allowing the town to suspect Josh and forcing him to endure gossip and scorn. Suspicion, once sown, died hard. I panted and ran on.

Around me, the light was fading fast. Soon it would be fully dark. I spotted a glimmer in the distance. If a fisherman was still docked at the Landing, maybe he would take me back to Wanakena. I stopped to rest, listening for signs of pursuit. Nothing rustled or crashed down the trail. I pushed on, reaching Janack's in time to see a man wrestling a tarp over his boat. Surprised by my appearance, he raised his hands in a warding gesture.

"Whoa! Where the Sam Hill did you come from?"

I pointed over my shoulder as I gasped out my request. "I need a ride. To Wanakena. Can you take me? Please."

He shook his head and continued with his chore. Tears of frustration leaked down my face. "Please," I repeated.

"Getting too dark unless you have running lights. This old cow's too plain for all that fancy stuff."

I searched my pockets for money, a credit card, anything to change his mind. I looked behind me. Movement down the trail caught my eye. I turned back to the fisherman. "Look, I want to be polite and all, but it's a matter of life or death. My employer, Carl Beamish, will pay you well when I get back, I promise."

That made the second outrageous statement I'd proffered in the last hour. He picked at his teeth. "Got a kayak you can use, if you promise to return it."

"Deal." I crouched to untie a boat from the stack piled on the grass. "Where's a paddle?"

He pointed toward a stack leaning against a shed. I snatched one, stuffed my pack in the kayak, and dragged the craft down to the lake. The beam of the flashlight dimmed. "Mind you stay to your left," he called, "or about ten yards from shore, you'll run into rocks. Follow the land around the point. When you see the pedestrian bridge, you'll know you're there."

"Thank you," I shouted as I settled into the boat. I had only gone a few yards from shore when the batteries in the flashlight gave out. I knew the shoreline, had memorized it from my outings with Gavin, but I had never navigated the lake in the dark. And, I realized, I had never been out without a life jacket. Too late to worry about that now.

I paddled farther from shore, then floated, waiting for my eyes to adjust to the dark before I peered at the compass dangling from my vest. I squinted, held the compass closer, and headed north across the channel. Lights flickered along the distant banks of Cranberry Lake. My vision blurred, still irritated from the bear spray. When it cleared, I saw land only a few yards away. I backpaddled, adjusted my direction to the east, and stroked harder. The adrenaline rush fueling me began to fade. My legs shook. Soon my arms did the same. I hummed every song that came to mind, from nursery rhymes to old Beatles' tunes. As I rounded the point, I spotted more lights across the lake. But I didn't dwell on how far I had to go. I only thought about Gus, staggering around in the dark, the necklace he intended to strangle me with lying somewhere along the Dead Creek Flow Trail.

Chapter 43

...the world falls apart...

The lights of Wanakena blazed like the Fourth of July. Once more Riley Finn was the cause of a crowd gathering on the lawn. I searched for a familiar face but didn't find one. Exhaustion made me reckless. Instead of landing gently, I ran the kayak straight up onto the swimming beach. When it tipped, I flopped onto the sand. Gavin reached me first.

"Miss Finn. Hey, it's Miss Finn." He motioned to those waiting on the lawn as he limped toward the water. Someone called for a medic. Then everyone was running toward me. I raised my head, pushed to my knees.

"Riley. Thank God." Josh pushed his way through, fell to his knees, and gathered me up. I tried to tell him about Gus, but before I could croak out the words, I passed out. I woke to find myself on his lap, swaddled in blankets, inside the store. Carl, Jesse, Officer Kellerman, Gavin, Ron, and Amy encircled me. The rest of Wanakena crowded behind them. Those who couldn't fit inside stood vigil on the porch, their inquiries about what was happening batting, moth-like, against the screens.

"What time is it?" I accepted a mug of hot chocolate, savoring the sweet warmth.

Josh tightened his hold. "Midnight. Riley, where have you been?"

I didn't want to blurt out the story in front of the whole group, but I had to alert someone. Gus might be hurting, but he was still dangerous. As I inspected their faces, Officer Kellerman tucked her thumbs into her belt and cocked her head. I touched Josh's cheek.

"Can I talk to you and Sandra alone?"

He inspected my face and, still carrying me, made his way to the storeroom. Kellerman followed. The crowd, eager for details on this, my latest crazy wilderness adventure, murmured their dismay. I didn't blame them. My ridiculous reputation was growing.

We settled on the same pallets Jesse and I had used for our conversation earlier. Carl poked her head in. "You sure you don't need me?"

"Soon, Carl." When she closed the door, I detailed all that had transpired on the trail. Despite my fear of hurting Josh, I didn't hold back the details. When I finished, Kellerman tucked her notes away and radioed for backup. Then she looked at Josh.

"Never suspected Jornigen, did you?" She waited for his answer. A muscle in his cheek ticked, but he didn't look away.

"Not for a moment. Gus was the one constant in all the scenarios. Quiet, hardly seen, but he noticed everything. Why would he want to harm you, Riley?"

"Because I kept asking questions. He warned me to back off. He was afraid I'd find out the truth, that he'd lose your respect, your friendship, maybe your love. And he was angry with Amanda, furious. She badgered him to help her with the drugs." I wrapped a hand around my neck. "Somewhere out there is a necklace intended for me."

Kellerman was already ordering a search party. Josh's jaw clenched as he inspected the wall above my head.

"What's wrong?" I forced his gaze back to mine. "What's bothering you?"

"It's my fault, all of it. Amanda, Gus. You. I should never have let him know."

"Know what?" He lowered his head. One more ghost of the past gnawed at him, colored all his actions, even now, as he held me close to his heart. I cradled his face in my hands. "Josh, I'll tell you my secret if you tell me yours."

"Not fair, Riley. Yours couldn't be as bad as mine."

"No, but just as hard to reveal." I held his face so he couldn't look away. "I'm in love with you, Josh Waylon. Totally. Madly. You need to know, even if you don't feel the same. No matter what you tell me, that isn't going to change. Ever."

He rested his forehead against mine. "Gus knew."

"What did he know?" I whispered.

"That I wanted Amanda gone. And, later, that I was glad she was dead."

The admission shuddered out of him, all the self-recrimination shining in his eyes. He blamed himself now even more than before.

"Listen to me, Josh Waylon. You are not responsible. Wishing a thing is not the same as doing it. Gus made his own decision. Now he'll pay the price for it. I love you. I love Timmy. Please don't push me away."

He set me down and headed for the door. I threw off the blanket and caught his elbow.

"Do you love me?" I held my breath. Officer Kellerman looked over, looked away.

"Before I answer," he folded his hands around mine, "there's something else. I have a child, Riley, a child with disabilities. I can't ask you to take us on."

"I'm a big girl, Josh, capable of choosing for myself." I waited for those blue eyes to meet mine. "Isn't that my choice to make?"

He lowered his voice. "What if Timmy's not mine?"

That stopped me. I had never considered such a possibility. "Why do you say that?"

"Gus knew Amanda was pregnant before I married her, and he suspected the truth about the child. He begged me not to make her my wife, swore she'd bring me nothing but chaos. She had a reputation even then, and I knew that, but I believed her when she swore the child belonged to me. I wanted Timmy to be mine."

"Does it matter?"

"Not to me. That boy is my son, no matter who fathered him. But I can't ask you to take on a family with so much baggage."

If I hadn't loved him before, his sense of honor and duty sealed the deal. "You haven't answered my question, Mr. Waylon. Do you love me?"

Kellerman headed off into the store. The clock on the wall ticked toward one. I closed my eyes and waited.

"I do, Riley, more than I ever expected to. But this won't last. Summer's passing. You'll go away. Timmy and I will be alone again." He raised my hands to his lips, kissed them, and walked out. I stood stunned, still wrapped in the blanket he had brought me, convinced he wouldn't leave me tonight. He'd come back. He had to.

Stepping back into the storeroom, Officer Kellerman urged me to go home. "It's late, Miss Finn. Why don't you go to your cabin and get some sleep?"

I pretended not to hear. The hours crawled by. I curled up on the floor and listened to footsteps come and go in the shop. The ache inside me grew until I thought I would break apart. My heart leaked sorrow like a cracked cup, then shattered against the wall of Josh's denial. I must have dozed off at some point. Carl roused me around five in the morning.

"Riley! Wake up, honey. I've got news."

I stretched and rubbed at the pain in my chest. "Is Josh back?"

"No. But they found Jornigen."

"Did he tell Josh what happened?"

"He can't say anything, dear. He's dead."

"No." My scream brought Jesse and Gavin to the storage room. "Not Josh."

"Hush, Riley. Hush, now." Carl patted my back. "It's all right. Josh is fine."

"He's not dead?"

"No." Jesse squatted to look me in the eye. "Gus is dead. He took his own life."

"I don't understand." And I didn't. Gus was dead. Josh was gone. Nothing made sense.

"Jornigen slit his own throat. He bled to death out on the trail. The search team found him next to the memorial for Amanda Waylon."

Chapter 44

...the trouble with bears...

Over the next few days, Wanakena boiled with gossip. Tales of the Wilderness Strangler made the newspapers all over the state. Thrill seekers and fans of the macabre wandered in, hiked Cat Mountain in hopes of seeing remnants of Gus Jornigen's demise. They shared photos of the memorial and of dark spots along the trail they swore were bloodstains. Unable to sleep, desperate to stop the turmoil in my mind, I kept to the work schedule, even gave up my Thursdays off. Josh didn't call. He didn't stop by. His silence told me more than I wanted to know. Tuesday when I went to Star Lake, Timmy didn't show for his lesson. I told my story over and over, to Sandra Kellerman, to an investigator from the State Patrol and to an FBI liaison. No matter how often they asked, I could only repeat what Gus had revealed. One of the searchers found the necklace he had threatened to use on me. I identified it, then returned to my brooding. My heart felt like it had been ripped in two.

Anxious to lift my spirits, Carl cooked up a storm. I didn't eat, barely spoke. The life I envisioned waiting for me only a few days ago had slipped away. I hate to admit how much I cried. My face turned blotchy. My pillow remained perpetually damp. I checked my phone every few minutes, hoping to find a text or emoji from my blue-eyed ranger. The screen stayed blindingly blank. I composed, then discarded, more than fifty messages.

By the third week after Gus's suicide, I moved through the day like a wraith, there but not there. Unable to deal with my moods any longer, Carl insisted I take the morning off, while she tended to the store. Any resistance I mounted was indeed futile. I moped around, tidied up the cabin, washed clothes. My fishing and kayaking excursions with Gavin had come to an end. He was busy packing to go home with his parents. No matter. I didn't feel like venturing out on the water alone. Unable to bear the emptiness of the cabin, I pulled on shorts and a tee and headed for the Moore Trail, the place I had first seen Josh, Ben, and Gus together.

August sunshine rayed through the pines lining the trail as it followed the river, lending a cathedral-like aura to the space. High in the canopy, the crows protested my intrusion. Ignoring the rustle of squirrels in the brush, the skitter of chipmunks, I listened to the gurgle of water rushing over the streambed as I stepped carefully around the rocks strewn along the path. Soon even the sound of the occasional car driving into Wanakena disappeared. I plugged in my earbuds and jogged on, up the inclines, down the needle-strewn dips. Each time my mind stuck on thoughts of Josh, I hummed them away, mouthing the words to the music playing from my list, uncaring of the tears that fell. My heart did a double-time beat. I ignored it. Who cared if I died here in the forest? *Nobody*, the headphones whispered. Mosquitoes buzzed my ears. *Nobody* echoed in my bones. Nobody knew where I was. Nobody waited for my return. I recalled a Neil Gaiman tale about a child named Nobody who grew up in a cemetery, raised by ghosts. I could be that kid. My parents hadn't contacted me once since I left Hopewell. I hadn't spoken to Emma for a week. Bedridden as she waited for the birth of her twins, my friend had her own concerns.

My self-pity had reached a high point when I caught sight of a brown blur off to the right. I slipped the buds from my ears, glanced over my shoulder, and almost fainted. Two bear cubs ambled down the trail behind me. When I stopped, so did they. That's when I heard the mother rushing at me. I pulled the cylinder of bear spray from my pocket and depressed the trigger. Only a puff. I pressed harder before realizing the canister was empty. I had used most of the deterrent on Gus.

The bear rose on her haunches and growled. I inched backward. The land dropped steeply to the river. I extended one leg behind me, lowered to a crouch, and balanced my foot on a rock. Without taking my eyes off the bear, I planted my hands on the ground and lowered the other leg. I slipped over the edge of the bank, grasping at roots and stones embedded in the dirt. The bear rushed me. I inched down the slope and cowered among the rocks. Above, the cubs snuffled. The mother halted her attack to chuff at them. I clung to the uneven hillside, pleading for the bears to go away before my feet slipped and I plunged into the water.

When the first raindrops pinged on the rocks beside me, I groaned. Above, clouds sailed east. The rain increased. The earth grew damp, then turned to mud. If I didn't climb up now, the bank might give way, sending me into the Oswegatchie. I berated myself for my stupidity, maneuvered upward, and peeked over the lip of the slope. The bears had moved on. How far, I didn't know. I crawled onto the path. The drizzle became a downpour. *At least*, I muttered, *it'll wash off the mud*. Wet, dirty, chilled, I slogged back down the trail. My tears mixed with rain until no one could tell the difference. A glance at the sky convinced me the storm would pass, but not soon enough. Desperate for a respite, I sheltered beneath a trio of pines. Their branches diverted the rain but did nothing to dispel the cold. Autumn, the forest announced, was coming. I slid down the trunk and buried my head on my knees. *Nobody* echoed in my brain.

I didn't notice his approach until I saw the boots. He crouched down beside me and lifted my chin. Josh.

"Wh-wh-" My teeth chattered. I swallowed and tried again. "What are you doing here?"

"Wrong question, babe. What are you doing out here by yourself?"

"I went for a run and got chased by bears and got stuck in the mud...and, and—" I ran out of breath and words at the same time.

"I'm sorry I left, Riley."

"Go away. You're nothing but a forest ghost come to torture me." I shivered so hard I bit my tongue. My hair dripped water down my back.

"No. I've come to take you home."

"I must be delirious. Nobody knows where I am." He covered me with his jacket and pulled me to my feet.

"You are the most stubborn, hard-headed, clueless woman I've ever met, Riley Finn. Everybody in Wanakena knows where you are. Amy called as soon as you passed the house. Ron followed you to the trailhead. Don't you know they care about you?"

I pulled the jacket over my head, stumbling against him as we walked. "Nobody cares."

"Wrong." He stopped. The rain had eased. "I'm sorry I made you cry."

"You did more than that, Josh Waylon." I gulped back more tears. "You broke my heart."

"I know, and I'm so, so sorry." He wrapped his arms around me. "I'll spend the rest of the summer making it up to you."

"I don't understand."

"Riley." He pushed my wet hair from my eyes.

"I smell like dirt and leaves and pine sap," I said, trying to squirm free. He kissed me anyway.

"I'll explain it all later." He pulled me closer, kissed me more thoroughly. "But we still have a mystery to solve."

I groaned. Not another one. "Right now, all I want is a shower." The thought of hot water sluicing over me prevented any more coherent thoughts. But then we reached the cabin, and he was soaping my shoulders. I knew I had entered a dream state when he spread his hands over my body, teasing and caressing. I wrapped my legs around his waist and welcomed him home.

Chapter 45

...do you want your job back?...

Carl prepared pork barbecue and invited the team over to discuss the next move. Gus's suicide, bolstered by the confession he made to me and the one he had scrawled in the dirt of the trail, had closed the case of Amanda Waylon's murder. At the barracks in Gouverneur, Kellerman showed me a note Gus had stored in a safe in his basement. Reluctant to come forward during the past year, he had planned to make a public confession if Josh were ever arrested and formally charged with Amanda's murder. Apparently, the man had contemplated suicide for many months.

Carl served the slaw and sandwiches as Jesse walked us through Ben Torvald's case. The professor swore he had nothing to do with planting explosives at the trailers. Investigators traced the material back to Jornigen's credit card, which placed the blame on Josh's former partner once again. And it must have been Gus who fired at Anton, perhaps in an attempt to warn him away before he tripped the wire.

"We still have no idea who killed the McMasters girl." Josh, shoulders tense, voice unsteady, rolled his glass in his hands. "They still think I had something to do with that."

"Explain to me again the main evidence against you." I drew lines on the tablecloth with the tines of my fork.

"You, Riley. Your statement puts me on the road close to the time of LeeAnne's death. You said you saw no one else as you drove back to the trailers, and you didn't pass any cars as you came into town."

My stomach clenched. I was nauseous at the thought that my testimony could damn the man I loved. Jesse cleared his throat.

"There is another suspect." We all turned toward him and waited. He shuffled his feet against the floorboards, no trace of gimpiness in his leg. When he looked at me, I detected danger. "You, Riley."

"That's preposterous." Carl huffed her way up and down the room.

Josh glared. "Not possible."

Jesse waved off their anger. "Riley has admitted driving down the road. Assuming the McMasters girl was already at the trailers, our Miss Finn had the opportunity."

"What's her motive?" Carl poked at Jesse's chest.

"That one's easy. She wanted the job. LeeAnne was her rival."

"No. I would never do such a thing." Dread slithered under my skin. Both Josh and I were suspects. My own testimony could damn either or both of us. I wanted to run away, to hide in the forest. "I didn't even know I had the job."

Carl moved closer, her chair screeching across the floor. "Riley, if there is anything else you can remember, anything at all, you need to tell us, and then let Sandra Kellerman know. She's been reassigned to the case and, believe it or not, she's on our side."

I stood up too fast. Blood rushed to my head, causing me to grab for the table. Josh reached for me, withdrew his hand when I waved him off. I moved to the fireplace and leaned against the mantel. The flight from Hopewell seemed like it happened years ago in a galaxy far, far away. Star Lake Wars reference. Save me. Wanakena had reshaped my heart. I had embraced this wilderness and the strong, loveable, witty people who lived here. Against all expectations, I had found a man who claimed my soul. I refused to be responsible for destroying his life. Ike wandered in from the kitchen. He nosed at my leg. I stooped down to pet him. Eyes closed, I relived the night I arrived.

I was lost. The instructions I'd copied told me to turn onto Route 61, but I didn't trust what I had written. And I needed to use the restroom. So, I turned at the marker for the canoe and kayak drop-off. As the road changed from pavement to dirt, I juggled a map, my phone, and the wheel. The road split. The right lane showed signs of tire tracks. I decided that meant civilization. I don't know how far I traveled. At least a mile, maybe two or three, when the narrow road opened into a clearing. Two trailers sat at the back of the lot. I saw no cars. I shifted into park and stepped out. I shouted a greeting. "Is anybody there? I'm lost. Can you help me?" My call sent a murder of crows climbing toward the sky. I looked back at the trailers. The curtain in the window of the left trailer twitched.

Josh moved to my side. He didn't touch me, but I sensed his warmth, his concern. "Think hard, babe," he said softly. I kept my eyes closed and continued revisiting that day.

Did I see a face? Not then. The silence gave me goosebumps. I scrambled back inside and locked the doors. I waited another minute or two, then circled the weed-strewn drive and headed back the way I had come. But I looked in the rearview mirror just before I left the clearing. And I saw...I saw.

My companions didn't make a sound. I gasped as an image grew stronger in my memory.

"I did see someone. Only I thought it was my imagination. A woman. She was frowning. I couldn't see her clearly enough to identify her features, but I think she had blonde hair, in a braid maybe. It fell over her shoulder as she closed the curtain."

Jesse cleared his throat. "Are you certain, Riley? You didn't include any of this in your previous statement."

I hugged Ike and stood to face the mayor. "I would do anything to clear Josh's name, Jesse. But I won't lie for him. I thought I had imagined it, but now I'm sure I didn't."

"You don't know who it was?" Josh joined me at the table. I took his hands.

"No, at least not then."

He waited a beat before asking his next question. "And now?"

Jesse laid a hand on the ranger's shoulder. "Don't push, Josh. We're going to find out who did it. Tomorrow, I'll take Riley to Gouverneur to amend her statement. No, you will not go with us. Now, it looks like Anton is going to survive. He faces a long recovery, but it appears his brain injuries were not severe enough to affect his memory or his ability to think. He and I will put our heads together and find a way to flush out our mysterious female."

"Maybe it was LeeAnne I saw." I scrubbed at the ache in my chest. Foolish heart, to cause so much pain and sorrow.

"They may have you look at some photos, Riley. Try not to worry."

Useless advice. Every word I uttered mired us deeper. Only one thing could save us. I had to find out who the real killer was. Maybe Josh read the thoughts clamoring at me. He sat me down hard and shook a finger in my face.

"Whatever you're thinking, Riley Finn, don't." All the color drained from his face. "If anything happened to you..."

Jesse settled next to me. He took my hand and clasped it between his own. "Riley, for what it's worth, neither Anton nor I believe that you or Josh had anything to do with the McMasters murder. We just have to prove it. So, promise you won't brood over this? Some introduction to Wanakena, isn't it?"

I didn't want to smile, but no one could resist the authority in him, the confidence. "That's an understatement."

"Good. We're going to keep working until we find the answer. Now then, didn't someone," Jesse winked at Carl, "say something about home-made ice cream for dessert?"

We trooped out to the porch, hiding our anxious thoughts, and directed the conversation to the approaching Labor Day festivities. Another party on the lawn, a final night of music under the stars. I sneaked a look at the calendar on my cell phone. Hopewell Schools would be back in session soon. Teacher workdays started in ten days. I sighed, saddened by the loss of the job I loved.

"What's wrong, babe?" Josh joined me on the porch swing. I made a face at my own musings.

"I should be going back to teaching in a few days. Instead, I have no idea where I'll be after Labor Day."

He started to speak when my cell chimed. Emma. I held up a finger to excuse myself, stepped off the porch, and strolled down the path toward my cabin.

"Emma? I'm so glad to hear your voice. How are you?"

"Fat as the Cheshire Cat!" My friend giggled in her contagious way. I smiled at her words. "The babies are fine. My blood pressure is behaving. Husband is pacing the floor like a caged tiger. And I have some great news for you."

"Please don't tell me anything about Warren Carstairs."

"Your ex's name will never pass my lips again. Are you sitting down, Ri?"

"No, I'm walking in the woods. Just tell me already."

"Fine. But you should be sitting down."

"All right." I sat on the steps leading up to my cabin. "Now. Talk."

She laughed again, louder. "You're not going to believe it, but the school levy passed in the special election, and the board is rehiring all the riffed teachers. So, girlfriend, here it is. Do you want your old job back?"

Chapter 46
...decisions, decisions...

Josh left shortly after Emma phoned. His parents had plans for the following day and couldn't stay to look after Timmy that evening. Jesse left, too, after calling the hospital to check on Anton. Carl and I danced around the elephant in the room until I gestured toward the bedroom I'd been sleeping in when I stayed with her. "Mind if I stay here tonight?"

She wrapped those moose-sweatered arms around me and held on. When she let go, I kissed her cheek and left her in the recliner, pondering the strange events that had turned her sleepy hamlet into a focal point of media coverage for the past two weeks.

No matter how many trees I counted, I failed to fall asleep. Instead, I traced and retraced my route to Wanakena, searching for one sure thing that would free Josh and me from the cloud above our heads. It wasn't until I read over my account of the meeting with LeeAnne's parents that I realized what I had forgotten. Faint as a snail's path, yet strong enough, if credible, to make the difference. I understood the risk, especially if I had figured it right. My rational side kept going back to Jesse and Josh's entreaties to stay out of it. I couldn't. Now that Josh had come back to me, I knew his life meant more to me than his anger. Besides, the carrot Emma offered dangled just within reach. Did I want to return to Hopewell? Did anyone want me to stay here? Too much to consider, so I put those questions aside. Tomorrow, in between customers I would make the calls.

*

The card read Jeremy McMasters, V.P. of Sales, Invesco Financials. I fidgeted through the automated menu, then pressed the number for his voice mail.

"Mr. McMasters, this is Riley Finn, the store clerk in Wanakena you spoke to about your daughter? Anyway, I don't know if you heard, but they caught the man who killed Amanda Waylon. He didn't harm your daughter. I'm so sorry. I want to help, and you said to call if I thought of anything. The thing is—"

"Miss Finn." McMasters's voice had that tinny echo of a man on speakerphone.

"Yes, sir."

"My secretary screens all my calls. She decided this one might be important. What more do you have to tell me?"

"Did you hear about Gus Jornigen?"

"Someone from the State Patrol called me, yes."

"The thing is, sir, I remembered seeing someone at one of those trailers that blew up. It might have been LeeAnne. And you mentioned she received a call from someone here. Have you found out who called her?"

"No. We already told you that. And you must be mistaken. LeeAnne didn't leave home until after five o'clock. It couldn't have been her you saw. Now, I'm a busy man, Miss Finn."

"Please, Mr. McMasters, before you hang up, I have one more question. Please. Although you don't know who called, how certain are you that it was a woman?"

"Interesting question, isn't it, Miss Finn? I didn't hear the conversation, but my wife did. She insists a female voice spoke to LeeAnne, and I believe my wife. Now, I have a meeting to attend, so I have one more question for you, and I expect you to tell me the truth. Did that voice belong to you?"

"No, sir, I swear it." Before I could say another word, he severed the connection. The air shimmered with accusation. No wonder Jesse said I was a suspect. LeeAnne's parents had identified a woman caller, and they thought it was me. But my phone records would prove I hadn't called. Unless I used a burner phone. *Too many TV cop shows, Riley*, I chided myself. Yet, it was a possibility the police had to consider. Which women would have had a reason to call LeeAnne? I ticked them off on my fingers...Amy. Carl. Birgit. All admitted to knowing the woman. What about her former boss in Cranberry or fellow waitresses at the Pine Cone? My head throbbed. The more I found out, the murkier things got. Or had they just gotten clearer? It wasn't Amy. She was a brunette. Plus, I didn't recognize her the first time I saw her in front of their house when she'd come out to call the boys, and she had absolutely no motive. Carl had been home when I arrived at her place. I doubt she had time to go all the way out to the trailers and back before I turned up. If she had, she'd have passed me on the road at some point. I re-visited Jesse's statement about motive, means, and opportunity. Maybe the woman on the phone lured LeeAnne to the site, but a male accomplice did the actual murder. I could see only one way to find out the truth. I paused to catch my breath, then dialed Officer Kellerman's number. After talking briefly, I agreed to come in the following day to amend my statement, and she reminded me I'd be looking at photos. That's when I remembered.

I hurried to open the picture gallery on my phone. I thumbed through all the shots I'd taken of the wilderness until I found the ones I had forgotten. There, at the trailers, I had snapped two quick pictures before I sped away. The first shot was blurry and out of focus. The second one was clear. Blown up, it might reveal the face of the woman hiding behind the curtain. But what did that prove? I messaged copies of the photos to Josh and Officer Kellerman. Then, I placed one more call. I left a message and shut off the phone to wait on a minivan of teens from the Adirondack Mission Church. Bill Harding, the postman, strolled down from the office on the far end of our building, his hands full of envelopes.

"Been meaning to drop off your mail, Riley. Carl's been a mite preoccupied and forgetful these last few weeks." He helped himself to coffee, bought a package of doughnuts, and ambled back to the P.O. I thumbed through the brochures and bills. Once again, no letter from my parents. But there was an envelope from Hopewell Schools, addressed to Miss Riley Finn. After Emma's call last night, I had a good idea of what it contained. I pried open the flap and read the greeting from the president of the school board, who indicated the administration would be pleased to re-hire me for the coming school year. I folded the letter and replaced it in the envelope. That decision would have to wait.

I hurried through dinner, ignoring Carl's comments about my weight and how I used to love her blueberry pie. She caught up to me at the back door and demanded an explanation.

"Riley, you're nothing but a will-o'-the-wisp. If you don't start eating, you're going to float away in the next big wind. What's going on?" When I didn't respond, she nudged me with her elbow. "Where're you going now?"

"I forgot something at the store. I'll be back in an hour or so. Thought I'd walk over to the pedestrian bridge and snap a few photos." I held up my cell as proof of intent. She narrowed her eyes, but she let me go.

I took my time walking into Wanakena. I lingered in front of the Lodge, remembering Amy and Ron's kindness to me, their children's joyful laughter. I paused at the sign for the Moore Trail, recalling the first time I saw Josh there. I counted the homes of the people I had come to call neighbors and friends, their generosity of spirit and love of a good time.

Up the road, the students at the Ranger School were learning how to care for the beautiful park they loved. At the Pine Cone, customers were sharing fish stories and contemplating the end of summer. If I guessed wrong, LeeAnne's killer might never be caught. If I left Wanakena, I might never return, drifting through the years yearning for what I had lost. Lights flickered on in the houses along the way. I read the street signs: South Shore Road, 2nd Street, 3rd Street, a perfectly defined world in the middle of a wilderness, fueled by the wild, beating heart of the earth. I reached the lawn that served as a gathering place for the hamlet right before dark.

She was waiting, her long body sprawled on the steps leading up to the pavilion. Her hair was braided, just as I remembered. In the deepening gloom, her face appeared as round as it had in the window the night I arrived.

"Hi, Birgit." I stopped six feet away, stuffed my hands in my pockets, and prepared for flight. If it came to a physical confrontation, I had no choice but to run.

"How did you know it was me?"

"Who else could it be? You told me yourself about the friendship, the necklaces, how Amanda recruited you. I called around, asked the people she worked for. You and she were friends. Until Ben changed everything."

Birgit examined her hands. Large yet graceful, calloused and strong, they were the hands of a woman used to hard work. "I warned you. I tried to get LeeAnne to back off, too, but she didn't want to hear it. Like all Ben's women, she thought she was special."

"I told you I wasn't interested."

"LeeAnne said that, too, until she changed her mind. She refused to let go. She wrote to tell me she was planning to seduce him, so I stopped her."

"How did you get her to meet you?"

329

"How did you get me to come here?" Birgit fiddled with the scarf around her neck. I didn't remember her wearing such a girly thing before. She advanced a step in my direction. "Self-preservation is a hallmark of our species, you know."

I barely had time to raise my hands when she struck. The scarf settled over my shoulders. She wrenched it tight and pulled. The pressure against my neck forced a gasp. I wriggled a hand under the cloth and tugged to loosen it. She reared back, lifting me off my feet. I kicked out. She winced, relaxing her grip, and I fell against the ground and rolled to my left. Birgit dropped beside me. She grabbed my free arm and, rising, dragged me toward the bridge. I kicked out again, hammering her shins. She stumbled. Once more, her hold slackened. I rolled free. Clawing at the grass, I scrambled to my knees and staggered up. She lunged for the hem of my jacket. I wheezed, slipped free of the strangling scarf, and raced for the store, my hand fumbling for the key to the secret back door, the one I had retrieved from the register right before closing. Muffled cursing followed me as I sprinted up the steps, ran toward the post office, and dodged around the side of the building. I had removed the bulb from the spotlight illuminating the flag. In the dark, no one could see me.

I trailed one hand against the structure until I reached the corner. I inhaled, held my breath, willed my racing pulse to slow. When I touched the tape I had placed around the hidden keyhole, I inserted the key. It refused to turn. I drew it out, turned it in my slick palm, and tried again. This time I dropped it. Faint sounds reached me from the front of the building, Birgit on the porch searching for me. I kneeled and patted the ground. If I couldn't find the key, I would have to run again. I swept my hands over the dirt. Finally, I found the key. Still kneeling, I fitted it into the slot and eased it to the right. The door creaked open. I slipped inside, set the lock, and barricaded the entry with pallets. Then I huddled behind a pile of empty beer cases.

My body shook. My bruised throat demanded water. I crawled to the closest shelf and patted the plastic wrapping until I found the bottled water. I tore at the cellophane, sobbing when it refused to give. I broke three nails before I freed a bottle. Taking out my phone, I listened to the recording of Birgit Sansdottor admitting she killed LeeAnne McMasters. Then I pressed the share button and emailed it to Officer Kellerman. As soon as the *Sent* message scrolled on, I shared it a second time, along with a message. *I love you.*

The front door thudded open. I shot to my feet, turned my phone back on, and shined it around the storeroom. There had to be something I could use as a weapon. The idea of taking down the Amazon warrior chilled me. I had acknowledged my size as a liability for as long as I could remember, but now, as I glanced around the storage space, I wondered if I could turn it to an advantage. If Birgit didn't find me in the store, she would look here. I had no time to move the barricade and escape out the back. Using bags of snow melt as steppingstones, I scaled a storage unit to the highest shelf and squeezed in behind boxes of cereal, cans of baked beans, and containers of powdered milk, making myself as small as possible. And I prayed.

Birgit pushed against the storeroom door. She cursed and shoved harder, toppling the items I'd stacked there, and flicked on the lights. She sounded like an enraged bull moose as she talked to herself. "Where is she?"

I ordered my body to stop shaking. My wayward heart began a rapid, irregular beat. I clutched my chest and took slow, deep breaths.

"Come out, come out, Riley, wherever you are." She banged her fist on a wall. Loaves of bread bounced onto the floor. She kicked through them to examine the barrier I had placed before the secret door. Unable to flush me out, she swept canned goods off a shelf. The thud as they fell drowned out her next words. Her steps retreated. She had almost backtracked into the store when my phone rang.

She returned to stand beneath the shelf where I was hiding. The phone rang seven times before it went to voice mail. My heart tripped over. This time I didn't think it was going to fall back into rhythm. But I wasn't coming down. If Birgit wanted me, she would have to climb up and drag me out. She raged at the boxes, flinging them down one by one as she built a stairway to reach me. I lay still, unable to think beyond the thumping in my chest. Her head popped up above the shelf where I lay.

"There you are, bitch," she said.

"Hello? Is anyone here? Riley?" Out in the store, Gavin, who should have been headed home with his parents, called out. If I had figured right, it was Birgit who attacked him in the woods. I couldn't let her hurt him again. I drew my knees up and kicked at the packages between us. They barely budged. I tried again, forcing the beans closer to the edge. The cardboard gave way, and the cans rolled onto Birgit's head and shoulders. She raised her arms to ward them off and fell to the concrete below.

I pulled myself to the edge to peer at her motionless body. Gavin shuffled through the open door.

"Miss Finn?"

"Call the police, Gavin, and the mayor. Do it now." I clambered down and squatted beside the fallen woman. I placed my fingers on her throat, checking for a pulse. Faint but still there. I knelt beside the body, rocking and coughing, feeling the unruly pumping of my own heart against my ribs.

Chapter 47

...closing the gate...

I lay in the hospital bed, eyes closed, listening to the heart monitor beep-beeping its way through the night. I think I slept, but the entire evening remained a foggy mash of voices and questions and people clamoring for explanations. What I did recall was the look on Josh's face as the EMTs loaded me into the ambulance, the way Jesse led him away. I asked where they were taking me, then insisted they go no farther than the emergency clinic at Star Lake.

"I'm not dying."

"Ma'am, we have a duty to provide medical care."

"Which I can get closer to Wanakena." I grabbed the guy's arm and pulled myself up. "I'm not having a heart attack. I have Afib. Please. Just give me a little more time."

"What if it doesn't correct itself?'

What if it didn't? I shrugged off his concern. I'd never had an episode like this, but then nobody had ever tried to kill me before. They caved to my incessant appeals and took me to the clinic, where the doctor on call placed me in a room and told me to relax. That was an order I couldn't follow. The events of the evening scrolled through my mind in technicolor. Josh tried to get in to see me. I heard him arguing with someone in the hall. So did Carl. The nurse refused to admit anyone other than family, so there I was, stuck in limbo, thinking about the job offer and Birgit's confession and what the future held for me. My heart jumped back into rhythm around six a.m., just in time for breakfast.

I signed the discharge papers, handed my credit card to a woman seated behind a desk labeled Billing, and walked into the lobby. Carl and Jesse bounced out of their chairs and buried me in a hug. Josh was stationed near the entry, arms crossed, head bowed. When he heard me cough, he took a step forward and halted. My boss and the mayor scooted away, promising we'd talk later. I chewed the inside of my cheek, uncertain if I had screwed things up for good.

"You should have told me what you were going to do." Josh dropped his arms, but he stayed where he was.

"If I had, the plan wouldn't have worked."

"You put yourself in danger, Riley Marie Finn."

Uh-oh. He'd used my full name, like a parent scolding a child.

"I'm not a child, Josh." I walked past him. "I saved your ass. Mine, too."

He wrapped his arms around me, lifted me off the ground. "You're not walking out on me, babe. Not now. Not ever."

"That sounds like a threat." I didn't fight him. It felt too good to be held again. He set me down but didn't release me. When I didn't look up, he tilted my chin until he could look into my eyes.

"It's a promise. Now, tell me what's going on."

"You mean, besides catching LeeAnne's killer and dealing with this stupid heart condition I have? Not much." I hesitated. If I placed my cards on the table, and he didn't care, what would I do? I clenched a fist and held it to my chest. The old Riley had flamed out somewhere on the water or along the wooded trails. I did not want to be that scared, immature girl anymore. "I got a letter from the Hopewell school district. They offered to hire me back."

Josh froze. A muscle in his cheek twitched. His intense stare ignited heat deep inside me. "If that's what you want, Riley, go for it."

I shifted in his arms. "There are two of us in this equation, mister. What do you want?"

"Damn it, Riley, I want you to stay in Wanakena. I want you to bake muffins, and go on picnics, and warm my bed. I want to make love to you every night."

"Every night?"

He blushed. "Okay, almost every night. Don't leave the wilderness, babe. Stay here. Marry me."

My heart took two giant leaps into the wild. "Are you sure this isn't a pity proposal?"

"No. I always propose to women who threaten me with blow dryers." His eyes sparked with mischief. "Besides, Timmy and my parents won't let me come back home until you say yes."

I could take the safe path, I realized, return to Hopewell, help Emma with her twins, run into Warren Carstairs and his Internet wife at various functions, pretend that conventional and unhappy was all I deserved. Or I could walk through this gateway to the wilderness, say yes to the man who had unlocked my heart and made me believe in dreams again. I stretched up as far as I could. "What I want, Josh Waylon, is you." I sealed my promise with a kiss.

A man coddling what looked like a broken arm walked in, saw us, and snorted his disapproval. Josh steered me outside. I touched my throat, conscious of the bruises there. When he saw me shudder, he scooped me up and carried me the rest of the way to his truck. He settled me inside, ran his hands down my thighs.

"I was afraid I'd lose you."

"No, love, not now, not ever." The kiss began sweet and ended with yearning, each of us aware of how much could have been lost.

"You're coming back to my place," he said as he pulled onto the road. "No discussion."

"All right." I croaked like a bullfrog. He reached for my hand. I needed to know one more thing. "Tell me what happened to Birgit."

"You really want to know?" I nodded, and he filled me in. "She suffered a severe concussion, a broken clavicle, and a punctured rib, but she'll heal. In prison."

Relieved that I hadn't killed her, comforted by his presence, I rested against the window and dozed off. When we reached Josh's home, Julia welcomed me, fussed over me like my mother never did, and refused to let me off the couch. Timmy snuggled beside me, and we watched Star Wars movies all afternoon. I ate supper with the Waylons, who were quietly thrilled at our announcement. His mother hugged me tight and whispered, "I knew you were the woman for him."

When Josh drove me back to Carl's cabin, Amy and Ron and the children, Gavin and his parents, and Jesse came out to greet us. After more hugs and yet another re-telling of my adventure, Josh shared our plans, which were greeted with cheers and a considerable number of toasts with Carl's best whiskey. Most of our friends were gone when Josh scooped me up and carted me back to my place. The lifting of the suspicion hanging over him had been worth the effort. The touchy ranger morphed into a wild and playful lover. He tucked me in, then slid in beside me. The whole incident with Birgit slipped away, replaced by the heat between us. I gasped out my pleasure as he kissed and nipped and licked me into a frenzy. I pleaded for him to come inside me, a request he granted only after he brought me to orgasm twice.

The following day, I called Emma and told her I wasn't coming back to Hopewell. I also asked her to be my matron of honor in absentia. Carl would stand in while Emma watched via Skype. We planned it for the Saturday of Labor Day. That way, Wanakena could celebrate with us during the weekend festivities. Timmy agreed to serve as best man, with Gavin as his assistant. Amy offered to watch the store. Whatever I thought I'd left behind paled in comparison to what I had discovered in Wanakena.

The Saturday of our wedding began with a light drizzle that changed to bright sunlight and temps in the high seventies. Mayor Jesse Livetree performed the ministerial duties. When it came to sharing the rings, Josh surprised me with a silver band inlaid with mother-of-pearl. Engraved inside were the words: *To my wild love. You hold my heart.* I surprised him, too. With Carl's help, I had driven to Lake Placid, to a jeweler who specialized in original designs. Josh's ring was also silver, but the words I chose told our story. *To Josh, my gateway to the wilderness. Forever.*

THE END

Acknowledgements

The ideas for stories rise from the most subtle of notions. This novel began in the town of Wanakena, when my husband and I spent several days there on a canoeing adventure. The real lodge, Packbasket Adventures, and its gracious proprietors, Ron and Angie Kovacs, inspired me to tell a love story that would reflect the beauty and the wildness of the Adirondacks. I am especially thankful to the hamlet of Wanakena, New York, "Gateway to the Wilderness." I beg the indulgence of the town for the changes I have made in distances and locations to accommodate this work of fiction. However, the stories of the suspension bridge are real. The inhabitants did raise the funds to rebuild it after an ice dam destroyed the landmark. I hope I have done justice to the place. Any errors of commission or omission are mine alone, along with some matters of poetic license necessary to fit the story itself. I hope Wanakenans will forgive me.

As always, I owe a deep gratitude to all who helped make this book a reality, from my first reader, my husband Gregg, who shared the original vacation with me and insisted this was a great story, to my editor, Donna Griffith, who always knows what I need to do to make a manuscript better.

I hope you, dear reader, find the joy that my characters Josh and Riley do. Let's hear it for wild hearts!

The New
Atlantian Library

NewAtlantianLibrary.com or
AbsolutelyAmazingEbooks.com
or AA-eBooks.com

www.ingramcontent.com/pod-product-compliance
Lightning Source LLC
Chambersburg PA
CBHW061917070425

24712CB00046B/710